NOT THE REAL JUPITER

NOT THE REAL JUPITER

A Cassandra Reilly Mystery

BARBARA WILSON

CEDAR STREET EDITIONS

Not the Real Jupiter
Copyright © 2021 by Barbara Sjoholm

Cover Design: Ann McMan/TreeHouse Studio
Text Design: Raymond Luczak

ISBN: 978-0-9883567-6-4 (print)
ISBN: 978-0-9883567-7-1 (e-book)

Library of Congress Control Number: 2020924877

To Sue O'Sullivan

1.

"*¿Qué es? ¿Qué es esto—esta maldita bola de lana?*" said Luisa Montiflores. "A goddamned farting ball of yarn, what the bloody hell is she doing on the cover of my book?"

Luisa's eyes blazed behind her fashionable bifocals and she ran a furious hand through long, wavy dark hair shot with white threads that hadn't been there the last time I'd seen her, four years earlier.

Luisa and I were sitting on the balcony of her eighth-floor apartment in the Pocitos *barrio* of Montevideo. The view was of the seaside promenade, the stiff-leaved palms, the beach along the Rio de la Plata. The air smelled of salt water and dry grass. It was early April, a warm autumn afternoon in the Southern Hemisphere. On the table were the remains of our salad, some fruit and Edam cheese from the pampas of Argentina, and half of a bottle of red wine from the high-altitude vineyards of Mendoza. Among the bread crumbs were the copyedited pages of my English translation of Luisa's new collection of fiction. We'd been going through the text, making small adjustments and alternately praising and castigating the comments of the copyeditor, when Luisa had turned on her laptop and opened an email from someone called Karen Morales, the marketing director at the small American press, Entre Editions, that was publishing her new collection.

Luisa read aloud, in increasingly sarcastic tones, the note that Karen Morales had sent along with the catalog copy.

> *Hi Luisa! Sorry for the short notice, but due to unforeseen circumstances, we're all a little bit behind here at the press. The catalog copy is due at the distributors very soon, so if you and Cassandra (who I think should still be in Montevideo with you) could take a quick look and approve, that would be great! Thanks so much, Karen. P.S. We made a last-minute change to the title after seeing the fantastic cover mock-up provided by our amazing designer.*

"And here is the disgusting and mendacious text she sends," said Luisa, turning the laptop in my direction so I could appreciate the horror of the cover illustration:

Luisa Montiflores, one of the lesser-known foremothers of Latin American speculative fiction, gives us a collection of radiant stories that surprise and enchant. The title story is a mysterious tale of maternal love and loss between Jupiter and two of her daughter moons, Io and Europa.

The background was blue-black, with galactic bursts of color. The ball of yarn—white, striped and swirled with pale orange—was obviously meant to suggest the largest planet in our solar system, with two strands pulled out and wound into two little yarn balls, one orange, one white. The original title in Spanish was *Júpiter y sus lunas,* which I had changed to *On Jupiter,* with Luisa's grudging agreement.

"We can't call your collection *The Moons of Jupiter,*" I'd argued. "That's Alice Munro's book."

"¿Y que?"

"Well, for one thing she won the Nobel Prize."

"So that gives her monopoly on the title forever?"

"In a word, yes."

"You know, Cassandra my friend, that my Jupiter is not the outer-space planet. It is a state of mind, coldness, attachment, loss. It is not the real Jupiter."

"I think that will be obvious."

Luisa and I had argued strenuously, but at the moment we were agreed: *Unraveling Jupiter,* the publishers' new title, was hideous, and so were the balls of yarn.

"We'll protest," I said. "I'm sure we can tinker with the catalog copy as well."

"I am not the lesser-known foremother of anything, and I am not a Latina foremother of speculative fiction in particular. What the hell is 'speculative fiction' anyway?"

"It's a sort of an umbrella for a lot of genres," I said, though I wasn't absolutely certain myself. "Not just hard science fiction, but other sorts of nonrealistic narrative? The supernatural, time-travel, stuff like that? It's probably just something the marketing director thinks will make your book will sell better."

"And what does she mean here, that 'The title story is a mysterious tale of maternal love and loss between Jupiter and two of her daughter moons, Io and Europa?' Is Karen Morales an idiot? Does she not understand metaphor? The story is about a human mother and her two human daughters. Cassandra, you told me that this editor of Entre Editions was clever, this Giselle Richard. You showed me the letter she wrote about how dazzling my writing was."

"Well, she *did* say that," I muttered in my defense. "And she *looks* intellectual in her photograph on the website. With the glasses and the dramatic stripe of white in her hair."

"We must change the title. We must drop Jupiter completely if that's confusing them. There are other stories in the book. We must choose one of those titles. What about 'The Lost Dog' or the 'The Empty Apartment'? I'm going to write this Karen Morales immediately. She must be Latina with that name. I'll write her in Spanish. And I won't spare her feelings."

"Please wait, please don't do anything rash," I begged, having been the recipient of a few letters from Luisa that did not spare my feelings. "Most of the stories are short but *Júpiter* is almost a novella—that should be the title of the collection—and Giselle *loves* the title story. She really was fascinated by the idea of the two moons—the daughters—and the remote mother. I'm sure there's a misunderstanding here. Let's not respond to Karen, but get in touch with Giselle directly."

"No, I'm writing Karen Morales and I'm telling her what I think of her cursed cover and title. I will *unravel* her, see how she likes *that*."

She made as if to start typing, then slammed down the lid of her laptop, and stood up. She was short in height but anger always made her larger.

"This is all your fault, Cassandra!"

Most things were, when it came to Luisa.

"I'm leaving!"

This, too, was familiar. A slammed door was a statement she had probably been making since childhood and certainly a dozen times in the almost twenty-five years I'd known her.

I didn't bother to respond—I knew in a few minutes, if I looked over the balcony railing, I'd see her dashing along the Rambla, a fifty-eight-year-old-woman in a black and white dress and a short red cardigan, expensive shoes, no purse, keys clutched in her hand, dark hair streaming behind her.

In an hour or two she'd be back. All I had to do was return to the copyedits and wait.

Instead I drained the rest of my red wine and went into the guest room to take a siesta.

2.

Some years ago I came to understand that a translator doesn't have to be as intelligent as the author she's translating. I credit this important and liberating discovery to my working relationship with Luisa Montiflores. In the beginning of my years of translating Luisa's fiction I used to spend hours in libraries hunting down references in books and encyclopedias and writing her long letters asking the meaning not only of certain words and expressions, but of tone and ambience. I asked her to send me photographs of Montevideo in the 1960s and early seventies, when she was a child. I read up on the era of repression and terror that had sent her, as a fifteen year old, into exile with her parents in 1975 to Rome. I read the work of other Uruguayan authors, those who came before her, those who went to Spain, Chile, or Sweden, those who returned home to Uruguay, and those who didn't.

I even—which shows how dedicated I was to 'background' in those years—attempted to read, in French, the first volume of *Écrits,* by Jacques Lacan, the French philosopher and psychoanalyst whose work had been so essential to Luisa's mother, Estella Montiflores, a psychoanalyst who had attended the master's famous seminars in Paris in the late seventies, and who had practiced a very Lacanian style of therapy in Montevideo from the time of her return to the capital in the eighties to her death in 2004. Jacques Lacan, the French re-interpreter of Freud, was especially interested in the child's formation of self, involving a mirror-stage and an Other. Lacanian psychoanalysis had a firm foothold in Uruguay, though it was even stronger in Argentina.

Yes, in those days I was fairly thorough, out of respect as much as due diligence. I wanted the authors I translated, as well as the editors I worked with, to see me as not just capable, but sophisticated. I felt I had to transcend a typical American high school education and two years at a Michigan state college, where modern French philosophy wasn't on the curriculum. I went to Spain during my junior year and never returned, traveling and picking up ideas about culture and history as I went, and learning to alternately remedy my ignorance or disguise it.

Most of the authors I began to work with initially were simply happy to be translated into English at all, and more than glad to offer me help, not necessarily in the nuances of style, since few Spanish or Latin American authors at that time were fluent in English, but in the hundred and one other details I needed to know to translate their stories and novels. The Spaniards told me harrowing stories about the Civil War, Franco, and the *Guardia Civil*. Some of them had lost family members or had grown up in exile in France. Just as Spain began to recover from the Franco years, desperate political exiles poured in from Uruguay, then Argentina, then Chile. Some of the Uruguayans had been displaced twice; after having first fled to Chile in 1972, they had to relocate again after Allende was killed in 1973. Barcelona, where I came to settle, on and off, in the seventies, was the city that many writers chose, because of the number of publishing houses. Some authors, especially the magic realists, became well-known, like Gloria de los Angeles, the Venezuelan author whose block-buster novel, *Big Mama and Her Baby Daughter,* was my great breakthrough as a translator. Other exiles languished. They tried writing popular fiction or literary criticism to make a living; they founded their own literary journals; they drank and smoked too much; they complained and ached for familiar tastes and smells, and some died early of heart attacks and homesickness.

I'd heard about Luisa Montiflores from some of the exile writers I knew in Barcelona. Younger than most of them, she'd been a child when her parents went into exile in Rome. They later divorced, and Luisa's mother returned to Montevideo in 1989. After taking a degree in literature at the University of Pisa and failing at an early marriage, Luisa followed her back to a home she barely remembered. Her novel *Diary of a First Love in Montevideo* won an important prize, but she found it hard to finish a second novel, preferring shorter forms. She was considered brilliant but *"arrogante," "pretenciosa," "demasiado inteligente para su propio bien."* Too smart for her own good. The usual sexist criticism only made me more intrigued. They also said that Luisa's Spanish was full of Italian expressions and borrowed concepts. *Todo Italo y no fuego,* someone said, referencing Italo Calvino, a play on "all smoke and no fire."

But few had ever met her. Only after her novel was translated into English and published by an American publisher did Luisa begin to appear on the international literary scene. I eventually encountered her in person in the mid-nineties, though by that point we had been corresponding for a few years. I'd read some of her short stories, had translated several, and, with her approval, placed two or three of the translations in literary journals.

We could not have been more different. I was tall, butch, disheveled most of the time. She was petite, straight, and always well-dressed. She would have been about thirty-five then. I was around ten years older, in her opinion a relatively clueless *Norteamericana* of mysterious class background, with no real sense of style. *Sin buen gusto*. Nevertheless we got on. It's true that we quarreled frequently, but then, Luisa quarreled with everyone. At first, in the world of letters, her feistiness was considered a rather charming example of the Latin American temperament. Later, her publishers and the organizers of literary festivals grew tired of her demands and tantrums.

If I lived in Montevideo I would have broken off the friendship long ago, or at least suggested she find a different translator. But time and distance have a way of softening all but the worst clashes. Our most serious argument happened many years ago when she found out I'd signed a contract to translate the first three mysteries in a series by a Spanish writer, Rosa Cardenes, which were proving as popular in the U.K. as in the rest of Europe.

Luisa despised writers of popular fiction who were successful with the public.

But since she didn't want to admit she felt jealous, she lit on another reason when she phoned me in response to a letter I'd sent her, regarding a story I was translating for a literary journal. I had detailed queries about psychoanalytic terms, about references to Calvino and Italian classical literature, about what certain metaphors meant to her.

We started out discussing my questions reasonably, though I sensed Luisa was irritated that I had to ask some of them. Then somehow Rosa Cardenes came up. Luisa said provokingly that maybe I didn't really have the time for her poor little stories any more, maybe I didn't really *want* to work with Luisa anymore. Childish stuff I'd heard before and had shrugged off. But then she attacked the letter I'd sent her, the questions that showed I didn't have a clue what her stories were about, and the next thing I knew she was shouting, "You are trying to understand me! You are trying to understand what you are too ... *unprepared* to understand.

Don't try to be more intelligent than I am, Cassandra. You can't be. Just get on with the translation. If you have time in between those bad crime novels that aren't even *literature*!"

I was fairly sure that the word she'd meant to use instead of *unprepared* was *estúpida*. I was furious. Hadn't I been doing my bloody best to read Lacan and a lot of other psychoanalytic rubbish, so that I wouldn't make a fool of myself in mis-translating the terminology of one or two of the recent stories? And how did Luisa think I supported myself as a translator if not by taking on authors like Rosa Cardenes, who was an extremely nice, *respectful* person by the way?

I hung up on Luisa, and for six months we had no contact at all. Even though I had to agree with Luisa, especially after finishing my translation of Rosa Cardenes' first mystery, that we were not talking great literature here.

Then I got a phone call from Luisa saying she'd been ill and was having surgery, hadn't been able to write for months, was miserable, and had treated me rottenly. I was the best translator she'd ever had.

I said I had missed her too, and I meant it.

She sent me a round-trip ticket to Montevideo, I stayed with her after her surgery, and we resumed working together, still with our ups and downs, but more or less nonviolently. I stopped trying to read Calvino in the original, but I never stopped being fascinated by her work and enjoying the challenges of translating it. Lacan aside, Luisa always wrote about mothers and daughters. I didn't have to be as smart as Luisa to understand that.

Now, years after our reconciliation, I lay on top of the bed in Luisa's guest room in Montevideo, with the copy of the Spanish paperback of *Júpiter y sus lunas* on my chest, staring at the cover, which was quite different from the proposed North American edition. A photo, touched with colors of blue and sepia, of a woman, seen from the back, holding the hands of two little girls, one slightly taller than the other. There was no mention in the brief copy of planets at all.

On Jupiter was a story of about fifty pages, divided into sections, some of them just a paragraph or two, some of them a few pages: scenes or fragments of scenes. The longer sections took place in Montevideo in the recent and less recent past, in an apartment that, as in a recurring dream, was the locus of half a dozen of Luisa's stories. Aside from the fact that the fictional apartment had many more rooms, which often changed shape and size and function, it was the same one Luisa had lived in with Estella for a dozen years. I knew, because I'd been to the apartment several times in the nineties and had met Luisa's mother there.

Estella had her office and consulting room in the apartment in what may have once been two bedrooms. She was short, like Luisa, but heavier, almost dense. Her clothes were well-tailored but severe and they fit her compact body like armor. I remember her thick hair, dry with reddish hair color, and her bleached moustache. Her eyes were large and opaque behind bottle-glasses, the eyes of an analyst who listened but did not speak. She displayed none of Luisa's vivacity and temper, but cast a cold shadow where she walked. We had lunch all together once at a long dining table. Estella ate sparingly of fish and boiled vegetables and drank only water, but she had a large bowl of ice cream afterwards. Luisa said she had problems with her dentures, and that was also why she didn't speak a great deal, because she was shy of showing her teeth.

One could recognize Josefa, the mother in *On Jupiter,* as Estella, though of course I didn't mention that to Luisa. She would have argued that Josefa was nothing like her own beloved mother, and anyway, the story had two daughters and Luisa was an only child.

The shorter sections of *On Jupiter* were mainly descriptions of the giant, gas-banded planet and two of its moons, Io and Europa. Each of these sections began "On Jupiter," or "On Europa," or "On Io," and seemed to be a recitation of facts ("Europa presents a frozen appearance, but it is considered a possible site of extraterrestrial life as there is water under its icy surface"; "Io has a colorful surface, sulfuric yellow spattered with volcanos, with red and green lava"; "The two moons orbit around Jupiter, always facing the planet, Europa and Io, reflected in the mirror-like face of Jupiter: *l'Autre.*") But over the course of the story the planet and her two moons formed a counterpoint to the story of Josefa and her two daughters, Jovina and Ana Maria. Jovina lived in the flat with her mother; she was obedient to the point of servitude, frozen on the surface, reflected only in the image of Josefa. Ana Maria seemed to support herself as a prostitute so she could paint; she lived with lovers and friends in a building for artists. But her independence was only temporary, given her volcanic temper, and when anything difficult happened in her life, she fled back to the solar system she originated from, her mother's apartment.

I knew that Lacan's theory of "mirroring," or how a child forms an image of itself, played a large role in the story. One of the governing metaphors was the distinctive manner in which the Galilean moons orbited Jupiter: her satellites didn't revolve, but kept the same "face" turned to her as they circled. It was also clear that Josefa, the mother, was Lacan's *l'Autre*, "the Other," and her daughters were lower-case "others." But, somewhat wiser now, I hadn't bothered to ask Luisa about her exact meaning.

I must have fallen asleep, because the next thing I was aware of was a rather alarming pale oval object hovering close above my face, like an asteroid bearing down on me.

The asteroid opened her mouth: "You should go to see them in person."

"Who?"

"Giselle Richard, of course. And her cowardly servant Karen Morales."

"What? In Portland?"

"It's the state up from California, it's next door." Luisa stared sternly at me, as I tried to rise to a sitting position and fell back. "You're flying to San Francisco in two days to your seminar. So why can't you go to Oregon? To meet these women face to face. To see what is going on and make sure they don't destroy my reputation." She had a long red leather purse in her hand and was waving it ominously in the direction of Portland.

"I know where Oregon is," I said. "And *next door* is not exactly how I'd put it. Anyway I'm only going to be in California for a couple of weeks, and I have things to do, people to see, a translation project to work on."

That was a mistake. "What project?" She loomed over me and I smelled her hairspray and irritation. "Who are you translating now? Not that idiot Rosa Cardenes again with the terrible mystery novels?"

As a translator you can't be monogamous, only discreet. I certainly couldn't mention the Chilean writer Claribel Montoya at this delicate moment, or I might find a red purse hitting my jaw. "You're always my first priority," I offered. "But a woman has to make a living."

"Just tell me it's not Claribel Montoya. I *loathe* her writing. And I know you've translated two of her books. I read the reviews of the Spanish editions. Which were not always positive, *incidentemente*."

"She's obviously not writing at the same level as you," I agreed. "Let's get back to *your* book. What can I do for you when I'm in California? Shall

I stop by the San Francisco Translation Center and see if they'd like to sponsor a talk or reading with you this fall when *Júpiter* comes out? Maybe one of the universities can invite you to lecture?"

"*Si,* okay," she said. "You can help with that. But you must do more, Cassandra." Her voice was firm, her dark eyes speared me. "You must talk to Giselle, remind her that the author has the deciding vote. In everything. That is the only way I'm prepared to continue working with these women at Entre Editions. If we can't resolve the cover, then I want to break the contract."

As with several other projects involving Luisa, I'd started out as the translator, but had ended up as her mediator, if not her literary agent. Having originally been approached directly by Giselle Richard late last fall about *On Jupiter* and having connected her with the publisher in Barcelona, Editorial Cielo, I was now caught between the foreign rights department of Cielo, which sold the English rights on Luisa's behalf, and Entre Editions, which had sent me a translation contract and paid me half my fee. I'd get the rest of the fee when the book was published in September. Therefore it was essential the book come out. An upcoming change in my living situation in London meant I might need all the money I could get my hands on.

"Well, I could at least call Giselle Richard from the Bay Area," I said in what I hoped was a pacifying tone. In my experience with editors, the only person who has less of a deciding vote than the author is the translator. "Can we continue with our copyediting now?"

"You continue if you like. I'm finished for the day. This is all your fault, Cassandra, and you need to make it right. Otherwise I can't go ahead. If there is a ball of yarn on my book, I consider the contract broken. I just came back here to get my purse. Now I'm going out again, to see a French film. You can come if you want. But don't sit near me in the theater. I want to cry."

I simply closed my eyes again. But a few minutes later she was back again with a glass of cool iced tea and a sprig of mint. She pressed her warm cheek to mine and kissed me on the forehead.

"Sleep, my tired old friend," she said in English. "My barking is worse than my biting."

3.

"I'm not sure if we can arrange something for Luisa," said Nadia Katz, the assistant director of the San Francisco Translation Center, while looking at her laptop screen. "We're pretty booked up. When did you say her book was coming out? September? That's sort of a crazy month, end of summer, all the fall titles. On the other hand, science fiction from Uruguay ..." She scrolled forward, "There's November, but that's rapidly filling too."

"In spite of the title, *On Jupiter* isn't really science fiction," I said, and then, lest she lose interest, "But you could call it speculative fiction. Entre Editions is hoping to market it that way." We were in her office in a building in the gentrified Mission District, and Nadia had moved a pile of galleys and finished books so I could sit down on the chair. It was good of her to meet me at short notice, but I had the feeling of competing with both the laptop and an actively buzzing smart phone on the desk.

"I confess, I've not read anything by Luisa," Nadia said, a rounded woman of thirty with hot-orange-framed glasses and very short black hair. "So maybe I should. Can you get me a galley? What made you choose Entre Editions?"

I didn't say that a dozen English-language publishers had turned down Luisa's book and that the foreign-rights person at Editorial Cielo had in effect gone into witness protection to escape Luisa's wrath. "Giselle Richard contacted me. She'd read my translation of Luisa's earlier collection, *Shadow of a Woman on the Sidewalk,* and loved it."

"Right," said Nadia, clicking on her laptop. Was she Googling me? "But aren't you one of the translators of Claribel Montoya? The Chilean? *Where the Fjords Meet*? Oh my God, now she's someone I'd love to have come to San Francisco and be part of our fall roster. Any chance of that?"

"I could certainly put a word in for you. Claribel's quite in demand these days. Later this month she's appearing at a couple of literary festivals in the U.K. I'll be on a panel with her. I'm also about to start translating her third novel, for her original British publisher Candleford. It was the novel Claribel wrote before *Where the Fjords Meet.*"

"Fantastic! She lives in Oslo now, isn't that right?"

"Yes, that's how my editor at Candleford came to hear of her. Janneken is Norwegian."

"But it was someone else who did the translation of this new novel, the one that's gotten such great press lately, wasn't it? Starred reviews, interviews, comparisons to Isabel Allende?" More clicking. "Yes, Penguin Random House." She read aloud the web copy, "Translated by Angela Cook. 'A contemporary masterpiece of exile and longing, set in modern-day Norway and Santiago of the early twentieth century. Magical realism re-envisioned through the eyes of a modern-day immigrant, a wrenching family saga, wholly enthralling in a brilliant translation by Angela Cook.'"

"Yes, that's right," I smiled through gritted teeth.

Janneken was still furious about how Claribel had slipped away from Candleford. "*I* discovered her, and *I* worked my ass to the bone to get her noticed." Janneken's English was almost perfect, but certain turns of expression took an extra turn when she was agitated. "And *you*—you, Cassandra. Why, if Penguin was going to poach Claribel, why didn't they ask *you* to translate?"

"Probably because the first two books didn't sell particularly well, and you sat on the third one, and then Claribel was named one of *Granta*'s 'Best Under 35 Spanish Language Authors,'" I reminded her. We both knew how it had happened. Unbeknownst to either of us, Claribel had written much of a fourth novel in a completely different style. She was invited to an international literary festival in New York, met the translator Angela Cook, found an agent in the U.S., and shortly afterward had a big book deal, with Angela attached.

"Do you know Angela?" asked Nadia, continuing to click and scroll. "I suppose it's always tricky when there are two translators competing."

"I wouldn't say we're competing," I said, wondering what she was reading. I hoped it wasn't the interview with Angela on the site *Words Without Borders* where Angela said that Claribel "had not been well-served by a previous translator."

"It's not about competition," I repeated, in an upbeat tone that didn't quite reflect my insecurity. "It's often a matter of schedule and priorities. I have a number of authors I work with, and I'm quite dedicated to the work and their careers. Not every author from Latin America can get an agent, or a big advance. Most foreign authors, like Luisa, don't have agents, as you know. It's usually smaller independent presses that really support translation."

"Oh, of course!" Nadia said, finally turning away from her screen and smiling a bit apologetically. "We're all about independent presses here at the Center. And that's fabulous about Entre Editions doing this book by Luisa. For a while it seemed like all they were publishing were French and French-Canadian authors. I think that Giselle originally wanted to reprint some of her mother's translations. Pauline Richard was a very well-known translator of French."

"You've met them then?"

"Well, I've met Giselle. At a translation conference four or five years ago here in the Bay Area. She's a really dynamic woman—you probably know that—and I'm impressed with their list. She's been branching out the last couple of years in some great directions. Korean women writers, a Polish author, and obviously—Luisa Montiflores. Definitely get me a galley and we'll see. What was it called again?"

"*On Jupiter*, in English. I couldn't use the Spanish title, *Júpiter y sus lunas,* for obvious reasons."

"But *not* science fiction, you say? Because it would be interesting to put together some kind of panel on Latin American sf. It's kind of a big thing now."

"I'll ask Luisa," I hedged. At least I could tell her I'd tried.

It was Friday afternoon and BART was standing-room only by the time I boarded a train to Ashby station in Berkeley, where my friend Kim was picking me up after her faculty meeting. The seats were already taken by people even more elderly and decrepit than me, so I held on to a pole, closing my eyes as jet lag combined with the swaying movement of the train made me dizzy. I'd come into SFO late Wednesday morning from Montevideo via Miami and Dallas, and on Thursday I'd attended a half-day seminar that Kim—Dr. Kimberly Lester, professor of Spanish and Latin American Studies at UC Berkeley—had arranged on Latin American women authors. The seminar was the reason I was in the States; Kim had somehow managed to get her department to pay for a round-trip ticket from London to San Francisco (I had converted it to a London-Montevideo-SF-London itinerary). I was originally supposed to fly over in March and stay two weeks, but Luisa had begged me to come and see her en route so we could work on the copyedits together.

After Kim's teaching assistant, Linda, lectured on the new crop of younger women writers from Mexico and South America, I discussed some of the more established writers, including a number I'd translated. From time to time Kim stepped in and filled in some political or literary history, and then monitored the discussion, which wandered into issues of identity, gender fluidity, and queer theory. Although I'd been a lesbian for about a thousand years, I was still a little confused when it came to queer theory, which often seemed to be about thinking rather than doing.

The discussion then veered into questions about translation itself, both the literary practice and the practicalities of it as a career. I gave some basic information about how to start making connections, and then I spoke a little about my own beginnings, back in the dark ages, when there were few translation programs, but still a lot of opportunity if you were in the right place at the right time.

I'd looked at the faces of the students, some eager, some skeptical, some just staring at their phones, and wondered what they saw as they looked back: a tall, thin woman, hovering around seventy, freckled with age, an untidy mass of gray-white hair, still wearing my all-purpose uniform of jeans, boots, a shirt and leather jacket, still butch in a world where there were fifty more nuanced gender designations.

After the seminar a group of us had gone out for dinner and had a lively time talking about travel and translation. We'd all drunk quite a bit of wine and in the end we'd left Kim's car in the university parking garage and taken an Uber back to her house in the Diamond district of Oakland, where Kim and I had a couple more glasses. Her long-time partner Dora was out of town. "I'm sorry you had to change your ticket," Kim said several times. "You hardly ever come to the States any more and Dora was so looking forward to seeing you." The third time she said it I realized that my change of plans had seriously put Kim's nose out of joint. I doubted that Dora was bothered. She was down in Guatemala doing community health work for a few weeks; she just assumed that she'd catch up with me some other time, she wrote me cheerfully.

But Kim was not like that. Kim didn't like changes at the last minute and she didn't like visitors as much without Dora to act the host. Kim had many wonderful qualities but spontaneity was not one of them.

I could tell, when Kim picked me up at Ashby station, she was probably wishing she could just go home and take a nap. She had dark circles under her eyes and her wavy gray hair needed a cut. She was approaching retirement age, she'd mentioned yesterday, and today she looked as if retirement couldn't get here too soon. She said she'd had an exhausting faculty meeting all afternoon. "Why the hell they schedule these things for Fridays is beyond me. We should definitely not have drunk so much last night."

I suggested going out for dinner, but she said she'd defrosted some enchiladas that Dora had made before she left. I couldn't help thinking that it had been a long time since I'd visited when Dora hadn't been around to make things easy. Dinner felt strained at first. Kim was still preoccupied with the faculty meeting and problems in the department. Finally, after we'd cleaned off the table and gone into the living room, she asked me about my visit to Luisa. Dora always found my tales of Luisa's eccentricities hilarious, but Kim wasn't quite in the mood to be amused, and I caught more than a hint of judgement when she finally said, "I've never fully understood your bond with Luisa. I mean, you persist for years in helping her with her career and mollifying her editors, and now you've managed to find a decent American publisher who apparently admires her work, and Luisa has a complete fit because she doesn't like the cover and says she's going to break the contract. I mean, why do you put up with that kind of behavior?"

"You're a professor of Latin American literature and you ask me why Luisa is temperamental? Besides, if I showed you those hideous balls of yarn you'd have a fit too."

"I'm not asking why Luisa is temperamental. I'm asking why you put up with it."

"I've known her a long time. She's fragile."

"Hah! Fragile as a piece of dried jerky. She's been in psychoanalysis for about thirty years, hasn't she? Surely that should have taught her some coping skills."

"I actually love her writing. And she's been generous, getting me invited to Japan and Finland. When she used to be invited to literary festivals. Besides, you have to admit, she's a fascinating, unusual writer. Yesterday I told your students that was my main criteria for translating writers: Are they deeply interesting? Do I love their way of using language? Luisa's writing haunts me."

"I noticed you didn't mention much at the seminar about that novel by Claribel Montoya you're working on. What criteria did you use for that?"

"My secondary criterion is *does it pay well?* But I'd rather those students kept some of their illusions for a while."

Kim laughed. "Most of them think a lot more and probably more sensibly about finances than you ever have. Though I agree with you, Luisa is a damn good writer and worth translating. But she's a troublemaker, too, isn't she?"

"Don't worry. I'll sort things out with Giselle Richard tomorrow on the phone about the cover and title. I'm certain we can find a compromise, though if I'm persuasive Luisa will get her way. And meanwhile I can spend a quiet week in your guest room, working on the Claribel Montoya novel. I'm somewhat behind with that."

"What's the novel about again?"

"A poignant satire of Scandinavian health care for mothers. It's not supposed to be making fun of postpartum depression, but of the Norwegian nanny state. So the author says. Poignant, yes, but funny? It hasn't made me laugh yet. *El primer año de tu bebé,* it's called. Janneken wants the title to be *Baby's First Year.*"

She guffawed. "I don't think the title is meant to be the funny part," I said.

"Sorry. I don't mean to come off as critical. I'm so happy you're here, Cassandra. I'm just a little tired tonight. It's been something of a brutal day."

I assured her it was fine, that she should just be however she felt. But of course inside I was wondering if it was going to be like this every evening, groping after shared ground, irritating each other, each of us wishing the other were Dora, so charming, so cheerful, so easy to get along with.

A little later we said good-night and I went downstairs into the guest room, brushed my teeth in the adjoining bathroom, got into my nightshirt, and hopped into bed. I opened my laptop's inbox and saw an email from Janneken, subject line: *Baby, Baby?* She wondered how Montevideo had gone and how far along I was with the translation of Claribel's novel. "I understand about wanting to get away from London to concentrate, but if you could just update me about your progress, that would be brilliant. I haven't heard from you for two weeks."

I had an uncomfortable memory of telling Janneken that when I returned from my travels I should have a draft of at least a hundred pages. I'd even persuaded myself I would have at least some time in Montevideo to work on it. I also thought I could work on the novel during the long flights. And then I'd promised myself I could really concentrate while in Oakland at Kim's.

The fact was, I wasn't all that crazy about *Baby's First Year*. The most I could say about it is that I did get Claribel's point: pregnancy and early motherhood perhaps weren't all they were cracked up to be, even in or perhaps especially in child-centered, parent-positive Scandinavia. Especially if you or your character, a female narrator from another country (with a warmer and more expressive culture) were already struggling to fit into Norwegian society.

Initially, Janneken hadn't wanted to publish it at all. "A tired novel by a tired mother," she called it. The tone was an off-key combination of arch and desperate. Each of the twelve chapters started with an apparent quote from a guide called *Baby's First Year,* written by a pediatrician. Juxtaposed with the narrator's internal voice, there were a lot of passive-aggressive scenes with Norwegian midwives, doctors, and home-help nurses, along with repetitive jokes about the Norwegian fetish for fresh air, which involved putting the poor little screaming baby in a pram and pushing her around in snowstorms. The husband was Norwegian and supportive, but there were also "jokes" at his expense. He knew how to change a nappy, but in fact he used most of his parental leave to watch international soccer games on television. The narrator, from Chile, missed her family, but a month-long visit from her accusatory and excitable mother was almost worse. Anti-depressants worked to some degree, but it was advertising for a nanny and finding Maria from Ecuador that really made life bearable. By the end of the novel the narrator was ready to start a new book, and looking forward to her next child in a few years.

Janneken, who had given birth to three healthy children and had apparently continued reading manuscripts during labor, didn't hide that she considered Claribel a complete whiner. "It is meant to be funny, but it's not that funny, it's lame and boring," she said. Adding, "No country has better health care than Norway." Janneken might publish Scandi-noir novels that painted a decidedly distressing picture of a society in the grip of dozens of deranged serial killers, but she was still a Norwegian chauvinist, even though she'd studied English lit at Edinburgh, lived in London for twenty years, and was married to a mild-mannered Scotsman.

Before Claribel had an agent, Janneken had been able to keep saying, "Yes, yes, we're still planning to publish your *Baby,*" but once the deal with Penguin was in place and *Where the Fjords Meet* turned out to be such a success, she had to act quickly. After all, it was Janneken who had discovered Claribel Montoya.

Janneken was sending Claribel's first two books back to press with new covers and blurbs, and she wanted the translation of the *Baby* yesterday. "I'm not saying drop everything you're doing," she said, but in fact that's what she hoped I'd do. If I *could* get it to her by May, June at the latest, she promised a bonus, and a slightly higher royalty percentage. It was February when I signed the contract and pocketed my much-needed advance. Now it was early April and I had only translated chapter one.

It wasn't as if I didn't need the money. My long-time pal Nicola Gibbons, who had always put me up in London whenever I was in town, had announced just before I left for Montevideo that she'd decided to move to Scotland. She was already looking at flats in Edinburgh. She'd buy one with a guest room, naturally. Of course, she understood if I'd rather keep my base in London, given that I was so often out of the country. She was willing to sell me her current two-bedroom flat in Islington for a below-market price. Or I could look into a place of my own to buy or rent.

None of these choices sounded good to me, and whichever one I made would be complicated. Yes, I had savings—more than most of my friends would suspect—but that was for a gracious old age, preferably in a sunny climate, not for buying real estate in one of the most expensive cities in the U.K. If I bought Nicky's flat in Islington I'd have to find a roommate who would be there all the time. If I bought another flat just for me I'd have to move out of London's center. And if I shifted my base to Edinburgh, I'd lose London.

I was about to write to Janneken to assure her that, although it had been harder to find the time in Montevideo than expected, I now had a good solid week plus two days in Oakland to make solid progress. I removed the extra *solid* and was about to hit send, when I noticed there was a second email from Janneken, sent at roughly two a.m., her time, subject title: *More!*

Cassandra,

I'm afraid there's a serious hiccough with the Baby and I need you to respond asap!! I heard from Claribel's agent late today. Claribel has gotten into her head that you're not the right translator for her, and she's making noises about dropping you and having this new translator, Angela Cook, take over. I wrote the agent firmly that choosing the translator is not usually the prerogative of the agent or even the author, especially if the contract is already signed with the translator and the translation is practically finished—and that's true, isn't it Cassandra? The agent came back just as firmly asking to see the chapters that are done, so that this Angela Cook can go through it. Apparently Angela Cook has raised questions about the quality of your work. Nonsense, of course. I know you're an excellent translator. But I'm worried about this whole thing. It's no good to us if Claribel gets her winds up, obviously. We need her onboard for publicity and just general good will.

I need to discuss this with the top dogs on Monday, but in the meanwhile, it would be very helpful to get whatever you've done on the manuscript so far so we can look at it and respond to the agent.

Janneken

P.S. Claribel worries that you do not get her "sense of humor."

Ten minutes ago I'd hardly been able to keep my eyes open. And now I was wide awake with irritation and the desire to simply chuck the *Baby* out with the bathwater. I didn't need trouble with Luisa *and* Claribel. But what if I lost *both* projects? I had nothing else on the translation horizon and my only regular income aside from these projects came from royalties that went straight into my savings account. My nest egg for my eighties, should I live so long. Irritation soon became panic.

I'd have to figure something out, write to contacts about other possible translating projects. No, I should get back to *Baby's First Year.* Immediately, tomorrow morning. But I should call Giselle too, first thing. Make sure that the cover problem didn't stand in the way of *Jupiter* coming out this fall.

I started to write to Janneken, then, I couldn't help it, I pulled up Angela Cook's profile on the faculty page of her modest Midwestern university. There I read that Cook, an adjunct associate professor, had received a National Endowment for the Arts Translation Fellowship, a PEN/Heim Translation Fund Grant, and residency grants from MacDowell, Yaddo, and the Banff International Literary Translation Centre in Canada. She had translated some authors I didn't know beyond the fact that I recalled they were also listed in Granta's list of Spanish-language writers under 35, and was the "award-winning translator of the dazzling Chilean author, Claribel Montoya."

The photo showed a woman of about thirty-five, a WASPY blonde, with a sharp nose and a squint, perhaps because she'd removed her glasses for the photographer, perhaps because she was what my Aunt Marie, who unlike my mother had a foul mouth, would have called "a right fierce hoor." Meaning sneaky with money and business, nothing to do with sex (said Aunt Marie).

Angela certainly didn't look like she had a "sense of humor."

Somewhat reassured, I tapped out a quick answer to Janneken that I'd received her message, not to worry, and that I hoped to send her something in a few days. I added that I believed I'd always had a very good working relationship with Claribel, and that I would be seeing her at the literary festival in Chipping Waldron in just two weeks, where we were doing a panel together. "We'll get all this straightened out," I chirped and clicked Send.

Then I lay there and hyperventilated.

4.

I did manage to fall asleep but I was awake at five. I crept upstairs, and banged around a bit in the kitchen looking for coffee, wishing I'd thought to ask Kim where she kept everything. I had just assembled the cone, the filter, and found some whole beans in the freezer, and was looking for a grinder, when Kim came stomping red-eyed from the bedroom. "Jet lag?" she asked, pulling out a fresh package of Peet's French Roast, already ground, from a cupboard.

"Sorry."

"It's fine. I should get out for a brisk walk and go to the gym anyway. I don't suppose you'd like to come?"

I shook my head: what a vile suggestion this early in the day.

Instead, I took a carafe of strong coffee back down to the guest room, resolving to get cracking on *Baby*. I opened my laptop, found the file of the first chapter I'd translated into English, and pulled out my copy of the original book in Spanish. The cover illustration was a photograph of a solitary pram parked on a sidewalk outside a city apartment. Snow was falling softly on the pram and street; there was not a responsible adult, much less a mother, in sight. It evoked a loneliness that was not humorous at all.

I couldn't imagine abandoning a baby outdoors on its lonesome. I couldn't even remember being outside on my own until I was about seven. My mother, with eight kids, did not believe in fresh air, but in keeping young children where you could see them, even if that meant everyone was underfoot all the time.

After two hours of translating, I allowed myself to look at email. A lot of it was the usual spam, but there were gems amid the rubble: intelligent queries from a magazine editor on a translated essay by a Spanish author, and a message from the author herself, inviting me to visit her in Granada. Good news came too in the form of a message from Rosa Cardenes, who'd won a prize for her latest Madrid-based thriller. She'd gone to Marseilles to receive it and she'd forwarded an interview where she praised her translators—all ten of us—for helping make her a success outside Spain.

Perhaps it was time to head back to Spain for a good long while? My old friend Ana had moved out of Barcelona to a small place on the Costa Brava. I missed her spacious, light-filled apartment on the Rambla de Catalunya, bought in the early 1970s when Franco was still alive, and home to Ana's art projects and her many friends over the years. But the coastal village where she lived now was pretty fantastic too. Maybe I could buy something in that village and rent it out when I was gone? Because I was far from done with traveling.

Coffee always makes me more optimistic. Buying a *casita* in Spain, why not? It sounded far better than a tiny studio on a terraced street in Wood Green or Deptford with a view of parked cars. I was in the midst of writing to Ana about coming to see her right after the literary festivals this month, imagining how I would settle into a marvelous day-to-day life finishing the translation of the *Baby* while looking out at the blue Mediterranean and swimming in the afternoons, relaxing with wine in the evening with Ana's friends, when a curt message popped up on screen from Luisa:

Have you called Giselle Richard yet?

Por dios, mujer, I just got here.

I thought about the back-and-forth I'd had with one of the students yesterday when she asked how I'd found a publisher for Luisa's book. I told her that the deal had gone through Editorial Cielo, but that I had played a role, as many translators did, in facilitating the connection with a publisher in the States. I didn't say that when I received Giselle's email, inquiring about the rights to *Júpiter y sus lunas,* I'd been staggered, since it came out of nowhere after two years of Cielo's presenting the book to English-language publishers and finding only rejection. Luisa's star had faded since the giddy days of her twenties, when she had won the award for *Diary of a First Love in Montevideo* and Cielo had sold translation rights to ten countries. They had kept publishing her since then, as did a few other editors at foreign houses. There had been two collections from two different university presses in the U.S., both of whose editors told me, when I informally contacted them on Luisa's behalf, that they couldn't muster enough support from their colleagues to do another of Luisa's titles, given the poor sales. I imagined "poor behavior" also had something to do with it.

Then came Giselle's enthusiastic letter. She'd read my translation of Luisa's last book, *Shadow of a Woman on the Sidewalk,* and raved about it in terms I knew Luisa would appreciate—"shimmering," "exquisite," "piercing"— and she wondered, since she understood that Luisa had another, newer collection out in Spanish, *Júpiter y sus lunas,* if I had considered translating it. If I would consider translating it for Entre Editions.

I'd gone to their website and had been impressed. Entre Editions, though only five years old, had quite a decent list, all fiction. Mostly women authors, which was unusual. Mostly French, but also Polish, Bulgarian, Korean, and German. On the website was a black and white photo of Giselle: business-like in a slightly glamorous way. Delicate bone structure and dark-rimmed glasses, a black pageboy with straight bangs and a thin stripe of white at one temple, like Susan Sontag crossed with Louise Brooks.

The Home-page description of the company was succinct: "Entre Editions is meant to suggest both the French word for *between*, as between languages, and also the word for *enter*. We invite you to come into the world of translation and stay a while."

But when I clicked "About Us" I found a more intimate tone. Giselle wrote about her mother, Pauline Richard, a notable translator for many years of both French classics and contemporary novels from France and Quebec.

I grew up in Montreal, in a home full of French and English books, and was encouraged to read widely from an early age. My American mother had studied and lived in Paris as a young woman, and married into a Francophone family in Montreal. She returned to France whenever she could, and one of the highlights of my early years was the school year I spent with her in Paris when I was eight. Her ear for French was finely tuned and most of all, she was a very good writer, as all translators must strive to be. When my grandfather grew ill, my mother moved back to her childhood home of Portland, Oregon, to care for him while keeping up a full schedule. I eventually followed her. Pauline Richard was considered one of the finest translators of French to English, and she is much missed since her death six years ago. She influenced me in countless ways—how I read, how I think, and how I think about translation. She knew a good deal about publishing as well, and schooled me early on in dealing respectfully not just with authors, but also with translators. Entre Editions is dedicated to my mother, to keeping some of her translations in print, and to discovering new voices from around the world.

I'd forwarded Giselle's email on to Luisa, along with the link to Entre Editions' website, and before the day was out I'd heard back from Luisa, who was thrilled, and from her editor at Cielo who was also delighted to know of the interest from an American publishing house. Although Luisa rarely acknowledged any insecurity about her writing or career, preferring to blame others for sabotaging her in some way, I knew she must be as relieved as I was that she might be taken on by an editor who seemed to understand her work and would promote it. It was the icing on the cake that Giselle, too, was so dedicated to the memory of her mother. *Of course* she would understand the underlying themes of *Júpiter y sus lunas.*

The website had mentioned a business manager, Jane Janicki, and two or three interns. There was no hint six months ago that a woman named Karen Morales would come to play a role in Entre Editions, putting balls of yarn on the cover and talking about speculative-fiction foremothers.

The business number I had for Entre Editions went right to voicemail, since it was Saturday after all, but I managed to locate an email from Giselle from several months ago that had her personal cell listed.

"Cassandra Reilly!" The woman's voice, with its subtle French inflection, was cordial but cautious. "Where are you calling from?"

I apologized for disturbing her on a weekend, but told her I was in Oakland and would be in the States for another ten days or so before flying back to London. I told her I'd gone through the manuscript with Luisa in Montevideo and that she'd been generally happy with the overall editing. Then, politely, I added that Luisa was *not* too happy with the proposed change in title (I emphasized "proposed") and *very un*-happy with the proposed cover design.

She sighed. "To be truthful, I'm not wild about the cover design myself. I prefer a more understated look. But Karen, the new marketing director, is very eager to boost our sales. I hired Karen to help us with audience development, the website, a more robust presence on social media. Speculative fiction is very big these days, in Portland and elsewhere. I think we want to find a way to balance appealing to new readers with preserving the integrity of Luisa's vision. But, of course, her opinion, and yours, is welcome. I really love her writing and I'm honored to publish it."

And then she launched into a bout of praise for *Jupiter*. How the title story about the mother and two daughters was so marvelous and the metaphors so striking. The conversation became animated as we talked about other writers we both admired, other books, other book covers. Finally she said she would talk to Karen and they'd start fresh with the cover design. And meanwhile, I must convey all the admiration she had for Luisa to her. Oh, she wished we could all meet up in person and talk this through,

When I told her that Luisa had suggested I might want to visit Portland on this trip, before returning to London, Giselle said, "Oh, definitely do come up to Oregon! How wonderful you're willing to make this effort! Maybe there are other translation projects you might want to do with us. We have very little on our list from Latin America and I know that's a specialty of yours. I'd love to talk with you at length about authors you recommend."

Other translation projects? More work? And with such a wonderfully intelligent editor who seemed to be so interested in women's literature?

I knew a half dozen women writers in Latin America and Spain who were eager to be translated into English. If I could promote two or three of them to Entre Editions that would make a trip to Portland completely worthwhile. Before I knew it, I was offering to fly up to Oregon in a week's time for a night or two. On the return trip to SFO I could connect with my British Airways flight to London. Even if I had to spend some money to meet Giselle, it might well be worth it if I came away with another translation contract for a book I could take on after *Baby* was finished. Personal contacts are everything, and I liked the idea of a personal contact with Giselle.

"Oh, Cassandra, I'd love to meet you! But is there any way you could come this week? In fact, if you could come this Monday or Tuesday, that would be super. I have to head off to New York on Wednesday night for a sales conference and some meetings, then I'm going to Montreal for the weekend." Her already warm voice turned delightfully coaxing. "Couldn't you change your plans just a bit? I know it's an expense for you, but I'd so very much like to meet you and this might be our only chance for a long time."

I quickly made a decision. I wasn't in the States that often, and if meeting Giselle meant I could persuade her to change the title back to *On Jupiter* and junk the ball of yarn, if it meant I could bring some deserving

Latin American women authors to her attention and pick up some work for myself, then I should go now. Besides, there was something about her French-accented, cajoling voice that seemed to put a spell on me.

"Why not?" I said. "I could fly up Monday, I suppose."

"Fantastic!" Then she paused. "The only problem is that I'm not in Portland at the moment. I'm on the Oregon coast. My mother left me an old cottage in Newport, a couple hours drive from Portland. I'm spending some time out here, catching up on a lot of reading, and also overseeing some repairs. I've absolutely got to be here Monday through Wednesday morning in case the window guy turns up. I know it's a huge thing to ask, but could you possibly come out here, to the coast?"

Swept up in her enthusiasm and pushing aside my intention to double down on *Baby's First Year* I agreed. I'd still have a week in Oakland when I returned

"Oh, marvelous," Giselle said, and then apologized, "Because of the construction I'm so sorry I can't ask you to stay, but there's an *absolutely* charming hotel here in Newport, not far from me, the Sylvia Beach Hotel. Yes, exactly, *that* Sylvia Beach! And since you're springing for the flight and the rental car, I'd love to book you for two nights at my expense. You'll love it, I promise, you'll never want to leave. They have a library on the top floor and mulled wine in the evening, and the beach goes on forever. And we'll have lots of time together to talk, I promise. I love to talk with other translators, and you're quite an important one—no, you *are*."

We arranged that one way or another I'd see her, Monday evening or Tuesday morning, and we'd spend Tuesday together.

I rang off, feeling pleasantly dazed by her warmth. Compared to the women I'd been around lately, the neurotic Luisa and the surprisingly stern Kim, it would be a nice change.

"I thought you told me you were going to keep your head down and translate all day every day while you were here?" said Kim when she came back from exercising and grocery shopping. "And I just bought a ton of food."

"It's true," I said, thinking of Janneken's urgent messages. "I should stay here and translate. But I'll get back to it when I return. Maybe I can even do some work in the hotel up there. I feel this is an unexpected opportunity. Giselle and I really seemed to hit it off, and she seems interested in discussing other translation projects I might want to do. You don't turn up your nose at that kind of thing. It's true, it will cost something to fly up to Portland and rent a car, but she's paying for the hotel room."

Kim paused, and then said, "If you're so keen to go then, why don't you take Dora's Subaru? That will cost you nothing but the gas. She just had it tuned up last week before she left. I think you could drive up in a day. Probably a long day, but you could manage it. If you didn't want to drive all the way back, you could drive to Portland and leave it with our friends there, Jill and Candace, and get a cheap flight to Oakland. That would give me and Dora a chance to go up there, visit them, and retrieve it."

"You'd do that for me?"

"Well, I think you're right. It's an opportunity for you. I mean, you can work on a translation anywhere, right?"

Probably relieved that we wouldn't have to spend the next ten days together, we enjoyed the weekend and bright and early Monday morning I set off for Oregon.

5.

It was exhilarating at first, driving out of Oakland on a fresh Monday morning on the wide open road. I had the radio tuned to a station that played only music, no news. The Subaru was comfortably beat-up, so I didn't need to worry about adding to the upholstery stains if I spilled anything. I removed a feathery thing dangling from the rear-view mirror, but I couldn't do anything about the many bumper stickers ("If You Cut Off My Reproductive Rights, Can I Cut Off Yours?" and "You're in California: Speak Spanish!") that caused some fellow drivers to smile and others to give me the evil eye, especially in conservative southern Oregon.

I couldn't help worrying, just a little, that Giselle might not be as friendly and amenable as she came across on the phone Saturday morning. What if she'd talked to Karen Morales and been persuaded that Luisa and I didn't know the market; what if they had decided to go ahead with *Unraveling Jupiter* and the big yarn ball and her baby balls? If Luisa didn't get her way, she'd be furious and this publication would end up like other times I'd worked with editors on Luisa's behalf: a tangle of threats, silences, recriminations, dashed hopes, and all the rest that made Luisa's existence (and by extension, mine) so fraught. Already, I thought, Giselle had been a bit less enthusiastic when I called her back Sunday afternoon to tell her yes, I was coming to Newport. I had a friend's car and should get there sometime Monday evening.

"Fantastic," she'd said, but she sounded harried. "I've already paid for your room at the Sylvia Beach for two nights. I'd love to see you Monday evening, but I'm expecting a long, crazy day getting ready for the sales conference. And the window guy said he'd be here Monday to finish up. Though God knows, at this point I really shouldn't be expecting him. You know how they are. They can take a window *out,* but they can't manage to put a new window *in.*" She laughed in a tired way. "Fortunately, it's just the bathroom window that's left, so if it rains, it's not a big deal. I've got plastic over it."

We agreed to meet Tuesday morning at nine thirty at the cottage. She later emailed me a confirmation from the hotel. There was none of the beguiling warmth of our first phone conversation in her message, but it was cordial.

By noon I'd reached the pretty mountain town of Dunsmuir on the Sacramento River, not far from the Oregon border. I passed Ashland around two p.m., and stopped for a latte. Recharged, I continued on through spring green hills to Roseburg, where I turned west. Kim had suggested getting off 1-5 so I could see more of the coast, even though it would take a little longer.

I soon regretted this choice as I found myself sandwiched in between logging trucks with actual giant logs swaying around the curves. The fact was, I was unused to driving long distances, unused to driving at all, in fact. I'd forgotten that the American West is lonely and empty for large swathes, broken only by endless signs for Taco Bell, Burger King, and McDonalds. The further I got from the urban mix of Oakland, the paler the faces became, and the more unsettled I felt by men passing the feminist-bumper-stickered Subaru in their big trucks that sported Stars and Stripes waving from the back. Most of the places I passed through were long, strung-out eyesores, box stores in vast parking lots, truck dealerships, shabby mini-malls, which emphasized the American habit of making even the most gorgeous places ugly.

In this landscape, I couldn't help chewing far too much on my current living situation, which suddenly seemed so wobbly. Ana had written back from the Costa Brava, enthusiastic about my idea of buying something in her village or nearby, but cautioning me: "I must tell you, *querida*, that prices here are much higher than when I bought my little seaside shack during the downturn a while back." She mentioned how much a small house belonging to one of her neighbors had sold for, a price that would wipe out my savings. I was back to my original dilemma about London.

I'd stayed with Nicky on and off for decades. We met when we were in our late twenties. By that time she'd been living in Olivia Wulf's house in Hampstead for almost ten years, ever since she'd first moved to London from Glasgow with a scholarship to the Guildhall School of Music. Nicky had noticed a small sign on the school's bulletin board about the well-known violinist needing some secretarial help. Olivia not only hired Nicky and gave her a room, she helped make her career, and in the end left the house to her when she died. Friends introduced me to Nicky and she offered me a place to sleep for a few days while I was doing some business in London. After that, whenever I was in England, I stayed in the attic room in Hampstead.

Eventually Nicky sold the house for a bundle and bought the two-bedroom terraced flat in Islington. It was a bequest she felt determined to share with me. Over the last years I'd been in Islington more often, and for longer periods. We rubbed along quite nicely, as we always had, ordering take-away and sharing the expense of a cleaner, since neither of us was particularly domestic. And on the rare occasions when we irritated each other, one of us usually apologized, remembering that life was short and friendships were precious.

It was perfect until last month when she told me one evening that she thought it would be better to get out of London before the country went to wrack and ruin. Scotland was bound to vote for independence and to stay in the EU.

"Oh, and you're planning to move back to Glasgow?" I laughed. She'd kept her accent and was proud of being Scottish, but she'd never had a positive word to say about the city. She'd grown up in a middle-class family that was strict and church-going and Nicky was anything but.

"No, Edinburgh," she said. "It's really cosmopolitan now, Cassandra. Tons of writers and artists and musicians. Not so stressful as London either. Smaller, less expensive, fairly tranquil for a large city, important when one's getting on in years."

"You don't like tranquility, you've never liked tranquility, I've never heard anything so ridiculous. Your whole musical life is bound up with London."

"I've looked at Edinburgh flats online. I could buy something lovely, with at least two bedrooms. I'm going to go up there for a week before my tour to Germany in a few weeks and talk to an estate agent."

Just after I arrived in Montevideo I heard from her. She'd just arrived in Edinburgh, was being shown the most scrumptious flats, half the asking price of what was available in London. She'd asked the estate agent to send me photos of the best of them, and that was the last I'd heard from her. By now, she had probably gone ahead and bought something. Five hours from London by train.

As I made my way steadily northward, the sky darkened to plum and gray, and heavy rain fell. I stopped for a sandwich and another espresso at a Starbucks in Florence until the rain subsided and became heavy fog again. Sometime after eight in the evening, around thirteen hours after leaving Oakland, I rolled blearily into Newport, its neon signs muted in the fog. I lost my way several times, which is when I discovered that the overhead light inside Dora's car wasn't working, and my phone was low on juice, so I couldn't get a map to come up. I rolled down the window and heard the breakers though, so I knew I was getting close to the coastline. Eventually at a quarter to nine, I pulled up to an enormous old wooden hotel, three stories tall, next to the edge of the bluff. Its bright, welcoming entrance, with daffodils gleaming in the lamplit fog, led to an old-fashioned reception desk.

"We've put you in the Edgar Allen Poe room," said the receptionist cheerily.

"Sorry?"

"Giselle, the woman who booked the room, thought you'd like that. I hope it won't be a problem. We don't have any other rooms left except Dr. Seuss."

Had Giselle mentioned the Sylvia Beach Hotel had themed rooms?

"I'll take Poe over Dr. Seuss. Did she leave a message?"

"No, don't think so." She gave me information about breakfast in the morning and the library on the top floor where hot mulled wine would be served a little later. Oh, and in case I didn't know, there were no televisions, radios, or regular phones in the rooms, and they didn't have wi-fi. There was cell phone coverage of course, but they discouraged phone conversations in public areas.

I nodded absently, filling out the form she gave me.

"Where are you from?" she asked, and I paused, as I often do. Years ago I would often answer, *Nowhere,* enjoying the disconcerted expression this invariably caused, but these days I kept things simple.

"Oakland."

"And you drove all day? Oh my, then welcome to a peaceful night here at the Sylvia Beach!"

I took the key and went up the broad wooden staircase to my small room with the single bed.

Red damask bedcover and red-patterned wallpaper. Bricked-up closet. Stuffed raven. Curved ax blade hanging over the bed ... wait, what?

I wondered if the universe was sending me a message (You should have stayed in Oakland), but I was too exhausted to think about it. I didn't need the mulled wine—I unkinked my bent body, took a hot shower, crawled right into bed, ignoring the pendulum overhead, and fell immediately asleep.

I woke up with my head still attached to my neck. In fact, I'd been dreaming so deeply that I hadn't remembered the pendulum at all. But when I opened my eyes to the blade hanging above me I hastily rolled away and jumped out of bed.

From the window I saw the gray morning beach at low tide. Far off, the breakers rolled in with a muffled roar, and innocent-looking frills of lace washed the dark sand. I pulled on my jeans, boots, and an all-purpose rain parka lent to me by the somewhat heftier Kim. Outside the hotel I found a wooden staircase leading from the bluff to the beach. Once on the sand I took great gulps of salt air and stretched yesterday's car-squeezed leg muscles to the limit with every step. Kim's parka flapped around me in the foggy breeze.

Only a few others were out this early, people jogging off in the distance and a woman nearby walking her golden retriever. I felt as if my eyes, so long trained to the small screen, had suddenly expanded to the size of the Pacific, as I took in the long, kelp-strewn shoreline, the gray and green bluffs. Through the light fog, I glimpsed a lighthouse to the north.

The long-leashed retriever bounded up and the owner and I exchanged a few words about the weather. She volunteered that she lived in Newport and walked her dog here twice every day, seven a.m. and seven p.m., rain, fog, or sleet. She had to open her shop at eight, a hair salon, she added, looking somewhat pointedly at my frizzy curls.

An hour later, after a long walk south in increasing sea fog, still not having washed my face properly or untangled my marine-misted hair, I was in the breakfast room, choosing muffins and fruit and yogurt. A boisterous crowd of gray- and white-haired women had taken up two of the family-style round tables, and were lustily sharing memories of times past in Portland. This seemed to be a kind of reunion of Second Wave feminists—they were easy to spot in their fleeces and jeans, without make-up but with plenty of laugh lines, and with an easy way of taking up space. Not for the first time did I wonder what my life would have been like if, instead of going to Europe at twenty, I'd moved west and become part of the lesbian and gay community in someplace like Portland. Would I have taken up hiking and gardening and volunteering at the food coop or the women's bookstore, instead of spending so much time sitting in European cafes with nervy writers and artists who bent my ear with theories and subjected me to years of second-hand smoke?

One or two of the women looked me over, more out of habit than interest, but I only nodded politely as I walked past their tables and took a chair at a table by the tall windows, next to a where a solitary older woman sat, drinking coffee. She looked up warily from her dime-store notebook.

I apologized if I was disturbing her, but she smiled and put her pen down. "This is the sort of place, this hotel, where you can come and write and be alone. But it's also an excellent spot to eavesdrop and meet the unexpected person you'll want to put in your novel."

"Would that be me?"

She had that unobtrusive but observant expression so many writers develop. I saw she'd taken me in entirely, photographed me in her mind, so she could describe me later, perhaps as "She was tall and willowy with an air of dignified deviltry."

"My daughter-in-law has hair like yours," she remarked. "I've always wondered how you get a comb through those kinds of curls."

"It's best not to try," I said. "That's what my mother eventually decided. We got on better after that. And by the way, I've already been a character in a couple of novels at least. Not to mention the movie that was made about me."

She laughed and held out her hand, "Nora," she said.

"I'm Cassandra Reilly." I took a leap since she'd introduced the idea of putting someone like me in a novel, "Are you an author? What's your last name?"

She seemed to hesitate before telling me, "Longeran. Nora Longeran."

She had straight, white bangs and a braid down her back, and seemed to be north of seventy-five; the green-gray eyes behind reading glasses echoed the pale aqua shawl that draped like a small blanket around her neck and shoulders, over what looked like a nightgown but was probably just a soft gray flannel dress. The scarf had an underwater pattern: waves and fish and maybe an octopus tentacle.

"I expect you're terribly famous," I said. "But I live in London ... for the most part. I don't keep up well. I translate, from Spanish."

She looked relieved. "I'm a little bit well-known, but only in some circles. I write for children." She sipped from her coffee. "But a translator, that's marvelous! Tell me all about it. I've known a few translators in my time. I even have a translator character in some of my books; she always plays a crucial role."

I moved over to her table soon, and we talked for well over an hour about translation. Her questions delighted me with their unpredictability. When most people think about translation, it's often individual words they focus on. They imagine that you have to know twice as many words as the average person, that every Spanish word, for instance, has an English counterpart, and it's your job to find that word and swap it in. But Nora was more interested in other, more distinctive aspects of translation. She wondered what my brain felt like when I translated: *Was I in two places at the same time? Was my mind reading Spanish when I was writing English? What did I do when I came to words or expressions that had no direct equivalent in English? How did I deal with that experience—intellectually or emotionally? Did my brain try to solve the puzzle or did my emotions tell me what the author meant and what that might feel like in English?*

When I asked her about the character she'd created who was a translator, she was reticent. *Oh, I'm sure I've gotten it all wrong. I don't speak any other languages, really, so I have to imagine how it is.* But what language does your character translate from? Into what language? *Oh, she's multilingual.* Then it was back to questions for me: *When did I begin to translate? Why Spanish? And weren't there many Spanishes, so to speak? Did I have to learn them all?*

Everyone else had gradually left the breakfast room until we were the only ones left and the servers were clearing off the buffet, yet we continued on, until suddenly I looked at my watch. I was supposed to be at Giselle's cottage at nine-thirty and it was nearly that now. I said I was sorry to leave, but I had some business.

"Business in Newport? What could that be, I wonder?"

"I'm meeting someone," I said. "About a translation I'm doing for her publishing company. Maybe you know her? Giselle Richard? She has a cottage somewhere near the hotel, on the bluff."

Under her blanket-like aqua scarf I saw her shoulders tighten but she said, in a calm, flat tone, lacking all the liveliness of our previous conversation, "Yes, an interesting young woman. I knew her mother, actually. Pauline. The family has had a summer cottage here for many years. The house has been vacant for quite a while."

"I think Giselle mentioned she's fixing it up. Replacing the windows at least. She seems to be using it as a place to work." The penny dropped. "Oh, then the translator you mentioned must be Pauline, I mean, the friend who gave you ideas for your character."

"Yes." For some reason her face had closed down, and I was uncertain why. I remembered the website Giselle had created with its paean to her mother. Had there been a falling out between Pauline and Nora somewhere along the line? Nora wasn't going to tell me anything, that was clear.

Awkward now, afraid I'd stirred up some unpleasant memory, I held out my hand. "Will you be around later? I'd love to chat again."

"I'm not sure I'll be available. Work, you know. But it was good to meet you, Cassandra Reilly. Good luck with your meeting. I'm sure Giselle will do a lovely job with your translation."

She opened up her notebook again with finality.

6.

Now I was seriously late. I dashed upstairs to the Poe room to brush my teeth and to jam the copyedited manuscript of *On Jupiter* into my shoulder bag. Giselle had given me her address and some directions, but I checked with the receptionist to get my bearings. "It's just a half a dozen blocks along Coast Street," she told me, but while I'd been having breakfast a thicker fog had moved up the bluffs, propelled by a strong wind from the sea that made me wish Kim's jacket had a hood. Hair unpleasantly dripping into my ears, eyes stinging from the salty gusts, I walked shivering along Coast Street for several blocks until I looked at the piece of paper with the address again. There was a SW Coast Street and a NW Coast Street and I was going south not north.

Once I was headed into the Northwest street numbers I found Giselle's cottage easily enough, just off NW Coast. It was the last residence near the edge of the bluff; the street ended in a wooden barrier. The cottage must have a stunning view when the sun was out, but now the battered gray shingles hardly stood out in the fog. It wasn't very large, one story with a dormer room upstairs. There were signs of remodeling: shingles removed around a couple of newly installed, unpainted sash windows at the front of the house, and bundles of cedar shakes in the sandy front yard. It didn't seem that the window guy had managed to get to one narrow window downstairs—perhaps that was the bathroom window Giselle had mentioned. It was covered with a thick, opaque sheet of plastic, not well nailed down, and fluttering raggedly at the top. In the driveway I saw a late-model Prius, but no house lights were on. Tarpaper flapped wildly on the part of the roof facing the sea. Up here on the bluff with only a few houses around, and no one in sight, the waves and wind combined to create a continuous roar, made more eerie by the fact that the ocean waves were invisible behind a bank of fog.

I knocked on the front door. I rang the bell. My watch said I was over half an hour late, but surely she wouldn't have gone off and just left me to stand here? Through the small windows at the top of the door, I glimpsed a hallway leading to a larger room with photographs on the wall and bookshelves. Maybe there was an office in back and she hadn't heard me knock or ring because of the sound of the wind and waves. I took out my phone and checked, then called and left her a voice message. Her recording reminded me of the seductive power of her voice, even though the words themselves were brief and business-like. "You've reached Giselle Richard and Entre Editions. Sorry, I'm out of the office right now, but will return your call as soon as possible."

I wondered for a moment whether the number I'd called was the right one. Wasn't her office in Portland? Her cell should be her personal phone, shouldn't it? Wouldn't she have her phone with her, even if she had gone to the hardware store to buy some duct tape, for instance, to stop the plastic on the bathroom window from ripping in the wind? Maybe I should go around to the back of the house and see if she was somewhere about. The wind was even stronger on the ocean-facing side, where I found a small deck with a couple of chairs knocked over and a metal table on its side. A sliding glass door to the house also seemed scheduled to be replaced, with the shingles removed all around the edges. Standing on the deck, I could see a small basic kitchen with a table and two chairs off to the right, while the glass door, undraped, opened directly into a living room that had been turned into an office with the addition of a modern desk piled with piles of paper and books. A laptop was open on the desk. I tried the rusty latch of the glass door and it squeaked open. I wasn't sure if it was broken or just not closed correctly, but I took that squeak as an invitation to enter.

Viewed from a neighboring house, my movements might well have looked a little suspicious. But I was sure Giselle had just gone off on an errand and would return shortly or was perhaps upstairs and hadn't heard me. I didn't think she'd mind if I slipped inside to get out of the clammy wind. I called out in friendly way as I slid the door open, "Giselle, it's me, Cassandra. Sorry, I rang and knocked and couldn't rouse you. Are you all right? Everything okay?"

It's often a good thing when breaking in to ask if someone is all right. It makes it seem like a wellness check.

Still no answer. I closed the glass door and although the house was old and beat-up and far from sound-proofed, the din of the surf and wind muted to a tolerable level. The important thing was that I was out of the howling wind. I wondered if it would be rude to look for a towel to dry my face and hair and decided that might be going too far. Instead I simply stood and looked around.

The ceiling was low and the walls were painted pale green with white trim. Aside from the glass door there were no other windows. The wood stove in the corner gave off no heat, and perhaps was rarely used. A small fat couch patterned in green and white stripes was against the largest wall, under a gallery of photographs, many of them black and white. I glanced at them curiously and saw a young woman of around twenty with a pixie cut and pale lipstick, and dressed in a Sixties-era sleeveless shift. Filterless cigarette in hand, legs crossed, she leaned back in a bistro chair and smiled buoyantly at the camera. I recognized that café on the Boulevard Montparnasse. The same woman, twenty-five years older and with her dark hair in a French twist, with big snap-on earrings, again smiling self-confidently, was photographed with two girls, one a teenager, the other four or five, in front of a modern apartment building. It must be Pauline Richard and her daughter, Giselle. Maybe a younger sister? The girls both looked like Pauline, especially the little one. Another picture, again in black and white, with a professional touch, showed the same woman, now in her sixties, sitting at a desk with bookshelves behind her. She was painfully thin, her head wrapped in a stylish wool turban, but she still had the same self-assured smile. Her camera smile.

There were other photographs in color, enlarged snapshots, nicely framed, including several of Giselle with an Asian woman who had long, prematurely white hair and a strong, unlined face. They had their arms around each other in one picture taken on the beach. I supposed that put paid to my vague fantasy that Giselle might be single.

Over in a corner, also matted and framed, was another color photograph, enlarged to 5 x 8, which I imagined had been taken half a dozen years ago or more. It showed three women on the deck of this cottage on a summer's day, a blue sky and bluer ocean: a younger Giselle, sans white stripe at her temple, wearing a white halter dress that showed off her tanned skin, holding the hand of her mother. Pauline was in pale blue pajamas, a light green blanket around her shoulders, her hair in a pageboy with bangs that looked too black and glossy to be real. The third woman I recognized as well. Nora, white braid and all, nut-brown and wrinkled in a one-piece bathing suit and flip-flops. I looked closer. The blanket that covered Pauline's shoulders was the felted aqua shawl with the images of underwater sea life that Nora had been wearing this morning over the gray flannel dress.

The grouping suggested close ties, at least in the past, and the shawl even closer ties with Pauline. Did they have the same shawl? Had Pauline given it to her as a present? Had Nora inherited it after Pauline's death? If the three of them were close, why did Nora's face close down when I mentioned Giselle? Was it true that she was unaware Giselle was staying in Newport, that she was working to repair the house? I didn't really know anything about Nora, not even where she lived. It wouldn't be here in Newport if she was staying at the hotel.

The plastic flapping at the bathroom window brought me back to myself. I'd have to return to the hotel and hope that Giselle called me with an explanation. I shouldn't hang about, poking around in someone else's things (I heard my eldest sister Eileen shouting at me through the years: *Get out of my room, you little sneak*). Still, I lingered a few minutes longer. I wondered if Giselle's desk had a mock-up of the entire print catalog so that I could see whether the cover of *Unraveling Jupiter* was included. I was quite careful to turn over papers and files without dislodging anything.

I didn't find the catalog, but while flipping through the file folders I did knock into the desk and with a start, like a person waking up from a nap on a reclining chair, the laptop screen lit up and revealed an email in progress. Who wouldn't be startled by catching a glimpse of one's own name?

Karen,

Let's talk about your ideas below before New York. I can then email Paul and run a few ideas past him about how we're going to present the fall books to the sales reps Friday. I know you'll do a great job with your part of the presentation, and they'll be as excited as I am by the new direction. I just want to give Paul a bit of a heads up so he knows what to expect and so we can fine-tune our pitches.

In other news, the window guy is driving me crazy. He was supposed to turn up this morning, but was a no show. Again. I told him if that bathroom window isn't replaced by Wednesday noon, I'm firing him. I have an unbelievable amount of stuff to worry about without fretting on our trip that someone could break in while I'm gone. I'll board it up myself if he doesn't come. I don't have time to tell you everything right now, but Jane's been raving again about the budget and bills. Oh, and on top of

*everything, that Cassandra woman is turning up tomorrow morning. I
know she's just the messenger, but I hope we're not going to have serious
trouble with Luisa about the marketing angle and cover. I'll take her out
to an early lunch and punt any decisions until she's safely back in London.
The sales reps will want to weigh in on the cover and publicity.*

Looking forward

And there the message stopped. I would have liked to scroll down and
see what Karen Morales had said in her earlier email, but I was afraid to
touch the laptop and delete or change anything by mistake.

I slipped back out the sliding glass door and walked away from the
cottage, back into the foggy winds, to the Sylvia Beach. Of course I
know there's always the chance that if you read personal email you'll find
out something you didn't expect, but to be referred to as *that Cassandra
woman* and *just the messenger* stung. What about the phone call we'd had
on Saturday, Giselle's warmth, her invitation to come to Newport, her
assurances that she herself didn't care much for the cover or the title? I
could still hear her voice in my ear, the slight French accent, the almost
caressing tone.

Yet the more I thought about the email message, the odder it seemed.
It appeared to have been written sometime yesterday afternoon with a
suggestion that she and Karen discuss ideas for marketing. Probably Paul
was a sales manager in another time zone. And Giselle had referred to me
arriving *tomorrow,* that is, today, Tuesday. Yet since the message was still
visible on the screen it didn't appear to either have been finished or sent.
Had the window guy suddenly appeared or something else happened to
interrupt her?

I supposed the likeliest explanation was that the email had been saved
as a draft and that it had never been sent yesterday. Perhaps it wasn't the last
email Giselle had written—she must have written many more messages
that were sent yesterday and this morning. But perhaps she'd decided to
call Karen instead on Monday or Karen had called her. In which case,
why save the message as a draft rather than just delete it? Could it be that
Giselle wanted me to find the message? Could she have saved it by mistake
yesterday but then opened it this morning and left it visible for me to
find? Was it possible that in some sort of devious, passive-aggressive way,
Giselle had intentionally absented herself from the cottage this morning,

had intentionally only semi-latched the sliding glass door, had deliberately left the laptop open with the message visible? Maybe it was all part of a sly negotiating strategy, one designed to throw me off my stride, and make me aware, without her actually having to say the words, that Luisa was not going to get her way.

This was all speculation, probably far-fetched, but whether or not Giselle had intended me to see the email message or not, I had.

And I had seen that Giselle considered Karen's opinion more important than mine or Luisa's. So it was going to be up to me to hold firm. No yarn balls, no idiotic title. *We'll see how she likes being unraveled,* Luisa had threatened. I would unravel Giselle and her flattery and make no concessions. But that didn't mean I still didn't want *On Jupiter* published by Entre Editions. I wanted that very much, and I'd make sure Giselle knew that when she finally called to apologize for not being there for our meeting.

A housekeeper was making up rooms on the second floor, including mine, as guests checked out and sounds of vacuuming reverberated throughout the old wooden hotel. I nipped into my bathroom and took a towel to dry my damp hair, and then went upstairs to the library that stretched across the ocean-facing side of the building. No one else was about, and I made myself a cup of tea and settled down. Fog washed against the tall windows, and I could see nothing of the beach below. I took out the copyedited manuscript and left my phone on.

Reason returned as I considered how very unlikely it was that Giselle would have left her house unlocked and her laptop open with a message to be read. For one thing the latch was rusty and it was only due to some rather pushy jiggling, I had to admit, that it had clicked open. The laptop was on, but quietly blank; it was only because I was a snoop and bumped the desk that the screen lit up. Giselle couldn't have predicted either that I'd come in or that I'd see that message. Maybe she was just refreshing her memory this morning about some correspondence about the cover and title. That was the likeliest explanation. As for her continued absence, something must have come up. Maybe she'd taken a walk and run into a friend and time had slipped away, maybe there was no duct tape at the local hardware store?

Time passed and the fog didn't abate, but the winds died down. I went over a few tricky issues raised by the copyeditor and drank my tea. It seemed to me once or twice that I heard sirens, but they could have been coming from Highway 101, which was probably not as far from the hotel as it had seemed last night in the dark.

Finally my cell buzzed with a text.

But it wasn't from Giselle. Instead, Janneken wrote:

Cassandra, Did you get my earlier long email? I imagine you're miffed. Rumblings about replacing you on the panel at Chipping Witteron. Fucking Angela Cook. Cursed agent!

What was this all about? I tried to access my email but couldn't get it to come up on the phone. Jannken must be talking about the panel in two weeks at the prestigious literary festival held yearly in Chipping Waldron, where Claribel Montoya and I were scheduled to appear. It was the first of two literary festivals that Claribel and I were attending together, but Chipping Witteron, as Janneken found it amusing to call it, was the bigger one, where name authors and sometimes translators had an opportunity to witter on about current books.

I texted back, "Can't open email, no wi-fi here. Details please," and another short message soon appeared:

Where are you that you can't get wi-fi? In brief, the agent is trying to get the Witteron organizers to oust you in favor of Angela Cook. She's on bloody sabbatical and has just arrived in London for a few months. I'm doing all I can to keep the arrangement as is, but it doesn't help you're not here to defend yourself. WHERE ARE THOSE CHAPTERS?!

How dare they want to kick me off the panel in favor of Angela Cook? My face felt so hot with irritation that I didn't need the towel to finish drying my hair. I also felt scared in the pit of my stomach, the way I'd felt when I hadn't done my homework in junior high, and the nuns would send me over to Sister Monica in the principal's office for a talk about the venial sin of sloth.

One thing was certain, I had to stop worrying about Giselle and Luisa and the cosmic balls of yarn and seriously get to work on *Baby's First Year.* Otherwise I was in danger of being un-invited to Chipping Witteron and of entirely losing this translation commission. And then I would be well and truly screwed. Not only would I soon not have a place to live, but I would have to break into my savings just to pay my bills.

I returned to the Poe Room, wanting to take my laptop to the nearest café and read Janneken's fuller account of this double-cross, but knowing I should probably stay here and wait for Giselle to contact me or else go back over to her house and try again. But when I looked out the window, I saw that the wind was increasing again, with heavy raindrops slicing through the mist.

I suddenly felt very tired.

The freshly made bed beckoned invitingly—I'd awakened early, after all, and was still not over my jet lag—but the pendulum still hung there. Even though it seemed to be made of tinfoil, with the dullest of blades, I didn't find it very reassuring in my present state of mind. Maybe it was time for some yoga.

I was an indifferent practitioner and in fact only knew about six poses, but sometimes they helped with the stiffness in my lower back and with general relaxation. I lowered myself to the floor, and in about five minutes was out like a light.

It took me a few moments to realize that someone was knocking lightly but distinctly at the door. Groggy, I called, "Just a minute," and checked my watch. 1:10. Giselle, finally.

Yet when I hauled myself up and opened the door it wasn't Giselle in the hallway. It was a bulky police officer with a badge and a holstered gun or two, who asked if I was Cassandra Reilly and introduced himself. Could he come in to ask a few questions about Giselle Richard? I was highly disconcerted to suddenly have such a large male in such a small space, with a pendulum glinting in the background. He requested my driver's license and studied it a moment. "Where are you from, ma'am?"

"London," I said. "But I'm an American citizen. I'm here on business. What's happened?"

"And your business is, Ms. Reilly?"

"It's to do with translation and publishing," I said. "I was supposed to meet Giselle Richard this morning here in Newport. I'm translating a book that her company is publishing. But she wasn't at her house, so I came back here to wait for her to call or come by."

"When was the last time you spoke with Ms. Richard?"

"Sunday morning, from Oakland. I drove up from Oakland yesterday. She booked me into the hotel for two nights."

I wondered if a nosy neighbor had seen me and reported me as a possible burglar. For surely Giselle wouldn't be reporting me. But then—where was Giselle? And how did the police know to come to the hotel and to ask for me?

"What time did you go to the house today?"

"Around ten. The meeting was for nine-thirty, but I got turned around a little in the fog with the Southwest and the Northwest and got there late. I tried calling her but she didn't answer. I figured there might have been some kind of mix-up." It would be best not to say anything about going inside the cottage. Alarm swept through me. "What's happened?" I asked again. "Has there been an accident?"

"Ms. Reilly, I'm afraid Giselle Richard is dead. She was found sometime after eleven a.m. down below her house, on the side of the bluff. We know you were in the cottage this morning. You were seen going in by the back way. Your appointment with her was on her desk calendar, along with the information that you were staying here at this hotel. You'll need to accompany me back to the station for a statement, if you don't mind. We'd like you to bring your phone and laptop. And your passport and travel documents, please."

The *if you don't mind* was proforma. I nodded, took my jacket and my shoulder bag with documents and laptop and went downstairs with him. I wasn't sure if I should turn over any electronics without professional advice. But I wanted at the moment to appear cooperative. Or else I was just stunned.

Giselle dead. Up until a few hours ago I'd so been looking forward to meeting her. Giselle with the white-striped black bangs, the clean-lined beauty, the slightly accented voice with the flirtatious edge, which had promised so much, including the possibility of more work.

But the chance to meet her was gone. As I would soon hear, Giselle's body had been discovered in dense scrub below the bluff. A walker had noticed a yellow scarf and left the path to investigate. Apparently she was found only about an hour after I'd been seen by a next-door neighbor mucking about her house in the fog and letting myself inside.

This is when you want a good lawyer, or at least not to be an expat queer translator in some beachside town where you don't know anyone.

7.

But, fortunately, I did know someone.

At the bottom of the stairs, in the small lobby of the hotel, was a wall mural illustrating the bookseller and publisher Sylvia Beach in profile, brown bobbed hair, light blue suit, manuscript in her hand, seated next to the man himself, James Joyce, dapper in a tuxedo suit, red bow tie, dark glasses, and eye patch. Behind them were painted shelves of books, and black and white photographs of authors from the 1920s.

Against this literary backdrop Nora Longeran, now dressed in Levi's, sweatshirt, and ball cap, like an overage Little League girl but with all her faculties intact, thank you very much, stood out pugnaciously. "I know why you're taking this woman away. The receptionist told me about Giselle's accident. Cassandra can't be a suspect. She had nothing to do with this. She was with me at breakfast. She told me she was going to a meeting with Giselle about publishing. Have you read Cassandra her rights? She's a foreign visitor from England. The British Consulate should be informed."

I wasn't sure if this broadside, delivered in the ringing tones of a good ACLU member, was really the best defense. Personally I always try to say as little as possible when I'm in trouble. On the other hand, Nora seemed very willing to act as a character witness on the strength of ninety minutes in the breakfast room.

"Ma'am," said the officer. "She's just coming down to the station with us to assist in our inquiries. Nothing to get excited about. Also, she's not a foreign visitor. She's American as you and me, so there's no problem there."

"It's fine, Nora," I said. "He's right. They just have some questions for me. I was born in Kalamazoo," I added, as we went out the door. "Let's keep in touch."

"I'm getting a lawyer," she called. "You have the right to remain silent."

An hour later I'd been fingerprinted, as well as fed a sandwich and offered a lot of very good coffee. Since this was far better treatment than I usually received when in police stations (except in Italy where the coffee was even better), I was inclined to cooperate, though I couldn't give them a completely convincing account of myself. An Irish-American with dual citizenship and an address in London seemed to be a combination inherently dubious.

Still, most things would check out, I hoped, mentally running through my actions the past week. I'd left Montevideo the previous Tuesday night on a flight to Miami, where I went through U.S. customs and passport control, and arrived in San Francisco via Dallas late morning Wednesday. I'd stayed in Oakland several nights with my friend, a professor at CAL, and had participated in a university seminar on Thursday. Saturday on the phone I'd talked to the publisher of the translation, Giselle Richard, she'd invited me to come up to Newport to discuss some issues with the book. I'd left Oakland early Monday morning and checked into the Sylvia Beach as soon as I got to Newport. Giselle was paying for the room. My plan was to leave the car in Portland with friends and fly to Oakland tomorrow. My flight back to London was next week, Wednesday. And yes, I had a ticket.

The officer who first interviewed me over a cup of coffee in a basic but comfortable room at the station seemed amiable enough. He introduced himself as Sergeant Pete Jones and took down my personal information.

"Retired?" he asked.

"Still working. I'm a Spanish translator."

He had flipped through my passport and seen multiple entry and exit stamps. "That must be a fascinating job," he said. He loved to travel, he told me, and had been to Asia often. His wife was Thai-American, and they visited relatives, but also had explored the Australian Outback and trekked in Nepal. He was a fit-looking man in his forties, with big blue eyes and a grin, easy to relate to. Which was probably the point, since soon he switched gears and began leading me through a detailed recap of my movements from the time I left Oakland on Monday through this morning. I was glad I'd gotten it all convincingly organized and clear in my own mind first, since he was thorough.

He paid special attention to the time of my arrival in Newport and asked me in an obviously offhand way if I hadn't stopped by Giselle's house in the early evening, just to say hello to an old friend.

When I said I'd never met her before, and that it was just a business meeting, he said, "Oh right. You did say you hadn't met her before."

"The receptionist at the hotel can confirm I arrived at around nine."

"Yep, got that," he said cheerfully, looking at his laptop screen.

Eventually he went off to print my statement out, and at first I thought that was the end of that. Maybe, in looking through my records, they'd come across a slight altercation I'd had with the I.R.S. some twenty years ago, when I'd been threatened with the loss of my passport over a misunderstanding about my taxes. And if they got into the Interpol database something might conceivably turn up, in Venice, in Venezuela, in Transylvania. But basically I imagined that he'd come back with the statement, I'd sign it, and I'd be free to go.

I still didn't know any details about Giselle's death beyond what Detective Jones told me, that Giselle was found late this morning on the bluff below her house. How she died, when she died, and most importantly why she died didn't come up. But surely they couldn't suspect me, could they? Or even imagine that I was a witness?

But the easy-going Pete Jones never returned. Instead Detective Harald Haakonssen ("two A's, two S's," he told me), came in and sat down across from me. He had my statement in his hand as well as some other material. Harald Haakonssen was well over six feet, in late middle age but trimly built, with thinning blond hair and large ears. Conservatively dressed. Gold wedding ring. I guessed him to be tenacious and by the book, someone who practiced martial arts in his spare time. I looked for a gleam of imagination in his steel blue eyes but saw only skepticism. It's the kind of expression that makes you feel you're lying even when you're not.

To begin with, he read aloud from the statement. "Here I see you told Sergeant Jones, 'I left Oakland around seven-thirty in the morning and arrived in Newport at nine in the evening.'"

"Yes, that's right."

He gave me a stern look. "I remember a trip I took a last year for work. I drove from Newport to San Francisco in eleven hours. It took me slightly less than that on my return. So, in theory, if you left the Bay Area at seven-thirty a.m. as you say, even accounting for morning traffic, shouldn't you have gotten to Newport between six and seven in the evening?"

"I imagine you were in some kind of official police vehicle traveling on 1-5," I countered. "But I left the freeway for the coast, and stopped a few times. I went the speed limit, and it was foggy. I'm lucky I got here in thirteen hours."

"I'm glad you drove the speed limit," he said. It was the first hint I had that he might have a sense of humor, albeit an understated Scandinavian version. He went on, "And once you got to the hotel last night you didn't leave? You didn't go out for dinner and a short walk?"

"I'd already had a sandwich in Florence," I said. "And the idea of wandering around in a place I'd never been before in the dark and fog just wasn't very appealing."

I wanted to ask him if all these questions about my arrival pointed to the strong possibility that they suspected or knew that Giselle had died last evening. But Haakonssen was not going to tip his hand. Instead he moved on to my actions this morning.

"You went out early, before breakfast," he stated. "The receptionist said hello to you at about six forty-five."

"I've been waking early since I got to the West Coast," I said. "But yes, I thought a short walk would be invigorating."

He went on, "And you returned around seven-thirty for breakfast. After which," he looked at the statement, "you went to Ms. Richard's house for your meeting, which you say was for nine-thirty. But you were late."

"Yes, I got talking to someone, a woman named Nora Longeran, at breakfast, then I had to run back upstairs and get the manuscript of the book and then I got a little turned around. That should all be in the statement."

"Tell me about Nora Longeran. She seemed to be shouting at one of our officers in the lobby. She said," he glanced at his notes, "that you were a foreign visitor."

"I'd told her I lived in London. She made assumptions. Our conversation wasn't that personal, it was more about books and things. I mean, she didn't tell me much about herself. She said she knew Giselle Richard's mother, Pauline. I gather Pauline died some years ago."

"Yes, I believe so." He showed no feeling about that, but returned to the facts.

"You were seen by a neighbor knocking on Ms. Richard's front door around ten. She says no one answered and you went around the back. She didn't think anything of it because the Prius was there and she assumed Ms. Richard was working in her office. She saw you walking away down Coast Street around twenty minutes later. Is that correct?"

"Yes."

"Do you make a habit of breaking into people's houses, Ms. Reilly?"

"The latch was already wobbly and gave when I pushed at it. It was very foggy and cold and I didn't want to hang about outside. To be honest, I was worried about her."

"Why worried?"

"I only meant—Giselle seemed eager to meet me. When a person doesn't answer the door and you have an appointment, you can imagine that something happened to them." This innocent concern for a woman's welfare seemed to strike Haakonssen as possibly sinister.

"How long were you in the house? After you realized she wasn't there? Where in the house did you go?"

"I just ... I was in the office. I thought she might have gone out on an errand so I waited about ten minutes. I didn't go into other rooms or upstairs."

"You're sure about that?"

"Of course I'm sure."

"And there were no noises upstairs or from one of the bedrooms?"

"I'd seen some tarpaper on the roof, waving around, but I don't think I heard it inside. Just some plastic flapping at the bathroom window." It crossed my mind that if anyone in the house had heard me fiddling around with the sliding glass door they could have escaped through that window. "Giselle mentioned that there was a window guy coming on Monday to install the last window, but it seems like he didn't fix it. Have you talked to him, this window guy?"

Haakonssen ignored the question. He returned to my forced entry. He asked me to describe in detail everything I'd seen. He was particularly interested in any shoes by the door, and the kitchen area downstairs.

"I didn't go into the kitchen," I told him. "I was just in the office for a short while and left."

"But surely you glanced that way in the, what was it, oh yes, twenty minutes you were there? There's a small table by the kitchen window."

"Yes, I think so." What was his interest in the kitchen? I'd only been in the office. There was no reason to mention that I'd studied the photographs on the wall, glanced at a few files, and read Giselle's email. He would have more questions if he knew I'd snooped around on the desk and looked at the computer screen. I wanted to keep this simple and not get any more involved.

But of course, given the fact that I've done a little amateur detecting in the past I couldn't help but be interested in the kinds of questions he was asking. It helped keep my mind away from the very distressing image of Giselle's body on the lower bluff. Did she fall and break her neck? Was someone else in the cottage the day or evening before? Had anyone looked at Giselle's computer? Had they seen that last message?

It embarrassed me to think of Haakonssen and others reading the email: *that Cassandra woman* still burned in my mind. And the tone of the email didn't sound as if Giselle was eager to meet me at all. And the tone of the other hand, it would confirm that Giselle had been expecting me Tuesday morning, not Monday night. They could sort out any other discrepancies themselves. Surely they'd be on to the window guy right away.

Haakonssen. With a name like that, as well as the gaunt good looks of a really tall Norwegian, the detective seemed to belong to one of those Scandi-noir television thrillers so popular these days. Nicky was addicted to these shows and when I was in London I'd spent many evenings with her watching cops race back and forth between Denmark and Sweden over the Oresund bridge or up around mountain-shadowed Norwegian fjords, chasing criminals who often as not careened off the road. Janneken had published a number of these kinds of thrillers as well, with troubled detectives who solved the most gruesome serial murders in between bouts of black-out drinking.

Was I suffering from some form of shock? Was I imagining myself in a cop show instead of sitting across from a police detective in Newport, Oregon?"

Haakonssen was still on about the cottage.

"You didn't go into the kitchen, sit at the kitchen table, have a drink of anything?"

"Why would I do that?" But as I answered him my memory went back to the kitchen table, and I remembered something. I said slowly, "I could see the kitchen table from the office. There was an almost empty bottle of Dewar's on it. Two chairs, but just one glass. A small glass. It was empty."

"Just the one glass? No plates or utensils? No other glass, in the rack over the sink for instance?"

"I told you, I didn't go over to the kitchen. I didn't look in the sink."

"And you didn't drink anything?" he repeated. "You said it was Dewar's."

"Just because I'm Irish-American doesn't mean I generally walk into someone's home and have a finger or two of Scotch in the morning."

But I thought about my great-grandfather in a little village outside Dunmanway in West Cork. According to my mother, who heard the story from her father, old Sean Kelly had done just that. He broke into an Englishman's house and drank half the liquor cabinet. He was sent to prison for a while, and later died of the drink.

Haakonssen glanced down at the statement again. "You said you called Ms. Richard from your phone at around ten a.m. this morning when she didn't answer the front door. Do you have your phone with you? Mind if I look at that record of your call to Ms. Richard? And we'd like to have a look at your laptop too."

"Look, I've told you the truth," I said, alarmed now. "I've answered all your questions as best I can, but I'm not turning over my laptop or phone. I'm also assuming you have Giselle's phone and if it's missing, you can get her records from her cell provider. There should be correspondence on her laptop as well. The records will corroborate I had a meeting with her about a book her company was publishing, that she invited me to come to Newport for a meeting and paid for me to stay two nights at the hotel, that I went over to her house in good faith to meet with her and she wasn't there. That's it."

I didn't think Haakonssen was going to give up that easily, not because he necessarily thought I was guilty, but because his nature was a dogged one, and there might be something I said that he could use. But someone knocked and came into the room and said quietly, "Ms. Reilly's lawyer, sir. He's just arrived and would like to see her."

8.

A short time later Nora's lawyer Tom Hoyt and I were sitting in a small coffee bar near the Sylvia Beach Hotel, and he was looking over my statement and asking me a few questions. He was around sixty, "semi-retired," he told me, adding that he only worked a few days in Portland most weeks, and spent the rest of his time in a small town about forty miles north of Newport. "By great good chance when Nora called me I was there in Neskowin and able to drive down."

Tom wore a suit and tie; he was pink from the sun, his light hair was sparse. He had kind brown eyes. His voice was remarkably deep for his rather slender frame. I wondered when Nora had called him and what he had been doing since he arrived. It was just after five now, and I'd been in the station for several hours. We'd ordered coffee and he had a stale-looking sandwich with cheese and a very tired slice of tomato. I wasn't hungry.

"Did you learn anything from the police?" I asked.

He'd picked up half the sandwich but put it down again. "Giselle Richard seems to have died sometime yesterday, probably early-mid evening. Which is why they asked you so many questions about your time of arrival in Newport. She was pretty banged up from the fall, but the cause of death was a broken neck. She was found this morning wedged between a couple of big rocks on the bluff below her house, sometime around eleven—so after you'd left the house and returned to the hotel. She probably would have been found sooner but for the heavy fog. The rain this morning didn't help," he added, taking a bite of the sandwich and washing it down with black coffee.

"A broken neck," I repeated, wincing. "From the fall?"

"They can't be sure yet. There's no obvious sign of foul play, no knife or gun wounds," he said, "There's evidence of a contusion on one side of her forehead, but that could easily have come from her fall. Newport is a small station, so they have to call on forensic experts elsewhere. Detective

Haakonssen told me that alcohol might have been involved, but they can't be sure until the toxicology tests come back." He paused. "Apparently the kitchen table had a nearly empty bottle of Scotch on it and a single glass. You saw that too, it seems."

I nodded. "So, they're thinking that she might have drunk too much? That she fell by accident in the fog last night?"

"It's possible. The bluff is steep there. Maybe, even if she wasn't seriously impaired in some way, she just lost her footing." He looked at me. "Anything you want to tell me?"

Hesitantly, I said, "I probably need a lawyer, but I can't afford you."

He waved that away. "Nora asked me to get you out of the police station and find out if you needed legal representation. Meaning a criminal defense lawyer. But I think that's premature. So consider this a favor for a client who's also an old friend. We're just having coffee."

I nodded. I'd committed no crime, so of course I wouldn't need a defense lawyer. I might as well talk to Tom and get my innocence established. "Until Saturday when I rang Giselle from Oakland, we'd only had email correspondence. She seemed upbeat on Saturday, when we made the plans to meet on Tuesday morning here in Newport. Sunday, when I confirmed my visit on the phone, she was a little more distant and distracted. She seemed stressed, but since I didn't know her, I thought maybe it was to do with the window replacements and remodeling. She told me that she was leaving Wednesday night for New York for meetings and a sales conference and then on to Montreal for the weekend. I don't suppose the police have talked to the window guy?"

"I don't know," Tom said. "But I'm sure the police will follow up all possible leads. Anything else come to mind?" He pushed away the rest of his sandwich. He probably sensed I was holding something back, something that wasn't in my formal statement.

After a moment—better to tell someone at the start of the investigation rather than have it come up later—I told him how I'd looked briefly through the papers on the desk hoping to find Entre Editions' fall catalog. The full story of Luisa would take all evening, so I simply said, "My author didn't like the new title and I wanted to see if Giselle and her marketing manager, Karen Morales, had gone ahead and inserted a mock-up of the new cover design and the terrible title in the catalog."

"And you found something that bothered you on the desk?"

"No, but while I was looking, careful not to disturb anything, I bumped into the desk and the laptop woke up. I saw an unfinished email to Karen Morales." I didn't meet his eyes. "The note confirms Giselle was expecting me Tuesday morning. There was some stuff about the sales conference. She did mention some worries about money, that her co-worker Jane was upset about their finances. The email was never sent, so I imagined Giselle had been interrupted. It wasn't signed."

Tom was writing this down in the margin of the statement. "Any idea when the email was written?"

"Sometime Monday afternoon ... I guess I should also add ... her reference to me wasn't completely flattering. I had the feeling that she thought the author I've translated, Luisa Montiflores, was a problem, and that maybe I was too."

Tom glanced at the statement and then at me with a slight smile. "Is that why there's no mention of the email message here?"

"Is vanity a valid reason?"

"Okay, I don't think we need to bring that up at this point. They'll have already started looking at Giselle's laptop, I'm sure."

"What's next then?"

"I gather her sister is arriving from Canada later today. She's the next of kin unless you know of anyone else?"

"I don't really know much about Giselle. But I think Nora knew her and her mother as well." I hesitated. "I had the sense, at breakfast, that Nora wasn't quite telling me everything she knows about Giselle."

Tom said nothing, merely looked down at the statement again.

"Maybe I can talk to her more about this," I suggested. "Back at the hotel."

"I believe she's already checked out. She wanted to get back to Portland."

It struck me suddenly that, being Nora Longeran's attorney, he would first be concerned about his main client. Was that the reason Nora had really called him—because there was something about Giselle's death that might concern *her*? Perhaps he'd driven down to Newport to give *her* advice, and only after that come to the police station to get me out.

"I don't think you have much to be worried about," Tom resumed. "On paper your story checks out, though they'll want to follow up on a few things. All the same, Detective Haakonssen told me they're going to want you stay in Oregon for the time being, if not necessarily in Newport. But if you go somewhere else, you'll need to let them know."

Although Detective Jones had said something about not leaving the country when he returned my passport, it hadn't completely penetrated. Now the realization sank in that I might be stuck in Oregon for weeks. My chance to appear on the literary-festival panels with Claribel was out the window. Angela Cook, snug in England, would continue bad-mouthing my translations. What a bloody disaster.

I explained, rather desperately, that I had a ticket to London, departing out of San Francisco next week. That I had important commitments in the U.K. Public appearances at literary festivals. Meetings with editors. A deadline to turn in a new translation. And most important of all, I was in the midst of probably going to have to buy a flat or at least move out of the place I was staying. Plus, my flight was non-refundable.

"Surely they can't force me to stay in Oregon against my will?"

"Let's just say it would be wise to comply. Otherwise they could figure out a way to hold you. Charging you with a break-in, for instance. If you're cooperative and stick around as they request for a week or two, you may have to answer questions if there's more evidence, but you can move freely. Better cancel that flight and see about rebooking when you hear otherwise. Hopefully, this will be wrapped up soon and you'll be on your way home to London." He gave me his card. "Just call my office in Portland if anything comes up and they'll find me."

We both stood up. The owner of the little coffee bar had been ostentatiously wiping down her counters, and as soon as we left, put up a Closed sign. We stood on the sidewalk outside. The fog had completely vanished; there was a blue sky and the sound of the surf was gentle in the distance.

"If you don't mind my asking," I said. "Why would Nora do this for me? I'm a total stranger to her. Unless there's something I don't know about this case?"

Of course Tom Hoyt didn't respond to that. He smiled. "Nora takes an interest in people and tries to help where she can. I suppose that's what happened in your case. She enjoyed chatting with you over breakfast, thought you were a foreign visitor, knew enough to realize you had no friends or anyone to help you here in Newport. She has a very warm heart," he smiled. "Though she hates anyone to know it. People take advantage."

As we parted, I thanked him again and asked if he knew how I could get hold of Nora to thank her as well.

"Nora doesn't give out her phone or email address," he said. "I'm sure you can understand why."

"Oh, sure," I said, though in fact I was clueless. "Well, please tell her I'm very grateful. And thank you as well, for driving down to help me. I might still be at the police station if you hadn't come."

"You have nothing to worry about," he said. "Let the police do their job, and you just relax and enjoy the Oregon Coast."

I walked into the foyer of the Sylvia Beach, but before I could go up to my room, the woman at the desk—fortunately not the one who'd seen me hauled off to the police station— stopped me.

"Sorry, might you be Cassandra Reilly?"

I hesitated and then nodded. It occurred to me suddenly that with Giselle dead, perhaps my second night at the hotel had been cancelled. Maybe I'd even have to pay for both nights.

"We'd like to offer you a different room," she said. "We had an unexpected cancellation and our manager thought you might be more comfortable in the Agatha Christie room. Given the circumstances. I mean, you might not want to look at ... the pendulum. There will be no extra charge. Your two nights were paid for by Ms. Richard. The Christie room is also free for the next several days if you'd like to reserve it yourself."

"I'll let you know my plans," I said. "It's kind of the manager to get me out of the Poe room anyway."

"It was Ms. Longeran who suggested it," the woman said. "She thought it would be fine to move your bag and things, so we went ahead. The Agatha Christie room is one of our nicest. It faces the ocean. It has a view to die for." She looked dismayed. "Sorry. It's a tragedy that poor woman fell."

"Did you know Giselle Richard?" I asked as I took the new key.

"Not personally, but the cottage has been in the family for a while— her mother used to come to Newport a lot, someone said. They couldn't remember the details, but I think she died here, in Newport. It was before my time."

In ordinary circumstances I would have been charmed by the Englishness of the suite, the dark green walls, rose-colored carpet, chintz-covered armchair, wooden roll-top desk, and love seat, shelves of mysteries, an expansive view of the ocean, lit now by the western sun. It was beautiful, but the wide beach below made me uneasy.

Suddenly, the spookiness of being in Giselle's cottage this morning while her body lay broken on the rocks below hit me. I started shivering, and got under the flowery duvet. I knew that I'd had far too much coffee today, and that I should probably eat something, but for thirty minutes I just lay there, enfolded in the soft comforter. Did Giselle have demons? Was she a drinker? Could she have committed suicide? All those thoughts, ugly as they were, paled next to the idea that someone could have killed her.

I would have to let Nicky know that I might not be able to get back to the U.K. next week. She couldn't throw me out on the street. For one thing, it was terribly important at the moment that I had a respectable address in London. I shuddered to think if I'd had to tell Pete Jones that I was homeless.

I certainly couldn't tell Luisa what had happened—at least, not yet. I could use the excuse that the hotel had no internet connection to explain my silence. Even so, knowing Luisa, I should make sure that *On Jupiter* was still going to be published before I contacted her, since that's the first thing she'd ask about. Which probably meant tracking down Giselle's employees Jane Janicki and Karen Morales.

Perhaps one or both of them had ideas about Giselle and how she could have fallen, jumped, or been pushed. Did she have enemies? Did she drink alone and too much? Of course the police would interview Giselle's employees, her family, and others who knew her, but it might not happen as soon as I'd like, or as soon as I needed it to happen if I were to get back to London on my scheduled flight.

I pulled myself together. I'd investigated a few crimes for friends over the years—disappearances and thefts mostly, but also a few unfortunate deaths. I didn't have to make a big deal of it, but couldn't I help move things along more quickly if I were to do some informal sleuthing? The sooner the answer to Giselle's death was found, the sooner I could be on my way. Because if I didn't turn up at Chipping Witteron and play my role as the better translator and all-around better choice than Angela Cook, I was in danger of losing my translation contract. The agent would force Janneken to fire me, and Janneken would be angry, never hire me again, and tell other editors how unreliable I was. I'd be back to translating business documents for multinationals in South America.

I didn't want to think about that, or about the fact that Nicky was about to disappear into deepest Scotland, leaving me adrift.

I threw off the duvet and sprang up from the bed. No, I'd set to work finding out more about Giselle. I already had an excuse to talk to Jane Janicki, the business manager at Entre Editions, about whether the publication of *On Jupiter* would go ahead, and if not, what we'd do about the contracts. If I went to their office in Portland, it wouldn't appear that I was investigating Giselle's death, just seeing to my financial interests, and meanwhile having a quiet look around and asking a few innocent but probing questions. Whatever I learned I could pass on to the police in Newport.

I'd already considered leaving the Subaru at the home of Kim's friends in Portland. Maybe they'd be helpful in other ways. I certainly couldn't afford to keep staying in the Sylvia Beach on my own dime.

I called Kim on her cell but she didn't answer. I punched in her office number at CAL, in case she was working late. She picked up, in a rush. She had revisions to a paper to look over and then was headed to some kind of faculty social event. But she was suitably shocked to hear of Giselle's death and how I'd been taken in for questioning. It was a lot to absorb all at once, though I tried to condense it. The last time she'd seen me was yesterday morning, waving as I pulled away from the curb in the Subaru.

At least I'd gotten to her before Jones or Haakonssen had called to corroborate my alibi.

"The lawyer I talked to said they'll check all the elements of my story, but if what I told them is true—and of course it is—they won't bother me too much. The problem is that they want me to hang about and be available until they finish their investigation. I'm hoping it will turn out to be an accident, but in the meanwhile, they told me not to leave the country. I thought it might be best to go to Portland. Be in a more familiar urban setting, near an airport."

"Of course you don't want to stay in Newport by yourself, you poor thing!" Kim's voice was sympathetic, and I felt myself steadying. "Go to Portland. I'm sure Jill and Candace will take you in. Jill and I have been friends since college. She's a professor at Portland State. She teaches entomology, and Candace is retired. They have a nice big house—I'm sure they'd have room for you. I don't like to think of you being alone up there, and obviously you don't want to pay a lot of money for a hotel. Let me call them and get back to you."

While I waited to hear back, I went over to the book shelf and picked out an old copy of a green Penguin paperback: *Miss Marple and the Thirteen Problems*. Was Nora Longeran sending me a message by suggesting that the staff move me into the Agatha Christie room? Did she suspect foul play? Why wasn't this beautiful room already booked; had it been Nora's room? Why had she left so abruptly?

I thought again about Giselle's unfinished email to Karen Morales, with its suggestion that all wasn't well at Entre Editions, and that there were issues with Jane, the business manager. Had Giselle and Karen talked on the phone? Or was there some possibility that Karen was supposed to come to Newport yesterday evening? *Looking forward …*

When I'd heard Tom Hoyt say that the time of death was evening, I'd envisioned Giselle's fall happening in darkness. Yet, as I looked out the windows at the sun nearing the horizon, I thought that didn't make sense. It was almost seven now and it was still light. Wouldn't someone have seen Giselle topple off the bluff and immediately have called 911? Especially if they'd seen her pushed? Of course, it had been raining and foggy last night. Still, wouldn't Giselle have screamed?

My cell phone rang.

"Good news and bad," said Kim. "The good news is that you're welcome to stay at their house. The bad news is that they aren't in Portland at the moment. They're in Palm Springs at a weeklong conference on beetles or bees or something, and then they plan to stay a couple extra days and hike around Joshua Tree National Park. But they said it's just fine if you stay there until they get back next Monday evening, and you can keep staying as long as you want."

"I hope it won't be that long," I said, grateful for Kim's help. "Anything I should know? I'd like to leave here fairly early tomorrow morning."

She gave me directions and Jill and Candace's cell phone numbers, along with the security code of their front door. A neighbor was checking their mail and pulling blinds up and down, so they'd let her know to give me the key. And there was something else: They wanted me to Skype with Candace when I got there, so she could explain how things worked. "Apparently they've had foreigners stay with them before, and someone broke the dishwasher."

"Foreigners? You *did* tell them I'm American?"

"Yes, but you don't come here that often, Cassandra. Things change, get more tech-y. I recall they like gadgets and apps."

"Okay, fine," I said. "But I'm a very adaptable houseguest. As you know, I hope."

"I do," she said. "But Dora and I are the old-fashioned kind of people who turn on lamps by hand and stand outdoors for a minute if we want to know what the temperature is."

"Don't worry," I said. "I've read about people who use an Alexa. They can be turned off."

"That's what I'm afraid of," she said. "Don't fiddle with stuff. And it's called Alexa not 'an Alexa.' Alexa is just the voice of the tube thing, the Echo."

"Yeah, yeah."

I heard someone knock on her office door and remind her of the faculty party. Kim paused and called out, "Yes, I'll be there," then to me, "Are you going to phone Luisa?"

"Oh my God, no. At least not yet. She's already steamed about the cover."

"One last thing, just to let you know, Jill told me that they have a friend who's a lawyer in Portland who could probably advise you. But you say you've already spoken with a lawyer? Someone you found in Newport?"

"No, he has a Portland office but he lives part-time on the coast north of here. Believe it or not a fellow guest here at the hotel, a writer I was talking to at breakfast, heard about Giselle's death and saw me being taken off to the police station, and she called this guy and got him to drive to Newport and get me released. She's my fairy godmother. I'm guessing she might be well-known, though I've never heard of her."

"What's her name?"

"Nora Longeran. I think she writes kids' books."

Kim burst out laughing. "Yes, I've heard of her. If you have a moment, go to Powell's Books when you're in Portland. You can see a few of her books on the shelves most likely."

9.

Jill and Candace Sabine-Noble lived in the Northwest district of Portland, a few blocks up from a shopping street, in a large, wood-frame house painted ochre with teal trim, much like the others on the block. But unlike the other houses, which were shaded by big old horse chestnuts and maples that dominated the postage-stamp front gardens, the Sabine-Nobles had put in a Mediterranean-style garden of grasses, sage, and lavender. On a warm late-spring morning the yard and house looked manageable and tidy. I retrieved the key from the neighbor and introduced myself. She was a young software designer who worked at home, and she seemed thrilled that I was going to housesit since a friend had invited her to Lake Tahoe for a long weekend and now, without letting Candace and Jill down, she could take off tomorrow for California. Together we unlocked the door and quickly punched in the security code on the box in the entryway. Then she left for her Pilates class.

Unlike the Craftsman bungalow style of the exterior, the inside of their house was modern, and the kitchen had been extensively remodeled to bring in more light. The countertop was colored concrete, and the appliances were all new. I resolved never to touch anything but the fridge and the toaster. Even the coffee maker seemed too complicated with its LED screen and many attachments. It would be easier to have my meals out, anyway. For now, there was an apple in a fruit bowl and I ate that.

I'd tried calling Nicky this morning and left a voicemail; soon after I'd sent a text. Normally I wouldn't be worried that she didn't get in touch, especially when she was on tour. Still, I tried to make my text a little more urgent than the voicemail.

INVOLVED IN MURDER CASE IN OREGON. MIGHT BE DELAYED ARRIVING HOME. DO NOT, REPEAT, DO NOT PUT MY DESK OUT ON THE STREET IF YOU ARE MOVING TO SCOTLAND. I'M STILL THINKING.

Here in Portland I called Entre Editions' office in my Contacts, but no one answered. Giselle's warm voice asked me to leave a message. Shuddering a little, I said I was Luisa's translator and needed to discuss some concerns about the book, then added that I might stop by soon, as I wouldn't be in Portland long. I was hoping to see Jane Janicki or Karen Morales. I didn't mention anything about having come from Newport or having been questioned by the police. Or about Giselle's being dead.

While looking at a map of the city on my phone and trying to figure out the best way to drive over to Southeast Portland where the office of Entre Editions was located—there seemed to be a lot of bridges here—the Skype tones sounded, and I answered.

The first thing that met my eye was the tanned, wrinkly cleavage of a woman in a bathing suit, with a slice of swimming pool visible off to the side. Then the phone was hastily raised to show the face of the woman, also tan, wrinkly, and a little embarrassed. "Sorry, the phone slipped. I'm Candace. Jill's in a session on pollinators. Welcome to Portland!"

"I'm Cassandra. Thanks so much for letting me stay here." We introduced ourselves as graciously as we could given that one of us was sitting in a lounge chair by a pool in Palm Springs and one of us was a stranger standing in her kitchen.

On the other hand we both knew Kim, who had vouched for me. After a few preliminaries, regarding the circumstances that had brought me to Oregon and some comparative discussion of the weather in Palm Springs and Portland, we got down to the instructions for my responsibilities as a house-sitter. I thought it would be mostly about compost and recycling, watering a few plants, some emergency numbers. But Candace wanted to explain the house room by room.

For almost an hour, as I heard the splash of people swimming in the pool in Palm Springs, we walked through the house, with our phones pointed at different appliances while Candace explained how the house worked, beginning in the kitchen with how to grind coffee beans, steam milk, and otherwise interact with the coffeemaker. The dishwasher had multiple settings, and the microwave was "very sensitive."

If the weather was hot, which was unlikely, it was important not to open the windows since they were connected to the security system. I could use a fan if I was warm. But if I was cold at night I should just use an extra comforter, because they'd turned off their natural gas heating for the summer. We visited the bathrooms together with our phones so she could explain the low-flow toilets, the towel warmer, and the radiant floor heating, and then progressed to the master bedroom where the king-size bed could be raised in two sections, if one sleeper wanted to read longer. I had to remind her I didn't think I'd be using that feature since I was in the guest room, which had an ordinary queen-size bed. We dropped in on the laundry room and I was instructed to turn my phone in the direction of the washing machine settings and cycles, so she could see them and explain. This went on for ten minutes, during which time I resolved never to wash any clothes if I could help it.

"The lights in the living room have been programmed to come on automatically at six a.m. and turn off at midnight. You can override that but perhaps it's best ..."

"Yes," I agreed. "I think it's best if I don't fiddle too much with anything."

"It's only that Jill and I stayed in a rental flat in London a few years ago," Candace explained. "It's all different there. The washing machine was in the kitchen, and it was so tiny. The toilet ran for ages. And everything was in centigrade."

"I don't suppose you have Alexa?"

"Well, we do have an Echo, yes. But it's turned off while we're away. I don't think you need it, do you? Just raise and lower the blinds, really."

An hour just to tell me to raise and lower the blinds? I tried to reassure her, "I'll take good care of everything." I was sorry they didn't have Alexa on tap. I had been looking forward to issuing commands and asking questions.

To close, Candace reminded me they'd be home Monday morning. "You're welcome to stay as long as you like. Oh, wait, did I tell you about separating the recycling?"

While I'd been talking with Candace, a couple of texts had come in. One from Kim, wondering if I'd gotten to Portland okay and offering to help however I needed her. The other was from Janneken, asking again whether I'd gotten the email she sent yesterday. Reluctantly I opened my laptop.

Janneken's long email was bad news, though only slightly worse than I'd feared. Claribel Montoya was now in the U.K. to promote *Where the Fjords Meet*, not only doing some of the lit fests, but reading at a few bookstores in London and surrounding cities, accompanied by Angela. Janneken had gone to one of the readings.

Angela wasn't unpleasant, she was in fact, rather quiet. All the same I did not care for her, especially when Claribel called her up front at the end of the reading and Angela put her bit in, quietly, about the art of translation. It always gets up my nose when translators make out their work to be some kind of great calling. I can only say I'm glad you don't make a big song and dance about translation being a spiritual connection, a co-creation, and rot like what a privilege, etc.

Anyway, the next day I took Claribel to a fancy lunch. She asked if Angela could come and I said no. In the nicest possible way. I said I wanted a more one-to-one conversation. Obviously you expect some change when an author gets attention the way she has, but I almost didn't recognize her. Remember how humble and excited she was about getting published in English? Well, now, she's considerably tougher. I found out she'd left her husband a year ago, soon before Where the Fjords Meet *came out. They're divorced now. The in-laws have temporarily taken in their little girl. Truth is, I don't think Claribel ever bonded with that child, and sees the girl as an obstacle now to her career. She's spending a lot of time in Paris, she told me, and I got the feeling she might have a boyfriend there.*

This is all to say she is a lot less about being grateful to anyone who gave her a leg up, and a lot more into getting the best deal she can for herself. Candleford isn't part of her vision and, I'm afraid, neither are you, Cassandra. It may be the influence of her new best friend Angela Cook and the American agent, but I'm afraid, since they can't break the contract for the Baby, *that they're going to try to find an excuse to replace you as her translator.*

Really, the only chance I see to salvage this is if you're quite far along with the translation, and then get yourself back over to London as soon as possible and throw yourself at Claribel's feet. I can't afford to alienate her.

Throw myself at Claribel's feet? Not bloody likely. I didn't even *want* to translate that supposedly satiric novel about a distressed little baby with her eternal crying. Let Angela Cook take it on and good riddance.

I thought I should probably respond as soon as possible, as reassuringly as possible. But what was I to say? That I was stuck in Oregon as part of a police investigation due to the death, by accident, suicide, or murder, of the publisher of Entre Editions? That barring a speedy solution to the mystery, I might be in Portland for some considerable time and God forbid, I might actually have to live with these gadget-glad lesbians when they returned from Palm Springs next Monday?

I couldn't actually imagine Janneken being that sympathetic. After all, she still had Claribel as an author, and she had lots of other spoons in the pots, as she often told me. It would be better if I let her continue to believe I was in the Bay Area, beavering away on *Baby's First Year*.

I didn't answer Janneken right away. Instead I scrolled through the emails looking for something that might cheer me up. There was an email from a stranger named Alistair Robinson-Sykes, with some jpgs attached. The subject line read: *Do you like the look of any of these?* I wasn't going to open such a suspicious email until I noticed that it had been cc'd to Nicky. Oh, the photos from the estate agent in Edinburgh, finally.

The pictures were a series of upmarket flats in terraced buildings in neighborhoods I knew nothing about: Dalry, Bruntsfield, Leith. Was Nicky really going to get so much money from the Islington flat that she could afford to buy one of these "charming, sunny apartments with period details on a leafy street, close to all amenities," in a sensible country that wanted to stay in the EU?

I tried to picture a room for me in one of these swanky flats on a tree-lined crescent. Maybe it wouldn't be so bad? Sighing, I emailed her: "Moving up in the world, Gibbons!" Was she back from the concert dates in Germany? Who knows, maybe by this time she'd already put in her offer and had it accepted. Maybe she'd already called the moving van, emptied the Islington flat, and sent my poor little possessions off to Oxfam.

By early afternoon I was across the river in Southeast Portland and pulling up in front of a large, yellow, two-story Craftsman-style house with a massive overhanging porch. I'd gotten a deli sandwich nearby and ate it as I drove. Unfortunately, I'd chosen a Reuben pastrami on rye with extra sauerkraut; soon it was all over my one clean shirt. On the phone-size map the route to an address near Laurelhurst Park had looked simple enough, straight along Burnside and over the Burnside Bridge but I hadn't accounted for lunchtime traffic and a demonstration taking place in the city center. In an effort to avoid the backup of cars and marchers I turned off into a side street and eventually found myself crossing the Morrison Bridge, with a spaghetti of street choices on the south side of the river.

I ended up jogging through miles of narrow streets with wooden houses and lots of electric orange and yellow azaleas and pink ornamental plums.

This house too had a nicely landscaped yard of azaleas in bloom that sloped up from the street. I hadn't thought about the fact that Giselle might use her house as her office. There was an older Honda Civic in the driveway and a couple of other vehicles parked out front, one belonging to an electrician and the other to a remodeling company, judging by the lettering on their vans. All was quiet in the neighborhood on this weekday, but when I rang the bell I heard the sounds of hammering inside as well as men's voices.

The woman who answered looked familiar and I realized she was the same woman in the photographs with Giselle at the cottage, the Asian woman with the prematurely white hair in a messy ponytail. She was maybe in her mid-forties. An oily dark smudge stained her forehead, her eyes were red from exhaustion or tears, and one of her thumbs was blue-black, from a misplaced hammer blow perhaps. She wore jeans and a denim work shirt a size too big. She stared at me without saying anything. My white shirt was marred by drips of meat juice and sauerkraut, I knew, but otherwise, wasn't I reasonably presentable?

"I'm so sorry to bother you," I said. "But I'm looking for the office of Entre Editions."

"This is it," she said.

"Oh, well in that case, I wonder if I might speak with the business manager, Jane Janicki?"

"You're looking at her. And if you're a reporter, I have nothing to say."

"I'm not a reporter," I said quickly, to cover my surprise. Okay, she wasn't Polish. "I'm Cassandra Reilly. The translator of the book of stories you're doing in the fall by Luisa Montiflores?"

"But aren't you somewhere in South America?" She had dropped the stern expression and just looked confused. Then she came out on to the porch and closed the door behind her. She gestured to one of two large wicker armchairs on the porch. I sat down, but she hesitated, then perched uncomfortably at the chair's edge. "I'm sorry I can't invite you into the office. It's something of a mess at the moment. I started remodeling my house a few weeks ago."

I nodded, uncertain how to take this. If Jane was just Giselle's employee, her business manager, why was the office in her house, the house Jane called "my house"? If it was their shared house, had they been romantic partners? In either case Jane must know Giselle had died Monday night. Then why was she talking about remodeling? *Of course* she must know Giselle had died in a fall at Newport. The police would have told her. Reporters must have been here too. Jane was certainly pretending ignorance.

Should I pretend too, act like I just happened to find myself in Portland today? I decided to keep it simple. "I know about the accident," I said. "I'm really sorry. It must be terrible for you. As her business manager … partner?"

Her face closed down protectively. "Business manager."

The banging started up in the back of the house again, along with a male conversation about voltage. Jane stood up.

"I'd better go see what they're up to," she said, moving to the door.

I couldn't let her go without trying again. After all, she was the business manager, she would know if Entre Editions would be continuing, wouldn't she?

"I don't want to be insensitive," I said, "but is there any possibility we could talk another time? Tomorrow, for instance? I'm only in Oregon because Giselle asked me come up from the Bay Area to discuss the marketing for *On Jupiter*. I'll be going back to London shortly. I'll need to tell Luisa Montiflores something … in case the book is postponed. Which I would understand, given the circumstances."

"I'm sorry that you came all this way for nothing," Jane said. "I really can't tell you much. I'm sure I have your email. I'll be in touch with all the authors and translators as soon as I can."

The door was almost shut when I said, "Then is there any chance I could speak with Karen Morales? Is she here? Luisa was very upset about the change to the title and the cover. I don't mean to sound judgmental but the balls of yarn are very problematic. I know Karen loves the new cover, but I just don't think it's going to work. The image is not"— I suddenly couldn't think of the word in English, for Jane had turned around and her face was no longer reserved but cold with anger—"*digna,*" I finished. "I mean, dignified. Appropriate."

"Karen doesn't work here at the office now, but from home. What changes in the title?"

I tried to explain in a few words, but Jane interrupted. "You'll have to take it up with Karen." She took out a piece of paper from her shirt pocket along with a pencil. There were some architectural drawings of a doorway on it. She wrote down Karen's address and handed it to me, seemingly unaware that her hands were shaking. "I can't remember her phone number."

"I'll go over there now," I said, hoping that I wouldn't get the same response from the marketing director, and wondering if there was bad blood between them. Or if there had been something between Karen and Giselle that shut Jane out of the picture. "And I hope we can talk again soon. Can I call you tomorrow?"

"Have a good trip back to London, Cassandra," she said and went back inside.

I walked down the path and steps to the sidewalk and the car, confused by this odd scene with Jane, and no further with my informal investigation. Would I get further with Karen Morales using the same excuse that I wanted to know more about the fate of Luisa's book? I hoped so.

From the directions given to me by Google maps it looked like the route to Karen's address, in someplace called the Pearl District, was straightforward: over the Burnside Bridge if I could locate it this time.

I was still standing on the sidewalk, peering at the phone, when a youngish man, balding but with a full auburn beard came up to the electrician's van and opened the back door. After he'd retrieved some parts and looked ready to head back to the house, I scraped some stray sauerkraut off my shirt and went up to him.

"Could you tell me how to get to Burnside Street?"

He pointed. "Just couple of blocks up that way. Where are you going?"

"The Pearl District."

"You're not from here?"

"No, I live in London, usually. I'm a translator. I was just visiting the office, for the first time, a meeting." I hesitated, then decide he was my best shot at finding out more. "Jane told me Giselle had had an accident, but she didn't give any details. Do you know what happened?"

"Broke her neck in a fall from the bluff at Newport," he seemed somber, but self-important and indiscreet, the way that people sometimes can become when they believe they're the first to share tragic news. "She was found yesterday around noon, the news said, though she probably fell the night before. It's pretty foggy over there, and I guess that's why she wasn't found right away."

"Oh, my God, I'm so sorry." Even though I couldn't act shocked, I did mean it. "But why didn't Jane *say* that's what happened?"

"Jane doesn't want to talk about it," he said. "She told me that this morning when I got here. *I don't want to talk about it, C.J.,* she said. She said the police came yesterday to tell her about it and ask some questions. She's also had a reporter or two here. I'm surprised she talked to you."

"Probably because she didn't know what else to do, since I came from so far away to see Giselle. I flew here from Uruguay, actually."

"So you didn't know she was in Newport, then?" C.J. looked puzzled. "But maybe it wasn't common knowledge. I think Giselle moved out a month or so ago. To have a quiet place to work while the remodel goes on. The contractor is walling off the office from the rest of the house and putting in an outside entrance. He's been there about two weeks. This morning he cut some wire by accident, so that's why I came over. He asked me if we should stop the job for a while. He doesn't know Jane like I do."

I tried to draw him out a little more with a sympathetic look. "It sounds like you knew them both well. They were a couple then, I take it?"

"Yeah, knew them both, knew the whole family. My dad had the business before he retired, and he was the Janickis' regular electrician. The old folks went into assisted living and eventually died. Jane had been living on her own but moved back in with Giselle about five years ago. My dad and I worked on installing some new lighting for them."

"Forgive me if I'm being nosey, but given Jane's age, the Janickis must have been elderly parents."

"They adopted her when she was four from an orphanage in South Korea that had some connection with their church. Mr. Janicki was Polish, her mom was Swedish Lutheran—lots of them in the Northwest. My dad remembered her from way back then, when they brought her home. Mr. Janicki was a loan officer at the local bank, so my dad knew him originally from that. They were good people but close-minded, real cautious and frugal. I don't know if Jane ever came out to them. My sister's a lesbian," he added. "That kind of thing is fine in Portland, you know."

"It's fine in London, too," I reassured him. "And Uruguay. Most LGBT-friendly country in Latin America. What about Giselle? What was she like?"

"Younger than Jane and lots of energy. Good at knowing what to say to people. Jane is more reserved." He looked up at the big yellow house. "I hate to think of Jane there all alone now."

We were both silent, then he shifted his tools into the other hand and said, "I'd better get inside. My dad always said we shouldn't talk about our customers, the things we learned from being inside their houses, but sometimes, it's hard to see unhappiness without saying something."

10.

Back in the Subaru and driving, I hoped, in the right direction, I considered what I had just learned and what had become more questionable.

Had Jane and Giselle been lovers or not when Giselle died? Jane had told me she was just the business manager, while C.J. had told me Giselle moved in five years ago. The photo of the pair, arms entwined, on the wall of the Newport cottage suggested love, not just friendship. So, had they broken up? When? And why?

Giselle's email message to Karen indicated some conflict about money. Who owned the press? Jane and Giselle together, or just Giselle? Why, really, had Giselle gone off to Newport a month ago? C.J. had suggested it was because they were remodeling the office. Giselle had told me on the phone that she was trying to fix up the cottage after winter storms. But Jane's peculiar coldness suggested that there might have been a rupture of affection.

If Jane had still been Giselle's life partner, wouldn't the police have contacted Jane immediately on finding Giselle? Wouldn't they have asked Jane to come out to Newport to I.D. the body? Wouldn't have Jane wanted to see Giselle a last time? And if they hadn't broken up formally, was it somehow in Jane's interest to pretend she and Giselle were only business partners, and to suggest that the police contact Giselle's sister in Canada as the next of kin?

What accounted for Jane's restrained, almost disconnected manner? Until I mentioned Karen Morales, that is.

My mind went back to the single glass on the table and the mostly empty bottle of Scotch, to how Haakonssen had asked at least twice whether I'd seen a second glass on the counter or in the sink. It seemed far-fetched to think that Jane had driven to Newport Monday afternoon, had a couple of drinks with Giselle, and then pushed her to her death, before returning to Portland and carrying on with the remodel, but I supposed it was possible. A more likely conclusion after the autopsy would suggest that Giselle had drunk too much on her own, had wandered off outside and had somehow tripped and gone over the side, breaking her neck on the way.

I remembered that Haakonssen had told Tom Hoyt they were treating it as an accident until further investigations suggested otherwise. That was perhaps because Giselle or her clothes smelled of alcohol. Maybe Jane's reluctance to talk about the death—to C.J. as well as a stranger like me— had more to do with shame than with personal reticence. If Giselle, for instance, was a habitual drinker, then perhaps Jane wasn't too surprised to hear about a fatal accident.

Yes, a verdict of accidental death brought on by drinking was probably in the offing. Maybe there was no need to cancel my flight. There was still the matter of Luisa's book, of course. But perhaps I could get some better answers from Karen. Maybe Karen would help me understand if they were going ahead with their fall list or whether I'd need to talk to Jane about breaking the contract. In which case, the question of the unfortunate title and balls of yarn would be moot.

The Pearl District, located near the train station, wasn't what I expected. Nor was Karen's address, on a block full of newly built, nicely landscaped four-story condo buildings, where I'd expected to find her living. From the way Giselle referred to Karen's hire six months ago, I'd supposed she was a former publicity intern, in her early twenties, who'd worked her way into a full-time job as publicist and marketing director. I'd pictured her in shared housing or a tiny studio.

I buzzed the name Karen Morales and, after a short silence following, "This is Cassandra Reilly, sorry to disturb you, but may I talk to you for a moment? Jane Janicki gave me your address," a woman said in a groggy voice, "Oh, the translator." She told me to come up to the top floor.

Her apartment was furnished in a style that wouldn't have been out of place in an upscale dentist's office, but with a few brighter elements: a blue woolen throw on the beige loveseat, a red leatherette sling-back chair. Over the sofa hung a large abstract painting in reds and blues. There were no personal photographs on the walls.

Aside from a dirty coffee mug on the counter that divided the kitchen from the living room, the apartment was spotless, but Karen herself looked terrible. She wore a limp, striped T-shirt and running shorts; no bra, no shoes. Bleached blond hair, dark at the roots, was pulled back into a loose knot from a strongly contoured face blotched with red. Her eyes were puffy. She was probably early thirties, but looked older. She had a sensual mouth: full, well-shaped lips. "Sparkling water, kombucha, ice tea, or beer?" she asked. "Personally I might have a beer."

"Just water for me, thanks. Before anything else, let me just say, I'm really sorry about Giselle. You and Jane must be devastated." I paused and added cautiously, "I don't know if you know, but I was in Newport the last two nights. I didn't get a chance to meet her though."

"I know you were," she said. "At least, I know Giselle was expecting to have a meeting with you Monday or Tuesday." She paused. "I really can't fucking believe this has happened. Any of it."

She poured me a glass from the tap, and then took out an IPA from the fridge and a plastic clamshell container with a large assortment of sushi, which she put on the bar counter. I sat down on a high stool across from her and watched her tear open a packet of soy sauce and squeeze it into a green lump of wasabi. She mushed it with her index finger.

"Help yourself," she said, before dragging a piece of California roll through the mixture. "This is breakfast. Sorry, you're catching me at a bad time. The cops were here yesterday evening, and I'm afraid after they left I got wasted and then was up half the night throwing up. Why have you come to see me?"

She was the complete opposite of Jane, that is, unnervingly blunt.

"As I said, I'm really sorry and shocked by Giselle's accident," I began. "Considering the circumstances, it probably seems really gauche to talk business. The trouble is, I'm just in Portland a few days. I came here this morning on the off chance I could talk to someone about Luisa's novel. I went over to the office, but wasn't able to get much out of Jane. I'm sure she's shattered by the news. I guess I'm wondering if Entre Editions will go ahead with the fall list." It sounded lame, and I added, "If so, we should discuss the cover. Jane told me to talk to you about it."

"Did she?" said Karen bitterly. "She hasn't answered my emails or phone calls since I heard on the news Giselle had an accident. No recognition that I might possibly care about Giselle too. That we *worked* together, that I'm a member of the team. I guess I'm fired. I shouldn't be surprised. She's been angling to get rid of me for months, before Giselle even moved to Newport. What a cold-hearted bitch she is."

"If Jane was going to fire you, she wouldn't have sent me over here," I pointed out.

"Well, I'm quitting anyway. Without Giselle, the press is fucked."

Karen took a long drink from her beer bottle and picked up another piece of sushi, this one with raw tuna. Slopped it in enough wasabi to make most people's hair stand on end. Bits of rice and flecks of muddy green wasabi dropped on to her already none-too-clean T-shirt.

I didn't feel too bad now about the pastrami stains on my own shirt.

"Sorry," she muttered after she'd swallowed, "I'm in some kind of shock trying to process this. I mean, Giselle was jazzed about going to New York. We were supposed to leave tonight. We had a sales conference on Friday. And then we were going to Montreal Friday night for a quick weekend. That's where she grew up. I'd never been. We had some things to discuss, but I didn't hear from her Monday. I didn't try too hard to track her down because I was getting a lot of promo materials together and was running around town. Had to check on my mom, she's had the flu. In the evening I had my writers' group. I tried calling and emailing Gisele Tuesday morning but there was no answer. I was surprised, but then I remembered you were probably meeting with her. Then yesterday evening around seven o'clock, a cop shows up here and says she's dead. No idea why they came to me, unless maybe there were emails about the New York trip. I couldn't get any more out of him except she seems to have gone over the bluff by the cottage. How is that possible? It's not like the house is perched on the edge of a sheer cliff or anything. There's a railing. It's not a high railing, but you'd have to actually climb over it."

It struck me for the first time that I'd not actually seen the surroundings of the cottage that morning because of the dense fog and rain. The surf had sounded so loud that I'd assumed the waves were almost directly below. I realized with a jolt my image of Giselle stumbling drunkenly out the door and right over the precipice was improbable. Still, couldn't someone with most of a bottle of Scotch in them stagger off a marked path, even with a railing, and lose her balance?

"The detective in Newport seemed to think alcohol might have been involved in the accident," I said carefully. "Do you know, was Giselle overly partial to Dewar's? There was an almost empty bottle on the table."

"The cop yesterday asked me about Giselle's drinking too. She hardly drank at all, I mean a few beers, some wine with meals maybe. Never drank hard liquor, neither do I. You say Dewar's? That same bottle has probably been in the cottage for years, back in the cupboard with a dusty old collection of Cinzano and Cointreau. Dewar's was Giselle's mother's drink of choice, she told me once." Karen stopped, as if remembering something, then shook her head, and shoved another piece of California roll into her mouth and muttered, "I don't think she fell by accident."

"What makes you think that?" I didn't like where this was going, because if Giselle's death wasn't an accident, then this investigation was all going to take longer than I cared to imagine. "Do you have any ideas?"

She took another a swig of beer to wash down the sushi. "Burglary was my first gut feeling. That's what I told the cop. I mean, the cottage had been practically empty since her mother died. Giselle only went down there occasionally over the years and her sister never used it at all. But since Giselle had decided to sell it, she'd started fixing it up, at first going down on weekends and then moving in about a month ago. Probably the housebreaker didn't realize she was there and she didn't have good locks. A lot of vacation cottages and second-homes have had to put in security systems, but Giselle never got around to it. She said there wasn't anything to steal. If the burglar came in and found her, she might have fought back, and been killed by mistake. And he panicked and pushed her body over the side."

I decided not to mention that if Giselle had been physically attacked, it was likely that neighbors might have heard something, or that there would have been physical signs of violence on Giselle's body. Karen's eyes were leaking tears, or else it was the wasabi.

"So, you think it was a stranger, a random intruder, nothing premediated?"

"I've thought about the guy who was replacing the windows. But he would be too easy to track down," Karen said. "There are a lot of sketchy people hanging around the beach, homeless people living around the bluffs. The police are probably going to find the person who did it."

Karen got up and went to the refrigerator. Under her breath, she said, "Unless Jane drove out there Monday and pushed her off the bluff." And more loudly, "I think I'll have another. Want one? I'll bring over the six pack."

"Sure, why not?" I wanted to keep her talking. I assumed she meant me to hear what she'd said. Was she trying to plant some doubts about Jane—had she told the police something last night about problems in Jane and Giselle's relationship? Did she really think Jane could possibly be involved?

"Why would you think Jane would push her girlfriend off a cliff? Did you tell the police that?"

"No, of course not, I'm joking, obviously." Karen sat down again, passed me a bottle, and popped the cap off her own. "I mean, come on, Jane may have been jealous, but to *murder* Giselle ... ?" She left the question dangling, to indicate that it was indeed possible.

"From the website," I said after taking a sip of beer, "a person wouldn't necessarily get the impression that Jane played a large role in Entre Editions. But obviously she did. So now that Giselle is gone, is the company Jane's? I only ask because of Luisa's book. I'm wondering what we might expect at this point."

"I'm sure Jane has the legal right to continue on her own, I think they owned it together, though Giselle has the larger percentage. But good luck with that—Jane has no real understanding of what people want to read and how to reach them. I honestly doubt she'll go on with it. Sorry."

"Well, presumably she could hire some other people for editing and marketing," I said.

"That's not the issue. Jane has *no* vision. Giselle's the creative one in that partnership."

"What are Jane's skills?"

"She was a business manager for a local magazine when she met Giselle. She knew how to deal with designers and printers," Karen said, grudgingly. "She does the bookkeeping, manages a line of credit, deals with the distribution. She's a penny pincher, though, and Giselle thinks bigger. It's because of Giselle that Entre Editions is on the map. She's a risk taker, she *was* a risk taker, I mean. She was amazing, seriously amazing, at making people believe in what she was doing."

"So you met them ... somehow ... and became their marketing director?"

"I met them first at a local conference for women entrepreneurs. They gave a presentation on Entre Editions and I was totally inspired, but I could see they really had zero idea of how marketing and publicity could give them a much bigger advantage in the marketplace. I'm talking social media, live feeds with authors and translators, book trailers, launch parties with food and drink from the country of the author. They didn't even have a Facebook page. No Twitter, no nothing. I went up to Giselle afterwards and said, 'I want to work with you. I want to be part of your team. You need me.'"

Once again, her eyes filled with tears, and she said, "I honestly cannot believe what has happened. I hope they find the bastard who did this and lock him up for life."

I waited a moment—was she overdoing it? "Did you know anything about publishing when you went to work for them?"

"No. But I love reading. And I'd just begun to write some fiction myself. I wanted to understand the process—how books get selected, edited, designed, and put into people's hands—so that at some point, if I ever finished a novel, I'd know how the business worked."

She stood up and went into the kitchen, rooting through a drawer to pull out a bag of potato chips, which she tossed into a wooden bowl. En route, she turned on the tap in the sink and splashed water on her face and ran some of it through her hair. When she returned to sit across from me she was calmer, though a few tears leaked out still.

"I remember when I went over to the house the first time," she said, crunching. "Jane wasn't around that day. Giselle and I talked for hours. The whole house downstairs, not just their small office in the back, was full of books. Review copies needed to go out, events needed to be arranged. They were struggling with growth and publicizing their titles. They had a rotating crop of interns who did publicity and manuscript reading them for them, interns that came from Portland State mostly. I could see what I could do for them. Giselle saw it too. She asked me if I'd consider working for them as a consultant, part-time, to help them with marketing. Eventually I was full-time. Not that I need to work," she added. "I was the marketing director of a local tech startup that was bought. There were four of us principals. We did well."

I had a couple of chips, and Karen took a handful, and went on, alternating chips with the last of the sushi. "Giselle was obviously the editor in chief. She listened to my ideas for repositioning the press differently. A noir mystery or two, some genre fiction, a little postmodern narrative, fun stuff—we would have attracted more readers. At first, when I brought these ideas up they were both resistant, Giselle a little and Jane a lot. Jane because she didn't want a newcomer to have any influence and Giselle because she genuinely *loved* the books they published. But eventually Giselle came around. This upcoming catalog was the first time I really had a hand in shaping titles and covers. I was *so* happy at the designer's take on *Unraveling Jupiter*."

I took another sip of beer. "I'm not sure Luisa ... you know, she thinks of herself as a literary author."

"Giving Luisa's book a speculative-fiction spin was my idea," Karen said, ignoring that. "It's clear that Luisa's roots are in Argentina's science fiction traditions." She ate the last piece of sushi all in one bite, so I couldn't quite make out the next words, something about Luisa and modernism, and then more clearly how much interest there was in Latinx sf at the moment. "And Jupiter! Everybody loves the planet Jupiter. I could have promoted the hell out of that book."

We sat for a moment in silence, broken only by crunching. Karen mourning her lost opportunity to sell copies of *On Jupiter* to unsuspecting sf fans; me, thinking of Luisa's horror at being promoted at a science fiction convention, among people dressed as aliens and starship voyagers.

"So." I tried to sum up where we were. "Basically Giselle wanted you to become a bigger part of the press, but Jane didn't like the idea. And at some point, their relationship turned sour. Leading Giselle to move out to Newport, for a while anyway. But she still planned to keep working with Jane in the publishing business. Or was Jane going to be ousted there as well?"

"If you think Giselle was leaving Jane for me, you're wrong," Karen said. She was now on her third beer. "But we did discuss restructuring the press, or even me buying out Jane completely. We were going to talk about it seriously on our trip to the East Coast. It might have been difficult to negotiate with Jane. But I was definitely willing to invest in the press for the chance to have a stronger voice."

"It doesn't seem surprising that Jane was sort of angry. I mean, the press had been her and Giselle's baby, and then you came along."

"Probably she *did* think Giselle and I were getting together, but it was more that Giselle and I had similar energy for the press. Jane was like, no, no, no, we can't do this, and Giselle and I were like yes, yes, yes, we can."

"Was Jane jealous and upset enough to ... hurt her? Had they broken up?"

"That's just what the cop asked me. He asked if Jane and Giselle had majorly quarreled. I told him that they were taking a break, trying to work things out. But I did tell him that I found Jane a very repressed person emotionally, so really, I didn't know how Jane was processing the separation." Karen's lips tightened. "Probably Jane told the cops that *I* did it. But I don't have any motivation, do I? Giselle and I were basically just friends having some fun, sharing a vision. That's all it was at this point. I wasn't in love and neither was she."

Just friends, and yet it was Karen not Jane who was blotchy from lack of sleep and crying and drinking beer in the morning—oh, wait, it was near five o'clock by now.

"And you don't think Giselle would have killed herself?"

"No way. Giselle was excited about publishing. Maybe she didn't love Jane anymore, but she cared about her. She was okay with the relationship changing to just business partners. Now Jane, Jane I could see doing something drastic—she was more dependent on Giselle emotionally, and she's a person who keeps a lot of stuff bottled up."

"Yes, I got that impression too," I said. "But back to Pauline, you said the Dewar's was hers, along with the other liquor in the cupboard. Can you tell me something more about Giselle's mother? Did she live in the cottage? I heard she died in Newport. How did she die? Was she ill?"

"Her mom didn't live at the cottage," Karen said slowly. "She went there one weekend. A friend found her the next day, Giselle told me. She died in her sleep. Her mom had had a couple of bouts of breast cancer already, in her sixties. A couple of months before her death, she'd gotten a CAT scan that showed a lesion in her brain. Giselle told me that her mom was scared of losing words. *Words were everything to Pauline,* that's how Giselle put it."

"Do you have any reason to think Pauline's death and Giselle's were related? I mean, Pauline had cancer, but Giselle was young and healthy."

"It's a weird coincidence, both of them dying at the cottage. That's all I'm saying."

I thought back to the website with its paean to Pauline, and to the photos on the wall of Giselle's mother, sexy in her Sixties sheath dress, elegant even in the turban and wig that must have been the result of losing her hair to chemo. The woman with the confident smile that persisted as she got older.

"Pauline seems to be a big part of Entre's story."

"Yeah, I thought maybe too much, though I tried to be diplomatic. I mean, I love my mom too, and would be crushed to lose her. But when I redesigned the website earlier this year I suggested Giselle tone down the "in honor of Pauline Richard" theme a little. That we start focusing on contemporary authors rather than republishing Pauline's translations. But Giselle was reluctant; she didn't want to let go of her mother."

"Her mother translated from French, isn't that right?"

"She'd married a French-Canadian doctor while she was studying in France. They moved to Montreal and that's where Giselle and her sister grew up. The sister is still in Canada, in Vancouver I think, but Pauline came back to Portland to live in the family house and take care of her dad during his last years. After he died and Pauline got breast cancer, the second time, when she had a double mastectomy, she asked Giselle to come to Portland too."

"When did Giselle move here?"

Karen shook her head. "Ten-twelve years back? Before she moved here, she worked for about three or four years in Boston as an editorial assistant for an independent press. That's how she got the publishing bug. Her mom died six years ago. It was from selling the house in Portland that Giselle had the money to start Entre Editions. She kept the Newport cottage, though she was thinking about putting it on the market after she fixed it up."

"What about the sister?"

"Giselle never said much about her. I don't even know her name actually. I don't think they were close."

The buzzer sounded and Karen jumped, and went to the intercom: "Yes?"

"It's Dani."

"Come up." Karen said, and then to me, "Shit. Dani is an intern from Portland State that Giselle and I took on in January. She's been continuing to help us this quarter."

"I won't stick around," I said, getting up.

We met Dani at the door. She had a colorful wrap of polished cotton around her head, a single hoop earring, and two tattoos on her upper arms.

"Cassandra Reilly," Karen introduced me. "She's the translator of Luisa Montiflores."

"Oh, I love those stories. Especially the title one!"

"Sorry I can't stay longer," I said, edging past her out the door. I didn't want to be there when Dani heard the news. "Karen, thanks for meeting."

"We'll be in touch," she said awkwardly. I wondered if she regretted telling me so much about Giselle and Jane. Perhaps she needed to talk to someone who had a connection with the press but whom she thought she'd never see again. Grief makes some people mute and some people garrulous and reproachful.

"Dani, what can I get you? Sparkling water, kombucha, ice tea, or beer? Personally, I might have a beer," I heard Karen say as I left.

I wondered if Karen was the most the reliable witness when it came to judging Giselle's alcohol intake.

11.

I washed my shirt in the sink, scrubbing at the sauerkraut and pastrami stains just like my Irish ancestors might have done, though perhaps they would have preferred to boil the shirt in a pot on a peat fire to get a taste of meat for the potato stew. I'd often washed clothes by hand in my travels, and not just in countries where a washing machine had been a luxury at one time. It was quick and easy compared to figuring out the instructions to the Sabine-Nobles' new-model Whirlpool.

I didn't plan to touch even the microwave oven tonight. Instead I walked down to Bamboo Sushi, ordered a bento box and read the restaurant's copy of today's *Oregonian*.

Like most city newspapers, the daily *Oregonian* was probably thinner than it used to be, with only a few articles of national and international news reprinted from the *New York Times* or the *Washington Post*. I skipped those and went right to the local pages.

Under a photo of Giselle, the same one as on the website, was this story:

> *Portland publishing entrepreneur and translator Giselle Richard, 41, fell to her death Monday evening in Newport, Oregon. Police say Richard's body was found the following morning in scrub and trees below the steep bluff of her vacation home. Neighbors say that Richard had been living full-time at the cottage for about a month and was often seen walking on the beach or in town. Richard apparently died of injuries from her fall in what police are treating as an accident pending further investigation.*

This was followed by a brief summary of the founding of Entre Editions five years ago, a small, independent press focusing on translation, which had been gaining not only national but international recognition. The head of the Oregon Arts Commission spoke of the loss to the book community, and a leading bookseller offered this: "She was so lively and outgoing, yet she had a serious side as well, and she was a total advocate for the art of translation."

The last paragraph gave a little more information about Giselle and her family. Born and raised in Montreal, Canada, Richard was the daughter of Pauline Richard, the noted translator of French literature and a former Portland resident, and her ex-husband Dr. Pierre Richard, a Canadian physician, both deceased. Giselle Richard was also the granddaughter of Angus Lawson, who had founded a chain of shoe stores in Oregon and who had been a pillar of Portland society in his time. After attending university in Montreal, Richard worked for a publishing house in Boston and then moved to Portland to start Entre Editions. She was survived by a sister, Jacqueline Richard.

Jacqueline. Karen had said Giselle's sister still lived in Canada, in Vancouver. Was Jacqueline in Newport now? Tom Hoyt had told me she'd been asked to come and identify the body. I wasn't sure how far to the north Vancouver, B.C. was but surely it was just a long day's drive.

Among the photographs on the cottage wall had been one with Pauline and two young girls who had appeared eight or nine years apart in age. Karen had said Giselle and her sister weren't close. Perhaps it was because of the age difference or the fact that Jacqueline appeared to have stayed in Canada.

I finished my bento box, paid up, and strolled leisurely back to the house along one of the streets parallel to NW 23rd. The cherry trees and magnolias were coming into bloom, the dog-owners were out, and the wide-shouldered porches of the boxy wooden houses had a welcoming look. This was a neighborhood that included brick apartment buildings with Art Deco or Spanish touches; both houses and apartment buildings had managed to keep some sense of their early-twentieth-century feel, though perhaps some of their interiors were as up-to-date as the Sabine-Nobles. As I carefully let myself into Candace and Jill's house I thought I might as well enjoy this lovely house in Northwest Portland, because it was certain that whatever I was able to afford on the outskirts of London would be the size of a large closet. And I certainly wasn't going to be able to afford anything if I didn't get to work on translating.

Once inside the front door, I took off my shoes, made a cup of green tea and sat down at the dining room table. I propped up *Baby's First Year* with its lonely photograph of the pram in the falling snow, and thought about Janneken's description of Claribel's essentially leaving her little daughter with her ex-husband's parents. While she went to Paris. I was reminded that Luisa's mother, Estella, had also left her young daughter to go to Paris to study with Lacan. Luisa often talked about her sense of abandonment—talked about it in metaphor, that is. If you were to ask her, she would say, "I am very proud of my mother for becoming a successful psychoanalyst. " Pauline had also gone to Paris on a fellowship, but she had taken Giselle with her.

Why had my own mother never gone to Paris, with me or without me? The farthest she ever got from Kalamazoo was Flagstaff, Arizona, when she drove all night to get me out of jail after I'd been picked up hitchhiking, age seventeen. Needless to say, we turned right around and drove back to Michigan.

I opened my laptop and dutifully went to where I'd left off in the translation. Chapter Three: "Failure to Thrive." The narrator was back at home now with baby and sports-mad husband, Knut. "Baby not gaining weight," said the Norwegian home-health nurse, an extremely tall woman with muscled arms, who often mimed her instructions, or spoke in basic Norwegian to the narrator, while directing most of her informational lectures to the lay-about Knut, abusing his parental leave in front of the television.

How should I render the nurse's insultingly basic Norwegian in English so as to show it was different from my English translation of Claribel's Spanish text? Should I leave in some Norwegian words? A few *Ja's,* anyway? A big fat *Nei* or two?

I knew that, for so many reasons, I had to crank out more pages of this novel over the next few days and send them to Janneken. But the pages couldn't appear "cranked out" if Angela and the agent in New York were going to look at them. If I made unintelligent choices or mistakes, Angela Cook would gleefully point them out to the agent and Claribel. "What Cassandra Reilly did with the Norwegian words is just *wrong.* It's not enough to throw in a *Ja* here and there," she might say. "I don't think Cassandra gets the satiric *intent* of this scene."

My reputation, not to mention my income, was on the line. But all I could think about was Karen Morales. I couldn't get a handle on her: What was I to make of Karen's use of the English language, for instance, *her* word choices? Like a lot of marketing people, she was probably quite adept at parroting others' words, maybe giving them a better spin. *Postmodern narrative,* would that have been how Giselle talked? *Speculative fiction,* maybe that came from Karen's sf circles in Portland. The New Age-y stuff about Jane being so repressed, whose language was that? The swearing, I was sure, was all Karen's own.

She was a mystery to me, at once slovenly and sexy, obviously very sharp, but possibly also a dissembler. She'd glossed over the fact that she and Giselle were having an affair of some sort, and that Jane could have been hurt and jealous. That insinuation that Jane could have pushed Giselle over the cliff? Her admission of the kind of wealth that could have gone to buying Jane out? Karen had seemed to point the finger at a burglar with violent tendencies, at "sketchy" homeless people. Did she really think a burglar had killed Giselle, or was she intentionally trying to misdirect me?

And why would she bother to misdirect me, a mere translator inquiring about next steps for Luisa Montiflores's collection of stories?

Though it was probably true, by this point, that I was clearly moving into the role of amateur investigator. I set aside Chapter Three and opened a new document to jot down a few notes, trying to recall what had happened since I first was so rudely awakened from my nap on the floor of the Poe Room.

I began with the two police officers who had questioned me in Newport, Sergeant Pete Jones, so good-natured and breezy, who brought me a sandwich and coffee, and acted as if this was all just a formality, and big-eared Detective Harald Haakonssen, with his repetitive questions.

What had been on Detective Haakonssen's mind as he went over and over my movements during the course of Monday evening and Tuesday morning? He'd seemed obsessed first with the length of time it had taken me to drive to Newport and then with every little detail in the cottage—as if the police didn't have cameras, as if they couldn't dust and fingerprint everything, as if they couldn't look in the sink themselves, as if they couldn't test the Scotch for drugs with the amazing facilities at their disposal.

I went back over his questions about the cottage and tapped them into the open document:

"Are you positive the lock on the sliding glass door was 'wobbly' already when you tried it? Does 'wobbly' mean that it was just not latched well, or could it have been deliberately broken?"

"What made you enter the cottage when no one answered? Why didn't you just come back or wait until she returned your call?"

"Was anything knocked over? Furniture? Lamps? Were there signs of a struggle?"

"Are you sure you didn't go into any other rooms upstairs or downstairs?"

"Can you describe what you saw during the time you were in the cottage?"

At the time I'd found many of his questions leaning toward the accusative rather than the merely interrogative. My ordinary actions on Monday and Tuesday seemed sinister in the interview room, and I'd found myself responding warily. Didn't an American, albeit one with dual citizenship, have the right to drive around her own country, at her own speed? Didn't Giselle's phone show my number several times, and once they got the recordings wouldn't I be proved a practically innocent bystander? What possible motive could I have for harming Giselle?

I was so busy defending myself during the interview that I didn't realize what I now saw more clearly: Haakonssen probably didn't suspect me at all.

He was only using me as a pair of eyes. And through the detailed description of the cottage that he'd drawn out of me, he'd been able to compare the cottage as it was around ten a.m. with what the investigation team would be looking at.

I remembered how he'd asked about the shoes by the door and how I'd told him I'd seen a pair of well-used walking shoes, but no indoor shoes, no sandals or slippers. I remembered how he'd asked me several times about the kitchen, especially about the table in the kitchen with the bottle of Scotch and the glass. The possibility of a second glass in the sink.

I had been irritated, but now, looking back, I recalled the interior of the cottage almost like a stage set, the props arranged to indicate a scene where a troubled woman drinks alone on a foggy night. Synge? O'Casey? But then it would have been Irish whiskey.

If Haakonssen had read the same email I had on Giselle's laptop why wouldn't he conclude, as I had, that Giselle had been interrupted, and had never gotten back to the computer. Was she having a drink with the window guy? Or had Karen, Jane, or some unknown person arrived later that day?

Aside from understanding that Jane and Karen were rivals in business and perhaps in Giselle's bed, I didn't know Giselle and her circle at all. A neighbor could have done it; a friend turned enemy; a disgruntled author (though not a translator, I hoped); one or another builder in addition to the window guy. Jane, Karen, the sister. That would explain why Giselle might have been wearing indoor shoes or slippers—she knew the person she was drinking with. It would have been easy, after Giselle had been pushed off the bluff, for the murderer to return to the house and remove the second glass or wipe it of prints. But who had a motive? I dismissed the idea of a violent burglar. There would have been signs of a struggle, and I had seen only a quiet little workspace piled with manuscripts and books.

It could have been an accident, just as the newspaper suggested, and as I'd wanted to believe. But if it wasn't an accident, then I needed to think what I could do to contribute to a possible murder probe. Anything, that is, which wouldn't draw unpleasant attention to myself and make me a suspect. Not for the first time, I thought of how being a translator had taught me something about following the trail of meaning while trying to keep my own footprint light.

It was almost eight p.m. before I gave up on getting further along with the *Baby* today. I had almost three chapters done now, fifty-five typed pages of a good draft. If I could do one more chapter in the next few days, that would be closer to the hundred pages I'd promised Janneken. For now I needed to give my inner dictionary a rest.

If I'd been back in London I might have flipped on the telly. The Sabine-Nobles had a big flat-screen television mounted in the living room and next to the smartly upholstered sofa was an array of remote controls. There were several pages in the house-instruction manual detailing how to access a few hundred channels but the effort seemed too great for the meager reward.

Besides, I had to email Luisa and tell her that Giselle had met with a fatal accident, which *might* mean delays to the fall publishing program, if not a complete halt. I typed a longish message to Luisa, ending with a few options—should we write to Editorial Cielo and let them know the situation? Ask them if they would undertake to contact Entre Editions and if necessary scrap the contract? Or should we wait to find out if Jane was planning to keep the publishing company going?

After I finished writing Luisa, but before sending the email, I searched online for the *Oregonian's* story about Giselle to see if any new information had been added to what I'd read in the morning's print edition. Yes, now there was mention of Jane Janicki as the co-owner of Entre Editions, and a quote from her: "Giselle co-founded the press in honor of her mother, Pauline Richard, and would want it to continue if at all possible in whatever form that takes." That didn't exactly sound like a ringing commitment to actually make sure it continued in the form it currently had. After all, why should Jane care about keeping alive Pauline Richard's legacy?

I inserted the link to the story in my email to Luisa and clicked *Send*.

I didn't expect to hear from her until the next day, and was surprised, twenty minutes later, while scrolling through other messages, to hear a ping and see a return email from Luisa. I tended to forget that Montevideo had only a four hours' time difference from the West Coast, not eight or nine hours like the UK or Europe.

She wasted little sympathy on me, as usual, and less on Giselle, before reminding me that she'd had a bad feeling about Entre Editions from the beginning (Untrue, she'd been thrilled). It was so far away, in a place unknown to most people, *Newportland* (True). The mess with the cover and title showed how unprofessional they were, and she hoped I had encountered Karen Morales by now and had told her to go jump in a lake (employing a Spanish phrase that put it a little more crudely). Yes, we (I) should immediately ask Cielo to break the contract, and we (I) should tell Entre that we were not giving back any money to them, because of their dishonorable behavior.

She closed with her usual *abrazos cariñosos* and the injunction to move quickly on this. While in the United States I had the perfect opportunity to find another publisher for her!!

With a sigh, I closed my laptop. At least Luisa now knew the situation. She could jump in a lake herself or *vete a la mierda* as she'd put it.

I pulled down the blinds, made sure the front and back doors were bolted, and checked that the security system was on. It had been a long day, and I was ready for bed.

I hadn't been upstairs since my phone-tour around the house with Candace on Skype earlier, but now I paused to look at the photographs hanging on the stair wall and along the upstairs hallway.

They weren't just random shots of the couple magneted to the fridge, but a carefully framed and curated collection of the lives of Jill and Candace. Here they were, at the bottom of the stairs, as children, with parents, grandparents, siblings; here they were at high-school graduations, Candace with long, smoothly ironed dark hair and a winning smile, clearly an A-student, but probably popular, and Jill, definitely a nerd, with over-large glasses, in an Oxford shirt. Did they have crushes on girls then? Jill did, I was sure of it.

At any rate, by their mid-twenties they were a loving couple. A blown-up color photograph showed them in the West-Coast-dyke uniform of the day—T-shirts under long-sleeved flannel shirts, jeans, hiking boots—and posed by a large waterfall, with short hair, bandanas around their foreheads, and day packs, looking incredibly happy.

The years passed: Jill matured into a handsome woman with a strong jaw and more attractive glasses, and Candace let her hair grow again and became slightly plumper. They must have done well professionally because holiday shots showed them in Paris, in St. Petersburg, and in Istanbul. And then there were the wedding photographs: three rounds it appeared. Before it was legal (a commitment ceremony in a backyard flower garden). When it was temporarily legal in Portland (at city hall with hundreds of other same-sex couples). And finally when it was the law of the whole land (at a Unitarian Church, perhaps, with a woman minister and a beaming congregation in the pews).

I might be, I confess, a little cynical at times about true love, but if ever a couple was committed to being committed, it was the Sabine-Nobles. And as I followed their trajectory from little girls in a dress (Candace) and cowboy outfit (Jill), to their last and binding marriage ceremony, I couldn't help feeling touched, even envious.

Few of my motley and beloved women friends around the globe had found such wedded bliss or had even been interested in wedded bliss. Nicky, for instance, had always been too preoccupied with her career as a bassoonist to look for a long-lasting relationship. She'd had flings, always with women, and enjoyed them hugely, but further than that she really would not rather go. "A shared life with another musician would be difficult, Cassandra," she told me. "But a romantic commitment to anyone who wasn't a musician would be *unbearable*."

I could count on one hand the number of married lesbians I knew in Europe or Latin America, but here in the U.S., they were legion. I certainly didn't want to be married and yet, staring at the chronological pictures of Jill and Candace's relationship on the walls I felt a not-completely-unfamiliar longing for what they seemed to have: a coherent narrative.

I padded down the hallway into the unpretentious guest room and was grateful for a nice box spring and reading lamp. The attached bath was modest, with nothing tricky about the shower taps, and plenty of hot water.

I was asleep by nine.

That night, in a small guest room in a comfy American bed, I dreamed of Jupiter and one of her moons, a small moon with a sandy beach, and a red-haired woman and a dog in the distance. The figures were always in the distance, no matter how fast I walked to catch up with them. I knew quite well in the dream that was the kind of thing common to this little moon—you could never close the distance between you and anyone else. Some dimension of time was involved, so although the figures were visible, they were not approachable. The woman with the dog was my mother, Frances, who had been born in Detroit to Irish immigrants and had died fifteen years ago.

She looked so young and her hair was so red in the dream, unrealistically fire-red. I'd never seen her looking this young, except in a few photographs from before her marriage to Dad. Already in the wedding pictures she looked pinched around the mouth, more like the mother I remembered, than this dream-like redhead who thought that love would make everything right.

I was up early and went out to a coffee bar a block away to get an extra-large latte. Then I got back in bed with Luisa's manuscript, intending to look at it again and think about which other publishers besides Entre might be interested, and how I would craft a query letter. It sounded to me like Luisa wanted to break the contract, whether Jane decided to throw in the towel or not. I supposed Luisa was right, given that from what Karen said, Jane would probably struggle to manage without Giselle's vision and apparent ability to persuade people to believe in her.

Something I had certainly experienced first-hand, since I never would have come to Portland, much less driven to Newport, without Giselle's cajoling voice in my ear, her suggestion that we'd have a lovely time, just the two of us, discussing many more translation projects I could do with them.

I wondered if in writing to some publishers I should I mention magic-realism or fabulism, or was *Latinx science fiction* the way to go? Karen had said something today about Luisa's roots in Argentina's science-fiction tradition before mumbling something I didn't quite catch about Luisa "as a modernist." But maybe Karen been talking about As-a-mov? As in Isaac Asimov? Hard to tell when someone had her mouth full of sushi.

Luisa's Jupiter was, as she had told me many times, nothing to do with the actual planet. Nor was her Jupiter related to the Roman god of war, and his sons, the moons. Luisa's Jupiter was round, creamy, and veined with pink and blue, with a volcano peak of dark brown at the center. A peak that spewed out lava that flew into space and formed the two moons that circled around Jupiter, two moonlets always hoping more lava would flow in their direction, so that they could reach the size of their mother and become planets in their own right, rather than just orbiters.

This sounds more poetic in Spanish, of course.

I was never sure whether Luisa was getting better as a writer or worse. Even after years of translating her work, I still had moments when I felt vaguely embarrassed by her lavish metaphors, and several such moments had come up in this collection. Yet I also knew that it was that very tendency to go a little too far with her allegories and symbolism that had endeared her to some scholars and literary critics in Latin America. With Luisa, there was always something to analyze. Some reviewers and academics would see Jupiter as a cruel and rapacious North America, holding its moons trapped in a punishing orbit of cultural influence. Jupiter might also be seen as the International Monetary Fund, which kept the moons of so many Latin American countries revolving in debt around its fat, round treasure chest. On the other hand, the brown volcano spewing lava, generating worlds like Io and Europa and all the rest of the many moons in Jupiter's orbit, might be seen as a reclaiming of Latin American creativity. In this reading Jupiter would be described fertile and generous, not chilly and withholding.

Literary critics specializing in the Southern Cone, particularly Uruguay and Argentina, were well aware by now that Luisa, like her mother Estella, had been influenced by Jacques Lacan during her years in Europe. On her return to Montevideo, Luisa had entered psychoanalysis (as far as I knew she had never exited; as for so many people in Uruguay, therapy was an on-going part of life, like going to the dentist). Lacan's image of the Big Other (*l'Autre*) and the little other (*l'autre*) had appeared before in her stories. "Jupiter and Her Moons" was a typical Luisa Montiflores example of fictionalized Lacanian psychology in the way the omnipotence of the mother led first to joy and then to fear of losing that joy. In this case there were two moons, two sisters—two selves, I suspected.

I could only "suspect" because Luisa rarely confirmed anything, not to interviewers, not to scholars who studied her, and not even to me, who was her translator image, her little moon, her *l'autre,* orbiting around her creativity and reproducing it, as skillfully as possible, within the limits of English. Rich in vocabulary as English was, it couldn't match the Romance languages for sumptuousness.

Giselle may not have gotten every single one of Luisa's metaphors and references to Lacan, but I was under the impression that she'd read Luisa's manuscript with an understanding of mother-daughter psychology. Of course she would, if she translated from French, and if her mother was such an expert in French literature. Still, it occurred to me that even though I'd looked at the online catalog of Entre Editions, I didn't have a clear idea of what Giselle had been most drawn to in French fiction. The two titles she'd translated were slim novels by contemporary authors I'd not heard of before. So should I pitch *On Jupiter* to an editor like Giselle, if I could find one? Or should I look for an editor with tastes more like Karen Morales? My mind went back to her untidy appearance, her red-eyed unhappiness, to the mess she'd made of the soy sauce and bright green wasabi paste. She knew a lot about Latinx science fiction, of that I was sure, but how much did she know about Lacan? I was now more inclined to think she'd said Asimov.

The one editor I couldn't go back to with *On Jupiter* was Janneken. She'd already rejected it once, and not only because she found Luisa personally obnoxious and her writing too precious, but because as an editor Janneken was highly attuned to what was selling. She'd made her mark in British publishing by discovering and promoting Nordic crime writers, with a few Russian and German authors thrown in. Now that she could see a post-magical realism boom of youthful Latin Americans getting international attention, she was interested in writers like Claribel. Young women authors on their way up, not older women authors who'd burnt a lot of bridges.

I knew that I should get cracking on Claribel's *Baby* right away. Not to send something soon to Janneken was to court my editor's wrath and possible dismissal from the project. If I kept my nose to the grindstone I could finish Chapter Three, "Failure to Thrive" in three or four hours and start on Chapter Four, "Colic" this afternoon.

But perhaps because of my dream, or perhaps because my spirit was just contrary at times, I felt more preoccupied with Luisa and *Jupiter.* It suddenly struck me as noteworthy that both works dealt with mothers and daughters. Luisa, of course, wrote as a daughter who had been neglected by her self-absorbed, withholding mother, while Claribel wrote as a first-time mother who felt "reduced, obliterated, subjugated" by the screaming demands of the endlessly hungry little being in her care.

I supposed the main thing that united these two writers was their discontent, their anguish that *their* needs were never met. And once again, I was back to wondering about Giselle and her mother, Pauline.

After I'd dressed—my hand-washed shirt was now sauerkraut- and pastrami-free, though wrinkled—I searched for Wikipedia's entry on Isaac Asimov. He wrote quite a bit about Jupiter, it seemed, including a children's book titled *Lucky Starr and the Moons of Jupiter.* Could Luisa possibly have read Asimov in her youth and been influenced by him? Was that what Karen meant?

I didn't want to check and see if she'd sent me any more messages. I needed some breakfast. I raised the blinds, unbolted the front door, and carefully punched in the security code to leave. After breakfast, I'd walk down to Powell's Bookstore. My main mission would be to investigate North American publishers that did translations and that might take a chance on Luisa. And while I was at the bookstore I'd check out Asimov's books and remember to look for Nora Longeran's children's novels.

I'd metaphorically park Claribel's baby in the pram and leave her outside the house, where I couldn't hear her calling me.

12.

"I have always imagined that Paradise will be a kind of library," Borges wrote, and if he had visited the labyrinthine rooms of Powell's in Portland, he might have called this bookstore another kind of paradise, where the supply of books was endlessly and imaginatively renewed, and where you could buy the books to create your own personal library paradise at home.

From outside, the block-sized bookshop looked unremarkable, ungainly in fact, cobbled together from two or three older buildings. But inside it expanded to near infinity with stairs and corridors to larger and smaller rooms on four floors: the Red room, the Rose room, the Blue, the Purple and the Pearl. The bookstore was so large and so initially overwhelming that paper maps were available, color-coded. I went to one of the information desks and learned that most translated fiction was shelved in the general- fiction shelves in the Blue Room. I was about to ask where to find the science-fiction section, but a heavily pregnant woman rushed up with a more urgent question—Where were the bathrooms?—and I set off for the Blue Room. I'd find Asimov later.

I had to admit, Claribel's novel, *Where the Fjords Meet,* had a handsome jacket, and the author's photograph on the back was nice to look at as well. Powell's had a pile of the hardcovers on one of their tables. I didn't pick it up, plagued as I was by envy of Angela Cook, the rhapsodic copy and blurbs, and a grim sense that I had been shunted aside to translate *Baby's First Year* when I could have been basking in the glow of stellar reviews of this "contemporary masterpiece of exile and longing."

I moved into the shelves, looking first under the M's for copies of Luisa's books. There was a single pristine copy of each of the two collections, reviewers' copies perhaps, never read. *Shadow of a Woman on the Sidewalk* was my favorite; I pulled it out for a look. On the cover was a print by the French photographer Sarah Moon, "Suzanne aux Tuileries," in which a woman deep in thought walked away from the viewer, trailed by a tiny dog. Sarah Moon used Polaroid film and worked from the thin black and white negative film to make her haunting prints, blurred at the edges, expressionist, otherworldly. Luisa had chosen the cover image herself. It was that loneliness in Luisa's writing that I tried to capture, that spoke to me like this photograph of the woman and the dog, and the deep afternoon shadows spoke to me. The *woman* Luisa was frankly impossible. Her *writing*—at least my writing of her writing—enchanted and moved me, not always but often.

I put the slender volume back and resumed my prowling of the shelves, discovering Latin American novels translated by the masters, Edith Grossman and Gregory Rabassa, and by newer names. Many were published by mainstream houses, others by university presses or by independent publishers. After long struggles on the part of us translators, our names were generally on the covers, albeit in small type under the authors' names.

Sometimes the blurbs on the jackets and back covers referred to the people who had written the books in English: "Fluidly translated by Arthur Smith;" "A fluent translation by Samantha Jones." These riverine modifiers were echoed in similar adverbs like "gracefully," "elegantly," "smoothly," and the dread "faithfully." The serious praise was reserved for the author: "bursting with inventive language;" "magnetizing prose suffused with brilliance;" "a captivating style;" "prose that dazzles on every page."

The invisible translator, whose captivating English prose it actually was, barely got a mention.

No marketing department had yet come up with anything like: "Now available to those who don't read German and don't propose to learn it anytime soon, in a magnetizing English version by Susan Bernofsky," or "Based on the original Japanese by [small-capped author's name], a stunning book by [LARGE-CAPPED TRANSLATOR'S NAME]." Attention to the translator was more likely in the case of ancient classics. Emily Wilson's new version of *The Odyssey* merited the written ovation: "A staggeringly superior translation—true, poetic, lively and readable, and always closely engaged with the original Greek—that brings to life the fascinating variety of voices in Homer's great epic."

Homer was merely great, while Wilson had produced something staggeringly superior—possibly even to Homer.

Still, some of the newer presses devoted to translation made more of an effort to foreground the translator. Previous translations were mentioned, along with awards and prizes. Many translators were professors and some had interesting hobbies ("She moonlights as a flamenco dancer"). Some translators, in generating controversy, were famous in their own right, like the contemporary duo of Richard Peavar and Larissa Volokhonsky, who'd given the boot to Constance Garnett when it came to the Russian classics. And some were famous first and foremost as fiction writers, like Jhumpa Lahiri or Lydia Davis. I looked inside the cover of my best-known translation from 1990, still in print, of Gloria de los Angeles's magical realism novel, *Big Mama and Her Baby Daughter,* which had been made into a film, and read the one-line description of myself: "Cassandra Reilly is a noted translator of Spanish."

"Noted." I guess that was something.

It can be difficult in a bookstore, if you've published a book in your life time, not to occasionally feel very small indeed.

I reminded myself that I was here to do some research, so I conscientiously searched for titles of Latin American authors I recognized or just translations that looked interesting. I had about twenty volumes in my shopping basket before coming to my senses and returning half of them to the shelves. I couldn't haul a load of books back to London. I already had piles of them that would soon have to go into boxes.

A sharp sense of loss floored me. No matter what my decision, I was probably going to be moving out of Nicky's flat, from the room she had always called "yours."

I'd noticed that there was a coffee shop at one corner of the bookstore: I'd have a cup of tea and settle my nerves. No need to go all dramatic about being thrown out to fend for myself. I was a traveler, wasn't I? Always had been, since I parted ways with my family at twenty. I didn't need my mother and sisters badgering me to comb my hair and give up my unholy ways. I didn't need Nicky to provide a home. I could rely on myself.

I returned fifteen of the books and paid for the rest, leaving all but one in a bag behind the counter at the register. This was a battered little paperback of *Lucky Starr and the Moons of Jupiter,* which I'd found on the Isaac Asimov shelf in the Gold Room.

Soon I was sitting with a cup of Assam at a table for two. I'd barely started the book when someone came up and said hesitantly, "You're Cassandra Reilly, aren't you? The translator?"

I looked up in surprise and recognized the intern who had stopped by Karen Morales's flat yesterday: Dani.

"Would you mind if I sat down with you? I'm on my lunch break, and I would love to talk to you—about translation and other things."

In her early twenties, slender, with wavy dark hair, loosely pinned up, and long, dangly earrings, Dani wore an off-the shoulder knit blouse that exposed one of her upper-arm tattoos, this one a Celtic pattern. I invited her to join me and she placed a latte in a wide cup and a peanut butter cookie in a napkin on the table, then shoved her backpack under her chair.

"That's lunch?" I asked.

"Sort of. I sometimes come here in between classes mid-day. Portland State is pretty close."

We talked about translation for a bit. I'd imagined that she was studying Spanish literature from her interest in Luisa and my other work, but her subject was contemporary German literature and she was working on an M.A.

"Giselle liked to take on interns who know one or more languages. My girlfriend Ren interned for her last summer, though just for a month because she's so busy. Ren is in the Spanish department. She's doing a Ph.D. and teaching part-time. She's also writing a novel."

"It sounds like Giselle tried to make it a good environment for interns."

"I learned so much," Dani said, raising her latte for a sip.

"What kind of things did you do there?"

"I was mainly assisting Karen, doing publicity, sending out review copies, helping organize some readings, but I used to help Giselle too. That was more interesting to me, the editorial work." She looked away. "I feel really upset, having spent so much time with Giselle and Jane. Ren too. She knew Giselle even better. She was the one who recommended Giselle publish Luisa Montiflores. After Karen told me yesterday about Giselle, and that the police came to see her, I've been wondering if they'll want to talk to me as well. Have they talked to you?"

I nodded. "Yes, they did. But then, I was in Newport to meet Giselle, at her request. When I went to the cottage, on Tuesday morning, there was no one there. Later a cop came along to the hotel and hauled me in for questioning," I saw from her face that this prospect frightened her. "But I just told them what I knew and they gave me some coffee and a nice sandwich and I was on my way again. Nothing to worry about."

Her shoulders relaxed slightly but she still looked worried, sipping on her coffee. She'd pulled apart her cookie, so that it resembled peanut butter crumble, but hadn't eaten a bite. I wondered if Dani needed someone to talk to. Maybe, if I provided an ear, she could tell me more about the relationships among the women at Entre Editions. After all, she'd probably seen more of their intimate daily life than most.

"So, when you were an intern, you'd go over to the office at Jane and Giselle's house?" I asked. "You probably spent a fair amount of time with them. Since January?"

She nodded. "I'd go to the house a couple of times a week at least. I never saw that much of Jane. She'd be on the computer in the office mostly. Giselle would be, like, '*Bonjour, chèrie*, come into the living room, sit down, let's talk, would you like some tea?' She was more my ideal of what an editor should be, you know, gracious, passionate about literature."

That was my ideal too, but I had rarely encountered it outside the pages of Edwardian novels. "So Jane didn't seem as interested in literature?"

"I know she wanted the press to succeed. But she seemed upset sometimes when she was talking on the phone, and she was frustrated with Giselle. Once," Dani put down her latte. "I heard them having a fight, about six weeks ago. They were in the office and I was still in the living room. There's a dining room and kitchen between the office and the front of the house, but I could still hear them. Giselle had told me to wait in the living room, she'd get a few query letters and sample translations for me to take away to read. But as soon as she went back into the office, Jane started raising her voice about unpaid printing bills and 'publicity expenses through the roof.' I heard Karen's name, something about 'she has so much money, let her pay for catering if she thinks we need it for the party.'"

Dani looked upset, remembering. "I wanted to leave. It was awful, like listening to my parents fight about money when I was little. Finally, Giselle came back to the living room, trying to act as if nothing had happened. She'd forgotten the letters and other stuff she was going to give me and I didn't want to remind her. So I just left. Afterwards, she emailed me and apologized."

I tried to imagine Jane shouting. She clearly had another side, perhaps a violent side? I said sympathetically, "That sounds awful. And so unprofessional. So, it was some time after that fight that Giselle moved out, to Newport?"

"Beginning of March." She still hadn't eaten any of her cookie, but had continued to crumble it into a nutty-scented paste. "Giselle told me it was because they'd decided to remodel the house so the office would have a separate entrance. In a way I wondered if it was so that things like that—someone overhearing them in the living room—wouldn't happen. Giselle said it would be noisy, so that was why she was going to her family's old place on the coast."

"Did you see Giselle or Jane much after that?"

Dani shook her head. "I started coming over to Karen's place instead, once a week or so. I still did editorial work along with publicity, but mostly it was from home. Giselle and I emailed. I haven't seen Jane since Giselle left."

"What about Karen's role at the press? If you don't mind my asking? She hadn't been working there very long, I understand. It sounds like she might have been the cause of the fight?"

"I think Giselle really liked working with Karen, I mean, I know she did. Karen had created a whole new website and knows all about social media. And they loved to talk about events. Karen always had ideas about holding catered book parties with music in unusual venues in Portland, like a Korean restaurant or Grandpa's Café at the Polish Hall, and bringing the author over from wherever and putting them on tour. So like with Luisa's book, Karen was fantasizing about renting the planetarium theater at the Museum for Science and Industry in Portland. Her ideas were all about trying to make Entre Editions stand out from the crowd. You know, not just another independent press, but more glamorous and hip." Having ground the cookie to powder, she balled up the paper napkin neatly and stuffed it carefully in the latte cup.

"Maybe Jane felt left out. Could she have been jealous?"

"No, I don't think Jane sounded jealous. It was more like Jane was freaking out about the costs of these kinds of events."

I was direct. "But if the police were to ask you about Giselle and Karen, what would you say?"

"I guess it's possible they were involved. I know that Karen used to drive out to Newport once in while, maybe more often. Giselle came into Portland for a couple of meetings over the last month, but I don't know if she stayed at her house, or if she stayed with Karen." Dani looked worried again. "Would the police ask something like that? I don't know Karen very well. She's kind of self-absorbed and moody. I've heard her blow up with people on the phone—she doesn't like to be contradicted. She can put on a good face, but you have to tread on eggshells sometimes. Maybe Jane stood up to her. I know they didn't get on too well. Maybe Giselle and Karen were making some kind of secret plan to dump Jane."

Clearly Dani had been thinking overtime about all this. "What would make you think that?"

"I met with Giselle once a couple of weeks ago to return some manuscripts and she seemed pretty upbeat."

"More than normal?"

"She was always positive, but that day she was more than positive. She was excited. She talked about some new directions for the press, 'repositioning,' she said; a possible investor, and ideas for funding. I've wondered if Karen was the investor. She's a millionaire, you know. But I've also wondered how that would go, because Karen can be so volatile. She and Giselle had already disagreed about some things too. You got the feeling that Karen might have bigger ideas. Maybe even that she'd like to take over the press herself. And I think Giselle would have been pretty resistant to that."

Dani trailed off, and she pulled her backpack from the floor to her lap, as if she was about to leave. Then she seemed to make a decision. "I haven't told anyone except Ren this, because it sounds silly, and I don't know why I'm telling you, except maybe it's not silly at all. Maybe it's something."

"Go on."

"Two days ago, early Tuesday morning, I went over to Karen's to drop off some stuff. I had to TA for a class at eight a.m., so I'd come early. It was before seven. She'd told me to buzz her door, but she wasn't there. The box was kind of big, so I wasn't sure where to leave it. Finally I thought I might go around the back of the building and see if there was an outside door to the condos from the parking lot, and just leave the box there and text her.

"But she must have forgotten I was coming, or something, because I actually found her in the little parking area back there, with a hand-held vacuum, cleaning the back of her SUV. I noticed when I came up behind her that there was sand rattling through the vacuum cleaner. She'd taken out some shoes that were all sandy, and a raincoat or parka, and they were on the sidewalk. At the time I didn't think much about it. I just assumed she'd taken an early walk somewhere and had just returned. I guess it crossed my mind briefly that she could have just returned from Newport."

"Did she seem at all ... furtive?"

"I don't think so. She was glad to see me and took the box. Thanked me. She said she had forgotten about me dropping it off. She was totally casual, so I was too."

"So she probably hadn't heard yet about Giselle?"

"I guess not. I only heard myself that evening on the news. There wasn't much. Just that Giselle had had an accident."

"Karen seemed really upset when I saw her yesterday," I said. "Still, you say she was fine on Tuesday morning?"

"Yeah. It was just all the sand that seemed strange. I mean, sand makes me think of the coast more than Portland."

Dani looked at the time on her phone. "Sorry, I've got to get back to campus. I have a seminar in twenty minutes. I feel better talking to you. I mean, I know it was probably just an accident, Giselle falling. But, still— if the police don't get hold of me, do you think that someone should let them know about the sand?"

"Up to you," I said. "But if you decide to share it, call Detective Haakonssen in Newport at the police department."

I watched her dash out, earrings flying in the breeze, cell phone in her hand, checking for messages as she darted across the street. No lunch and she didn't even eat her cookie. An unwholesome image of Karen popped into my mind, Karen walking at night along a sandy beach to the rocks below the bluff where Giselle had fallen or been pushed. Sand in her shoes, sand in her car.

Had she been cleaning her car Tuesday morning to get rid of evidence? But what was Karen's motivation to kill Giselle? Could she and Giselle have quarreled that afternoon or evening in Newport, either about their new relationship or about the direction of the press? Perhaps Karen had some kind of financial hold on Giselle already and Giselle was balking. Still it was difficult, remembering Karen's swollen eyes yesterday, to think she could have tried to hurt Giselle on purpose. But if she had the volatile temper Dani had suggested, maybe an after-dinner amble on the bluff had ended with Giselle over the side, and with Karen, freaked out, scrambling down to the beach to try to help her, then discovering she was dead, and hightailing it back to Portland.

The trouble was, Karen had told me she had her writers' group on Monday night. And unless she was a psychopath, would Karen have been cheerily vacuuming the sandy evidence from her SUV early Tuesday morning?

Unbidden, I recalled the woman and the dog in my dream last night, walking on the sands of Io. I'd thought the woman might be my mother, but now recalled my own walk on the beach at Newport, Tuesday morning before breakfast, before meeting Nora. The fog had been light then and I recalled the two joggers in the near distance. And then there was the woman in the blue parka and watch cap, with her golden retriever. We had chatted and she'd said, what had she said? I couldn't remember, except that she told me she walked her dog twice a day. And that she had a hair salon. I remembered her face well enough to recognize it again.

Perhaps there was a chance that this woman and her dog had seen something early in the morning. Perhaps I should mention this to Detective Haakonssen? And tell him about the sand in Karen's SUV and her early morning vacuuming, in case Dani decided not to call him?

First I wanted to talk to Jane again, about breaking the contract for Luisa's book, and once I was in the door, I'd try to figure out how to question her about her quarrels with Giselle and Karen, and about Entre's financial problems. I had to help this case along a little faster. I didn't have the time to wait for the Newport police to figure it out.

I took the streetcar up the hill to Jill and Candace's to collect the Subaru and put the bag of books into the passenger seat, without going in the house. There are only so many times you want to hear the scream of a security system that scares the correct numbers out of your head.

13.

The yellow house set well above the sidewalk was quiet, as was the whole neighborhood. The same Honda Civic sat in the drive, but unlike yesterday no vans were parked on the street. Neither C.J., the young electrician with the auburn beard, nor the builder seemed to be here.

I rang the bell, then knocked. Jane's car was here, but apparently she wasn't. Or else she was avoiding me. It was this suspicion, along with a justified fear of Laurelhurst neighbors who probably took their responsibility to keep an eye on crime seriously, that deterred me from going around to the back of the house and checking to see if anyone had forgotten to close a window or door.

I'd already reaped the consequences of my innocent reconnoiter at Giselle's cottage in Newport Tuesday morning.

Instead I got back in the Subaru and drove out of the neighborhood to a larger street where I found a café in a turn-of-the-century wooden building. The weather was nice enough to sit outside but I saw that the high-ceilinged interior had more comfortable looking armchairs and even a velvet sofa. I ordered a bowl of lentil soup and settled down to read for a while. On a whim I'd picked Asimov's *Lucky Starr and the Moons of Jupiter* out of the top of the book bag.

Great Galaxy! Soon I was absorbed in the adventures of earthling David Starr, aka Lucky, and his sidekick, Bigman, a pouter-pigeon of a short-statured Martian, both of them en route to Jupiter to save the galaxy. In their spaceship they also carried with them, in a special tank of carbon-dioxide-saturated water, a small being from Venus called a V-frog. After some preliminaries, Lucky and Bigman landed their craft inside one of the moons of Jupiter, where a large spaceship powered by a force called Agrav was in production. They were met by a hostile commander and a lot of unfriendly workers. Someone on this moon, called Jupiter 9, was a spy for the lawless Sirians of the galaxy and was attempting to steal the secrets of the anti-gravity spaceship. It was Lucky Starr's mission to find the spy, human or robot.

The V-frog intrigued me. The way that Asimov explained it, the frog, despite its small size and vulnerability, had no enemies or predators. This was because it was able to make any sentient being in its vicinity like it or love it by generating waves of telepathic love. The frog could also pick up emotions from others, magnify the emotions, and broadcast them out in waves that affected everyone in the vicinity, for good or ill.

Lucky Starr had brought a V-frog with him to Jupiter 9 as a kind of stealth weapon. The V-frog would project good feelings onto erstwhile enemies, but it also might be able to pick up the emotions of the people on the planet, one of whom could be a spy and or saboteur. If such a person existed, the V-frog might alert Lucky and Bigman of his presence, unless the spy was some kind of robot. And if the spy *was* a robot, the V-frog would be helpful in identifying him, since robots couldn't feel human emotion, only fake it. And if there was no emotion, the V-frog couldn't transmit it.

Two young mothers and their fleece-wrapped infants came into the coffee shop and soon the noise level increased. Reluctantly I put the paperback in my jacket pocket and headed out again. I had decided to call the Newport police station and I didn't want my conversation overheard.

I parked about a block away from Jane's house while I sat in the Subaru and made my call. I said I had some new information on the case and was immediately put through to Pete Jones, even though I asked for Detective Haakonssen.

"Cassandra Reilly," he said. "What do you have for us?" There was less bonhomie now than when we were first chatting over coffee and a sandwich about his travels to Thailand and my fascinating life.

I told him I'd now remembered meeting a woman on the beach Tuesday morning, and that she'd mentioned she walked her dog twice a day along the same stretch.

"Yes, we've talked to her," he said. "She called us yesterday afternoon and she told us she'd met you Tuesday on the beach, very early. She also described being on the beach Monday evening around seven thirty and seeing a woman matching Giselle Richard's description who was walking toward the hotel."

"What? I thought Giselle was already, you know, over the side by then."

He ignored that. "I know you've been over this with both me and Detective Haakonssen, but I'd like to ask you once again: You're sure you didn't encounter Giselle outside the hotel and talk to her before your check-in at 8:50 p.m.? You said you arrived in Newport sometime after eight and wandered around 'lost' for half an hour. That's a long time to be 'lost' in our small town."

I hadn't expected to be on the defensive again. Was it my fault the coast was fogbound and that American cities were so confusing to navigate with all the strip malls and lack of signage? "No, I didn't encounter her. I didn't go down to the beach. I didn't even know where the beach *was* at that point. Definitely not."

I felt thrown by this new information. The lawyer Tom Hoyt had told me they thought Giselle died around six p.m. Monday evening., but if she'd been seen walking on the beach ninety minutes later, what did that mean? Probably the woman with the dog was mistaken. Even though it wouldn't have been technically dark, it would have been so cold, damp, and misty that everyone would have been wearing parkas with hoods that hid their faces.

I'd wanted to ask Haakonssen whether the investigative team had read the email that Giselle had been writing when she was interrupted. I'd wanted to ask him if he had theories about who could have interrupted her. They must have interviewed the window guy by now, and scoured the neighborhood for witnesses to any sketchy characters hanging about in the scrub and rocks under the bluff or sleeping in vans nearby.

But I didn't want to have a long conversation with Sergeant Jones that might have unseen traps. I decided to keep my mouth shut about Karen and the sandy boots as well. That would sound at this point like a feeble attempt to direct suspicion away from myself. Surely if Karen had come to Newport that afternoon or evening in broad, if foggy, daylight, someone would have noticed her or her car. The neighbors had noticed *me*.

Instead, as nonchalantly as I could, I said, "The newspaper said her death was being treated as an accident? Is that still true?"

"We're keeping all possibilities open." He paused. "Someone has come forward to help us in our inquiries, that's all I can say for now. We realize you have commitments in London and I'm sorry you've had to cancel your flight home. But as we've told you, Ms. Reilly, we're requesting that you don't leave the state at this time. We have your address now in Portland, but we may have to ask you to return to Newport in a few days for a follow-up interview. Please let us know if you leave your current address. Agreed?"

Of course, I had not mentioned that I hadn't yet cancelled my flight, but I still wanted to appear cooperative. And I had more questions now: Who had come forward? Was someone claiming they'd seen me on the beach Monday evening?

"Would you still like to talk to Detective Haakonssen?" he said.

"I don't know. For now, I just wanted to check in and tell you about the woman and dog on the beach. I'm sure you're working as hard as you can to solve the case, but I do feel a little worried that ... Can you at least tell me who has come forward?"

"I'll tell Detective Haakonssen you called," he said, and hung up.

Disgruntled, I clicked off and checked email and texts. Return to Newport in a few days? What would I do if this investigation dragged on for weeks? A vision of a room in the library at Chipping Witteron arose: three comfy chairs and a couple of small tables with cups of tea. Seated in one chair was the moderator, and in another chair the now blonde Claribel, sleek with her international success. In the third chair was Angela Cook, squinty-eyed and pointy-nosed, hinting that the last translator (who unfortunately was detained in a murder case, the murder of an *editor*), had not quite been up to the job of conveying the layers of meaning in Claribel's earlier novels.

It was time to write Janneken:

Got your messages. Yes, looks a bit dire, doesn't it? But never fear, I'll be on the plane in just a few days and can meet with Claribel and assuage her concerns. Meanwhile I'm not far from being able to send you the first chapters as requested. Tell Claribel it's a wonderful satire. I'm loving it!!!

Once I'd sent this message, I scrolled through texts I'd missed this morning. Finally, something from Nicky. I read the text quickly:

Sorry for the silence, busy, busy, still in Germany. After the tour we came back to Berlin for a few days. Such a fabulous time performing with Petra and Sally. Sally's from Winnipeg, remember her, the violinist? Well now she's got a place here. Raves about Berlin and I see why. It is so central. Glad you liked the Edinburgh pix. Alistair the posh estate agent was supposed to send them to you two weeks ago. To be honest, I'm a bit off Scotland at the moment, it rained the whole bloody time I was there. Reminded me of my childhood: Gray. What would you think if I did something mad and rented a place in Berlin for a while? You'd love it here. Meanwhile there's been an informal offer on the Islington flat. Actually, it's a Russian we met on the train from Hamburg back to Berlin. He seems to have plenty of money and would take it right away. I told him I'd see what your plans were. Cheers, N.

P.S. You're having me on, aren't you, about this murder business?

I wasn't surprised that Nicky had gone off Scotland and was suddenly enamored with Germany. She did get carried away at times, especially by violinists. But to give up her home and flit off to Berlin? That was unlike her. She couldn't be having a midlife crisis, since she and I were the same age. More likely it was early Alzheimer's.

And what was this completely bizarre idea of selling the flat to a Russian on the train? That sounded like something from a John le Carré novel. He must be a money launderer or a spy. This was far worse than the Edinburgh idea. In a pinch I could have handled Edinburgh, especially in an "airy apartment on a tree-lined street," even in the rain. But to imagine Nicky with no place in the U.K. to call home, and thus no place for me to call semi-home?

It was unthinkable.

I was just starting to respond to her text in what I hoped was an even-tempered way, when I saw a white compact pull up in front of Jane's house, its motor running. I slipped out of the Subaru and tried to get closer to the car, hiding behind a large tree shading the sidewalk. The two people inside the vehicle continued talking for a few minutes, then the passenger got out. White ponytail, blue shirt, jeans: Jane Janicki.

The car drove in my direction. It must be an airport rental, with a Washington plate. I didn't get a close look at the woman at the wheel, just saw she had dark hair to her shoulders and bangs. But from the photographs at the cottage and the family resemblance, I could be fairly certain it was Giselle's sister Jacqueline.

I managed to reach Jane while she was still on the front porch.

"Hi, Jane!" I said. "Do you have a minute?"

I was there to discuss whether it was possible to break the contract for Luisa's book—that is, if Jane wasn't going to publish it. But of course I also hoped to ask a few other questions. If the woman in the car was Giselle's sister Jacqueline and if Jacqueline had driven here from Newport, was there any news about Giselle's death yet? Any information as to whether it was an accident or murder, any suspects, anything that would make it possible for me to make my flight to London?

Yet the sight of Jane's face—desperate was the only word for it—stopped me cold.

"Are you all right?" I asked instead.

She shook her head. Her cheeks and eyes were swollen from crying and her jaw quivered with the effort of keeping her emotions in check. I'd believed yesterday that Jane had taken Giselle's death less dramatically than Karen. Now I wondered if Jane had bottled everything up inside for fear of completely breaking down. Had talking to Giselle's sister uncorked an emotional storm?

"Come," I said. "Sit down here." I guided her to a wicker chair and perched on the one next to it. "Did something just happen to upset you?"

She nodded. A few strands of her white hair had come free of the ponytail and she absently tried to brush them from her cheek. She was wearing the same clothes as yesterday and I imagined that she'd probably not washed or changed since then. Perhaps she hadn't slept either. She sank down in the chair and made an effort to pull herself together by gripping one hand over the other and squeezing. She rocked back and forth in place. I felt for a second as if I were watching a child try to contain emotions she couldn't reasonably be expected to handle.

Then Jane focused her eyes on me and said, gulping for breath, "Giselle's sister, Jacqui, doesn't want a memorial service. She said Giselle doesn't deserve one. She told me some awful things about Giselle and her mother, how they treated Jacqui. Things I could hardly believe."

"So that was her sister—Jacqui—who just dropped you off?" I asked. Naturally I was curious about what these hardly-to-be-believed things were, but I was afraid of Jane rushing back in the house if I came on too strong.

"Yes. She wanted to see me, we had lunch. I couldn't really eat anything."

"Did she drive here from Newport to see you? Is there any news about how Giselle died?"

"She said the police don't know yet if it was an accident. Jacqui identified Giselle's ... body, that's the main thing they wanted from her. She couldn't tell them much else. She said the age difference between her and Giselle meant that she hardly knew her sister. It's awful," Jane said again, still gripping her hands, but no longer rocking.

For the moment, all I could think to do was start talking, in as soothing a voice as I could, about whatever came into my mind, which was this neighborhood of well-kept houses and gardens. I told her it was autumn in Montevideo, so it was a surprise to see flowering magnolias and azaleas.

Gradually she seemed to calm down, and I took the opportunity to say, "It was probably a shock to see Jacqui. Had you ever met her before? I believe she lives in Canada, in Vancouver?"

"I'd never met her," Jane said, her voice steadier. "Giselle was in contact with her both in Montreal and Vancouver and tried to help her. Most recently she had tried to get Jacqui back in school, in a community college. I know Giselle tried to be patient, but she said that Jacqui was always a problem, always had been. She had temper tantrums when she was a baby, and later on did a lot of acting out and some self-destructive behavior. I always had the impression Pauline had tried to help Jacqui when she was in trouble as an adolescent, but I didn't know the details."

"But you're saying Jacqui has a different story about her relationship with her mother, with Giselle?"

"I'm not sure what to believe. I'm trying to put what Jacqui told me together with some other things I've found in our accounts that seem irregular. Things Giselle kept hidden from me." She paused, "Financial problems that will make it impossible to keep publishing."

"Maybe I could help? I mean, I don't understand your exact situation, but I do know about publishing."

Jane began to shiver. She stood up as if she was wondering why we were sitting on the porch and went to the open door and picked up a last few envelopes on the mat. I thought she was going to close the door in my face, but perhaps the urge to talk, to share with someone, made her change her mind.

"Come in," she said. "And excuse the mess."

14.

I followed Jane through the house. The living room, dim from partially closed wooden blinds and half-drawn drapes, was dominated by an Arts and Crafts fireplace of stone and tiles. A hand-loomed area rug glowed softly in cobalt and gold over the warm, polished fir floorboards. The colors were echoed in the abstract designs of the sofa and slipcovered armchairs, each with its bronze table lamp. Several paintings, boldly figurative, hung from the walls, along with a large, framed, black-and-white photograph of Pauline Richard. I recognized her from the photos at the cottage. Here she was older, perhaps in her late thirties, glamorous in a sort of doomed Anne Sexton way.

What did Jane mean, excuse the mess? The Mission-style coffee table in front of the sofa was piled with literary magazines and a few hardcover novels. The cobalt blue couch looked inviting—this must be where Giselle had discussed manuscripts with Dani and other interns, and with translators more fortunate than I. But Jane kept going, through the kitchen and into a back room, and soon I could see signs of remodeling and disorder. Two desks, one with a desktop computer and a supersize monitor. Several tall file cabinets next to shelves attached to another wall, filled with manuscript pages. Posters and bulletin boards taken down and leaning against the walls. A labyrinth in the center of book boxes, piled shoulder-high. Everything covered with dusty plastic. A blue tarp hung down where the separate entrance was framed in and sheet-rocked, but not taped or mudded yet.

Jane pulled the plastic covers off a couple of chairs and the desk with the computer monitor on it. She gestured to me to sit and she did too.

"I understand why you're here, Cassandra. I imagine that you and Luisa may want to break the contract. In fact, I'm sure you will when you hear my situation. Yesterday I told you that I was putting things on hold. Today I've come across some new information. I just want to explain that I'm not the kind of person who has ever had big financial problems. That's not how my parents raised me. My father was a bank vice-president and had a lot of stories about people whose lives were ruined by debt and loans they couldn't pay off. Five years ago when we started the press, it seemed like we had so much—more than enough. Giselle had sold her mother's house for such a lot—and I didn't owe a penny to anyone."

She abruptly got up, which relieved me, since our knees had almost been touching in this crowded space, and stood between two tall piles of boxes, as if they could prop her up and protect her as she spoke. "It's not just that I don't feel able to carry on without Giselle. I wouldn't want you to think that I'm incapable. I've more or less been running the press from the beginning, in terms of managing production schedules and bookkeeping. It's that, financially, it's not possible. I'll try to honor all the agreements we have with foreign publishing houses and authors for all the books published up to now including the spring list, but we have about ten contracts signed for books meant to come out this fall and next year. I'm going to have to cancel all of them. And even then, it will be a struggle to meet my obligations."

Although I'd come here with the intent of breaking the contract, I didn't feel relief that it was so easy, only sympathy when I saw Jane struggling like this in a mire probably not wholly of her making. I tried to make it easier for her and told her that if I could help, I would. "I know the Spanish publisher, Cielo, will be disappointed, but they'll probably appreciate knowing sooner rather than later. Of course you won't get the initial advance back from them."

"No, I understand that," said Jane moving to another corner of the boxy labyrinth, and adjusting a pile that was unevenly stacked. "And I wouldn't think of asking you to return the first half of your translation fee. I'll try to get the rest to you as soon as I can, even though it may not be immediately. After all, you finished the translation, you put a lot of work into it."

"No worries," I said. "I'll try some other publishers now that the rights are going to be free again. I'm sure someone will be interested." I was not sure of that at all, but I was grateful Jane was even considering my situation as a translator, and wanted to be gracious in return.

There was a long silence, and then some sounds deep in her throat. Was this my cue to leave? Our business was concluded, yet she'd said on the porch she wanted to show me something.

Suddenly she burst out, "It's not fair. She's gone, and I'm left to sort everything out. I took out a homeowner's loan to remodel the office. And the press is in debt to printers and the money isn't coming in fast enough, and now I'm responsible. You know about publishing—is it always like this? You spend and spend and spend—the money goes out and doesn't come back for years, if at all."

"Publishing is a challenging business," I said. And then, seeing a chance to probe a little deeper, "But you said you started out pretty well capitalized. That Giselle had invested the proceeds of the family house sale into starting the press?"

Jane remained standing among the boxes and I only saw a sliver of her pale face and white hair. "She did invest a lot of it originally. We had a business plan. But of course there were estate taxes and some medical expenses connected with her mother's illness to settle. And Giselle wanted to have income to live on for at least two years while the press got going. And, finally, she gave money regularly to Jacqui."

"You said that Jacqui didn't share in the proceeds from the house sale?"

"Giselle said it was because Pauline knew Jacqui was bad with money and assumed that Jacqui would just fritter it away. She'd done drugs in the past and was clean, but still struggling. Moved around a lot, worked a bit as a housecleaner, did some art. I think she'd finished high school but never went further. Giselle didn't like to talk about her. I know that Jacqui would contact Giselle from time to time asking for financial help with something or other. It could be first and last rent at a new apartment, or a workshop she wanted to take, or it could be to buy some new clothes. She liked to shop. Jacqui felt her mother and sister somehow owed her for what she'd gone through as a child. Giselle told me that."

"What had Jacqui gone through?" I asked. I wished Jane would come out of the boxes—it was a little strange to be talking to a cardboard wall with a head semi-visible—but if it made her feel safer to speak, perhaps that's how it had to be.

"I can't share what she told me today," Jane said. "It was hard to hear. And, anyway," she added in a sterner tone, "I don't completely believe it. It must be exaggerated or made up. I never met Giselle's mother, but Giselle always spoke of Pauline with such love. And the way Giselle talked about Jacqui always made it sound like she was sort of erratic, with mood swings. No, I can't believe it, and I'm not going to feel sorry for whatever happened in her past. Childhood is one thing, but when you're an adult you to have to take responsibility."

Silence again. I thought about a four-year-old girl from a Korean orphanage arriving in Portland, coming to live with the Janickis. Not knowing English. Everything strange, big, lonely.

"Responsibility," said Jane again, coming out from the boxes and moving over to the blue tarp hanging over the new door to check that it was tight across the opening. I supposed it was boarded up on the outside. "Anyway, I'm not talking about Jacqui and whatever she's upset about from her childhood. What I'm saying is that when we started Entre Editions, we made a business plan based on Giselle's investment from the house sale. That was to cover doing five books a year for two years, enough to get us launched. Giselle also had her own personal checking account, like I did. In the beginning she paid for a lot of extra things. Redecorating the house, traveling to book fairs on her own dime." She sighed. "When it was her own money, what could I say?"

"That probably added up," I said.

"Giselle had worked for a publisher in Boston. She knew the importance of how a publishing house presented itself. Booths at trade fairs, attending European book fairs. It's not how I would have necessarily done it, but I could see it got results. We were reviewed a lot. Giselle was interviewed. She cultivated the right people. All according to plan." Jane drifted back towards me, her eyes on a pile of papers on the desk where she'd been sitting.

"All according to plan," I prompted.

"Yes," Jane said flatly. "We weren't in bad shape, and some of the books sold surprisingly well. One got a prize. We were on the map. We worked hard, didn't take salaries until the second year. If we didn't, Giselle said, we'd burn out. So that became an added expense. Payroll taxes, health care, insurance added up. Then in year three she contracted with a freelance publicist for the bigger titles. Okay. Then last fall she proposed hiring Karen as a marketing consultant."

Jane moved off again, in the direction of the boxes, but then turned, her face flushed with indignation. Good, now we were getting to Karen. This must be what Jane had wanted to tell me: how Karen had ruined them financially and stolen away Giselle's affections. I shifted forward to listen better, as Jane continued pacing through the small aisles created by the box stacks.

"Even before Karen went full-time and started with her nutty ideas about book launches costing an arm and a leg," Jane went on, "I was feeling stressed out about money. Giselle told me she was going to sell the cottage in Newport. The location alone would bring in a small fortune. But she dragged her feet all winter. Meanwhile she'd persuaded me to remodel the office here, with the idea that when the cottage was fixed up and sold in the spring or summer, everything would balance out. In early March she decided to move to the cottage to oversee repairs." Jane swung back towards me, her mouth a tight line. "Stupidly, I agreed. We weren't getting along very well and I thought maybe some time apart would help. I had no idea that Karen was going out to Newport to see her, that she was coming into Portland to 'meet' with Karen."

So Jane knew about the affair. But how? "Did you see her over the last month or two that these ... meetings were going on?"

"No. We emailed, talked on the phone. I saw Karen a couple of times when she came by to pick some books up. Karen and I weren't ... we weren't very friendly. But it was only when I realized they were planning to go to Montreal together after New York that I put everything together. Some credit card charges for restaurants in Portland in March that Karen claimed were business meetings with booksellers, and various excuses from Giselle about times when she didn't pick up her phone. I don't know how Giselle thought I wouldn't notice reservations for two airfares to Montreal, and a hotel booking that were cc'd to the office email. Maybe that was her way of telling me we were finished as a couple."

"I'm sorry," I said. "That's not very kind."

"There's worse," Jane said bitterly. "I had noticed—how could I not notice?—that from around the first of the year Giselle had started writing herself checks from the business account, for cash. When I asked her about it, she said that it was for the cottage. She was paying a contractor under the table to replace the windows and fix the roof. We argued about it a lot before she left for Newport. At some point she told me she hardly had anything left in her personal checking from the house sale. But she told me that she didn't see why she couldn't take money from the business for the cottage and for some of her own expenses herself, after all, it was really *her* money originally." Jane's voice was subdued now. "I don't know if I should have made such a big deal about it. After all, once she sold the cottage, I was pretty sure we'd be back on track. She'd promised to put at least half the sale money into the press. But I was starting already not to trust her. Now I know I was right to be suspicious. She lied to me more than I thought."

Another long silence and then Jane came back to the desk, to the piles of paper, and picked up a folder. "I guess it's common, when someone dies, that you find out a lot you didn't know."

"And you found something in Giselle's papers?" I wasn't sure why she was telling me this, but I didn't want to stop her. This might be information I could pass on to Haakonssen. I didn't want to believe Jane was involved in Giselle's death, but the facts needed to come out, all of them.

"I was going through her files early this morning, looking for a will to see what her wishes were for ... a burial. I didn't find any instructions, but I thought she might have put it in her safe deposit box at our bank, since I was pretty sure she had a box. I wasn't originally going to look at all her bank records; I was just looking for the number of the box, a key, something like that. But all I found were files of bank statements from her personal account. And statements from another account in Canada, something I didn't expect."

She stared down at the papers, and I repeated, "Something you didn't expect ... ?"

"Starting years back, around the time the money from her mother's house became available, there were automatic monthly transfers to an account at the Bank of Montreal. Five hundred a month, for about five years. Then, last year there are no more transfers to the Canadian bank. Instead, money begins to come *into* Giselle's checking, from the same account number. Several large transfers, five thousand each time."

Agitated now, Jane pulled out another folder. "Here are statements from the Bank of Montreal. The account is with the bank's trust division. The balance shows there's still about a hundred thousand dollars in there. I had no idea this account existed or why. There's no paperwork for it in her files here at home."

"Did her father leave her his estate?"

"No. At least Giselle told me he only left her a small legacy in his will. She used it to live in France for a year after college. He remarried after he and her mother divorced. His second wife got everything. According to Giselle." Jane looked suddenly doubtful.

"Did you call the bank in Montreal?"

"I called them this morning. I explained that Giselle died in an accident and I was her business partner. They couldn't give me any information."

Jane had sat down again by now and rubbed her forehead. "I had better luck at our local bank here in Portland. It's the same bank where my dad was a vice-president. I called a woman there who's the loan manager. Liz was the one who gave me the loan to remodel. She also knew my dad. She'd heard Giselle had had an accident, and understood I'd want to find the will. She checked the box rental agreement and I wasn't on it, but she did tell me that she saw Giselle in the bank as she was signing in to open her box, and they'd chatted a little. Liz said she'd seen Giselle leaving with a big manila envelope a little later. I suppose that could have been the will and/or other papers. Giselle must have come to Portland without telling me."

I said, "Do you think she might have taken the papers to the cottage?"

"Probably," Jane was silent. "I felt so humiliated talking to Liz. Like a lot of people, Liz thought Giselle was just about the most wonderful, delightful person you'd ever want to meet. I wasn't going to tell her that I'd started suspecting my girlfriend was two-timing me with Karen, and had been lying to me about her financial situation, or that maybe the missing papers had something to do with her death. "

"What about Jacqui?" I asked. "Did you ask her about the trust account? Do you think she could be the beneficiary? Maybe it was something that Pauline or Pauline and Giselle together set up for her. You've said that Giselle tried to help her sister. Maybe there's some kind of explanation for the trust account being in Montreal. I don't know much about these kinds of things, but I believe there are grantors and trustees. Could you ask your Liz at the bank about that? Or maybe you need a lawyer."

"I don't know. Yes, I should get a lawyer. I don't want to talk to Liz again about this. I'm embarrassed." Jane's face fell again. "And as for Jacqui, no I didn't ask her about her financial situation. She overwhelmed me right from the beginning. She told me a lot of horrible stuff about Pauline, said she wouldn't come to a funeral for Giselle, much less plan it. And then she asked me for a thousand dollars to cover her expenses while she's down here. As if I had that kind of money. I gave her the cash I had in my wallet, a couple of twenties."

"Is she staying in Portland?"

"No, she's in Newport still. She just came here for the day. I ended up feeling like all she wanted from me was some money. She expressed almost no interest in me, how I might feel about losing Giselle, and no convincing sadness about her sister. She said she'd talked with the police and was sure it was an accident. That they thought it was an accident. The only time she showed emotion was when she talked about her mother. I don't even want to go into it, what she told me. Half of it made no sense and the rest was simply unbelievable."

I wanted to press Jane further, but before I could, Jane's cell rang and she took the call.

"Yes, thanks for getting back to me. I want to talk about the building permit. We need to change it—I won't be putting in an outside door after all. Can I put you on hold just a second until I get the blueprints? Thanks." She put the phone down. "I'm really sorry, but I need to take care of this."

Jane's voice was oddly professional now, with no trace of the emotions that must still be roiling her. I had no choice but to follow her back into the kitchen and dining room, into the living room, and to the front door. She opened it for me.

I said, "Well, we'll consider that the contracts for Luisa's collection of stories are effectively cancelled, shall we? You'll have to write a formal letter to the foreign rights people in Barcelona, but I'll drop them a line too to explain the circumstances and that I've met with you. And I'll start contacting some other publishers, and we'll hope for the best."

"Thanks for understanding," she said, still business-like. "That's one project cancelled then. Believe me, it will help."

"I'll be in town for a few more days." I handed her my card. "I've written the cell phone number I'm using in the States on the back. If you need any advice about dealing with foreign publishers, I'm glad to stop by again and help draft a few letters."

"Thank you, but I don't think that will be necessary," she said. The raw confusion, anger, and desperation of the last half an hour was vanquished, and her face was now as blank as yesterday. "What a cold-hearted bitch she is," Karen had said.

Cold-hearted enough to kill her lover? Or just self-protective, the way an orphan is, in an untrustworthy world?

15.

I went back to Kornblatt's on NW 23rd. They served breakfast all day, and a plate of scrambled eggs with onions and lox sounded just right to me. Along with some rye toast and a strong cup of tea.

After I'd eaten and was drinking a second cup, I pulled out a small notebook and scribbled some of what I remembered from the hour or more I'd spent with Jane. At the end I noted in no particular order a few puzzling matters I wished I understood better.

Richard family: A trust account with a healthy balance at the Bank of Montreal. A five-hundred-dollar monthly contribution from Giselle for a few years after Pauline's death. Who originally set up the trust and when? Who's the beneficiary? Could Pauline have set it up for Giselle? Or for Jacqui? Or both her daughters? Was it within the terms of the trust for Giselle to begin to transfer money back to herself? Was this fraud or was it to help Jacqui? Is this something I should even be pursuing? What's the story with the safe deposit box: What was in it? Where are the agreements and wills?

Giselle's relationships and finances: Was she in over her head with the publishing company and with monthly payments into the trust? She didn't let Jane know about those payments, why not? Was Giselle looking to raise money? She was fixing up the cottage, a valuable piece of real estate. Perhaps to live there, but probably to sell. But maybe she was looking to raise money in another way—from Karen perhaps.

Karen/ Jane/ Giselle: Was it romantic/sexual/monetary, or all three? Were Karen and Giselle scheming to buy Jane out? Were they using their week away to discuss this? Was there any reason other than a fun time that the two of them were going to Montreal? Something to do with the bank account? If Jane found out about this plan, she's more likely to have a murder motive than Karen. But maybe Giselle changed her mind about Karen. Maybe Karen lost her temper and gave Giselle a shove. Dani said Karen's volatile. Dani also said there was sand in her SUV.

What's the story with Jacqui? Why so angry with Pauline and apparently Giselle? What happened in the past? Who would know this besides Jane, who isn't going to tell me? Would Karen? Surely Nora would know something about Pauline's family. Did Jacqui have a reason to kill her sister? If she has no money wouldn't she be the obvious one? Too obvious, if she's a beneficiary of the trust or the next of kin who might inherit everything. Besides, she lives in Canada.

Nora: I haven't forgotten about her and her immediately calling her lawyer to come to Newport. She was cagey about Giselle too, acting as if she didn't know her well when the fact of that photograph on the wall suggests otherwise. Does Nora know more about Pauline's death than she's saying? What was she really doing on the coast the evening Giselle fell? Why did Nora leave Newport so abruptly?

I didn't add Pauline to my list of suspects, for obvious reasons. Yet Karen had made me curious today by telling me that Pauline died in her sleep at the cottage six years ago. A woman with a brain lesion could well have died naturally, but something about what Karen *didn't* say made me wonder. Had Giselle confided some kind of suspicion to her? Certainly, Giselle benefitted financially from her mother's death. Everything went to her and nothing, according to Jane who heard it from Giselle, to Jacqui. I thought about the large photograph of Pauline dominating Jane's living room. I hadn't seen pictures of the Janickis. Who was Pauline Richard, really? What had been her relationship with her two daughters, and should I try to find out more about her?

From a professional standpoint, my meeting today with Jane should have been sufficient. The dissolution of the contract for Luisa's collection was underway and I doubted Jane would change her mind. I could now with a clear conscience look for another publisher. The other questions I had about Giselle's death could probably wait until tomorrow. At least writing them down had put them in perspective.

Meanwhile I'd return to *Baby's First Year*. Last night I'd made a lot of headway on Chapter Three. It was only four p.m. Buoyed by my plate of scrambled eggs and starting to get a buzz from the second cup of English Breakfast, I decided that I'd finish the chapter and send all sixty-plus pages to Janneken tonight, with the promise that more was coming in the next few days.

I'd have to tell Janneken about the detective with the Norwegian name out on the remote coast of Oregon. No, on second thought, then I'd have to tell her I was, against my wishes, involved in a murder case. And that would send Janneken over the edge. She, like most people, preferred their murders on a television screen or between the covers of a book. And she also preferred me to meet my deadlines.

Back at the Sabine-Noble house, I went straight to the dining-room table and opened my laptop. I didn't mess about with email or searching for more exacting definitions on my online dictionary. I just banged out six pages of "Failure to Thrive," without trying to overthink my translation. It went quickly because there was a lot of dialog.

Me: Knut, I think the baby is hungry, but she won't attach.

Knut (not removing his eyes from the screen): Just a minute, this play is about to wrap up. GOAL, you bastards, get it in, get it in!

I was only a page from finishing Chapter Three when my phone rang. I was tempted not to answer it, but then I saw the caller: Detective Haakonssen.

"You phoned earlier," he said without preamble. "Sergeant Jones told me you had new information."

"I remembered I'd talked with a woman on the beach early Tuesday morning. But the sergeant already knew that. And he said the woman had seen Giselle on the beach Monday evening. He also told me that someone had come forward to assist with the inquiry, but didn't say who. I assume it's Giselle's sister?"

He paused. "And what makes you say that?"

I realized I had a choice here. I could share what I knew from spending half an hour with Jane in the office of Entre Editions, about Jacqui and her mother and sister, and about the financial statements from the Bank of Montreal, and in this way possibly help the investigation move more quickly. Or I could say nothing, for fear that I would become more involved than I wanted to be. I usually avoided the police as much as I could. But my inclination to remain on the sidelines was overcome by a stronger impulse to see this case wound up as soon as possible.

"I went to see Jane Janicki today," I said. "I saw her yesterday briefly as well. And Karen Morales."

"Continue."

"It's partly why I came to Portland, to try to sort things out about the translation and publishing contracts with the book I was doing with Entre Editions. So that's why I was over at the office, in Jane's house. When I arrived Jane was just being dropped off by Jacqui, Giselle's sister. Jane was very upset, she didn't tell me all the details, but said Jacqui didn't want to have a memorial service for Giselle, based on things that had happened with her mother and sister."

He was rather unnervingly silent. I wondered if he already knew that Jacqui was upset with her family. After all, he would have interviewed her in Newport. Was she staying in Newport? Did he know she'd come to Portland to see Jane?

I went on anyway, trying to be as concise as I could, telling him about what Jane discovered in the statements about the trust account at the Bank of Montreal. "She was looking for a will, and information about the trust—who set it up and who's the beneficiary. There's a safe deposit box at their local bank in Portland, with a key somewhere. But Jane found out from the bank that Giselle visited the bank a couple of weeks ago. So, you might want to follow up with that. Maybe all those papers are in the cottage."

This time Haakonssen broke his silence with some unexpected praise. "I appreciate this information, Ms. Reilly. This is more than we knew, and we'll certainly pursue it."

I should have gone on to tell him about Karen and Giselle's planned trip to Montreal, and about my supposition that they may have been planning to buy out Jane or oust her in some way, but my mind had gone back to Karen's story about Pauline's death: "Do you see a link between the deaths of Pauline Richard and her daughter? And I'm curious about Nora Longeran. Is she a person of interest? She knew both Pauline and Giselle pretty well, I suspect."

"I'm afraid I can't discuss the case in any detail with you. It's still ongoing," he said with familiar firmness.

"But what about Karen Morales?" I said. "Did you hear from her intern, Dani? Dani told me that she'd seen Karen vacuuming sand from her SUV early Tuesday morning. A lot of sand."

"Yes, we've heard from this young woman," he said, somewhat

dismissively, and then he cut me off before I could rattle on with any more questions about Karen or anyone else. "As I said, I appreciate the information about Jane Janicki, and I understand you're in a position to learn more about their business operations. We would be glad, if you'll let us know if you have any further conversations with Ms. Janicki about financial details that might have a bearing on the case."

I made one last attempt to wrest a little information from him. "But has the coroner decided if Giselle's death was an accident or something more suspicious?"

"Thank you, Ms. Reilly. We'll probably be contacting you soon for a follow-up interview, either on the phone or, preferably, in Newport."

"Soon? Do you mean, like, in a day or two? Because I'd really like to get on with my life. In London. Obviously, you don't think I had anything to do with this?"

"Thank you, Ms. Reilly," Haakonssen said again. "Good-bye."

We disconnected, but almost immediately the dulcet tones of Skype sounded.

It was Candace. I'm sure I looked disgruntled, because the first thing she said was, "Bad time to call?"

"Sorry. I just got off the phone with the detective on the case."

"Oh right," she said, as if she'd completely forgotten what had brought me to Portland. This time Candace was fully dressed, in a crisp, white shirt that showed off her tan. She appeared to be sitting in a chair on the balcony of their hotel, with a technicolor desert sunset and the swaying fronds of two palm trees in the background. Next to her was a tall drink of something clear with ice: sparkling water or even a gin and tonic. It was like looking at a postcard that said *Wish you were here.*

Candace was just checking in. I did plan to stay in Portland all weekend, didn't I?

I answered, possibly a little gruffly, that I wasn't going anywhere.

"No problems with any of the appliances?"

"They're all still in working order." I didn't say that I hadn't touched anything with an electronic panel and had mostly eaten out.

She seemed disappointed that I didn't have any questions about the washing machine or the convection oven.

"Did we talk about watering?" she said, in an effort to keep the conversation going. "Remember, if it's warm you might need to water the pots on the porch. Rain doesn't touch those pots and the porch can get hot in the afternoon because of the angle of the sun. Don't worry about the garden. That should be okay. It's supposed to drizzle or rain this Friday, maybe Saturday."

I assured her that so far it hadn't been too warm on the porch. I tried to recall if I'd seen any pots on the porch. Had they been stolen? I'd have to go out and look in a minute.

"But don't overwater them."

"No, no."

We stared at each other wordlessly for a moment before she said again, "Well, I just wanted to check and make sure you were fine and enjoying the house and that everything was okay before I go meet Jill and some of her bug friends for dinner. Ha ha!"

I remembered in time that Jill was an entomologist, and smiled creakily back. "Have fun. Yes, I'm enjoying myself. Thank you so much! Bye!"

Suddenly exhausted, I lay down on their couch with its array of colorful pillows. I threw half the pillows on the floor. I'd check the pots later. It was possible, with all I had on my mind, that I just hadn't noticed them. I started flipping through some issues of the *New Yorker,* looking for one of those insanely long and well-written articles about some topic I wasn't remotely interested at first, but that gradually felt more and more important to be up on. Pickling and fermentation, maybe, or new forms of money laundering.

I didn't feel up to continuing on with the translation of *Baby's First Year.* I'd done enough today. And I still had to figure out how to respond to Nicky and this loony idea of giving up her base in England or Scotland. If she thought I was going to stay with her in Berlin when I was in Europe she was sadly mistaken.

But what if she didn't think that? What if the little flat she imagined buying in Berlin had no guest room earmarked for Cassandra Reilly?

I didn't get beyond the "Talk of the Town" before my phone rang again. This time, it was Kim.

"I just had a call from Candace. She said you looked stressed. Nothing's wrong at the house, is there?"

"No, nothing's wrong at the house!" I said. "For God's sake, I'm unwillingly part of a criminal investigation, Kim!" We weren't Skyping so I didn't have to modify my grumpy expression. "Right before Candace called I was on the phone with the detective in charge of the case in

Newport and he told me he wants a follow-up interview in Newport. Soon, but I don't know when. It's more than irritating."

She listened to me vent for a while and then reminded me that she and Dora were available to help me. "If you need us, we're here for you. Dora doesn't get back for another week, but I could fly up to Portland Saturday if it would help to have some support."

I thanked her and said I'd think about it. I certainly didn't want to be here when Jill and Candace came back Monday morning. I was sure they were very nice, but I didn't think I'd fit into their lifestyle.

"I'm hoping it will be wrapped up shortly, I'm just not sure how," I told Kim. "I have a couple of ideas about what may have happened. It may have been an accident, but I can't help wondering. There's so much that seems murky and the more I find out, the less pleasant I suspect it will all be."

"Well, a suspicious death isn't all that pleasant for anyone, especially the deceased," said Kim. "But be patient—they'll figure it out. And if you get a chance, could you call Luisa? She's been bugging me about you."

"I just emailed her yesterday and told her about Giselle. I don't need to talk on the phone to Luisa about the contract again. We'll be able to break it."

"Yes, but she seems eager to talk to you. She called here twice. She's afraid your phone isn't working well in the Oregon wilderness. I told her I'd let you know."

"Okay, I'll call her soon."

But Kim went on, "We ended up talking on the phone for awhile. I made the mistake of telling her that I'd written several articles about Cristina Peri Rossi. Why did you never mention to me that Luisa dislikes Cristina?"

"Well, I don't know if dislike is quite the right word. Respectfully loathes and completely rejects her maybe. If they've ever met, Luisa isn't saying, but I know Luisa has written a couple of very critical reviews of Cristina's books. At bottom, she thinks Cristina should have come back to Uruguay. She got that from her mother. Estella thought everyone who didn't return to Uruguay when the political situation began to improve was a coward and unpatriotic. Plus, Luisa has always been offended by Cristina's impressive publication track record."

Kim had met Cristina Peri Rossi long ago and had been quite taken by the clouds of cigarette smoke and metaphors the woman generated.

She defended her now: "For Cristina there was no 'back' to return to! She was in her twenties when she left—she was in danger of death or prison if she'd stayed. In Barcelona she made a new life. After fifteen years she wasn't just going to throw that away for the uncertainties of Uruguay."

"I know. I know. But you can't really argue with Luisa. She's invigorated by her aversions."

"Luisa is stuck in a past that doesn't exist any longer," said Kim. "The new generation of young Latin American authors doesn't think like that. They live in New York or Mexico City or Berlin. If Luisa is going to be envious of anyone, it should be writers twenty or thirty years younger!"

It was true, I realized with a jolt. Luisa Montiflores, approaching sixty, wasn't part of the current scene. She still saw herself in opposition to the earlier generation of magical-realists and political exiles, some of whom were no longer alive. She had yet to realize that her time had passed and that younger writers had overtaken her. In that light maybe it made sense that Karen and Giselle had tried to reposition her as "a lesser-known foremother of Latin American speculative fiction" and thus set her up to be rediscovered and reintroduced.

After the phone call with Kim, I milled around the kitchen and living room, restless and weary. I pulled all the books I'd bought at Powell's from the canvas bag and placed them on the coffee table, but I felt no desire to do more research today. In fact, I didn't even feel like reading any of these novels; all the recently published fiction from Argentina, Chile, Mexico, and Peru that had seemed so tempting this morning now seemed overwhelming. Yes, I might find another publisher for Luisa, but would she be grateful?

The conversation with Kim had affected me unpleasantly, not just because it made me question my responsibility to Luisa, but because it made me feel dated. Just as authors aged out of fashion, so did translators, I suspected. I might be cosmopolitan, but I was probably too unsophisticated and too lazy, not to mention too *old,* to work with a younger generation of Latin American writers.

For now, my advancing years didn't seem to matter to the British publishers of the popular genre novels I often worked on. As long as Rosa Cardenes was producing a mystery novel every year or two, I'd probably remain her English translator. But how long could I keep this up? At what point would I begin to be seen less like one of the "rock stars of Spanish translation" as a sweet young student in Berkeley had called me, and more like a rock? A fossil?

I put all the translations back in the canvas bag and instead picked up the Asimov space opera and started again from the beginning. There was something about the funny little V-frog from the carbon-dioxide-saturated oceans of Venus, the "small mind-reading and mind-influencing animal" that fascinated me. One V-frog could do little—apparently thousands of the creatures were needed for true telepathy—but Lucky Starr still believed the frog might come in handy in investigating a conspiracy on Jupiter 9, rooting out a spy for the enemy Sirians, and distinguishing humans from possible robots. One V-frog, he explained to Bigman, might be able to catch "whiffs of strong emotion."

I had an image of the V-frog as a kind of translator. Catching the meaning of a foreign text isn't just a matter of words, it is capturing the emotional tone of the prose, the feelings behind the words. The process of translating fiction in particular relies on feeling the emotions engendered by the original text and conveying them in English.

Lucky Starr and the Moons of Jupiter was a quick and exciting read. Although the poor V-frog didn't make it alive past the first chapters, there were other aspects of the novel that intrigued me—the descriptions of Io and Europa, for example, and the fact that no one could land on Jupiter or come near it. It could only be observed from a distance. That was very much like Luisa's perception of Jupiter: a giant planet with a force field that held its satellites in a firm grip. At the time Asimov wrote his Lucky Starr books, in the fifties, Jupiter was only known to have nine moons. His preface to this edition, written in 1978, mentioned that now there were thirteen.

It occurred to me for the first time—I was no cosmologist—that in calling Io and Europa Jupiter's closest moons, Luisa had forgotten to mention Amalthea, a very small moon that orbited closer to Jupiter than the two bigger sisters. Amalthea, called Jupiter V in Asimov's book, played a significant role in the plot, when eventually the Agrav (anti-gravity) spaceship had to land there.

More than once I had the peculiar feeling that I was encountering phrases and sentences that seemed familiar. "A perfect circle of creamy light," Asimov described Jupiter from a distance in the first paragraph. And a few pages later, "a planet of poison and unbearable gravity." It wasn't surprising that Luisa had also called Jupiter *creamy* or spoken of it as *poisonous*—but *unbearable gravity*? I remembered that from somewhere in the story. *Gravedad insoportable*. I had translated it as "intolerable" Coincidence most likely.

The plot was very exciting and I cruised along in enjoyment. Asimov was an amusing writer, a born storyteller. Even if some of the dialog was hackneyed, there were descriptive passages that were surprisingly lovely. Yet from time to time I continued to have the feeling that I'd read certain phrases before. And then, finally, came the distinct sensation that I had written one of the sentences myself: "Now the sky turned black and belonged to the stars."

I got off the couch and went to find the copyedited manuscript of my translation and paged through it. Yes, there it was: "Now the sky turned black and belonged to the stars," I'd written. I picked up Luisa's original book in Spanish and found the sentence: *Ahora el cielo se convirtio en un espacio negro que pertenecia a las estrellas*. Literally, "Now the sky became a black space that belonged to the stars." I'd chosen to simplify it in my translation.

Strange.

Of course the plot and the descriptions of the planet and moons were very different from Luisa's *Jupiter*. Io in Asimov's book was soft and white with clouds of ammonia. The Agrav spaceship landed on it, too, where in Luisa's story the planet and the two moons were always described as if she were looking at them from a revolving ship in the sky; sometimes they were closely observed, sometimes they were distant.

I thought back to Karen's sushi-muffled comment about Luisa's giving a nod to Asimov and *The Moons of Jupiter*. I'd assumed, once I figured it out, that she was referring to this book about Lucky Starr. But perhaps it was more than just *a nod*. If Karen was well-acquainted with Asimov's work, then she had noticed what I'd noticed, that some sentences, some descriptions appeared in the same or slightly altered form in Luisa's story.

Karen may have assumed it was intentional—that Luisa was conversant with science fiction and its tropes. And perhaps that's why Karen thought *On Jupiter* or *Unraveling Jupiter* might find a wider readership if it were marketed as speculative fiction.

But *was* Luisa consciously referencing Asimov? And if so, why hadn't she ever mentioned that to me?

I almost opened my email program again and sent her a note to ask, but I was nearing the end of *Lucky Starr* and wanted to find out how it ended.

16.

I woke up around midnight, when the downstairs lamps automatically turned themselves off. All the pillows were on the floor, along with pages from the copyedited text of *On Jupiter,* and the blinds were still open. I had a crick in my neck. I got up and closed the blinds and pulled the drapes, but not before glancing out. Yes, there were two large ceramic pots on the porch, with some kind of gigantic bronze plants in them. Their sword-like leaves gleamed eerily. How could I have missed them? In the harsh white porch light they looked like they came from another planet.

I went upstairs to the guest room, took off my clothes and tossed them on a chair, and jumped between the sheets, intending to take up my dreams where I'd left off.

But now, of course, I couldn't sleep. I couldn't decide what to believe about Giselle. Was she simply an idealist, like so many small publishers, the gradual victim of her own optimism that eventually there would be a bestseller to make up for all the titles that had bombed or languished on an ever-lengthening backlist? Was it her idealism that had caused her to put most of the proceeds from the Portland house sale into Entre Editions and persuade Jane to work for free for two years and to drain her savings to get the press off the ground? Or was there something more calculating about Giselle?

Had she persuaded her depressed and aging mother to make a will in which she got the house and cottage, and her sister Jacqui nothing? Had Giselle simply been using Jane for a few years to launch Entre Editions and, now that Jane's resources were depleted, had Giselle been looking elsewhere for investors? Had Jane gotten wind of the relationship with Karen being both sexual *and* economic? But if it *was* economic, wouldn't Jane be glad to have an investor like Karen or even to have been bought out so she didn't slide deeper into debt? Furthermore, from a financial point of view, it wouldn't have served Jane to push her partner over the bluff because Giselle's death left Jane worse off. After all, Giselle was going to sell the cottage in Newport and use the money to pay off the remodeling loan on the Portland house, or so Giselle had said. The motive then—if Jane had had anything to do with Giselle's death—must have been jealousy. Anger at Karen and Giselle, loss of trust, and jealousy powerful enough to want to murder.

I could only hope that Haakonssen would move quickly on the information I'd given him by at least finding out who the beneficiary of the trust was. He could draw his own conclusions about the Giselle-Jane-Karen triangle. I didn't want to get into discussing the intricacies of lesbian relationships with him, that I knew.

For my own part, I still found myself wondering about Pauline, the beautiful big Other in the story, the mysterious mother planet around whom her daughters circled, drawing them to her with unbearable gravity.

I finally fell asleep and woke up again to sunshine that turned the pale curtains lemon yellow. Barefoot, in the same clothes from yesterday, I padded downstairs, and made myself a cup of tea using the electric kettle successfully. Braving the toaster with mixed results, I blackened the onions on a bagel I'd bought at Kornblatt's yesterday. I took the tea, slightly scorched bagel, and a container of cream cheese, along with my laptop, out to the small deck off the kitchen. It too had pots and the dirt looked dry, but I counted on the forecast of rain later to help me out. My responsibilities to this house, light as they were, still weighed on me.

I opened my inbox with a sense of dread and, sure enough, there was a menacing email from Janneken. Well, not menacing per se. She said she'd gotten my text yesterday, and wanted to make sure I understood the *gravity* of the situation vis à vis Angela Cook, the new agent in New York, and the panel at Chipping Witteron. She was expecting the hundred pages or whatever I had *immediately*. "It doesn't have to be perfect," she said, "That's what editors are for."

I decided to take this as permission to finish translating the last page of Chapter Three and to cast a quick and forgiving eye over the whole sixty-two pages before sending it to her. Yes, I could depend on Janneken to fix whatever was wrong; she was not afraid of the red pencil. I wrote a quick note to encourage her to do whatever polishing was needed, and simply added, "More to come in a few days. Thanks, Cassandra."

But the relief that flowed through my veins after pressing *send* was short-lived. I not only felt the brutal reality of the fact that I now had

180 pages—nine more chapters—to go, but I was anxious about what everyone would think about *these* chapters. Janneken's admonition to me about the *gravity* of the situation brought me back to language issues I'd encountered in *Baby* having to do with the state of being pregnant. Spanish-to-English dictionaries give several options; one is *grávida* and the other, more frequently used, is *embarazada*. Luisa, for planetary reasons no doubt, consistently used *grávida*. Claribel, on the other hand, always used *embarazada*. As many beginning Spanish students know (to their embarrassment), it's common to say *Estoy embarazada* instead of *Tengo verguenza*. The second means "I'm embarrassed;" the first, "I'm pregnant." However, you can also say *Estoy embarazosa* to mean embarrassed, with a tinge more of unease than shame. In *Baby's First Year,* the word *embarazada* was occasionally supplemented with the word for unease: *embarazosa.*

I hadn't worked out how to find any equivalent in English, and wondered if it was because, in fact, I felt an uneasiness with Claribel's prose, with her story, with her. I had met her just once, and although we had exchanged friendly emails and she'd seemed pleased enough with my translations of her first two books, we had never clicked completely. I wished that I *had* formed a better connection with Claribel, so that I could write to her directly and ask her what she wanted to say. Now there were all these other people interposed between us, inserted into what should be a reciprocal relationship between author and translator. One of the interpositions was bound to be Angela.

I don't have to love every word of an author's text. Rosa Cardenes, to be truthful, was really writing the same mystery twenty years along, with a likeable detective, who didn't age and didn't really mature either. Readers were happy that the detective had found a love or two over the years and gotten a much nicer apartment in Madrid and had solved a case involving her old *abuela* that brought a tear to the eye. They didn't require much more, and, as Rosa's translator, I tried not to require more either. Still, I adored Rosa herself, thought her plots more or less hung together, and always felt a sense of cozy orderliness when I immersed myself in her detective's world. Rosa had a sunny deposition and an absence of neurosis that was always a balm. My job, as I saw it, was to convey that essentially positive spirit and spritely dialog to her legions of English-speaking fans.

If I had a book by Rosa to translate here in Portland, I would not feel so gloomy. I was sure I'd feel, in fact, that the case of Giselle would soon be wrapped up, and that aside from an unfortunate murder or two, life was pretty darn *genial,* a favorite word of Rosa's.

But *Baby's First Year* was a tougher case. Janneken had told me that Claribel seemed to have abandoned her child to the Norwegian in-laws, if only temporarily, for a career and a boyfriend in Paris. My suspicion was that she hadn't originally written the novel to raise a laugh, but to describe her fear, her loneliness, and her sense that her life as an independent person was over. Only after the Spanish reviews began to call the novel a satire of the Norwegian way of dealing with pregnancy, birth, and the baby's first year, did Claribel, no longer hormonal, vulnerable, and afraid, try in embarrassment to reposition the novel as a kind of comedy.

Did Janneken see that? Would Angela? Or would they just feel that I did not have a sense of humor about the ups and downs of postpartum mamas? Better not think about the poor *Baby* right now. It only brought up inchoate professional angst, along with fears that I was losing my touch as a translator and would soon be reduced to begging for the kind of bread-and-butter translation work I'd done in my apprentice years, while people like Angela Cook went around slagging me off and getting prestigious awards and fellowships.

Instead I'd turn to my other task at hand, researching several of the American independent presses that specialized in translation, one in Brooklyn, another in Minneapolis, and two in the Bay Area. Their online catalogs looked intriguing, full of international authors I'd never heard of, blurbed by other authors I'd also never heard of. There were photos of melancholy Ukrainians and pensive Japanese, Hungarians, Francophone West Africans; high-cheek-boned young novelists from Latvia and Finland—a whole new generation of unsmiling, serious foreign writers in translation, who had already won prizes for their work, prizes I'd also never heard of.

How would Luisa fare in such company? She hadn't won any prizes for years; she was really only prominent in Uruguay. Like many writers who create some excitement with their first literary work, she'd only been considered promising for a limited time. Her work was anthologized; she was invited to conferences; she had a small international profile for a while. Critics found much to explore in her work. At the same time she'd never really established herself as a part of a movement. The university presses that had previously published her in English hadn't known exactly how to market her—that was one way of putting it.

I went to the "About" page of the presses' websites. Most of the presses were non-profits, and their goals were admirable: *to make international literature available in English; to cultivate the art of translation; to open borders; to cross borders; and to cross-pollinate across borders.* This was all very inspiring, especially in these times of closed borders and xenophobia. Information about how to order books or to donate to the publisher was readily available on the sites, but information on submitting manuscripts was either not available or couched in cooler language.

I saw before me the dispiriting prospect of writing query letters puffing up Luisa's achievements, and attaching the title story. And then, most likely, hearing nothing for months. If ever. One press warned, "Because of the volume of submissions, we are unable to respond to phone, fax, or email inquiries about the status of queries or manuscripts."

When did translation queries become such an overwhelming *volume of submissions?*

While I was not looking, obviously.

Dani had told me that it was her partner, Ren, who'd mentioned Luisa Montiflores and her work to Giselle, but interestingly Giselle had contacted me rather than the publisher in Spain because she'd read *Shadow of a Woman on the Sidewalk* in my translation. She'd told me that she often preferred to identify a translator first. That was one of the things that had struck me at the time—that and her personal interest in Luisa. "I suppose I have a weakness for the brilliant but neglected author on the margins of world literature. But I never choose to publish an author *only* because they represent a part of the world or a language less translated. Their work must speak to me. And Luisa's does."

I had never quite identified what it was in Luisa's work, particularly the title story, that spoke to Giselle. Was it something about the way Luisa wrote about her mother? Had Giselle been the moon to Pauline's planet? What about Jacqui, the second moon? If Giselle was the Lacanian *little other* to her mother's *Big Other*, then where did that leave Jacqui? Was she the *littlest* other? In Luisa's story, there had been two sisters. Was Jacqui Europa or Io, or another moon entirely? Was she Amalthea?

I was back to thinking about Giselle and her family, and about Giselle and her colleagues/lovers, Jane and Karen. I was missing some essential part of their work and personal relationships with each other. If I could understand it, it might help me in solving the mystery of why Giselle had died.

I started by doing a basic Internet search on Karen Morales.

There was ample evidence that she was who she said she was, a techie who'd lucked out. In her twenties Karen had been the only woman executive at a "scrappy little startup" here in Portland, a business that had figured out a new way to track housing values and consolidate information on sales from the past. When the startup was acquired by a big Silicon Valley company, the four people involved in the company from the beginning, all of them under thirty, walked away with millions, in both cash and stock options.

Karen had been interviewed several times at the time of the sale, including by a reporter who quoted an unidentified woman who had been a coworker of Karen's, though apparently lower on the totem pole. The reporter asked if Karen was a role model for girls interested in tech, and the employee said, "Sort of. She's really smart and she could be helpful to other women. As the company grew she pushed to hire more women and pay us well. Still, she wasn't *one of us,* if you know what I mean. She had some streak of ruthless ambition in her—I don't know what other words to use. It meant she was able to stand up to the two top bros in the company and shrug off their sexism. Not all of us are able to do that, they'd just fire you. So we admired her toughness and competency, but she was hard to be around. Is that the role model we want?" Asked to comment on this, Karen Morales said, "My grandmother was an immigrant from Colombia who cleaned motel rooms. My mother wanted to go to college but married and divorced young and had to raise us on her own. She scraped and saved so my brother and I could study and not work after school, and get the scholarships we needed. I'm not ruthless, but I am ambitious. There's a difference. A lot of girls in tech haven't had to fight for what they want and they don't know how to get it. I do."

I found it hard to square the tough, extremely competent Karen of this article with the red-eyed, hung-over, wasabi-stained Karen of the day before. But I supposed that standards for cleanliness were different at startups, where what was prized was the willingness to work constantly and break things rather than to look attractive. It actually made me like Karen more to think that she could buck expectations of how women should act at the workplace, until I thought about some of the synonyms for ruthless: callous and cold-blooded, to name a couple.

Karen popped up in a few other contexts—she contributed substantially to a program for LGBTQI youth in downtown Portland; and she'd given a talk at a high school and met with Latina high school girls interested in tech careers. On LinkedIn, I saw that after having worked most of her twenties for the startup, she'd come to Entre Editions last October, which fit with what she'd told me.

Her name also came up as one of the contributors to an anthology of Latinx science fiction, published this past February as the result of a Kickstarter campaign. The anthology was available online and I bought the e-book version.

Karen's story was more interesting for its ideas than for its literary style. It took place on Earth, in a dystopian future, and it explored power struggles between the matriarchal human *wozens* and the *transbottens,* gender-neutral, semi-autonomous robot-slaves. I wasn't sure whom to root for. Matriarchal societies are supposed to be good, aren't they? But these wozens had gone down a dark path. They wanted all the minerals in the former Amazonian rain forest and other perks for themselves and their progeny.

There was a lot about how the wozens conceived their progeny, which confused me. Added to that was the strong implication that Earthling civilization as we know it was not around any longer, due to dust storms and plagues. Things are hard enough on our planet without suggesting it could get much, much worse.

I didn't think the story was going to offer evidence that Karen had been involved with either Jane and Giselle's break-up or Giselle's death. But it did suggest that Karen's interest in taking Entre Editions in a more science fiction-y direction was personal.

I continued to scroll through search results for Karen Morales, now adding the names Jane Janicki and Giselle Richard. At the top of the list was the Entre Editions' website, followed by various news items and notes about book reviews and events, many of the more recent taken from Karen's press releases. But lower down I found an article in the monthly newsletter of a Portland network of women entrepreneurs, describing a presentation given by Giselle and Jane. The title of the article was "Entre (editions) preneurs: Translation publishers *extraordinaire.*"

The article, from September of last year, opened with a photo of Giselle and Jane flanking Karen Morales—who was, according to the caption, the social-media manager of the entrepreneurs' network. In the photo they all seemed the best of chums, professionally attired, smiling at the camera. Karen especially looked much better turned out in the photo than she had in person yesterday. Her hair was dark then and her brows neatly plucked. She wore an expensive-looking jacket with slacks.

In the newsletter account, Giselle got the most coverage; she seemed to have a knack for the snappy but sincere phrase. Jane was mentioned as the co-owner, however, and praised by Giselle: "Jane has a great talent for business; she's fantastic at the day-to-day overseeing of production and keeping us on track to meet our goals. If I have a talent, it's for thinking big, so it's good to have someone else to rein me in."

But in the end, it appeared, thinking big had won out. I suspected that had something to do with Karen.

By nine-thirty, I'd grown tired of doing electronic research. I checked my email to see if Janneken had gotten the *Baby* chapters, but there was nothing. I ignored some messages from Luisa. They were red-flagged *high priority*, but I knew that only indicated high anxiety.

I wondered if there were anything I could do to help the case today. After all, Haakonssen had indicated that he would be interested in learning more about the business operations and finances of Entre Editions. I couldn't see myself going back again to Jane's house, since we'd more or less concluded our discussion about Luisa's book contract. But maybe I could find a pretext to visit Karen again. I could tell her Jane was cancelling *On Jupiter* and that I was looking for a new publisher. I could ask for her help in finding that new publisher. At the same time, perhaps I could find out a little more about her relationships with Giselle and Jane and about, for instance, the trip to Montreal. Anything I could pass on to the Newport police that might help resolve the investigation, one way or another, was something I wanted to try.

I texted her on the number she'd given me yesterday, asking if she could give me a little of her time. I had some questions about placing Luisa's book, now that Entre wouldn't be publishing it. I'd be happy to meet her wherever she liked or come to her condo again. Five minutes later she answered *Ok. Come in 30 min. My place.*

17.

I put on a light jacket and a scarf and stepped out into the spring day, heading down the hill to Karen's condo in the Pearl District. I buzzed three times at intervals before she answered and let me in.

It occurred to me that my text might have woken her; if so, she'd made an effort today to look more presentable. She'd taken a shower and her short hair was wet; she was wearing a shirt and clean pullover and jeans. The skin around her eyes was tender and pink, and her finely molded lips were a little chapped. I wondered how they would look with lipstick.

I apologized, "I know this is terrible timing, and publishing is probably the last thing you want to talk about," I said. "But I don't have many days left in Portland, and now that Jane has canceled *On Jupiter,* I know Luisa would want me to make an effort to locate some other possible publishers. I get the feeling you're really good at what you do, and I imagine you've done a lot of research on how to best market Luisa's book."

"Coffee?" she asked without responding directly to my attempt at flattery. I nodded and she poured us both a cup. "So, what you're telling me is that Jane is throwing in the towel? But maybe I shouldn't be surprised. Jane didn't really have the knack for publishing. She should have gotten out while she could."

I didn't want to tell Karen that Jane seemed to have found herself swimming in debt as a result of Giselle's profligate spending. So instead I just asked again if Karen could offer me a little advice. I needed a new publisher for Luisa Montiflores. How should I go about it?

For fifteen minutes, over coffee, she enlightened me. Not with specifics about possible presses exactly, though she mentioned a few, but with the angle I should use to get in the door.

"What you've got to remember, Cassandra, is that the eventual catalog copy is designed to appeal to the sales rep who has one minute to make the sale to the buyer for the bookstore. Same when you're approaching a publisher to make your pitch. Tell them in as few words as possible who is going to buy this book. Give them a title, like *Unraveling Jupiter,* that will make them sit up. Do not, I repeat, mention Lacan and all that shit."

I had a notebook with me for cover and pretended to write some of this advice down, knowing all the time that Luisa would blow her top if she knew what Karen was saying. Luisa would immediately remind me of her position in Latin American literature, her long-ago prize for *Diary of a First Love in Montevideo,* and her positive review in the *New York Review of Books* (which was actually just a positive mention, really, in a longer article about Clarice Lispector). Somehow I had to get the conversation around to Giselle and Jane and money and Montreal.

I pasted an admiring look on my face and said, "This is great information. You really seem like you've mastered the art of the pitch. How did you decide to change careers and get into publishing translations?"

"It wasn't so much about translations, it's about publishing," she said, as if explaining something obvious. "Publishing—books—making books—it's cool. Yeah, I'm good at tech, and I made a million dollars by helping sell an app that allows real estate companies to track sales—but who the fuck cares, really? I don't care about real estate, I could have helped market software for just about anything. But publishing—people write manuscripts, they become books. That's different."

"And you write, as well," I said. "You've written at least one science fiction story. And it was published, too. That must have felt wonderful."

"Oh, you saw that anthology!" she said. Her expression suddenly brightened. "Are you a writer, too?"

I was sometimes asked this question, but the answer I could have given, that translation *was* writing, would be unconvincing. You could call yourself a writer if you wrote a story about matriarchal wozens and robot-slaves with sentences like, "But Xaryha, you will never be human, don't you understand that? You will never be one of us!" But if you spent a few hours attentively laboring over the most effective way to render a single complex and beautiful Spanish paragraph into equally complex and beautiful English, you were somehow never acknowledged as actually writing that paragraph.

So I just said, with a regretful smile, "No," and tried to steer the conversation back to the subjects I was interested in. "You were saying something about Jane earlier, that she should have gotten out while she could. Did you mean that about the press, selling her share, or about their relationship?"

"Both, but definitely the press. Look, Giselle was fed up with Jane. She was convinced Jane was too cautious. Jane was always trying to put the brakes on. It's not easy to get a new business off the ground, but Giselle's basic strategy was working. Entre Editions was attracting attention and sales were increasing. Higher-profile authors and agents had taken notice. The main problem was that Giselle had used her own money, and that money was almost gone. Giselle kept saying that all they needed was to discover an international star, like Elena Ferrante, and Entre would be profitable. But the fact is, the company was running short of the necessary funds to function, much less expand. Giselle's suggestion that I buy out Jane wasn't something I hadn't thought of myself."

"So that was Giselle's idea, that you buy Jane out? Were they equal owners??"

"They were sixty-five/thirty-five on paper, but it was Giselle who'd put in all the seed money. What did Jane do?"

"Worked for no pay and provided the office and equipment? Gave Giselle a home?"

Karen shot me a sharp look as if realizing suddenly that perhaps my intentions in coming here were not quite as benign as she'd thought and that perhaps I was even critical of her. Rather too late she activated the V-frog in her pocket, as Asimov might have put it, and a guileless warmth flickered to life and flowed in my direction.

"I suppose that's one way to put it," she said mildly. "People always have choices."

But once having begun to escalate my questioning, I didn't back off. "Did you know that Jane took out a loan to do the remodel, and was struggling to pay off the printers?"

"If Jane had been more reasonable, I could have paid that printers' bill in a second. I could have found us an office and paid the rent. Money's not the problem here. No, it was control."

"Jane didn't want to give up control of the press to someone she didn't trust. So you took Giselle away."

"That's not how it was! It was all about publishing! Giselle was willing to take a chance, she was a risk-taker."

"You started an affair with Giselle to get rid of Jane and play a larger role in the press, didn't you?" I deliberately made my voice more accusing. "But maybe things weren't working out the way you expected. How much did Giselle ask you for beyond buying out Jane? Maybe you didn't like the idea of putting up the money and having only 35% control. Maybe you wanted a bigger percentage or to be in charge of managing the press. Maybe Giselle got cold feet when she realized how ruthlessly ambitious you could be!"

The volatility I'd heard about from Dani was suddenly on full display. Karen's eyes went up in a dark blaze and she jumped off her stool across from me. She wasn't that tall. I could take her if necessary.

"What's your game, Cassandra? Where the hell do you get off coming over here and making accusations about my intentions? Okay, I saw an opportunity to help Giselle and get experience in publishing. I was sure I could run the business side of things better than those two, but I was also fine about just getting rid of Jane and putting the company on a better footing. And okay, Giselle and I were occasional lovers. But it was no big deal, just some fun. And I fucking did not kill her if that's what you're insinuating."

"*Calmete, mujer*," I said, peaceably. "I was just testing you."

"¡*Qué mierda!*" But she did calm down, though it took an effort. She went over to the fridge and took out a beer, without offering me one. She also took out some blueberry yogurt and a large flat box of left-over pizza. She placed the box on the counter between us and opened it. Even cold, pepperoni has a distinct smell. She then found a spoon and ripped off the foil top of the yogurt cup.

"I apologize," I said. "The thing is, the police seem to have me on their list of suspects. They won't let me leave Oregon while the investigation is going on. And I really need to get home for work. So it occurred to me that I could maybe make things move a little faster if I tried to do a little asking around on my own."

"Why would they suspect you?" she asked, alternating bits of pizza with blueberry yogurt. A dab of purple remained on her upper lip.

"No idea. Well of course I *was* at the cottage Tuesday morning about an hour before they found Giselle. Other than that, I'm as innocent as you are. They're talking to everyone—it's horrible, isn't it?"

"Well, you can cross me off the list. I told you about my writers' group, didn't I? Every other Monday night, six to eight. I'd been over at my mom's before that to bring her some groceries, and the police can just ask her if I came by. After the writers' group, I went for a walk to get some exercise. Then I was up late doing more work to get ready to go to New York. I absolutely have an alibi for Monday afternoon and evening." But something in her voice made me wonder what she might not be saying. Was it general knowledge that Giselle had died Monday evening?

She went on, "I'm sure the cops have checked me out. But they came back last night around eight p.m., and asked to look at my car. The next thing I knew they produced a search warrant and drove off with it. It's impounded. As if I would drive to Newport, kill Giselle, drive back to Portland, and go check on *mi madre*?"

Now that I had seen Karen's temper, I didn't feel like testing it again. I wasn't going to mention Dani's call to the Newport police, or that I'd seen an email from Giselle to Karen left unfinished on her laptop.

She had polished off a second slice of pizza. The smear of blueberry yogurt was joined by a fleck of tomato on her lip. I felt the vibrations of the V-frog when she looked at me, but she only said,

"If I were you I'd be asking myself why Pauline and Giselle both died at the cottage in Newport. Don't you think that's suspicious? I told the cops but they weren't that interested. All they wanted to talk about was the Dewar's on the table that day. And my fucking car."

I sat up a little straighter. "You told me the other day that Pauline died in her sleep. Natural causes, most likely as a result of the brain lesion. Are you saying something else now? Did Pauline take her own life? Is that what Giselle thought?"

"It was recently, when I went to Newport to meet with her. Giselle and I were in the kitchen drinking beer, and Giselle started to talk about Pauline's death. How she had suspected that her mother didn't just die in her sleep, but that she overdosed. Giselle was never sure if her mother did it on purpose or if she simply didn't realize how strong the combination of pain meds and alcohol was. I had a feeling Giselle thought someone else might have been involved."

I immediately thought of Jacqui. "What about the younger daughter? Could she have had anything to do with it?"

"Giselle almost never talked about her sister. I got the feeling that Jacqui had been a big disappointment to her family. Maybe it was just that she wasn't intellectual like Giselle and Pauline. I had the sense she was developmentally a little slow, even kind of crazy at times. She'd used drugs as a teenager. Giselle did tell me that. She was a lot younger than Giselle, so she probably came along when Pauline was over forty. But as far as I know, Jacqui was out of touch with her family. How could she have been involved in Pauline's death?"

I thought of what Jane had told me yesterday, about Jacqui's tantrums as a baby, her self-destructive behavior as an adolescent.

"You haven't seen Jacqui here in Portland then? She's been to Jane's. Told Jane that Giselle didn't deserve a memorial service."

"No, I haven't ever met Jacqui. There'd be no reason for her to contact me, and I have no idea what she means about Giselle not deserving a service." For the first time this visit, Karen looked truly sad. "I know it must be awful for Jane. If I were a better person I'd reach out to her. I mean, Giselle was a complicated woman, but she was really inspirational and smart, she really gave a lot to the literary community. She needs to be remembered. People would *want* to come to a memorial service."

"It seems like something that you'd be really good at organizing," I said.

She sighed and her eyes got a little pinker, so I changed the subject. "Have you thought at all what you'll do next?"

Karen's answer took me aback. "Oh, I want to stay in publishing. Writing and publishing. I've got a novel in mind. Same planet and cast of characters as the story, only this time I would do a lot more with the transbottens. I'm fascinated by the concept of A.I. and the moral implications of robots who are programmed to be 'good workers.' What if a transbotten rebelling against being a good slave and a wozen rebelling against the corrupt politics of the ruling matriarchy got together to try to change the world?"

I pretended to listen attentively, but eventually the plot line was too much for me. Karen's physical appearance and habits repelled and attracted me in equal measure. Make that sixty-five percent repelled and thirty-five percent attracted. Why did someone with pink eyes, puffy skin, and dry lips look so kissable? She was half my age, so that was never going to happen.

"I've considered starting my own publishing house," I suddenly heard Karen say as she closed the pizza box. "There would be a learning curve, but I'm sure I could get up to speed in no time. And I'd hire good people to work there, no more of this depending on interns for one or two quarters and then they're gone. I'd have consultants—maybe you might like to be a consultant, Cassandra? Because I'd definitely like to publish translations, at least translations from Latin America, along with science fiction from here in the States. And why not start with Luisa's novel?" she went on, with growing enthusiasm, thinking aloud. "I mean, it's more or less edited, right? And the cover's designed and the copy's written. Before Jane said no, I'd booked the Planetarium for a launch party in October. I could contact them again about a date. We could get you and Luisa over, no problem. Maybe it could be a launch party for the new publishing company."

I told her I'd better get going, but added cautiously that Luisa and I would consider her proposal, though it might be a hard sell, given that Luisa was a little ambivalent about being presented as an sf writer. To myself I thought, no way would Luisa accept *Unraveling Jupiter* as a title, much less having her North American launch at a planetarium in Portland.

But that reminded me, "Two days ago, you remember, we talked about Luisa's writing. You said something about Luisa and Asimov. Did you mean his book *Lucky Starr and the Moons of Jupiter*? Do you think Luisa was referencing him in some way?"

"You may not know everything there is to know about Luisa's process of writing," she said, a little playfully. "Let's just say I don't think her choice of Jupiter is random. She's read Asimov, I'm sure of it."

She walked me to the door. "If you're free tonight?"

Startled, I said nothing, and she continued, "I'm giving a reading with two other science fiction writers at a local bookstore. I'd love it if you could come."

She kissed my cheek and I went off with a faint smear of purple yogurt on my face, having told her I'd try to make it.

18.

On the sidewalk in front of Karen's condo I checked my phone, hoping for a text from Janneken to at least say she'd received the three chapters (*Thank you so much, Cassandra. And as usual you've done a splendid job!*). No, nothing. Of course, it *was* Friday evening in London, and she was probably at a book launch or something to do with her many children; all the same, she could still let me know, couldn't she?

I trudged back up the hill to the Northwest neighborhood. The sky had clouded over since earlier this morning; perhaps there would be a rain shower and I wouldn't have to worry about the potted plants outside. But I didn't feel like going back to Jill and Candace's house and the prospect of buckling down to Chapter Four. How could a colicky baby possibly be amusing? Maybe I should skip ahead to Chapter Seven, where the narrator simply left the baby in the hands of the home-health-care nurse and checked into a hotel with a spa outside Oslo for a couple of days.

I walked slowly, preoccupied with what Karen had told me. I hadn't managed to get anything significant from her about Montreal; according to Karen the weekend jaunt was no big deal. That was not how Jane saw it. I wondered if the reservations for the airfare and hotel were really the first Jane knew about the affair. Really, wouldn't she have noticed something between Karen and Giselle much earlier? Maybe there was something else about Montreal, some reason Giselle had given Jane for going there in the first place? Montreal had other associations besides the bank. Giselle and her sister had been born there, had grown up there with Pauline.

The most interesting things about my conversation just now with Karen had to do with the problem-child Jacqui and with Pauline's death at the cottage. I hadn't known before that Giselle suspected an overdose, much less that she had hinted to Karen that someone could have been involved in Pauline's death. Why hadn't the police been interested in that? Or maybe Haakonssen *had* been interested and had just not allowed Karen to see it.

I decided that I'd call Tom Hoyt and see if I could wheedle Nora's phone number. Fortunately I had punched his number into the contacts on my phone. I stood just off the busy street and talked to his office receptionist, who put me through to his voice mail. I told him I'd like to get hold of Nora, since, in the course of my—I didn't want to say "investigation," since that might make him hesitate—conversations with the co-owner of Entre Editions and my offer to write a short article for a translation journal about Giselle, I was hoping to learn more about Pauline Richard's influence on her daughter as a translator. Nora had told me they were friends. Before I rang off I also added, "Since you're a lawyer, I imagine you know a bit about trusts. Specifically the different between a grantor and a trustee? Thanks!"

While waiting for him to call back, I visited a few shops on the northern edge of NW 23rd and had a slice of quiche at a patisserie. After this light lunch I continued to wander up hilly Thurman Street. The small businesses and bistros turned into short blocks of spring-foliaged narrow lots dominated by older wooden houses, shingled, painted, wide-porched, gradually growing even larger and more decorative as the street climbed into what appeared to be a dense forest at the summit.

After a few blocks I happened to glance across the street and saw, charging quickly along the opposite sidewalk at a speed greater than mine, a familiar figure in an all-weather parka and jeans. What luck! Wearing hiking boots and a ball cap with her white braid snaking out the back opening, Nora Longeran was bent under a daypack that looked heavy. She seemed preoccupied with her own thoughts, and looked up in alarm when I crossed the street to join her.

Then she recognized me. "Cassandra the translator, isn't it?"

I wondered if she was regularly accosted by fans, young and old, when she was out and about on Portland streets. She didn't stop, but waved that I was welcome to accompany her up the hill. I wondered if she was taking a walk or returning home from shopping with that heavy pack.

"I'm so glad to see you," I said. "First of all, I wanted to thank you for sending your lawyer along to the police station in Newport. And for the Agatha Christie room. I'm staying in Portland now."

Her legs were shorter than mine, but her pace was faster. Puffing slightly, I continued, "I was really shocked that the police took me in. I suppose you were questioned by the police too?"

"You were at the wrong place, wrong time," she cut me off. "I knew that. Tom could see that. Don't worry about it. What can I help you with?"

Since I'd already developed the story for Tom Hoyt about writing an article about Giselle and Pauline as translators, I used that, adding, ""You said at the Sylvia Beach that you'd known Pauline Richard. It sounded like you were good friends. Was that here in Portland?"

She slowed and glanced at me warily, before answering in a neutral tone, "Yes, we were good friends. We knew each other as girls, lost contact, and then reconnected later in our lives. Eventually she moved back to this neighborhood in Portland, where I'd also bought a house."

"So you saw a lot of her? You knew her well?"

"We were kids who liked books, then women who loved them. Friends who love books never run out of things to say to each other." Nora shifted the daypack forward on her shoulders. "I've just been down to the library on Lower Thurman for my weekly fix. When Pauline was alive, we used to walk down Thurman together to the library and then take the bus back up. She didn't have my stamina. She only gave up smoking after the second time she got sick." She speeded up again.

I wasn't sure I had Nora's stamina either, but I took a couple of long strides and caught up. "How did you and Pauline meet?"

"In a French class our first year in junior high. Right here in Portland. We actually weren't close friends at first, far from it. She came from a 'better' family, lived in a big, fancy house. Her father had a shoe store chain, and my dad was a plumber. We were both good in English. I outshone her in science, but I had to concede defeat in French. I've never had much of an ear for foreign languages. I can invent them for my books, and imagine what they might sound like—but as for going to Paris and asking the way to the *bibliothèque,* I'm about where I was when I was thirteen."

"But you bonded over reading?"

"Yes, in our English classes. We studied together, at her house or mine. We went to the library on weekends, we loaned books back and forth. Neither of us was very athletic, and at the time we weren't that interested in boys. Or I should say, I wasn't. Boys liked Pauline, she just found them *immature.* Once she got to college and then to Paris, she felt differently."

I thought of the photograph of Pauline with her cigarette in the café in Montparnasse.

"When was she in Paris?"

"She went to Reed College in Portland for a couple of years, did her junior year in Paris, then she finished her degree at the Sorbonne. She married a French-Canadian medical student and when he finished his studies and internships they moved to Montreal."

"But you kept in touch?"

"No, not really. Our lives went in different ways. I got married early, never finished college—I'd had a scholarship to the University of Oregon in Eugene, but blew it. My husband left me. I was a single mother of two and had to rely on my parents for a while." She paused. "I was nobody and nothing, just a working mom with a secret dream, to be a writer." Nora halted. "Don't put that in your article. It's not about me."

"No, no," I said. "It's going to be about Pauline's work as a translator. But it is interesting to know where she got her start. To see where she, where both of you, grew up."

We had by now come to a two-lane iron bridge over a deep ravine, wooded on both sides, with a path winding down below. The houses had become much grander, two and three stories, with carriage houses and vast porches. Nora stopped and looked down. With her jeans and backpack, her small stature, the pale braid and baseball cap, she looked in profile almost like a young student again. "Most of the houses around here were built in the early years of the twentieth century. Mansions, some of them. The new rich are buying them. That's Portland nowadays."

I prodded her. "You said eventually you did get back in touch with Pauline."

"We reconnected in the early eighties. I was giving a talk in Toronto, she asked me to come to Montreal. I met her daughter, Giselle, that is, and her husband, Pierre. Later she got divorced. By then, we were both in the literary world, in different ways. For about ten years we wrote and saw each other when she came to visit her parents. Her mother died, and her father asked her to stay on in the house in Portland, so she eventually did. That was 2001. We were both fifty-eight. Her father died, and she remained."

"And Giselle moved out to Portland around a dozen years ago?"

"Something like that. Pauline had a small lump removed and treatment for breast cancer a couple of years after she moved here from Montreal. It was caught in time and she seemed fine. Then, about three years later, the cancer returned. She had to have a double mastectomy and chemo. That's when Giselle moved here, to take care of her."

"So you knew Giselle for quite a while too," I said. "What about the other daughter?"

Nora didn't look at me as she said, in a less than forthcoming way, "She lived in Canada. Didn't visit. She and Pauline weren't close. Jacqui was difficult in some ways, always had been."

This was the third time I'd heard that Jacqui and Pauline weren't close. Jane had told me. Karen had told me. And now Nora. But what did that mean? What did it mean that Jacqui didn't visit? Did it have something to do with the divorce? Maybe the father had custody or Jacqui preferred to live with him in Montreal? And what did it mean: "difficult?" Just a pain in the neck, or seriously unbalanced?

Nora had started off again, but more slowly, as if she were caught up in complicated memories. We walked about a block in silence while I tried to screw up my courage to ask more probing questions. If anyone would know about Pauline's death in Newport six years ago, Nora would. She'd know if Pauline had been suffering from depression after she'd gotten the news about her cancer spreading to the brain. *Words were everything to Pauline,* Giselle had told Karen. Nora might have a clue whether Pauline had intentionally taken an overdose—or whether someone had helped her along the way. She might even suspect, as Karen did, that there was some connection between Pauline's death and Giselle's.

Suddenly Nora turned to face me and gave a brief, jerky wave to the left. "Do you want to see Pauline's family's house? Giselle sold it after her mother died."

The streets up from Thurman were very steep, the sidewalks buckled with tree roots. "Pauline's father came from New England," Nora said. "Built up his shoe stores with hard work. Even during the Depression he did well. He used to say, 'You can put on an extra sweater and go without a coat, but you can't go outdoors barefoot.' Pauline was their only child."

The old Lawson house was set high above the street, with stone steps that numbered at least twenty. Teal green, recently repainted, three stories with gables and gingerbread, surrounded by even taller evergreens, big leaf maples, and a giant magnolia, with leathery leaves and brown suede buds, some beginning to flower into fragrant white petals. The home looked as if it could house a family of eight and their servants.

"It's magnificent."

"Yes," Nora said. "You can imagine how intimidated I was in junior high when I came here. At home I shared a bedroom with my older sister: bunk beds, hardly room to turn around. Pauline had chintz, a doll collection, books, a view of the forest behind."

We stared at the house. Nora said, "It was a lot more dilapidated before the new owners bought it. When Pauline's father retired, he sold the shoe stores to someone who defaulted on the payment. Long story, only important to say Pauline's parents were nearly broke for a while, which was another reason Pauline ended up moving to Portland to take care of them. But before her mother died and her dad went too gaga, Angus remembered he had some stocks to sell. So her folks had enough for their declining years, and Pauline inherited something too. It would have been better if her parents had sold the house rather than just letting it crumble. Pauline should have sold it as well, but it seemed like a lot of trouble. She wasn't a very practical woman. Giselle took after her in some ways—she was a dreamer. But Giselle could be sharp about money. Pauline didn't bother much about that kind of thing."

"Giselle sold the house soon after her mother's death, isn't that right?"

"Yep, right away. You can understand it, of course. Far too big for a single young woman with no means of repairing it. I'm sure Giselle didn't want to live in this house after her mother was gone either. But it was ... there was something unseemly about the haste. There was an estate sale. Everything went. Nice old furniture, family china and silver, tons of books. Giselle got rid of most everything except some of her mother's books and her desk."

"But everything was on the up and up, I mean, Pauline's will *did* leave Giselle the house?"

"Oh, I'm sure it was all above board. Pauline had told me several times she wanted the house to go to Giselle. She'd made other arrangements for Jacqui. But Pauline adored Giselle. They shared the same interests. She would have been proud of Giselle using the money to start a publishing company that specialized in translation. It was something the two of them often talked about. Giselle brought a number of Pauline's translations back into print."

Nora sounded as if she were trying to convince herself of Giselle's good intentions. But it sounded to me as if she had some doubts. Did they have to do with real estate or with Pauline's declining health before she died?

"Do you have any reason to think that Pauline wasn't capable of taking care of herself by the end?"

"Pauline was perfectly capable of taking care of herself. She was by no means a doddering old lady!" said Nora tartly. "It's true, the second experience with cancer, the mastectomy and all that, hit her hard. But she pulled through, she kept working, translating. We both of us believed in work. I'm almost seventy-six and still going strong. Translation and writing are careers you can have far beyond retirement age—as you must know yourself!"

"Yes," I said, wondering how old she thought I was. I generally thought of myself as looking ten years younger. "Particularly if you haven't saved any money along the way, it's handy to have a skill. But back to Pauline. I've understood that Pauline could have suffered from depression ..." I began, and then halted. Nora's greenish eyes were stormy under the white brows.

"Who told you that? Pauline had full control of her mental powers. We had a book club meeting only a couple weeks before she died in Newport. Pauline was brilliant and insightful. As usual."

Before I could apologize, her cell phone started ringing. She fished it out of her pocket and answered. "Hello Tom. What's up?"

"No," she said, suddenly looking over me with a glare. "Nope. Same policy as always. I only give my number to people I *want* to have my number."

She clicked off, turned her back on me, and started walking quickly down the hill to Thurman.

I stumbled after her down the steeply angled narrow street, and finally caught up with her. I said I know what she must think, that I had been stalking her or something, but it wasn't like that. I was staying with friends of friends in the neighborhood and had just happened to see her.

"But I did want to talk to you," I said, as we came to the main street, and she finally stopped and faced me, a troubled look on her face. "Here's the deal, Nora. The cops in Newport would prefer that I didn't leave the country while the case is active. They won't tell me anything about how it's progressing or who they suspect or even if they think it's no accident. I've been over to the house Giselle shared with Jane Janicki, to their office, to talk about the contract for my author's book, and *she* doesn't know anything either. And I've talked to Karen, the marketing director, and she thinks there might be a connection between Pauline's death six years ago and Giselle's. You are really my only hope, Nora. You knew both Giselle and Pauline, what do you think? I'm hoping that if I can give Detective

Haakonssen more help that they'll let me get back to London and get on with my life."

To my relief, Nora didn't go striding off, but stood, small and bent, under the weight of her daypack full of books. "What do you need from me?" she said. "There's only so much I know myself. I lost touch with Giselle after Pauline died. Well, not at first, but eventually."

"Did you help her get the publishing company started?"

"Not directly. Certainly, I was glad to see she was reprinting Pauline's works. I put in a good word to several reviewers, and I wrote a short piece about Pauline for a local literary journal. I saw Giselle at readings and so on, but we rarely spoke more than a few words. I've not often been to Newport in recent years. I understood from friends that Pauline's cottage was mostly vacant."

"But recently Giselle had started working on the cottage, possibly to sell it."

Nora chose her words. "I heard Giselle was thinking of selling it. I had a fleeting thought that I might buy it. Use it as a place to write. That's why I went to Newport last weekend actually."

"Did you see her there last week? Talk to her about selling it to you?"

"No." Nora paused. "You might as well know. I did walk by the cottage early Sunday morning. I saw Giselle through the windows, at the desk where her mother used to sit. She looked so like her mother, I was frightened. It was like going back in time, to when we were in our early forties and became friends again. I practically ran away. I knew I could never live in that house. I never contacted Giselle about buying the house if she put it on the market. I spent Sunday at the aquarium, my favorite place in Newport."

The drizzle promised by the darkening skies was upon us and she pulled up the hood of her rain parka, and tugged the hood's elastic cord so that the ball cap that had made her look younger was hidden and her face peeked out like that of a gnome. I made a mental note that my own fading claim to very late middle age, my springy, still thick curls, should always be visible. I wanted to ask her more questions—about Jacqui in particular—but she was moving away.

"Sorry," she said. "You need to get somewhere dry and I need to get home asap." She looked at her watch. "I have a phone meeting very shortly with my editor about a book scheduled for next year."

Disappointed, I thanked her for making time today to talk with me.

"Really, I wasn't tailing you. I just had had some quiche at St. Honoré Bakery and came out and there you were. I mean, I know you're a well-known writer, but before this week I'd never heard of you!"

"Your honesty is refreshing," she said with a slight smile.

I felt a bit embarrassed. I should have looked at her books at Powell's, instead of messing about in the Gold Room with Asimov.

"I wish you well," she said, then added, as if she was regretting the words as they popped out, "Give me your phone number. There's more to tell you about Pauline and her daughters—but it will take time."

I handed her my card. We looked at each other.

"Listen," she said, speaking quickly, "I like you, Cassandra. And I do feel the need to talk to someone, maybe someone who doesn't know me. I too would very much like this investigation to wind up, however it happens. I'm sorry about what I said to Tom. You wanted to know something about grantors and trustees? I might be able to help you. Maybe this weekend?"

"Thank you," I said. "But can't you just tell me now—was Jacqui the beneficiary of a trust set up by Pauline and Giselle? Were they the grantors?"

"Yes to both questions. They set up the trust for Jacqui's education and general welfare. But now I've really got to go!"

I watched Nora scamper off into what was now a steady rain. I should definitely ring Haakonssen again, ask him about Nora Longeran and what her role was in all this. Was she under investigation too?

I needed to find out more about Nora. And I needed to get out of this weather.

Someplace dry. Someplace with books. The library down the hill on Thurman, where Nora had just come from, and where Pauline had been a regular, was the obvious answer.

19.

"Can I help you?" asked the librarian at the information desk. She had chin-length white hair, as thick as mine, but straight and tidy. Neat arched brown eyebrows over brown eyes. Freckles merging into slight age spots on her face, an upturned mouth, which indicated she might still have something to smile about in her sixties. Always a good sign.

I thought she looked familiar and it seemed that she was trying to place me as well. She made the connection first. "Oh, you were at the Sylvia Beach Hotel a few days ago, at breakfast, weren't you? Talking to Nora Longeran?"

Tuesday morning she'd been, like most of the rest of her mates, in a fleece pullover. Today she wore slacks and a striped blue-and-white Oxford shirt with a sweater vest. **Arlene Zink** read her name badge.

"That's right," I said, then hesitated. This didn't seem like the right place to get into a conversation about a possible murder case. I wondered if the librarian knew I'd been taken to the Newport police station for questioning, or if she and her friends had all returned to Portland and had only learned about Giselle on the news Tuesday evening.

But librarians have a gift for discretion. Probably it's part of the curriculum in library science. Don't comment on the material patrons check out. Don't ask them why they want to know anything. Don't ask their age, their sexual preference, their political leanings. Arlene Zink had probably seen Nora in here an hour or so ago and was curious whether my appearance in the library was connected to that, but she merely nodded and asked again with a smile (was it a routine professional smile or a sly sort of dyke-recognition smile?), "Anything I can help you find?"

"I'm wondering if you have some of Pauline Richard's translations published by Entre Editions? Actually, if you have them, I'd be interested in *any* translations the library has by Pauline Richard. And by Giselle Richard."

Arlene Zink checked the online catalog. While Pauline's older translations weren't at this branch, all of the translations of hers that Entre Editions had reissued were available here, along with a translation done together by Giselle and Pauline. Seven titles in total. As she walked me to the correct shelves, the only question she asked me was whether I'd like to do an online request for Pauline's original translations, of which there were eighteen, held either at Portland State's library or at the central library downtown. She seemed slightly disappointed when I told her that wouldn't be necessary.

I took my stack of books to a table off on its own, and settled in. The rain was streaming down the windows and drumming faintly on the roof. A real spring storm. Sitting here felt safe and familiar, as intimate as a recurring dream. No one knew me here, no one knew I was an American who had passed most of my life abroad. In the library here in Portland I was just an ordinary patron, quietly turning my attention to the subject at hand.

The earliest of Entre Editions' reprints of Pauline's translations were three novels originally published in Quebec in the late 1970s. They must have been among Pauline's first efforts when she was living in Montreal with her husband, before she had children. Giselle had also republished her mother's translation of a collection of stories by Guy de Maupassant, and two novels by a French woman writer. The bio was the same in all six reprints: Pauline Richard had been born in Portland and educated at Reed College and the Sorbonne in Paris, where she had lived throughout the 1960s. She moved with her husband to Montreal in 1970 and eventually began a productive and much admired translation career. She died in 2013, in Portland, Oregon.

Pauline was certainly productive, but was she "much admired"? I'd have to look up more about her later on my laptop. Meanwhile I turned my attention to the actual texts and read a few pages in all of them. Then I looked at the translation that carried the name of both Giselle and Pauline Richard. *Unforgettable* was by an author named Alain LeMoyne; it had originally been published in French in 1989. This was its first translation into English, Giselle had written in a short introductory note.

My mother was a particular fan of this writer and of this novel, Alain LeMoyne's last. She first met him during a sabbatical year in Paris in 1987-1988, and later translated samples of the novel for possible publication in English. After LeMoyne's untimely death in 1989, she

abandoned the attempt to find a publisher for him and set the novel and her
twenty pages of translation in a folder, along with clippings about him and
some biographical notes. Years later, when she and I were going through
some of her things, she found the box and was moved to start translating it
again. In her last years, my mother grew determined to finish this novel and
persuaded me to help her with it. I too became an admirer of LeMoyne's
compressed, almost violent literary style. It was the only project my mother
and I undertook together, and although her death meant she never saw the
final version, I am sure she would be pleased to know that finally her dear
friend Alain LeMoyne was published in English.

The back cover summarized the novel as the story of a passionate, adulterous love told more in silence than in dialog, and compared it to Marguerite Duras.

Pauline's dear friend? Or something more?

What did Giselle really remember about that year in Paris, I wondered. According to the newspaper's account of her death, Giselle had been born in 1978, when Pauline was in her mid-thirties. Giselle would have been nine or ten. From the photograph of the girls in the cottage, it looked like Jacqui was a decade younger. Could Jacqui have a different father? Someone named Alain LeMoyne, who died an untimely death in 1989?

It was possible, but it would also mean that if Pauline moved permanently to Portland around 2001, she left a young teenage girl behind in Montreal. Why wouldn't Jacqui have come with her?

Arlene Zink had walked by me once or twice, helping an elderly man find the large-print-fiction section, and pointing out some cozy mysteries to another patron. When she noticed me staring into space, thinking about Pauline and Giselle, she came over and asked if I needed anything more or she could help in any way. No one was sitting near me, but we spoke in lowered voices out of library habit. I asked her if she'd worked here a long time.

She nodded. "Since this branch opened, around eighteen years ago."

"Then you probably remember Pauline Richard."

"She was a frequent patron. She'd use our dictionaries and encyclopedias. I could order anything she wanted through interlibrary loans." Arlene hesitated, "She might have been looking for company as she worked. I think she found the house up the hill too big and empty after her father died. I hope that's not too personal."

"Not at all. I've been hoping to find someone who knew her," I said. "I'm also a translator, and I'd like to write something about the Richards, Pauline and Giselle, since they both played such an important role in the field of translation."

Arlene nodded, "They deserve attention. What do you want to know?"

"Well, what was your impression of Pauline?"

"Physically—she was tall, elegant, always very well dressed. A few years after I met her, she had treatment for breast cancer. She lost her hair. But she had fabulous scarves and turbans. Not everyone could carry that off. I remember her sitting here at one of the tables in this turban, and a child of about seven asking her father if the lady was a fortune-teller. But she sort of reminded me of Simone de Beauvoir."

"You said she seemed lonely? Was she depressed?"

"Did I say lonely? I only meant that when I first knew her, she seemed solitary. She'd lived in Portland as a child, but had been gone a long time, and had lived a very different life. Then, after she got ill, her daughter—Giselle—moved out here to care for her. Giselle had been working for a publisher in Boston and managed to continue doing some editing for them, as well as getting involved with the literary scene here. That was wonderful for Pauline."

"So, Pauline didn't seem lonely or depressed the last years of her life?"

"No, not at all. She might have been sometimes in low spirits before Giselle came, but after that she got a new lease on life. She and Giselle were very close—you'd see them at events together, readings, and concerts. And Pauline and Nora Longeran used to spend regular time together. They were longtime members of a book group that met at the library. I was surprised when Pauline died, it seemed sudden. Giselle told me the cancer had come back and spread to her brain."

"Did Giselle seem distressed about her mother's death?" I asked.

Arlene looked puzzled. "Of course. Though I suppose she'd been expecting it. Afterwards Giselle sold the house, left the neighborhood, and started the publishing house. It happened quickly."

A woman came up and asked if Arlene could recommend a good historical novel, and they went off together.

It happened quickly—Nora had noted that as well. Had someone helped Pauline to die? Could that someone even have been Giselle? Was there a chance Giselle had given her mother extra painkillers in her drink, to ease her passage or to get hold of the real estate more quickly—or for both reasons? Did someone then suspect that Giselle had killed her mother? Had Giselle been being blackmailed over this? Was there any connection between Pauline's death and the payments Giselle made monthly to the Bank of Montreal, which had begun six years ago? This is where it would be important to know the beneficiary. Still, it didn't make sense: Giselle was the trustee. She wouldn't be blackmailing herself, would she? Not even the guiltiest daughter would think of that.

Arlene returned. Now the library was getting a little busier and she had to keep an eye on the main desk, where the other librarian was answering questions and checking people's books out.

I asked how well she'd been acquainted with Giselle.

"Not super well, but Giselle was always friendly. What always struck me was that the two of them were very alike in some ways—dressed well, gracious, intelligent. But Pauline was tall, and Giselle was much shorter. Maybe it's because Pauline had been quite a smoker, and probably smoked during pregnancy—sorry, I shouldn't gossip."

I smiled to show it was quite all right. "And Giselle was an editor and publisher as well, with a background in publishing."

"Yes, she'd worked for a long-established independent publisher in Boston. I think her mother might have helped get her the job, since that was the publisher who originally did a lot of Pauline's translations."

Arlene touched one of the books on the table, the novel by Alain LeMoyne, *Unforgettable*. In French, *Inoubliable*. What was it that could not be forgotten? Arlene's hands looked strong and capable, the fingernails short but neatly kept, buffed, not polished. She wore no rings. Librarians had public hands, like bank tellers and cashiers, not like translators.

"Giselle was quite an addition to the literary scene in Portland. I can still hardly believe she died at the coast. Is there going to be any kind of memorial service? Did you know her?"

"Just professionally," I said. "Entre Editions was going to publish my translation of a collection of stories by a Uruguayan writer. I've talked with her partner, Jane Janicki. Devastated, of course. Do you know Jane?"

"No, I knew Giselle was running the press with someone else, but Giselle was always the public face of Entre Editions, the one who was interviewed in the papers and radio. I guess Jane was more behind the scenes. And I didn't know them socially—they were younger. A different generation, really."

"What about Karen Morales, their new publicity director?"

"That name sounds familiar. I don't suppose she's one of our library patrons?"

"Somehow I don't think Karen is a library regular," I said. "She's a techie."

"There's a lot of that in Portland," began Arlene, but just then a small boy came up with his mother, asking for a book about dragons, at the same time that Arlene's colleague at the desk pointed at her wristwatch.

"Sorry," Arlene told me after directing the boy and his mother off to the children's section with a few suggestions. "I've got to take over for Judy for half an hour while she does an errand. I'll be at the desk if you have more questions."

"Thanks."

I watched Arlene head back to the counter near the entrance: a purposeful tread, but a willingness in her shoulders and the tilt of her head to stop and patiently answer any question put to her. I couldn't imagine working in the same place for such a long time, back and forth from stacks to counter, books in and books out. Or rather, I could imagine it—but in an alternate reality where I had taken up some useful employment as my high school counselor had urged.

Her face came back to me now. Mrs. Greensleeves, concerned eyes behind unusually small glasses, a little like Ben Franklin, with the lens ovals far down her thin nose, near the allergy-reddened tip. "You don't have the grades for a full scholarship out of state, Catherine, but I think we could get you some financial aid for Western Michigan if you applied yourself your senior year and made some time for extracurricular activities. Anything interest you? Basketball team? The school yearbook? The newspaper? Have you thought any more about what you'd like to major in at college? English [here the glasses slipped off her nose as she bent over my list of classes and grades, and she caught them with a practiced hand] seems to be your best subject. I know you told me you didn't want to be a teacher, but what about library science? That's always a good steady field of employment for a girl."

In those days I'd never heard of anyone becoming a translator. I'm sure Mrs. Greensleeves had never heard of that either, unless she associated it with the U.N. I was taking Spanish in high school, originally because everyone said it was meant to be the easiest language to learn, later because I was infatuated with my teacher, Miss Dede Paulsen. I liked speaking

Spanish right from the beginning, especially when we were acting out our dialogs and I could play the role of José, a businessman from Mexico City, or Francisco, an architecture student in Madrid. It never occurred to me that Spanish could be a profession—unless you counted teaching it to awkward teens like myself. For me Spanish was only a brief respite fifty minutes a day, five days a week from being my mother's daughter, Catherine Frances. Was it in Spanish class that I first came up with the idea of changing my first name?

It was only a few years later, in Barcelona, that the language itself became more than an escape from an Irish-American identity in a Midwestern city. When it became a kind of fluctuating identity in itself, fluctuating because I gradually realized that there was no single Spanish language to immerse myself in, but many Spanish languages, each carefully constructed from a writer's memory and imagination, each longing for an echo in English, an English that also changed with every project to match the expressive text of different individuals. My spoken Spanish, built on drills and dialogs in high school, shifted sometimes in accent and vocabulary over the years, depending on where I lived in Spain or South America. But it remained a second spoken language, usually more serviceable than poetic, at times colloquial, more often straightforward except when I had a Spanish-speaking lover. It was in written translation, hovering between two languages, that I discovered and tried to express the richness of many different kinds of Spanish: terse, ornate, flowing, withholding, bold, bawdy, secretive. It was in reading Spanish that I felt the emotional intensity and intent of the author. And it was in translation that I became the writer herself, if she could have written in English.

I wondered if Pauline felt the same. What could she express in translating from the French, in translating from the words of another, that she couldn't express in spoken French, much less in English? I caressed the cover of *Unforgettable* with my rough index finger. If I weren't an ethical person, at least when it came to libraries, I would be tempted to just take this book with me to read overnight.

Instead, I stacked all the translations neatly on the table and stood up to stretch. The query about the dragon novels had reminded me that I wanted to find Nora Longeran's kids' books. I headed into the children's section where the mother and her son were pulling out picture books. I supposed Nora's novels would be on middle school or YA shelves.

I wasn't prepared to see a whole shelf of them.

Many of her books were part of a series called *The Lands Beneath the Sea,* which told the story of Aggie and Rognvald, two friends from a remote island off the Scottish coast, who fall into the ocean during a boating accident and are saved by the sea-breathers. In order to survive they turn into sea-breathers themselves and, no longer able to return to their homes on dry land, they grow up underwater. The series first started in the eighties and seemed to be continuing.

Some of the books were hardcovers, with illustrations of the two children underwater and the fantastic sea creatures they did battle with, like the *Draugr,* a monstrous beast with a head of seaweed. They also seemed to be friendly with a blue whale, a codfish, and a giant octopus. Some were paperbacks with more modern covers and additional material at the back. In the first paperback volume, *The Sea-Breathers,* there was a short afterword written by Nora Longeran about how the idea originally came to her:

My grandparents on my mother's side emigrated from the Shetland Islands, from the island of Unst. My grandmother was named Agnes and she'd had a brother named Rognvald. She came from a storytelling family of fishermen and sailors and was a great storyteller herself. She married Alistair Inkster, a well-known name in those parts, and my mother was called Nora Inkster before she married my father. Although the Shetland Islands now belong to the United Kingdom, they are located far to the north of mainland Great Britain, as close to Norway as to Scotland. In medieval times Shetland was part of the Norse world, where ships traded with the Faroes and Iceland. There are still many place names in the Shetland Islands connected with medieval times and the language once spoken in the islands, called Norn.

People often ask me if I know Norn, and I have to say, not personally. I don't speak any language well, but at the same time I'm utterly fascinated by languages and translation. That's why I invented the character of the Inkster, a translator who has learned dozens of languages, including Norn, Old Norse, every dialect of English old and new, Gaelic, Welsh, Norwegian, Danish and so on, from drowned sailors over the centuries. She also knows French, Spanish, Basque, and Portuguese, even Russian and Greenlandic. Of course, as readers know, the Inkster can't speak these languages. She only writes them, in strands and swirls of ink through the water. In real life the octopus shoots the ink out of its sac, to deter attacks, but in my books Inkster uses her arms to write out translations as needed.

Arms? As in tentacles?

I flipped through the book's pages. Yes, here was Inkster, the octopus translator, explaining to the children Agnes and Rognvald that, because they were old enough to have learned to read English before they fell overboard, they were lucky. Inkster could tell them everything they needed to know to navigate their new watery world.

"I see you're taking a look at *The Lands Beneath the Sea* series," said Arlene, coming up behind me. "We have multiple copies of all the books. People have been reading them for ages. It's one of the most frequent questions I get from kids, *When will there be a new book?*" She laughed. "I don't suppose you could give me a clue?"

I shook my head, still rattled by the discovery that the translator character Nora had mentioned to me in Newport was a cephalopod.

"Did you want to check out anything? I noticed that you left the pile of books by Pauline on the table."

"Um, no, I don't have a library card."

This was clearly shocking news, but then she drew the obvious and obviously disappointing conclusion. "Oh, you don't live in Portland."

"I'm just passing through," I said, adding in a conciliatory way. "Portland is a wonderful city. I wish I could spend more time here."

"Where's home?"

Well might you ask. "I drove up from Oakland," I said.

"That's not far." Her smile came back, grew wider. "You said you're a translator. I hope I'm not prying, but have you published any books that we should know about at the library?"

"A few," I said. "The one by Gloria de los Angeles, *Big Mama and her ...*"

"Oh, that's still very popular!" said Arlene. "I confess, I never read it. But I did see the film. Wow, and you translated that!"

I smiled. "I'd better get going," I said. "Is it supposed to clear up later?"

"Not until tomorrow, I think. I don't suppose ... how long are you staying in Portland?" And then with the look of someone leaping across a chasm, "Are you free this evening? It's only that, I was only wondering if you might be interested in ..."

I interrupted her, "I'm so sorry. I'm booked this evening. I mean, I have a ton of work to do, translation stuff, a deadline."

She turned red, "I didn't mean," she said a little stiffly.

The truth was, she interested me, with those young-old freckles, those helpful brown eyes, the extremely clean fingernails. But not enough to want to do something about it. I wasn't sure why, but I suddenly felt almost claustrophobic with the desire to get out of the library and away from Arlene. I wanted to be on my own. Pick up something to eat, get back to Jill and Candace's, and open up my laptop. Ideas were swirling like a cloud of octopus ink around my head. Pauline and Giselle; this French writer Alain LeMoyne; Jacqui; not to mention Jane, Karen, and the crafty Nora Longeran and the Inkster.

I was grateful that three children under seven and their harried mother came hurtling toward us. Two of the kids rushed to the picture books and the third demanded the bathroom. I took the opportunity to quickly thank Arlene for all her help and to grab my jacket and head out onto Thurman Street again. It was now two p.m.

The heavy rain had turned back into a drizzle. I backtracked to a coop grocery I'd passed and filled a bag with healthier food than I'd been eating, then carried on to the house on Sawyer, which at the moment seemed a peaceful haven.

I felt I'd had a narrow escape from something dangerously tempting, not to do with Arlene's physical charms exactly, but her very manner of relating to me, with kindness and interest that already hinted at comfortable domesticity.

It started with signing up for a library card, and the next thing you knew you were joining a book group, getting together for potlucks, going to the Sylvia Beach Hotel in the company of a bunch of fleece-covered dykes, most of whom were probably married, and made jokes about you joining the club one day soon.

That was not for me. It was a life, in fact, that I'd firmly rejected in favor of near constant vagabonding, with close friends to anchor me.

Friends like Nicky, who unfortunately seemed to want to move her anchorage.

20.

I planned to begin my Internet research with a closer look at Pauline Richard's life, but I became distracted by what was meant to be a brief online search of Nora Longeran's series, especially the Inkster character. I landed for a long time on a site maintained by a blogger, who, ten years ago, had posted a long piece about Inkster and her possible biological, historical, and literary origins, with the title: *Inkster as the Kraken of the North Sea: Squid or Octopus?* Dr. Kevin McConnell, an associate professor in marine biology at the University of Newfoundland, maintained that Nora had gotten her inspiration for Inkster as one of the sea creatures in *The Lands Beneath the Sea* from the myth of the Kraken, a monster mollusk said to live in the waters off Norway and Iceland. The myths originated in sightings of a giant cephalopod by mariners, and were described in writings by Pliny the Elder as well as the Icelandic saga writers. Invariably the Kraken sought to do harm, wrapping its immense arms around ships at sea and dragging them to the bottom. The Kraken, likely a giant squid that can grow to over forty feet long, was also popular in literature and illustrations of the nineteenth century. Melville, Tennyson, and Jules Verne all described the Kraken in malevolent terms, and it was usually depicted as looking like an octopus, with eight thrashing arms, a head like a blimp, and two huge eyes.

Dr. McConnell sought first to untangle the difference between a giant squid and one of the octopus species in the Atlantic of which the *common octopus* was the most, well, common. This octopus was, however, not all that large, compared to the squid that roamed around the North Sea, being only around four feet long or wide and weighing around twenty pounds. He then attempted to prove that in spite of her Shetland ancestors, Nora Longeran had probably not been to the northern British Isles when she wrote her first books, including *The Sea-Breathers,* which introduced Inkster. She had probably been influenced more by her reading of sea myths than by actual biology. Perhaps, as someone who grew up and lived in Portland, Oregon, she was more familiar with the Giant Pacific Octopus, which could grow as large as twenty feet and weigh over a hundred pounds.

There was nothing in the article about Inkster as a translator.

Typical.

However, what was interesting about the blog post and what kept me reading for so long were the numerous comments. Unbelievably, there were several hundred, including some that were written as recently as this year. Most of them written by fans, a few by marine biologists or other specialists in oceanography, and a surprisingly large number by residents around the North Atlantic. *Hei, I am Jon, from Lofoten Islands. We know Kraken from long time back. It took my old grandfather and his bat. This was seen by many people also in bats who got away.*

I was pretty sure Jon meant boat.

I scrolled through a long discussion about octopuses in the North Atlantic, whether it was possible for the *common octopus* of the British Isles to be found farther north than the south coast of England and whether global warming would be increasing their range. There was some discussion of which animal was more intelligent, the squid or the octopus, with links to scientific papers on cephalopodic brain power, tool use, and some hanky-panky. There were multiple accounts, and photos, of a small octopus in Germany named Otto, who apparently juggled hermit crabs and shot streams of water at a lamp that was left on in the aquarium at night, thus short-circuiting the entire electrical grid of the building. A pedant from Newcastle was at pains to point out to the scientifically impaired that neither squids nor octopuses shot ink from their arms, but from their arses.

I looked to see if Nora had responded to any of these comments, including some good-natured digs about her having used "octopus tentacle" interchangeably with "octopus arm" in the first novels in the series. Otherwise all I discovered were a couple of references to Nora's preface to another writer's collection of Northern Atlantic sea myths, where she had obliquely addressed some of the criticism about the octopus-squid controversy. She was quoted as saying she'd taken inspiration both from the myth of the Kraken and from her visits to the Newport aquarium to spend time with the Giant Pacific Octopus in order to create an *imaginary* [her italics] character, Inkster.

By this time I was quite eager to read some of her books and thought about downloading one or two to my laptop. Then I remembered that in actual fact I was in Portland because of an investigation into Giselle's death, and that I didn't have time to sit around reading children's books.

I called the Newport police first, to be told that Detective Haakonssen was out all afternoon. What about Sergeant Jones then, I asked. He was gone too, out on a case, but should be back around six. Did I want to speak to another officer? What is this regarding?

"If you could ask Detective Haakonssen to call me this evening or tomorrow morning, I'd appreciate it," I said. Haakonssen, though practically monosyllabic, and unlikely to tell me all he knew about Nora Longeran's presence in Newport on the day Giselle died, or about her friendship with Pauline Richard, would at least know what I was talking about if I floated the idea that Nora might know something about Pauline's overdose—if that's what it had been.

Pauline Richard didn't have a Wikipedia page, but I found a profile and an interview online, written by a student from Reed College in the late 1990s. It discussed her career as a translator, first of French-Canadian authors and then of literary novels published in France.

In her interview Pauline repeated a few phrases common to translators, including the trope about "one attempts to serve the author's text," which always makes me think of translation as some kind of unsuccessful catering business. But Pauline also showed a deeper and more personal side to her career, one that mirrored my own journey and probably that of many other translators.

When I started out, I was hesitant and very worried about misunderstandings, about getting things completely wrong. A language isn't just words, as you know, it's a whole galaxy of customs, history, ways of being and thinking. The French insistence on le mot juste *was challenging and frightening. Not just the 'right' word, but the word that gets as close as possible to the meaning. I think, if I had continued to live in France, I would never have become a translator. I would have been too intimidated! But when my then-husband and I moved to Montreal in 1970, I felt freed up. My Parisian French was considered a bit snooty, so I began to speak differently to fit in. I also studied the literature of French Canada for a year and grew quite passionate about making it available to the Anglophone world. That period was very fruitful for me, and helped me retain a certain fluidity and freshness when I returned to my French-language roots, so to speak, and began translating classic and contemporary authors in France.*

I too might not have begun to translate Spanish had I stayed in Spain, but within a few years of first arriving at the University of Salamanca for my junior year, and then moving to Barcelona, I was off to South America, then on to Australia and Indonesia, and then back to Chile and Argentina. When I returned to live in Spain, I began to connect with the Latin American exiles and expats. I found their willingness, their eagerness to work with me gave me a certain freedom. Almost everything Pauline told her interviewer had been my experience as well. It was only when I took on translating a slew of exiled Latin American writers that I felt I came into my own as a translator.

Along with the interview, I found a link to the short piece Nora had mentioned writing for an Oregon literary magazine after Pauline's death.

We first met in a French class when we were thirteen. Pauline was already tall, with a swan-like neck. She wore her dark hair in a pixie cut. One day the teacher called her Audrey and that stuck. She did look like Audrey Hepburn at that age. My hair was in a long braid, pretty much like I wear it today. Sort of a pioneer-girl look. You can't imagine two more different girls.

She seemed incredibly worldly (a pose, I later found out) and picked up French as if she were born to speak it (not a pose at all). For a long time I hated her, the way only a seventh-grade girl can hate someone she admires. Then, suddenly, we became close friends. And although we lost touch for some years after she moved to Paris and Montreal, our friendship resumed, especially after she returned to Portland around 2000. Hardly a week went by the last years when we didn't speak on the phone or meet for coffee to talk books. She read widely and was always recommending something by a new author, an author from another part of the world, an author whose latest novel wasn't up to much, but "still quite marvelous in some ways, Nora." For Pauline, there was always something marvelous in literature. She never ever lost that.

Nora then spoke briefly about Pauline's effect on her as a writer:

To the question of whether Pauline influenced me in writing something about translation, I can't say. Obviously I write for children and Inkster is an octopus who tells the stories of the drowned in their many languages. But my translator does write, even if it is in ink in water. Inkster believes in being faithful to language and being inventive with language at the same time. And that concept, of faithful inventiveness, seems to me to sum up Pauline's attitude to translation.

It appeared to me that no one—except Giselle, of course—could have been closer to Pauline than Nora. So what more did Nora have to tell me? Phrases from our conversation standing in front of the house came back: "unseemly haste," "sharp until the end."

Could Nora possibly suspect Giselle of having hastened her mother's death? Could there be any possibility that Nora pushed Giselle over the railing Monday night out of anger or revenge for killing her childhood friend while her friend was still "sharp"? Or for selling the house and Pauline's furniture and memories far too quickly? Bestselling authors rarely murder anyone, it's true, but it could have been an impulsive act. Having seen Giselle in the cottage on Sunday, she could have returned late Monday afternoon to discuss the possibility of buying the cottage, and then, triggered by memories of Pauline, ended up confronting Giselle and giving her a push.

I tried to envision this, and failed. The librarian Arlene had said Giselle was short, but Nora was *quite* short, and thirty-five years older. Even though she looked in good shape, it would have been difficult to upend Giselle, unless Giselle was drunk or otherwise incapacitated. And, even though it could have been raining, wouldn't someone passing by have noticed Nora dragging a semi-conscious woman to the side of the bluff? "Hey, stop that. By the way, aren't you the famous children's author, Nora Longeran?"

I wished I had taken a better look at the cottage before I'd left Newport Wednesday morning. I had no real idea what the railing looked like, or how steep the drop-off was.

I thought back to what Nora had said just before we parted today, "There's more to tell you about Pauline and her daughters—but it will take time."

No one—that is, not Jane, not Karen or Nora, or Haakonssen—had said Giselle and Jacqui were half-siblings, rather than full. I looked up Jacqui Richard and Jacqueline Richard on the Internet. There were a few Jacqueline Richards that looked like possibilities, but all of them were born in the States and lived here. Not a trace of a Jacqueline Richard in Vancouver B.C., though there was one in Montreal, twenty years old, who was too young. I also found a mention of a Québécois pianist and conductor by that name, but she'd been born in 1928, and would be over ninety. Maybe Jacqui had a different last name now, through marriage or choice.

I tried looking up Alain LeMoyne. All the links were in French, and there weren't many of them so many years after his death. He was unknown in the States except for the one novel that Pauline and Giselle had translated. He'd been well-regarded in France, but there were no interviews and precious little biographical information aside from an entry in a literary encyclopedia. He'd written five novels and quite a lot of literary criticism. In 1987-1988, when Pauline took Giselle to France for her sabbatical, LeMoyne would have been around forty-eight or forty-nine. The entry said he had been married twice. His second wife would have been alive when he died at age fifty. He apparently had no children.

I found one grainy photograph. He had a big nose and a grin, not a handsome guy, but perhaps more passionate that Dr. Pierre Richard back in Montreal. Did Jacqui resemble him? I'd only seen a photograph of her as a child in the photograph on the wall of the cottage in Newport. She didn't have a big nose, but then, young children rarely did. There would be a birth certificate somewhere in Montreal. Did I want to go to the trouble of looking for it? Even if Alain LeMoyne were Jacqui's true father, did that have any bearing on the case?

I searched for Jacqueline LeMoyne and found only the obituary of a woman who had recently died in Kentucky, a horse trainer.

Jacqui X. Supposedly living in Vancouver B.C., not close to either mother or sister. Karen had suggested that because Pauline was older when she'd had Jacqui, the girl was developmentally a little slow. Nora said Jacqui was difficult growing up, and Jane seemed to think she was unstable and unpleasantly angry now. What were the chances that Jacqui had masterminded the murder of Giselle—or for that matter, of both Pauline and Giselle?

Slim, I thought. She would have had to drive hours from Vancouver to Newport on Monday, murder her sister, then drive back to Vancouver to wait for a call from the police, then fly from Vancouver to Portland and rent the white compact and drive out to Newport to identify her sister. That meant she would have had to cross the border three times. Wouldn't that have been noticed?

Little of this made complete sense to me. I closed all the open search tabs and logged off. I was too far from whatever investigation might be going on in Newport, and I feared that all the question-asking I'd been doing in Portland was pointless. I was no closer to figuring out why Giselle had died. Sure, I could go back to the library and spend the evening reading Alain LeMoyne's novel and seeing if there were any clues there, but it might be awkward if Arlene was still there, after she'd more or less asked me out. I'd claimed I had a translation deadline.

Because I did have a translation deadline.

Outside it was raining hard. It was probably raining in London too, but I would rather be there. I felt very homesick for Nicky's terraced flat in Islington and for all the nearby take-aways and cafes and shops. For the two cozy chairs in the living room with reading lamps. Would I ever get back to London, and would Nicky be there when I finally did manage it?

On impulse I started writing her a letter, which grew rather long, about the case and why I was stuck in Portland and how much I missed her, and how I was afraid if she moved to Germany I would never see her again and then our long friendship would gradually disappear into nothing. Of course I didn't send it; Nicky and I didn't have the sort of relationship where we talked about our feelings for each other. We didn't have to say the obvious.

But across the miles that divided us, Nicky was sleeping—probably with the violinist Sally from Winnipeg in a charming flat in Berlin—totally oblivious to what I was going through. She wouldn't look at her email until tomorrow, if then. Why was I bothering?

I ended up just sending three sentences in the end, "Miss you. Miss London. Don't go off to Germany. Cheers, C."

I had barely begun to translate Chapter Four, "Colic," when the phone buzzed. My mind must have still been on the case, as I'd been describing it to Nicky, because I assumed it must be Nora, calling to urge me again to come to Newport with her. Without bothering to look at the number I answered.

"Oh. Luisa."

"Surprising news, my friend. I have found the solution to the problem of Giselle's death."

I thought she must be joking. How could she have possibly solved a murder from Montevideo?

"I'm sorry I haven't been in touch," I said. "But I did talk to Jane yesterday—Jane Janicki, the business manager—and we agreed to break the contract. She's going to write to Editorial Cielo shortly. Kim told me that you called her in Oakland, wondering about me."

"*Sí, sí,* I was trying to find you, because I was worried about your phone reception, if they had problems in Oregon. But I just had a call from Portland and Karen's voice was completely clear. Like in the same room."

"Karen—not Karen Morales?"

"Yes, who else? And she has found the answer. Can you guess?"

"*Estoy confundida.* I'm at sea." If Karen knew what happened to Giselle shouldn't she be calling Detective Haakonssen?

"She's starting a publishing company of her own, she decided. A bigger and more commercial business, not just translations, but all kinds of fiction. Especially the speculative and fantastic."

I was dumbstruck. The solution to Giselle's death, in other words, was the solution to Luisa's personal problem of losing her publisher. Even for Luisa, that was insensitive.

Luisa misinterpreted my silence. "You are surprised, I know. Because I spoke very harshly about Karen in Montevideo, when I saw the cover and the text of the catalog. But now we've had a wonderful conversation!" Luisa sighed expressively. "A meeting of the minds. She doesn't speak perfect Spanish but she knows a lot about Latin American literature. The names she brought out, the old forgotten names of writers of the imagination, amazed me. They take me back to my grandparents' library, my mother's childhood home, to the novels of Jules Verne, Robert Louis Stevenson, Mary Shelley that were translated into Spanish. And Argentinean writers. She has read Angélica Gorodischer, and she mentioned a book I remembered from childhood! *The Marvelous Voyage of Señor Nic-Nac,* from 1875. My grandfather had that same book. He liked science fiction very much. He had all the classics."

Luisa continued on enthusing in this vein, about authors I'd not heard of as well as authors she'd never spoken of during our long acquaintance. Suddenly, after years of her talking about Borges, Lispector, and Lacan, she was talking about space travel and Utopias. About Jules Verne and Señor Nic-Nac, whoever that was.

Meanwhile my mind churned with the implications of what Luisa was suggesting. If Cielo agreed to break the contract with Entre Editions and make a new contract with Karen's company, fine. But what if *I* didn't want to make a translation contract with Karen? Once again, Luisa, after essentially forcing me to act as her agent, was doing an end run around me. Out of the goodness of my heart I'd met with Jane Janicki and I'd been researching other American publishers. But work with Karen on *Unraveling Jupiter*?

I interrupted Luisa to say, "You know nothing about Karen. She comes from a tech background, she's new to publishing, she doesn't even have a name for her publishing company."

"Yes, she does. It's Planeta B."

"Catchy, but ..."

"Cassandra, you know I don't like it when you are sticking pins in my balloon. You are in Portland—you can talk to Karen. You'll see she is very serious."

"I *did* talk to her," I said. "This very morning, in fact. Besides, you hated the cover and the new title."

"Yes, I told her that. She is fine changing it to something else. More like a real picture of Jupiter and its moons."

I was reminded suddenly of Isaac Asimov.

"Luisa, I've been meaning to ask you something. Yesterday evening I was reading a book I bought here in Portland, and I had the strange feeling from time to time that some of the sentences I was reading were familiar from *Júpiter y sus lunas.*"

"¿Qué?"

"You don't think that in your mother's or grandfather's library, or somewhere in Rome you could have come across the work of Asimov?"

"A Russian?"

"An American science-fiction writer, very well known, and translated to many languages."

"*Querida,* what are you hinting about? That I stole his ideas? But I've never even heard of this Ass, this Asimov."

"Not the ideas, but perhaps, unconsciously most likely, you borrowed something of the language at times, and your title is similar. His title is *Lucky Starr and the Moons of Jupiter.* It's about Lucky Starr and his companion Bigman, and they have a creature with them that can read and transmit emotions called the V-frog. *La rana-V?*"

Now it was Luisa's turn to be silent, confirming my suspicion that long ago, perhaps so long ago she hardly remembered it, she'd encountered Asimov's little book in her grandfather's vaunted library. "I'm not saying you've plagiarized. Of course you can pass it off as post-modernist borrowing. Still, I'm wondering now that I've noticed it, if this is something we should talk about."

"The connection is bad," she said finally, in an artificially faint voice. "Cassandra, are you there? Okay, good-bye for now."

"Luisa, I only want to suggest that ... ." I realized I was talking to air.

Grumpily I went into the kitchen and pulled out the prepared pasta and vegetable salad I'd bought at the coop on the way back here from the library. The fusilli looked tired and the carrots and bell peppers pallid. In the freezer I found a box of Boca Burgers and decided to heat one of them up in the microwave. To my relief nothing started blinking or blew up.

Not a very inspiring dinner, but filling enough. It was about six and the rain was falling heavily and grayly, even though it wasn't yet dark. What to do now with my Friday evening? Aside from tending to the *Baby* and her colicky cough? In the absence of a message from Janneken today, I felt only anxiety that she hadn't liked what I'd sent her, or that she'd sent it off, without editing, to Angela Cook, or that I'd already been canned from the Chipping Witteron festival and that she just didn't have the heart to tell me.

Instead I logged back on to check email. There was a message from Karen Morales, perfectly friendly and civil, explaining that she'd called Luisa "just to chat. In the course of the conversation, which was fascinating by the way, I mentioned to Luisa that I was mulling over the strong possibility of starting a publishing company of my own. Luisa seemed enthusiastic about my plans. She said she'd talk with you. So, I thought I'd give you a heads up. Nothing is firm—all I have for the company is a name."

At the end of the message she pasted a link to an event at a bookstore on SE Hawthorne Boulevard. Karen and two other Latinas would be reading science fiction stories. "This is the reading I told you about. Would love to see you there!"

I noticed that one of the other authors was Ren Redondo. Could that be the partner that Dani had mentioned the other day at Powell's? Maybe short for Renate? The Ren who was getting a Ph.D. in Spanish Literature, writing a novel, and had recommended Luisa to Giselle?

Just as Karen would love to see me tonight (if only to swell out the audience numbers on a filthy Friday night), so would I love to see her again, mostly to ask more questions. If she was really serious, if she really had the money, if she would really take that ball of yarn off the cover ... perhaps it was the best solution? Not to Giselle's death, but to the perennial problem of finding a publisher for Luisa.

I could also press Karen a little more about why exactly she thought the deaths of Giselle and Pauline were related. And if Dani was there with Ren Redondo, I could ask Dani whether she'd talked to Haakonssen about the sand in Karen's SUV and what he'd said. He was clearly not going to call me back by the end of the work day.

I glanced at the clock and searched online for directions to the bookstore, dreading the thought of getting into the Subaru and finding my way across town in the evening traffic in the pouring rain. Then I saw that the number 15 bus could drop me off six blocks from the bookstore.

I pulled down all the blinds and grabbed my umbrella.

21.

By the time I managed to find my way to the little bookstore from the bus stop on Belmont, the first reading was already underway and there was standing room only. I squeezed along one side and found a spot against a bookcase of new and used fiction; Philip Roth dug into my lower back.

At the back of the store a young woman in an embroidered blouse and jeans was reading in a monotone, only raising timid eyes occasionally in what seemed like supplication: *Help, why I am here, please let this be over soon.* I couldn't follow the story very well, but I believe it had something to do with time travel to Mayan Mexico—but not the real Mayan Mexico, because they had self-driving cars.

But perhaps it was just me. The audience was sympathetic, and once or twice I heard a supportive murmur or friendly laugh. The bookseller asked for a round of applause for "Marí" as she threw herself into a chair between a gray-haired woman and someone I'd seen a good deal of this afternoon: Arlene Zink. The librarian bent her head towards Marí and whispered something probably very encouraging, and I was left a little embarrassed that I'd jumped to the conclusion Arlene had been trying to make a date with me. The older woman was probably Arlene's partner, and perhaps Marí was their granddaughter. Arlene had merely been trying to drum up another audience member, most likely.

I took the opportunity to shift my position and squeeze away from the book shelves to a place on the rug nearer the small lectern. Arlene saw me and gave me a look of surprise, and then a genuinely warm smile, which I returned with a nod to indicate that Marí had done well.

The second reader came up to the lectern: Ren Redondo. I'd already glimpsed her in the small crowd, sitting next to Dani. Tall, with slicked-back, short black hair, she wore a white vintage jacket and red bow tie with a red and blue flowered shirt. She had us in the palm of her hand as soon as she began to read, hardly looking at the pages. The dialog was witty, the tone ironic. I wasn't sure at first where the story was set except the future in another galaxy, but they did speak mostly Spanish there, of a Cuban-inflected variety. It turned out the planet had been colonized by Cuban doctors and mechanics, sent there because their health care was excellent and they were adept at making do with spare parts. The audience laughed at the jokes and applauded enthusiastically.

Lastly, Karen bounded up to the front, in an expensive but casual yellow print shirt, black leggings, and short boots. Bleached hair brushed and gelled, some eyeliner, dangling earrings. No lashings of green wasabi or tomato paste on her face, no reddened eyes. Karen thanked everyone and then began to read her own story, self-assured at first, and then more nervous, perhaps reacting to the puzzled expressions on several faces. This was the story about the wozens and transbottens. Realizing it was a little long to read in whole, she began to skip around, so that it became harder to follow. She made unnecessary explanations and ended abruptly, with an unconvincing laugh:

"Well, if you want to read the whole thing it's available online! And eventually it may turn into a novel. In addition to writing, I'm also planning to edit a new anthology of speculative fiction written by Oregon writers. And, while I'm at it, I want to take the opportunity tonight to let you all be the first to know about a new publishing venture, Planeta B. I think it's time we had a press that focused on the work of homegrown Latinx writers as well as Latin American writers."

There was some applause at this and Karen looked confident again. She glanced at me, almost affectionately, "Additionally I'm so pleased that tonight in our audience we have a Spanish-language translator who I very much hope will contribute to our efforts to bring speculative fiction from Latin America into our lives. Cassandra Reilly, wave your hand."

Reluctantly I raised my hand, as Karen went on to describe her anthology, "And/OR Latinx, the first collection of *Oregon*-based Latinx writers of sf." Karen welcomed submissions and spelled out an email address. She suggested people take a look at the Facebook page she'd set up. Was it possible she'd thought all this up just this afternoon? I had to admire Karen's chutzpah in coopting me into her marketing spiel. It certainly came naturally to her, perhaps more naturally than writing talent. She glowed, she smiled, and an aura of opportunity shimmered around her. Planeta B sounded like it was bound to be a huge success— why had no one thought about this before?

Or perhaps she just had a V-frog or two in her pocket, Venusian amphibians helping her create such a lovely sensation of well-being in the cozy bookstore with the rain drumming on the windows. Even I began to think that maybe Planeta B could be the very best thing that could have happened to me and Luisa. That *On Jupiter,* minus the yarn balls, could be a publishing sensation and that Luisa could for once be satisfied.

The reading seemed to be over, though the bookseller invited everyone to stay, browse, and have a glass of wine or juice from a table set up in the back. Karen encouraged those interested in talking with her about the anthology to meet up near the drinks, effectively sidelining the other two readers. Marí slipped out the door with the older gray-haired woman, Ren and Dani went to get glasses of wine, and Arlene made her way over to me.

"I'm so glad you could make it. I should have known you'd already be aware of the reading. Wasn't the second writer, Ren, just great? I could have heard her read for a bit longer."

"I thought the first reader did a very good job, too," I said. "There were a couple of bits about the self-driving cars in the Mayan pyramids that sort of distracted me."

Arlene shook her head, and lowered her voice. "I couldn't make head or tail of it actually. Marí is the granddaughter of my friend Dolores. This was her first public reading so we came to support her. I'm afraid she left kind of upset. The third reader—did you understand any of that stuff about the *wozens*? This Karen wasn't on the initial slate to read tonight. Marí is in a writers' group with her and says she's always throwing her weight around. Has a ton of tech money apparently."

Arlene was in the clothes she'd worn at the library; her toast-colored fleece jacket with a pale orange scarf around her neck brightened her brown eyes. She really had a wonderful smile; how was it possible for the corners of her lips to still tilt up after the usual amount of trouble and strife a woman faced in the world?

"Dolores and I have been members of the same book group for about twenty years," Arlene. "But we don't usually read science fiction, though I'd certainly pick up a book by Ren Redondo. Are you a fan? I know you've translated some books of magical realism in the past. And other things."

"I'm interested in non-traditional narratives," I said. "I'm Cassandra, by the way. Though I guess you know that since Karen pointed me out."

Arlene blushed slightly, confirming my suspicion that she'd looked me up online soon after I left the library. Maybe she'd gone deep into the Google mines and learned other things me besides the fact I'd translated Gloria de los Angeles. Yes, I'd been sniffing around the Internet for background on Pauline, Giselle, and Karen the last two days, but that was business—sort of. I suspected that a librarian had better research skills than I did and perhaps another motivation. She liked me, I was sure of it.

"Well ..." said Arlene. "I guess I should get going, unless you want to have a cup of tea somewhere? I meant to ask you since you came in looking sort of rained-on, do you have a car, do you need a ride anywhere, because I could ... I'd be happy to ..."

I didn't let her finish, even though a hot cup of tea or something stronger would be welcome at this point, and God knows I wasn't looking forward to trudging back to the bus stop on Belmont Ave through the driving rain. I supposed I could always call an Uber. I'd put the app on my phone, but I wasn't very adept at it. Yet I wanted to catch Dani and Ren before they left, and I knew I should talk to Karen as well. I didn't want to do that while asking Arlene to wait for me.

"Sorry," I said. "I see someone I know waving at me, and since I came here in part to talk to her I probably should go over."

Arlene turned her head and to my relief, Dani actually did give a wave. Ren was chatting with someone else.

"That's totally okay," she said, hiding her disappointment. "See you at the library if you're here a few days longer. Maybe we could go out for coffee or something then?"

"Lovely," I said, just to be agreeable. "I'll probably be around."

Ren and Dani made a stylish couple. Dani wore a sleeveless sheath dress that showed tattoos on both shoulders, while Ren—take away the red bow tie and flowered shirt, give her a corduroy jacket and black-rimmed glasses—had a more professorial look.

I said I'd enjoyed her reading and wondered if the story she read came from a longer work.

"I'm trying to write a novel." She flashed white teeth. "Like a lot of grad students I was under the mistaken impression that staying in school for years would give me a lot of free time. Not that I don't enjoy teaching. I even enjoy working on my dissertation when I get the chance. It's about Latin American science fiction, maybe Dani told you?"

I nodded. "And she also told me that it was you who recommended

Luisa's book to Giselle. Good taste! How did you hear about Luisa?" "Giselle and Jane were trying to expand the list, gathering names of writers from some different parts of the world. I happened to have read *Sombra de una mujer en la acera* and so I gave Giselle your translation to read. She loved it, as you know. So I told her Luisa had a new collection out and she asked me for a reader's report."

"Ten pages or something, wasn't it, Ren?" Dani emphasized. I noticed that she was glancing in the direction of Karen, now swigging some wine over by the table with a crowd around her.

Ren nodded. "I liked it a lot. I probably got a little carried away, since most of my reader's reports for Giselle were just a page or two. But I thought Luisa's style was very evocative, and her imagery, even when it was slightly over the top, was beautiful. And because I'm into science fiction, I talked about some writers from the Southern Cone who were influenced by or wrote speculative fiction, especially a few Argentineans: Borges, Bioy Casares, Luisa Valenzuela, Angélica Gorodischer. You know of Gorodischer, I'm sure. Ursula Le Guin was a big fan of hers and translated her novel, *Kalpa Imperial,* into English."

"Oh yes. Gorodischer," I said, though this English translation was news to me. On top of all her many achievements did Le Guin translate from Spanish as well?

"Did you say anything in your reader's report about Señor Nic-Nac?" I asked.

"Oh, probably, yes," said Ren. "Along with a Chilean novel published around the same time, in the 1870s, *Desde Júpiter,* by Francisco Mirelles. 'From Jupiter: The Curious Voyage of a Magnetized Man from Santiago.' Neither the Magnetized Man nor Señor Nic-Nac has anything do with Luisa, really, but it's an occupational hazard of graduate school to want to put in details for context. Or maybe just to show off."

"Did you say anything about Isaac Asimov?"

"I don't think so. Though he was pretty fascinated by Jupiter. Well, all those hard-science writers loved the planets, didn't they? Mars, Saturn, Jupiter. They knew enough to throw in all kinds of facts, at least the facts that were known then. Whereas modern sf writers tend to be a lot more interested in gender, race ..." I felt Ren might be sliding into a lecture, so I interjected, "What about *Lucky Starr and the Moons of Jupiter?* Any connection to Luisa's book?"

"His adventure series from the 1950s?" Ren looked puzzled as to where I might be going with this. "I wouldn't have thought Lucky Starr highbrow enough for Luisa. Unless she wanted to reference Asimov in some postmodern way."

"I've wondered," I said, "if Luisa might have taken lines or images from *Lucky Starr* and used them in her own work."

"Great galaxy!" said Ren, and her eyes lit up.

"I wouldn't call it plagiarism," I said. "Coincidence probably, or a vague memory."

"Or homage," suggested Ren. "I should take another look at her *Júpiter* and at Asimov's book. Fascinating!"

"The point *is*," interrupted Dani, "Ren wrote up a brilliant ten-page editorial review of Luisa's book and suggested to Giselle it would fit with Entre's list. As far as I understand, that's why Giselle contacted you, Cassandra. But then Karen starts working at the press and gets hold of Ren's editorial review, takes her ideas, and starts talking the book up as a cross-over title that could be marketed to a wider audience. I seriously do not believe that Karen has ever actually read Luisa's whole book or cares anything about it."

Away from the power of Karen's V-frog I supposed I shared Dani's opinion of Karen's serious interest in literature, but I said, "I should probably tell you that Karen called Luisa this afternoon and offered to publish *On Jupiter*. Luisa seems enthusiastic. It won't be my decision, but I wonder what you think? About Planeta B and everything?"

Dani started to answer, but Ren put a calming hand on her bare arm. "Karen certainly seems to have money," she said equitably. "I don't think she'll publish the same kinds of books Giselle and Jane did. But is a press focused on speculative fiction the worst new venture to pour your cash into? I'd say it could be a wonderful thing for Portland to have a publishing company with some financial resources."

"I wouldn't trust Karen," muttered Dani. "And if you think she's going to publish good literature—like your novel when you finish it—with this Planeta B, you're crazy. She's going to publish stuff about wozens and transbottens. It's all about her. Everything is. She basically pushed herself into this reading. Just called up the bookseller yesterday and said she wanted to be part of it. Swaggered in with a guy half her age and didn't say a word to me. Glared at me. After we'd been working together for months! She must have figured out I told the police in Newport about the sand in her car. Ren, don't get mixed up with her and this Planeta B thing."

Ren sighed. "We'll see, Dani. I don't like to make unnecessary enemies. I learned that from my relatives."

"You didn't learn that!" Dani sniffed. "Your dad still hates the Castros. And he was born in Los Angeles."

"Let's say I learned by example how I don't want to be."

"Well, I don't trust her. She's fake, she's duplicitous, she's ..."

"Cool down," said Ren. "Her spaceship is approaching."

Karen was indeed descending into our air space, with a glass of wine and an entourage of three younger people. "Ren, Ren," she said, completely ignoring Dani. "What a fantastic reading. You're brilliant, *mi amiga*. I laughed so hard. I want that story for my anthology."

Ren gave a gracious, though slightly distant reply, thanking her, and then, taking Dani's arm firmly, added, "Sorry we've got to duck out, Karen. Nice to meet you, Cassandra. Early classes and all that."

"Send me that story!" Karen called as they left. Then she gave me a big hug. "Thanks so much for coming, Cassandra. You're a true friend," she said, as if our last two meetings had merely involved social pleasantries. I noticed she didn't ask me how I liked her reading.

"I want you to meet my friends from the writers' group. Marí is in the group too, but I guess she's left. Ren comes sometimes, but she's so *busy* these days with her teaching and so on. What did you think of her story? I liked it, I didn't absolutely *love* it though. Because you know, Cubans, mechanics, a little obvious maybe? And that girlfriend of hers, Dani? Out of the goodness of my heart I trained her in publicity and then she turns on me. Anyway, here's Allie, Carmen, and Yash. Get to know each other and I'll be back after I talk with someone, and get a top-up. Maybe we can all go out together afterwards?"

They all looked to be in their twenties. I asked the group how they'd met Karen.

"Twitter," said Allie. "Karen is big in some science fiction circles."

Carmen added, "Ren was in our group, and somehow Karen heard about it and wanted to join. Then Karen asked Yash. Our one guy."

"I knew Karen through the startup," Yash said. I wondered if he'd been an intern. He appeared to be about twenty-two or three, slender and dark in a checked shirt and vintage sweater with pockets and elbow patches, distractingly good-looking, but also earnest, with big ears.

"Yeah, he and Karen made a mint when it was sold," said Carmen, and caught his eye. "So it makes sense that they like to hang out and talk about how to spend their money." She and Allie giggled and went off together to talk with someone else.

Yash seemed embarrassed. "I'm not one of those tech millionaires who's going to spend the rest of my life doing nothing just because I was lucky," he assured me. "I mean, someday I'll retire, like you, and just enjoy life. But right now I'm just exploring everything I can. Screenwriting, trapeze, architecture. I'll probably invest some money in Karen's new gig, now that we're involved."

"You're involved with Karen?" I couldn't help it that my jaw dropped, likely making me look even more elderly than I was. I was ashamed to say that I wasn't retired yet.

"Yeah," he said, trying not to look too utterly pleased with himself. "Look, I know she's a few years older. More experienced. But however long it lasts, it's cool."

And all this time I'd been assuming that Karen was not only a lesbian, but was having a serious affair with Giselle, serious enough perhaps to make Jane jealous and even murderous.

"I see," was all I could muster at first, then: "When did this happen?"

"Well," he confided, perhaps under the wrong impression that I was a close friend of Karen's, "it's just started. We've known each other for a few years, but I always thought she was way out of my league. So—Monday night actually. We hooked up after the writer's group. Had a couple more drinks at another bar and decided to go to the beach." Now he looked positively smug. "Collins Beach on Sauvie Island. You know," he added, since I still seemed clueless, "the nude beach. We stayed till the park closed. Then we spent a few more hours together. Well, until two a.m."

Which would, I suppose, account for the sand in the car.

Karen reappeared, the glass she'd topped off now almost empty again. "So, Cassandra," she began.

"So, Karen," I said. "I understand you spoke with Luisa today."

"Yes, and what a fascinating person!"

"She called me to tell me about your publishing company and your offer to publish her."

"Isn't Planeta B a great name?" Yash said. "Karen's been thinking about it for a long time. That's why she started to work for the other publisher, to make contacts and get experience, so she could strike out on her own."

"Yashi, be an angel and get a glass of wine for Cassandra. I see she's not drinking."

When Yash had left, Karen said in a lower voice, "Why shouldn't I start my own publishing company now Giselle is gone? Jane's made it clear I'm not welcome to continue with her. My suggestions were never popular. Jane just wanted to do everything in the most efficient way possible. 'We don't have the budget,' she was always telling me. 'It's not within our budget.' Well, fuck that. Now I decide. There will be no financial obstacles. There will be no one constantly holding up the SLOW sign, saying there's no money to implement good ideas. I have plenty of money and will make my own decisions."

Taking a leaf from Ren's book, about not creating unnecessary enemies, I said, "I know Luisa enjoyed speaking with you today. Of course she'll want to discuss your offer with her publisher, Editorial Cielo. I don't really have a say when it comes down to it."

"Yes, but you play a huge role, Cassandra," Karen turned on the charm again. "And you told me yourself that Jane was relieved when you suggested breaking the contract with Cielo. It's already translated and copyedited, and I've already put energy into writing publicity copy for it and researching the markets. This way, *Jupiter* could come out this fall. I'll just make a new contract with Cielo, and one with you."

She put her hand on my arm as if to pull me closer. "Don't worry about the translation fee. I'll pay you the same that Entre Editions was paying—more, if you like. I'd like to keep you happy, Cassandra. Maybe there are some other translations from Spanish, of science fiction from Latin America that you'd like to do? It could be a whole new opportunity."

Could I take advantage of this friendly mood to dig a little deeper into the question of Giselle's finances? "Well, I admire you—you certainly don't let grass grow under your feet. Though it must be really hard. I mean, if all this hadn't happened you'd be in Montreal this evening. It's such a beautiful city."

She looked pained for a moment. "Yes, I was looking forward to it. But like I told you, it wasn't some torrid romance. In fact, she wanted to go to Montreal for other reasons—something to do with a trust account that she could tap for funds. I'd told Giselle that I was willing to bail Entre Editions out of its current difficulties and invest more, but I wasn't going to do it unless I had the majority share. We weren't on the same page about that, in fact, we were arguing about it the last couple of weeks.

Finally I gave in when she said she'd put in another fifty thousand if she could keep control."

"Did she say more about the trust?"

"Not much. Just that Pauline and Giselle had set it up when Pauline had her mastectomy and chemo, to help Jacqui in case Pauline didn't make it. Giselle was the joint grantor for that reason. Giselle told me that Jacqui didn't need help now in the form of a trust. It was too complicated, Giselle said, and she wanted to talk to the bank about closing it down and setting up something easier for Giselle and Jacqui to access. I have no idea what the provisions were or how much was in the account. But obviously it was the source of the fifty thousand."

"Did Jane know about this account, do you think?"

"No, I don't think so. Otherwise Jane wouldn't have been so upset about the budget all the time." Karen looked into her empty wine glass and around for Yash, then lowered her voice. "The thing is, our friend Giselle wasn't an open book. At first I thought it was sort of intriguing, the woman of mystery with the cute French accent. But her secrecy started bothering me. Keeping secrets from Jane about the trust money. And her weirdness about her sister. There was definitely some secret about Jacqui. The last time I saw Giselle was in Portland a couple of weeks ago. She came to my condo for a meeting and then we went out to lunch. She wanted to stop by her bank too, and get something out of her safe deposit box. She got back into the car with a thick manila envelope and put it in her bag. I asked what it was, and she said, "This and that. Maybe a bargaining chip." I assumed it was something to do with Jane, but she wouldn't say more. I had to think—is this the kind of person I should be in business with? The way she treats Jane?" Karen's eyes narrowed. "But I'm a lot tougher than Jane. If you want to know the truth, I was actually starting to think that after New York and some fun in Montreal, I might just finish up publicizing the fall books, and move on. Do my own thing and just let her and Jane be."

Yash came up with a half glass of red wine in a plastic cup. "I scrounged the last of this. We'll have to go out." He gave Karen a hopeful look.

Karen had forgotten the wine was supposed to be for me and downed it in a gulp. "Yup, let's go." She smiled. "Yashi gave me a ride here, since I don't have my car back yet. What do you say, Cassandra? Is it a deal with Luisa's book?"

"I'm flattered that you want me on board, but as I said, it's Luisa and her Spanish publisher you need to talk to. But I'll put in a good word for you."

"Cassandra is the translator of that collection of stories I told you about, Yash, by Luisa Montiflores, the book about Jupiter. We're discussing Planeta B doing that translation, and maybe some other books in future."

"Wow," said Yash to me, "I guess you're not retired then. I mean, that's great you're still working."

"Don't mind him. He's twenty-seven, though he looks about eighteen. He's a total doll, but he thinks *I'm* old. No, I know you do." She put an arm around him. "I'll be in touch, Cassandra. Call me Monday. Once I've decided on a plan, I like to move forward as quickly as possibly."

"I do too," I said. "But it's good to be careful as well."

22.

The side streets off Hawthorne were dimmer now and the leafing trees over the cracked sidewalks dripped on my umbrella. Unfortunately, my cell had completely run out of juice due to poor planning, so I'd have to wait to check for phone messages until I was back at Jill and Candace's. But the lack of cell connection meant I couldn't call a ride, either. Never mind, it was just six blocks to Belmont Ave and the bus stop.

As I trudged along in the dark under my umbrella, I thought less about Yash's well-intentioned words about retirement (*If only and where and when??*), than his indiscreet confessions about the nude beach on Sauvie Island and whatever happened afterwards, possibly at Karen's condo. There was always the possibility that Karen had driven to Newport after their tryst, woken Giselle up, pushed her off the bluff, and driven home in time to be seen vacuuming out her SUV by Dani, but I considered that unlikely, given the time of Giselle's death. Even if it was possible that Karen had been using Yash as an alibi, there was still the writers' group from six to eight on Monday.

There was also the problem of Karen's motivation. If she really wasn't in a sexual triangle with Jane and Giselle, then the element of furious jealousy that can drive people to murder was probably missing. Perhaps the affair had only been a ploy on the part of Giselle and Karen to make Jane jealous and unhappy enough to want to leave the press, in which case Karen would buy her out. Unless Karen was lying, and I didn't think she was, she didn't want to invest without getting something in return. She hardly needed to kill Giselle to walk away from Entre Editions and start her own press.

Jane, on the other hand, was domestically and financially enmeshed with Giselle. She'd labored alongside Giselle to make the press a success and the result was that she'd spent all her savings and had had to get a bank loan to remodel the house to make the office that was probably Giselle's idea. And Giselle had repaid her by having an affair with Karen, by moving to the cottage, and by keeping secrets from her.

Would Jane have been angry enough at Giselle and Karen, after learning they were going to Montreal after the sales meeting in New York to kill Giselle? One thing was for certain, Jane had no alibi for Monday night that I knew of. And Karen did.

I set that line of inquiry aside for now, and considered what Karen had told me about the main reason for the trip to Montreal. Giselle wanted to talk with the bank about closing down the trust account and meanwhile she wanted to take out fifty thousand dollars so that she could keep control of Entre Editions. It sounded like Karen had thought about buying Jane out of the business, but perhaps some of the money from the trust would go to Jane. Was that the "bargaining chip" Giselle meant?

But what about Jacqui's right to the money? The trust had been created by Pauline and Giselle with the intention to help Jacqui. What kind of help had she needed that, according to Giselle, she didn't need any longer?

I thought about what Nora had told me this afternoon, the dates she'd given me. Jacqui was born in 1988, the same year Pauline divorced her husband, Pierre. Jacqui must be thirty-one now, ten years younger than Giselle. That meant that when Pauline moved to Portland Jacqui was only thirteen. Who was taking care of her? Giselle wasn't living in Montreal then. According to Nora, Pierre Richard didn't seem to have wanted to have anything to do with Jacqui aside from giving her his name at birth, but if he had put his name on the birth certificate, wouldn't he have had to pay child support? Five years after arriving in Portland Pauline had a second bout of breast cancer with surgery and intensive treatment. By then Jacqui would have been eighteen, still living in Montreal, I supposed. It made sense that Pauline had set up the trust in Montreal for Jacqui if Pauline believed she might die. She would have wanted to provide for Jacqui's future. Probably that was the reason that Giselle had ended up as a joint grantor. This was just speculation but maybe the trust was set up with money left from old Angus Lawson.

But Pauline didn't die. At least not right away. She'd continued paying into the account, and had obviously asked Giselle to continue as well. Could there have been some kind of agreement between Pauline and Giselle that Pauline would leave Giselle the house and cottage if Giselle kept paying into the trust fund and continued to take care of Jacqui in some way? Jane had told me that Jacqui would ask for money from time to time from Giselle. Had Giselle doled it out from the account? Did Jacqui even know she was the beneficiary and that there were thousands of dollars in the account, according to the statements Jane had found? What I'd heard about Jacqui wasn't reassuring. She was troubled, difficult, unstable, people said. Giselle had seemed to feel responsible for her. And yet, again according to Jane, Jacqui had been furious with her mother and sister. For something that had happened in the past?

Or for something that had happened more recently?

I wondered what Haakonssen made of Jacqui? I still thought she was the "person who has come forward to assist," but was she also a suspect? Should I let him know about my conversation with Karen, that one of the reasons Giselle was going to Montreal was to talk about closing this trust account down? That she had taken out some papers from her safe deposit box?

At the bus stop I waited under the shelter as the rain pattered down loudly. Yes, I'd call Haakonssen as soon as I got back to Jill and Candace's. It was possible that everything was close to winding up, and that I'd be arriving in Heathrow Thursday morning, taking the Tube to the Angel and a bus along Upper Street. Even if Nicky weren't back from Berlin, her familiar pillows, shawls, shoes, and magazines strewn about would be welcome reminders that I wasn't alone in the world.

A car came slowly alongside me and stopped. The driver peered across the passenger seat and then made a gesture to open the door. At my age shouldn't this kind of thing be long over? Then I realized it was Arlene Zink offering me a lift. I didn't think twice, but left the sidewalk for the street, opened the door and got in.

A fire crackled in the hearth. Arlene had lit it right after we arrived and now we sat in comfortable slip-covered armchairs on either side of the stone fireplace. She'd offered me a towel for my wet hair and slippers for my damp feet. She'd brought out a bottle of red wine and a few plates with crackers and hummus, fruit and fig bars, and put them on a small table between us. While she bustled back and forth from the kitchen, I looked around. Arlene's home was probably the same era as the wooden Craftsman houses belonging to Jane and the Sabine-Nobles, but it was less posh, with the original fittings. The furniture was older and didn't match, and the drapes were limp velveteen. The rugs were a bit threadbare over the original, scuffed wooden floorboards, and the light fixtures were an odd assortment, mostly old, but with newer reading lamps introduced by the sofa and chairs. There were books everywhere, on shelves, on the floor, in boxes by the door on their way to a new home somewhere. It reminded me of friends' homes in the English countryside, except that it was much warmer.

"This neighborhood in Southeast is where all the alternative types rented or bought houses back when," she told me, sitting back in her chair. "They didn't cost much then. Natalie, my partner, and I bought this house together. We lived here for almost thirty years. We always thought we'd remodel it a bit, but mostly we just gardened. The lot is oversize. Nat loved her veg garden. I try to keep it up."

An older tabby wandered in and ignored us, but lay down on a cat bed near the fire. "Vita," said Arlene. "She's almost eighteen. She had a sibling, Virginia, but she died a couple years ago. Nat died five years ago."

Not a hold-out against marriage then, but a widow.

"I'm listening," I said.

They'd met in college and had been together ever since. The first bout of breast cancer came soon after they bought the house, when Nat was only in her thirties. It reoccurred in her mid fifties; she fought it for two years and died at fifty-seven.

Arlene didn't have to go into much description. I'd seen it and known it in my own friendship circles, inner and outer, from London to Melbourne to Santiago.

Arlene put another log on the fire. "I had to take a leave from the library at the end. Afterwards—there was a lot to do as well. Suddenly I looked up, and I was living alone." She smiled when she saw my face. "No need for pity. I've continued working, of course. I'm involved in progressive politics, supporting women running for office. I read a lot, see friends, have season tickets to concerts and plays. My sister's not far away, in Seattle. She and her husband have a daughter and son and grandkids there, so I always have somewhere to go for the holidays. Friends sometimes introduce me to other women, but nothing has clicked. I never really dated women before I met Nat, so I'm not that good at flirting."

That accounted, perhaps, for the awkward hovering at the library.

She smiled ruefully. "Why do I have the sense that your experience has been entirely different?"

"It's true," I admitted. "I don't have a partner, never have. I suppose

I had enough domestic closeness when I was growing up to last me a lifetime. Most of that intimacy involved people shouting at each other— in a friendly way. There wasn't anything violent, just the usual swat from my mother to settle a fight between siblings. There were a lot of us. My dad died when I was in high school. We didn't have much money. I shared a room with two of my sisters, Maureen and Nell. Our oldest sister, Eileen, had a tiny little room of her own. I longed for nothing more than to have a room to myself, an hour to myself in that house, without someone commenting on my appearance or my behavior. When I was older I wanted a lot more than an hour. I wanted a day, a week, a lifetime just to think my own thoughts and do whatever I wanted. I wanted to be wild, adventurous, and independent. Selfish, that's what I wanted to be, and women aren't supposed to be selfish."

"It doesn't sound selfish at all," she said. "But perhaps, it's been lonely sometimes?"

"Now and again," I said. She seemed to be waiting for me to say more, so I went on. "I know it looks like I might be a loner, but that's not really the case. I have a network of friends and colleagues. Of course, I don't see everyone frequently. We talk though, and write. Some of them are authors I translate."

"And you're okay with that? Just seeing friends occasionally? What if you get sick? Who do you call on?"

"A doctor. I know a couple of nurses, though. My oldest friends in Europe are in Spain. And there's Nicky, in London. I have a room at her place."

"You rent from her?"

"Sort of. We've been pals for years. Sometimes I don't see her for months at a time. She's talking about moving out of London, even out of England. But I hope she doesn't. For one thing, I wouldn't have a place to crash when I'm in London. But for another, well, I'd miss her a lot. We're sort of like family, we've known each other so long. She's a really good friend."

I went silent. Who was I kidding? Nicky was not sort of like family. She *was* family. I depended on her. I needed her to be there. I loved her like a sister. And I was crushed to think that she could ever think of moving and leaving me behind.

Arlene poured me more wine. "Well, to good friends then!"

★

I woke to the sound of chickens. Urban chickens contentedly clucking and scratching outside the window. Morning sun poured onto the queen bed with a quilt in a purple-and-white diamond pattern. The sheets were lilac, and the pillows were many. I remembered, after a few disoriented seconds, that I wasn't in the guest room, but in Arlene's bed, where we'd ended up after that bottle of wine.

"Good morning! Coffee?" she said from the doorway, holding out a steaming mug. "Or would you rather have tea?"

She was in a robe and slippers, and her hair was damp from a shower. I remembered that at one point last evening she'd said, "You can sleep here, if you want. I have a guest room." And since by that time—midnight—asking her to drive me back to Northwest Portland might be rude—I'd said fine.

And it had been fine, better than fine. This morning she had a grin on her freckled face, so I suspected it had been fine for her too.

Over a relaxed breakfast, which was an omelet from eggs she'd collected this morning from her hens, Arlene told me that she was free today and if I wanted, she could show me around Portland. There was a Saturday Market for farmers and artisans, walks by the Willamette River, a Japanese teahouse and garden, and in the evening the Living Room Theater, where you have a meal while watching first-run films.

By my second cup of coffee, more memory was returning in bits and pieces, of two bodies together, of her eagerness and uncertainty, my surprised pleasure. I told her that I'd love to see more of Portland, but I should find my phone first. I'd plugged it in when I got to Arlene's house last night, but with one thing and another had forgotten to check for missed calls.

There were three voice messages. Detective Haakonssen first, returning my call at seven-thirty last night. He apologized for the lateness and said he would be available Saturday and would like to speak to me. He'd be at the station all day. If I could possibly come to Newport, he and Sergeant Jones were re-interviewing a few people about the case.

The second call had also come in the previous evening, fifteen minutes after Haakonssen, from Nora. She was being recalled to Newport Saturday, she said "because of the investigation." Tom Hoyt would be meeting her there from his place up the coast. And she would very much like me to drive with her so she could talk to me and get my opinion about a few things. Maybe I could give her some advice. She added that she'd booked me a room at the Sylvia Beach, and not to worry about the cost. She'd also see that I got back to Portland on Sunday.

The third call had come this morning, around eight. Nora sounded a little harried, almost curt. "Hi, thought I'd hear from you. Anyway, I'm heading out now, so I can't take you along with me. It's just a lot easier to talk about things in person. So, if you can manage it, come to Newport. See you, I hope."

I was uncertain what to make of all this: I could understand that Haakonssen might want to re-interview me. I had been in the cottage at ten, an hour before Giselle's body was found, and I had arrived in Newport the previous evening, around the time she had been killed. But why was he summoning Nora Longeran? Why did Nora need a lawyer with her for these interviews?

I decided to wait to speak to Haakonssen until after I'd talked to Nora and had gotten a sense of what this was about, but when I called her, her phone went to voicemail. I said I'd be in Newport as soon as I could, I had some things to take care of first.

Arlene had cleared the table and was putting dishes in the dishwasher.

"I'm sorry, I don't think this is going to work out," I said, adding "I mean, the wonderful things you've planned. I've got to go back to the coast today, to talk to people. It's in connection with Giselle's death."

"I'll give you a ride back to Jill and Candace's," she said.

So I must have mentioned them last night, that's right: Arlene had told me she knew them well, they'd once been in a women's health collective together. She had gone to two of their weddings.

I opened the door of Jill and Candace's house and turned to wave, but Arlene was already gone. She'd surprised me on the drive here when I'd begun gently to explain myself, to make her understand that it wasn't *her,* it was that I was just generally unable to make commitments. And besides, I didn't even live in the States and didn't know when I'd be back, especially to Portland.

But as it turned out, she didn't really seem to care. "No need to apologize," she said, rather unnervingly cheerful. "You came along at just the right time. I was in a marriage so long I'd forgotten what fun sex could be. And the great thing is, you don't live in Portland, so it won't be embarrassing if you come into the library. There can't be any expectations. I won't even see you again!"

"Oh," I said. "And here I was imagining, if it turns out I have to stay in Oregon a bit longer ..."

Self-interestedly, it had occurred to me that Arlene might provide the hospitality that I would not enjoy from Candace and Jill when they returned.

She didn't take the bait, so I quickly added, "But I'm sure I'll be on the plane to London Wednesday. Or soon after."

"I never had a one-night stand before." She was quietly beaming. "And now a kind of block has been removed."

"Happy to have helped with that," I said. But I gave her the kind of kiss I hoped she'd remember.

Inside the house, I threw everything into my bag and wrote a note to the Sabine-Nobles. I'd debated whether to Skype Candace and had decided against it. With any luck I'd be back by Monday morning at the latest and they'd never know I had left the house abandoned, with the blinds down.

At the last minute I opened the Audible app on my phone and downloaded the audio version of one of Nora's books in her series. Not the first one, but the third novel in *The Lands Beneath the Sea*, with Inkster playing a significant role.

Message in Ink.

Finally around eleven I was in Dora's Subaru again, stopping only for gas on the way out of Portland, heading west.

23.

The drive to Newport was made shorter by listening to *Message in Ink,* even though sometimes I lost the thread of the plot when a semi-truck roared past me. The traffic to the coast on a Saturday morning was brutal at first, but eventually it quieted down and the voice of the audio narrator worked its magic.

The summary of events in the previous two novels was woven into the first chapter. Briefly, Aggie and Rognvald had set out one bright August morning from their home on the island of Unst to check on the small flock of sheep that their parents kept there during the summer months. Aggie was ten and Rognvald twelve. They'd made the trip two or three times before on their own this summer, and often in earlier years with their mother, a champion rower. But they had never made the crossing in a storm, and a storm is just what blew up suddenly soon after they'd pushed off shore for the return journey. That was the last they knew of the Dryland.

It wasn't clear to me whether Aggie and Rognvald had drowned—of course they had to have drowned—and whether the book told a consoling myth like many of those myths from the North Atlantic and other maritime cultures, of humans who continue to live beneath the sea in villages and cities very similar to those on earth, in houses made of stones and shells, and farmyards made up of seahorses and sea cows. Sirini the mermaid gave them a potent drink of rare ingredients that turned their ears into gills. Now they could breathe underwater, but they couldn't hear, nor could they speak with their mouths. Instead, Aggie and Rognvald learned to communicate with the help of a giant octopus, who could read their thoughts and those of other creatures, translate them into English and write them out in ink.

The plot of *Message in Ink* concerned a Norwegian ship carrying a princess fleeing enemies of her father, the King of Norway. I wasn't sure if this was a princess of olden times, or a more modern royal escaping from the Nazi occupation of Norway, since there seemed at one point to be an underwater submarine that shot a large hole in the side of the ship. Needless to say, Inkster, with the help of Aggie and Rognvald, saved the princess from drowning and managed to get her to the Scottish coast.

Rain had spattered my windshield outside of Portland, but by the time I pulled into the parking lot of the Sylvia Beach, the sky was a windy blue with only a few dark and distant clouds to the west over the ocean.

"We've booked you into the Melville room," smiled the receptionist. "There was a last-minute cancellation, so your friend Nora was pleased. Usually we're full on weekends."

I asked about Nora, and the receptionist said she had gone out but she'd left me a note, so obviously she'd gotten my message that I was coming to Newport.

"Off to my favorite place," she'd scribbled. "See you later."

I was on the third floor, next to the library, in a room with a nautical theme—and a lot of whale paraphernalia. Etchings and paintings of sperm whales, framed, on the walls. A massive bed and dark furnishings, a comfortable-looking chair facing north, in the direction of Giselle's cottage. I thought about walking along the beach to the bluff where she'd fallen. I also thought about heading immediately to the Newport police station to talk to Haakonssen. But my curiosity about what Nora wanted to tell me was too great and I went back downstairs.

I wondered where Nora's favorite place was—a café most likely—and was planning to ask the receptionist about coffee places in the neighborhood when she finished her personal conversation on the phone. But then, in a stand of tourist literature, I saw a brochure for the Oregon Coast Aquarium. Hadn't Nora said an octopus in Newport had given her the inspiration for Inkster? In fact, hadn't she told me last Sunday that after walking by Pauline's cottage and noticing Giselle in the window, she'd gone to the aquarium, to her *favorite place*?

The brochure had a map; the aquarium wasn't right in town, but south on 101, across Yaquina Bay, over the same bridge I'd crossed last Monday night in the fog and dark and mist coming into Newport. Ten minutes later, I was in the parking lot.

One of the appeals of large public aquariums is their dimness, along with their tang of fish and salt. The entrance is like walking through the portals of sleep, into a dream, and these buildings are often designed like the curl of a nautilus shell, with spiral corridors that take you below ground, so that you can see the fish from different levels: the circling sharks and sea turtles shooting through glinting daylight, the schools of magical yellow and blue fish, thin as paper, the showy blossoms of the anemones, down to the sandy floor where the night sky is inverted with starbursts of ochre and purple in splendid repose.

The Oregon Coast Aquarium did this immersion in the ocean sensation one better, with a huge, clear acrylic tube for visitors to walk through, traversing a series of massive tanks. Schools of silvery sardines swam above and below in one tank, while sharks and manta rays cruised purposefully in another. I wondered if the aquarium's architects and designers had read the Sea-Breather series.

I looked for Nora in rooms with tidal creatures washed by periodic artificial tides, pink and green anemones fluttering their tentacles, orange and purple sea stars. I passed by moon jellies bobbing and blowing in a large clear column of seawater and a tank of sea pens—a sort of coral with a feathery stem that withdraws into its foot, buried in the sand, in case of danger.

Finally I wandered outside into an aviary of puffins and auklets. The sky was darker now, the wind continued. No sight of Nora anywhere. Then I saw the sign pointing to the "octopus cave," and there outside, on a brown cement bench built into a series of rounded cement structures with openings, was Nora, tapping on her phone. As in Portland she was unobtrusive in a jacket and jeans, wearing sneakers and a ball cap, with her white braid over her shoulder.

"Oh, you found me," she said, but she didn't seem surprised. "Just a sec. Have a seat."

She finished what seemed to be a text message and pressed *send*, then stood and stretched. Where was the urgency I'd felt from her on the phone this morning?

"I'm sorry I wasn't available last evening," I began. "But I did get your message. It seemed like Detective Haakonssen wanted to talk with you. He left a voicemail for me too, to come to Newport if I could. So here I am. What's up?"

"Did you see the octopus yet?" she asked.

"Sorry?"

"She's not in the main aquarium, if you were looking for her there." She gestured for me to follow her into the barely lit cement caves. Even though I found it hard to imagine that Nora had designs on my life, she was making me a little nervous. She repeated impatiently, "Come on, it's fine. She's behind glass, in her own tank, here inside the caves."

"That pinky-orangey thing?" I couldn't help exclaiming, "looking like a very large, shriveled peach? *That's* a Giant Pacific Octopus? I thought they were huge. Where are all the tentacles?"

"Sort of tucked up somewhere at the moment I expect. Lucy's shy. She just came on exhibit a few months ago. She's relatively young, but growing fast. They don't have a long life span, and the aquarium replaces them usually after two or three years. Since they're native to the Pacific Ocean here, they release them in the same area they found them, so they can mate. Male octopuses usually die very soon after mating. The females lay their eggs and get them going in life, then they die."

I nodded. Still, I mentally complained: the octopus I'd imagined from just listening to the audio version of *Message in Ink* had seemed far more substantial than this bulbous, soft-suckered, glass-clinging sea creature. I peered closer and saw a lidded dark eye appearing to stare back at me from what was, I supposed, the head.

"Lucy is friendlier one on one. But she's no match for the octopus they had last year. Cleo would reach out and touch your arms, kiss them with her suckers." Nora grinned to see my face. "Really it's quite an amazing experience to connect with an intelligent animal with a consciousness so different from ours. Most of the neurons are in the tentacles."

"I read an interview with you on the Internet, about the origin of the series. Did you get the idea for Inkster as a translator here?"

"No, no. It was in the library near my house. I was reading lots of books on underwater myths of the North Atlantic and on marine animals. In the first couple of books in the series, Inkster was sort of a minor character. I hinted that she might be malevolent, a daughter of the feared Kraken. I did have the idea that her ink should play a role as writing somehow—sort of the oceanic equivalent of invisible ink—but it wasn't too developed at first. It was at the end of book two that Aggie and Rognvald figured out that Inkster was trying to communicate with them, and that she was skilled at many languages. It was right around then that Pauline, who was now a translator, came back into my life. You remember, I told you yesterday, when I went to Montreal and met her husband and Giselle, before she went to Paris?"

Okay, now we were getting somewhere. I was about to push her to tell me the whole story of Pauline and her daughters, when a volunteer walked by who seemed to know Nora well. They exchanged a few words about the social butterfly Cleo who was now swimming and mating somewhere off the coast. While they spoke the current show-and-tell cephalopod Lucy unfurled a tentacle, tentatively, down the side of the glass. I had a strange feeling she was reaching out to me, and I pressed my hand against the glass.

After the volunteer left, Nora said, "Early on I was criticized about the messages in ink that Inkster writes with her arms. First of all, I was slammed because I called them arms, and then you know, the ink comes from a sac, not from the tentacles. I responded defensively by reminding everyone that this was a fantasy. But of course now I really wish I'd taken more care with the actual biology and known about some of the research that's come out more recently about the ways that cephalopods telegraph messages on their skin with color and pattern. Really, I should have made Inkster a large cuttlefish, with a big body resembling a sort of computer screen."

"As a translator," I said, "I think the octopus and ink captures more of the actual experience of translating. Trying to grasp at meaning that's continually dissolving.

"Speaking of which," I turned to face her, "I really wish you would tell me what's going on. I drove three hours to see you because you asked me to and because I'm getting a bit desperate to make my flight on Wednesday. Is there a reason for all this mystery? Because I could have been having a really pleasant day at the Saturday Market in Portland with a charming and well-read librarian."

Nora nodded, "It's complicated. Even though I *want* to talk about it. Let's go visit the sea otters."

I couldn't help myself. I waved to Lucy, hoping her one waving pinkish white tentacle might wave back. For a moment she reminded me of Jupiter, imagined as a ball of pinkish-orange wool, with a stray strand of yarn signaling our connection. Then she drew her arm close and was just a remote, wrinkled-up peach again.

A few moments later Nora and I stood in front of a large outdoor tank with a few sea otters frisking and swimming by. Fur glinting with water and sun, they flipped onto their backs and then dove below, where you could half-see them through the glass.

"I appreciate you coming back to Newport," she said, her eyes on the otters. "I thought it might be easier to explain here, where so many things happened, starting with Pauline."

Now she had my attention.

"I told you that Pauline and I lost touch, the way people do when their paths diverge. But I was the one who deliberately let the friendship go, mostly from embarrassment at comparing myself to her. At first, when I was twenty, it was fun to have a friend in Paris. I loved her aerograms and the photos she sent of herself by the Seine. Usually with some good-looking guy gazing soulfully at her. She was my glamorous friend who was studying in Paris. Then she wrote she wasn't coming back. She was going to stay and study at the Sorbonne. Right about that time I became pregnant and dropped out of college, got married, had a child, then another. My husband, who had once given me soulful looks too, left me to live in a commune in New Mexico with the new love of his life. I stopped answering Pauline's letters, and when I didn't write back, she stopped too. I didn't know she'd moved to Montreal until the early seventies, when I got a Christmas card. By that time I'd written a couple of fantasy stories and had gotten them published, and that gave me a little confidence. Then one day I came across a book in the library about Scottish legends of the sea, and I started writing *The Sea-Breathers*. That changed everything."

"How old were you by then?" I had been staring at the sea-otters, zooming underwater and popping up again, to shake their fur in our directions.

"Around thirty-two. My kids were nine and eleven. Great kids, funny, good students. They helped me find time to write, cheered me on. Always. I mean, I couldn't have been luckier. To my surprise, I got a three-book contract. I was able to quit my job and buy a car, and eventually I bought a house. If I thought of Pauline much, it was mainly a sort of 'So there,' feeling. All I really knew about her, from another Christmas card, is that finally she'd had a baby, Giselle, in 1978."

Nora paused a moment and wiped away a drop or two of salt water that had splashed on her face. She went on, "Years later, she told me she'd been upset I broke contact with her. That she'd missed me. That she'd followed my career and had wanted to call me when she visited her parents in Portland over the years. She thought I was angry at her, and she was right. A friendship needs to be equal in some way. As far as I knew, Pauline had had an easy life, always getting what she wanted.

"Then, one Christmas, 1986 I think, I got a letter from her. She'd heard I was one of the main speakers at a children's book festival in Toronto in February. She told me how proud she was of me. How she'd love to see me, if my trip took me through Montreal. I decided to visit her. It was like we'd never been parted. There was so much to say. We talked about our school days and what had happened since, and about writing and books and translation. I could see pretty quickly Pauline wasn't happy, even though she was really attached to Giselle, who would have been about eight or nine."

"Her marriage wasn't a good one?"

"Pierre was an arrogant bastard. They lived in a beautiful apartment, but he was hardly around and when he was, she was nervous. By then Pauline had an established career as a translator, but he treated her like a house servant. She was excited to tell me she'd gotten a fellowship to go to Paris for nine months to work on translation, starting in August. I got the impression she was longing to be free. She told me she planned to take Giselle with her, so Giselle could go to a French school and be immersed in real Parisian French. This time, I wasn't jealous to think of her in Paris, I was glad for her."

"And from then on, you kept in touch?"

"Yes, the letters from Paris resumed. There were lots at first, about writers she was meeting, publishers and editors, parties and dinners. Projects she was being asked to undertake. If she'd had her druthers, I suspected, she would have just stayed in Paris, but she returned to Montreal. A few months after she returned she had a second child, Jacqui. And within six months she was divorced."

"So Jacqui was not ... ?"

"Not Pierre's child, though he did allow his name to be on the birth certificate to spare them both the scandal. He paid child support, as little as he could get away with. He could have helped raise Jacqui. But he refused. He turned against Pauline, would only communicate through a lawyer. Pauline got the apartment and support for Giselle."

"Who was the father?" I asked, already knowing the answer.

"A writer she was working with, Alain LeMoyne."

"Did Pauline love him?"

"Oh, she was madly in love with him. Now that we were close friends again, I heard all about it. But unfortunately he was married. He promised Pauline he'd leave his wife, but that didn't happen, though eventually he told the wife about Pauline and the child. This drama went on for well over a year. The birth, the divorce, long-distance phone calls, promises from Alain that he'd move to Montreal, Pauline's plan to move to Paris with the girls even if he couldn't divorce. Then, suddenly, Alain dropped dead in Paris of a heart attack. He was only fifty."

"And after that," I suggested, "Pauline raised Jacqui on her own, but perhaps without the love she should have given her daughter?"

Nora nodded, but before I could ask her if she knew anything about a trust account that Pauline could have set up for her younger daughter, her phone buzzed, and she looked at the text message. "Hmm, okay," she said to herself, but made no reply.

"It's hard to share some of the rest of the story," she said slowly, turning away from the sea otter tank and finally looking at me. "It's about Jacqui."

I made a guess. "Was that Jacqui sending you a message?"

Nora nodded. "She's here in Newport, yes. I was asked to come to Newport to talk with Haakonssen again. Tom Hoyt was with me this morning. Just routine. The detectives are re-interviewing everyone who knew the Richard family well. But the other reason I'm here is because of Jacqui. She wanted to meet me and I thought I should. We're going to have coffee later this afternoon."

"Why would she want to meet you?"

"I was her mother's oldest friend." Nora evaded my look. "She has some questions. About her mother. Giselle seems to have never really told her what happened to Pauline, and didn't invite her to the funeral."

"But as far as I understand Jacqui wasn't close to either Giselle or her mother. Why does she want to talk about Pauline? Isn't it Giselle she should be wondering about? It's just last Monday that Giselle fell."

"I don't know," she said. "I go around and around in my head about what might have happened to Giselle, and whether Jacqui could possibly be involved. It seems so unlikely. But then, I've never met her."

"Did you get the impression she's emotionally unhinged?"

"No," said Nora. "We only spoke briefly and then texted. I had told Haakonssen he could give Jacqui my number."

"What does Haakonssen think about all this?" I asked. "He's certainly met Jacqui by now."

"He didn't say."

"No, he never really does, does he?" I was reminded that I was supposed to go to the police station again myself. I would do that soon.

At least in Nora's case it seemed like the interview had been just routine. Who else would he be talking to besides me? Jane? Karen? Jacqui?

Nora began walking away. "Let's go somewhere else. After a while of looking at the otters, I only begin to feel sad. Even though they zoom around so delightfully, they're still in a tank and not in the ocean."

24.

I followed her to a platform overlooking the estuary of Yaquina Bay. It was humid now, and the sky had a gray and purple tinge that cast a shadow on the reeds and water-logged tree branches along the banks below us. The surface of the bay rippled in a strong westerly breeze.

As we'd walked here along a nature trail to get away from some of the crowds, Nora had said, "I know I'm taking up your time. But it would help me to tell someone about Jacqui before we meet later."

"I could come with you," I offered right away. "You shouldn't be alone, I mean, just in case she gets upset or something. Jane told me that Jacqui was in a terrible state, hostile and accusing, when they met up in Portland two days ago."

"We're meeting in a public place," said Nora. "That café on Third near the Sylvia Beach. I should be all right. Why was she angry?"

"Jacqui told Jane that she didn't want to have a memorial service for her sister. That Giselle didn't deserve it. There were other things too, but Jane didn't pass them on to me. It sounded like Jacqui was carrying a lot of trauma from her childhood."

"It was traumatic for Pauline too, for a lot of people," said Nora. She hung over the side of the railing and watched a redwing blackbird. Her white braid looked yellow in the sunlight and again there was that sense she was both old and wrinkled and somehow young, swinging her foot a little.

"I don't know if it was Pauline's age when she had Jacqui, or just her depression about losing Alain, but they didn't bond. Pauline wrote me that Jacqui was emotionally off somehow. Tantrums and crying spells, wet her bed until she was five, refused to eat, slow to learn. Pauline had to deal with that as a single mom, and then she had her elderly parents to cope with. Mother with diabetes, father fading into dementia. So on top of everything else Pauline had to fly back and forth to Portland. I'd see her when she was in Portland and she was a worn-out wreck, trying to take care of everyone. Pauline tried to make it all work by hiring a nanny for Jacqui in Montreal."

"And did that help?"

"Too well," said Nora. "Because pretty soon Jacqui only trusted the young nanny, Suzanne. She probably felt that Suzanne loved her more. She certainly behaved a lot better with Suzanne. Whatever maternal feelings Pauline might have had for Jacqui got weaker and weaker. At first Suzanne lived with Pauline and the girls in their apartment. But eventually Suzanne married and had a place of her own, and they all got into the habit of letting Jacqui stay over at Suzanne's quite often. Suzanne got pregnant and had a child that Jacqui loved, at least when it was an infant. Suzanne had another child later. By the time Jacqui was thirteen, she was living full-time with Suzanne and her family. That's when Pauline left her to move to Portland."

"Pauline moved to Portland without Jacqui," I repeated. That squared with what I'd guessed. "Where was Giselle by the way?"

"She'd finished university in the States, in Boston, then took a year or more off and traveled. Lived in France for a while, then went back to Boston to work as an editorial assistant for a literary publisher. She had a life of her own. I don't know if Giselle played any role in what went on with her half sister, but she was no longer in Canada when things went so wrong for Jacqui."

Nora paused, and stared down into the murky waters of the estuary below. "You have to understand Pauline's dilemma. There were no easy choices, especially since Jacqui wanted to stay with Suzanne. I have to *believe* Pauline felt she was leaving Jacqui in good hands."

"What happened?"

"Adolescence. Drugs. Lack of supervision. Suzanne's husband went off to Edmonton to work in the oil industry and Suzanne had two active young kids. A lot of Jacqui's earlier attachment problems resurfaced—maybe she felt that she was experiencing the same rejection she remembered as a child from Pauline. Anyway, she ran away and when she was finally located she had a drug habit and was seven months pregnant. She was only sixteen. It was too late for an abortion, obviously. She was really in bad shape, and Pauline ended up having to put her in a clinic for adolescents with mental health issues. She stayed there until she was eighteen. Suzanne was devastated and wanted to take Jacqui and the baby back, but Pauline refused and since Jacqui was a minor and sort of out of her mind for a while, Jacqui didn't have a say. The baby was adopted out."

Nora's face in profile was somber. "I'm not saying she did the right thing. But the doctors told Pauline that it would be dangerous for the baby to be alone with Jacqui. So the choices were that Pauline would need to become the baby's legal guardian, or that the baby would need to go into foster care, or be given up for adoption. There was support, even pressure, for Pauline to let the baby 'have a chance in life,' as they kept saying."

"This was all going on soon after Pauline moved permanently to Portland?"

"Yes." Nora looked over at me for the first time. I could see more clearly that her eyes were red with unshed tears. "I knew the whole story, but I didn't get involved with her decisions, just tried to support her in other ways. I told you at first about all that envy I used to have toward Pauline? It was gone. Vanished. I saw for the first time what bad luck and suffering really looked like. It was just one thing after the next. Alain's death. The divorce. Jacqui a runaway, then pregnant and addicted and half crazy. Jacqui's baby. Pauline's father losing his mind and finally dying. Pauline's rounds with breast cancer treatment."

"It seems hard to imagine that on top of everything else," I said.

"Yes, though she said, especially after the mastectomy, that it clarified the important things in life. I got the feeling that she'd made her peace with Jacqui. They were estranged, but at least Jacqui's child was being cared for by loving parents. The couple lived in Montreal. Meanwhile Pauline became closer to Giselle; she was grateful that Giselle moved to Portland and into the house. They began to work on translations together and Giselle made connections with the literary community. She worked as a freelance copy editor along with translating. Pauline was so proud of Giselle. And it meant the world to her that she could share her love of translation with her daughter—with that daughter anyway."

"And Jacqui?"

"Gradually Jacqui seemed to get better. At eighteen she left the clinic and lived in a group house for a while. She didn't go to college but she managed to pass a high school equivalency test and started taking art classes. She fancied herself an artist. But I gather that she struggled. Pauline was sometimes in contact with her, sometimes not. Jacqui didn't use hard drugs anymore, Pauline said, but she hung around with people who weren't good for her. She didn't have the best relationships with men. Sometimes Pauline helped her financially even beyond the trust fund."

"Tell me about that trust. How did she fund it to start with?"

"The last of her father's money. I mentioned the stocks. Some of them did pretty well. Pauline sold everything to set up the trust. It was for Jacqui's further education should she want to go back to school, but also for her ongoing support if needed. Pauline didn't give me figures, but she was adamant Jacqui be taken care of in case she died. Giselle was onboard with that, according to Pauline."

"Did Jacqui know she was the beneficiary of the trust? Did she have any idea how much was in the trust fund?"

Nora shook her head. "All I know is that Pauline felt responsible for Jacqui to the end. I'm not sure about the relationship, financial or otherwise, that Giselle had with her half-sister after Pauline died." She paused. "I can imagine she felt it as a burden sometimes. After all, she probably didn't know her sister all that well."

"You said something about it being unseemly that Giselle sold the family house so quickly. Do you think there's any possibility that Giselle could have ... helped her mother to her death? Or that the two deaths were connected?"

"No, I don't believe that Giselle killed her mother." Nora's voice shook a little. "But as for Giselle's death, I just don't know. Haakonssen didn't tip his hand when he talked to me this morning. He asked about Jacqui and I told him most of what I've told you, about her not being Pierre's child, and some of her problems growing up. I couldn't tell him anything about what she'd been up to as an adult. He also asked a few questions about Giselle and Jane's relationship. I couldn't say anything about that either. From articles about the press I understood Jane was a partner in the publishing house, and that's about the size of it."

"Do you think Jane could have been involved in Giselle's death? Something to do with Jacqui?"

"Why would you say that?" said Nora.

"The press is in financial trouble. In Portland, I visited Jane twice, and she was trying to understand what Giselle had been hiding from her. It seems that she had no idea Giselle was paying regular sums for a long time into the trust account in Montreal. You say the trust account was set up for Jacqui. But Jane didn't know that. Giselle never told her anything much about Jacqui except that she was difficult."

"I hardly know Jane," repeated Nora. "I saw her here and there at readings. She'd be at the book table, quietly selling the books, while

Giselle was mingling and networking. As for Jacqui, all I know for sure is that, according to Pauline, Jacqui would go through periods where she never mentioned the baby and then other periods where she seemed to get obsessed with the little girl. She knew her baby had been a girl. But whatever Pauline knew about the adoptive parents she wasn't telling Jacqui."

"You said she'd made her peace with Jacqui. Was Pauline still troubled about what had happened?"

"Yes. Pauline seemed fine, most of the time. But she had blue days. She would sometimes talk about Alain and brood about what a different life she could have had if she'd stayed in Paris with him, even if his wife wouldn't divorce him. How much better it would have been for Jacqui, how Jacqui would have been cherished. She berated herself for not being there emotionally for Jacqui. Over time, especially when Pauline had been drinking a bit in the evening, more came out. I think she began to feel that time was short and that maybe she should do more to help Jacqui.

"It was one of those times, when she'd been drinking, that she told me that she had the names of the adoptive parents: George and Helene Martin. A social worker had apparently given Pauline some written information—not the adoption papers, but enough information to go on should they ever want to find the daughter. As her health deteriorated, Pauline wrote to the Martins. They answered and sent a photo of the girl, now called Aimée Martin. Pauline showed me the photo. Aimée might have been five or six, she looked a little like Pauline, gamine, with short hair, a way of holding her head. Mostly it was the smile I recognized. It was painful for Pauline, but also reassuring to make contact with the family. Pauline wondered if she should tell Jacqui, but she said she was afraid of how Jacqui might react."

"Did Pauline tell Giselle?"

"I'm not sure, but even if Pauline didn't tell her about Aimée, it's possible Giselle could have found the names of the Martins, and the photo among her mother's papers. Maybe she even had contact with the family herself later."

"You said that Giselle didn't have anything to do with her mother's death six years ago. What about Jacqui though? Could Jacqui have killed Pauline for what happened to her around her baby? Maybe she didn't want Pauline's money. Maybe all she wanted was revenge."

"You keep asking me about Pauline's death. As if it's just a conundrum to be solved. As if she wasn't my dearest, oldest friend. As if I wouldn't have done anything for her. As if I could have said no."

I stared at her in astonishment. And then it all made sense.

"I need to get out of here," said Nora. "Follow me back to the Sylvia Beach in your car? We can talk more then."

Five or ten minutes later we were at the hotel, but after I'd parked Nora said, "Let's go down to the beach. I want to see the rain come in."

It was now about four o'clock and the air had cooled rapidly, especially over the ocean. There were others on the wide beach, many with dogs who were still swimming out to fetch balls or running hard after pieces of tossed driftwood. The rain had begun to lash the waves offshore, but still hadn't quite reached the sand.

We walked down the stairs and headed north, in the direction of the lighthouse and the cottage up on the bluff. I remembered what Karen had told me. That Pauline had gone to the cottage one weekend. She'd just gotten a CAT scan that showed the cancer had spread, that there was a lesion in her brain. Giselle suggested to Karen that Pauline had overdosed, with pills and Scotch. A friend found her the next day.

It had not occurred to me to ask who the friend was.

Now I said, "I understand that shortly before she died, Pauline found out she had a brain lesion."

"Yes, that's right." Nora had her hood up over her ball cap, so I couldn't see much of her face.

"She was frightened of losing words. *Words were everything to Pauline,* that's how I heard it put. She told that to Giselle. Did she tell you that as well?" I asked.

"Yes."

"She didn't ask Giselle to help her though."

"No, she didn't believe Giselle was strong enough. She didn't want Giselle to feel guilty."

"So, she asked her oldest friend. The girl she'd known from the time she was thirteen, who was so famous that no one would ever suspect her of helping."

"That's not completely correct. Giselle suspected. I never told her the truth. But I did tell the police a version of the events. It wasn't Haakonssen back then, but someone else. They had to investigate me, because I found Pauline, you see. So there was an incident report, which Haakonssen and his crew immediately saw on their database. A bit suspicious, wouldn't you say, me being in Newport then, and again this past Monday when Giselle died?" Nora smiled unhappily. "He wanted to interview me on Tuesday. And then again this morning. I told him what I told his predecessor. I didn't assist Pauline. I merely found her."

I waited, as the wind whipped at my hair and Nora's hood, and her words were half carried away by the rain-spattered wind.

"Pauline had it all planned. She didn't ask my advice. All she did was ask me to come out to the coast with her, but not to stay with her in the cottage. She had some business she wanted to talk to me about. Business and a favor. She asked me to get a room at Sylvia Beach, and that evening we had dinner out, at the Deep End restaurant. She told me about the CAT scan and said it was likely that she didn't have long. Worst case scenario she would, because of where the lesion was located, lose the ability to speak in a matter of months if not weeks." Nora's voice choked up, she couldn't continue immediately.

"The business she mentioned?"

"It was about the cottage. She'd left the cottage to Giselle in her will, with the verbal promise that Giselle either had to keep it in the family or give me the first option to buy it, soon or down the road. In the case of a sale, to me or someone else, she hoped that Giselle would take into account Jacqui's situation and invest part of the money for Jacqui. She didn't want to just leave the cottage to Jacqui, because she didn't think Jacqui would be able to manage it from Montreal.

"I thought that was the favor Pauline was asking," Nora went on. "Of course I said yes. I told her though that I hoped it would be a long while before that point came. There was so much modern medicine could do. Surely the doctors would suggest radiation, chemo, and so on. I'd help her through this. I told her I loved her and would do anything she needed me to do.

"'I know you do, old friend,' she said. "And that's when she asked me the real favor. All I had to do was come over to the cottage the next morning. And to make sure I was alone. And to make the necessary call."

I waited a minute, shaken, and then said, "You didn't try to talk her out of it?"

"At first. But then I agreed. I knew she didn't want a stranger to find her. Or worse, for Giselle to be worried and to come out to the coast looking for her. It was the saddest night I ever spent. Several times I almost went over there ... thinking that maybe she'd lost courage, or hadn't taken enough of whatever she was going to take. But I stopped myself. I did as she wished. I went over there in the morning, didn't touch her. Didn't touch anything. Just called 911, and told them how I'd found her. Told them she'd been terminally ill with cancer, but that we'd had dinner the night before and she hadn't given any indication of planning to die. But she'd left a note for me and one for Giselle that made it pretty clear her actions were intentional. There was no autopsy; the verdict was suicide."

We walked on without speaking for a bit, as the waves crashed onto the shore driven by a front coming in. My heart ached for Nora waiting through the long night and following her best friend's instructions not to come and check on her before morning. Yet I still was confused about one or two things. If Jacqui had the trust fund, then why would Pauline want Nora to buy the cottage from Giselle in order to help Jacqui? Did Pauline suspect that somewhere along the line Giselle might stop paying into the trust?

"I suppose Giselle wouldn't sell you the cottage," I said finally. "And you couldn't tell her that it had been Pauline's last wish, because then Giselle would be even more suspicious that you had something to do with Pauline's death."

"I went to the memorial service," Nora said, "and I gave one of the eulogies, which Giselle thanked me for. She also thanked me for what I wrote about Pauline in a literary magazine. But she seemed to change after I wrote her a friendly letter to say that Pauline had 'once' suggested I buy the cottage, so the money could go to help Jacqui. Giselle was quite clear that wasn't going to happen. She wrote back that her mother had left a will, and that she'd inherited both the house and the cottage, and that she planned to make sure Jacqui was taken care off. Then she emptied her mother's house, didn't offer me even a small keepsake, and sold it as fast as she could. She used the money to start Entre Editions, but she didn't invite me to the launch of three of Pauline's translations. I went anyway, of course. She was cool. I know she suspected me of helping her mother die. Maybe she began to suspect me of killing her mother so I could buy the cottage, I don't know. It wasn't very pleasant to feel so mistrusted. I left her alone after that."

Nora had stopped walking. The rising wind and spatters of rain, combined with her genuine grief, were taking their toll on her energy. I decided not to push her further on Giselle's and Pauline's deaths. She had told me a lot already. Instead I asked, "When did you first hear from Jacqui?"

"Yesterday. Jacqui had returned to Newport and asked if I might be coming over to the coast again. She really wanted to talk to me in person about her mother."

"She must think you know something."

"I do know something. Much more than 'something.' I know about her real father. I know about Pauline's decision to put Jacqui's baby up for adoption. I know the names of the couple who adopted her daughter. It seems right—if she seems calm enough—to tell her some of what I know. I suppose the papers Pauline had, with details about Helene and George Martin and the photo of Aimée, are somewhere in Pauline's or Giselle's things. Jacqui might find them in the cottage."

"Is she staying there, in the cottage?"

"I don't know. Isn't it a crime scene? She might be in a motel somewhere."

"How did she sound on the phone?"

"Polite and hesitant. She has an accent or a way of speaking that's a little odd." Nora had turned back into the direction of the Sylvia Beach towering high above the shore. Cold and pinched in the wet salt wind, her face showed every wrinkle of her seventy-six years. "To be honest, she sounded only as awkward as one of my fans. She's texted me a couple of times today. She can spell, I know that. She told me she had read some of my books—not as a child, but while she was a teenager. Well, there's nothing to be done at this late date," she said, as if to herself. "And now I must head to the hotel, wash my face, and go meet Jacqui at five thirty. I'm pretty sure I'm going to be exhausted afterwards, but if you want to get together later, just knock on my door. I'm in the Mark Twain room. It has a clawfoot tub. Maybe I'll take a bath later. It's been a long day."

25.

After Nora turned back to the hotel, I kept walking, even though by now it was starting to rain. What else did I have to do this afternoon but wander around a sandy gray-and-green world at the edge of the continent, chewing over what Nora had been telling me for the last few hours?

My immediate reaction had been to believe everything Nora had said about Giselle and Jacqui, and about the evening Nora spent with Pauline the night she committed suicide.

It seemed that Pauline had acted with remarkable tact and foresight, making sure that she and Nora were observed in pleasant conversation over dinner. Making sure that Nora returned to the Sylvia Beach so the receptionist could note her presence.

Making sure, at least in Nora's telling, that her old friend escaped any taint of suspicion.

Giselle might have wondered why Nora just happened to have been in Newport that weekend, not staying at the cottage with her mother, but in a hotel. She might have wondered why it was Nora who conveniently was there to find her mother the next morning and call the police. But in the midst of her initial grief Giselle wouldn't have asked too many questions, most likely. She knew her mother was very ill. She knew her mother drank Scotch and probably took something to dull the pain or get to sleep. And she had a last note from Pauline that must have explained why she had decided to take her own life before she lost her ability to read and speak.

It was only when Nora broached the idea of buying the cottage from Giselle, in order to give Jacqui part of the money, that Giselle suddenly showed some misgivings. She might have had no idea how much Pauline had confided in Nora about Jacqui and her problems. And perhaps she thought that Nora was going to be monitoring what Giselle did with her mother's property, in order to make sure Jacqui got her share. Or perhaps she had some crazy idea that Nora had killed her mother in order to get the cottage.

Was it a completely crazy idea?

I'd sympathized with the unfairness of Giselle's treatment of Nora, how she'd sold the house so quickly, how she hadn't even given Nora a keepsake. It was only now, as I continued walking in the darkening wet sand, that I wondered whether Giselle's actions were as unreasonable as Nora portrayed them. How did I know, in fact, that what Nora had told me was completely true? What if Giselle had discovered that Nora really had had a larger role in her mother's death?

What if Giselle knew Nora had killed her mother? What if Giselle had blackmailed her, and Nora had then finally had enough and pushed Giselle over the bluff? Of all the notions I'd entertained about this case, this scenario seemed least likely. It's true that Nora had been jealous of her friend's good fortune at one time, but that was years and years ago. I had heard in Nora's voice how much she'd loved Pauline. No, there were other scenarios that were more likely—I just couldn't see them yet.

By this time I was actually at the base of the bluff. I looked up at the houses on top through the rain that was now streaming down my face. I saw only the upper floor of the cottage, with its weathered gray shingles and newer ones around the dormer window, and the roof. The wooden railing looked tall and sturdy enough from this angle, not an obstacle you would casually flip over even after a few glasses of alcohol.

Only five days ago I'd stood up there on the bluff, fresh from my interesting breakfast chat with Nora, copyedited manuscript of *On Jupiter* in hand, excited by the prospect of meeting the woman with the white streak in her dark hair and the cajoling, lightly accented voice.

I felt reverse vertigo looking up, as if I were watching a black-and-white film or acting in my own dream. The drop wasn't straight down, but it was abrupt at the edge where the railing stretched. Below the railing were scrub junipers and salal bushes, thickly green in the rain, here and there an animal track that could have been a path. From here I saw no signs of illegal habitation. I supposed the police would have been all over the side of the bluff, looking for clues.

I saw a figure pass by on the top of the bluff by the Richard cottage. The woman was wearing a rain parka, but I caught a glimpse of her head under the hood. Dark bangs.

It would have been foggy on Monday night, the fog obscuring the bluff as the increasing rain was doing now. I could almost see Giselle struggling with someone and then being overpowered and pushed over the wooden railing. Tumbling over rocks and scrub until her neck snapped. Did the killer just leave Giselle there? Who would do such a thing?

The parka-clad figure on the bluff had vanished. Could it be Jacqui up there? There was only one way to find out, to climb up the bluff by means of the sodden sandy path.

As I hiked up, being careful of my footing, pushing away branches of sticky-wet thorny leaves, I thought about all Nora had told me today. Jacqui as a challenging baby, Jacqui as a tantrum-prone toddler, Pauline as a distant mother preoccupied with the loss of Alain LeMoyne, her divorce, her career. The different ways that Pauline had treated her two daughters: Europa, covered with ice; Io sulfurous, volcanic, erupting. Europa, the small moon, was more distant; she made two orbits around Jupiter for every four orbits that Io made. Why were they so unalike when their bodies must have broken off from the same mother planet?

Jupiter had many more moons than these two daughters of course. For starters, there was Amalthea, the moon that Asimov had described in *Lucky Starr and the Moons of Jupiter,* which played such a decisive role in the adventure story. Asimov had called her Jupiter 5, only a hundred miles in diameter, a tiny moon, caught in the strong gravity of Jupiter. Was Jacqui's baby the third moon of the drama? Amalthea—Aimée Martin?

My mind went back to something Nora had said on the beach a short while ago, about papers with information about the Martin couple who'd adopted Jacqui's baby. Could these papers be in the cottage? I'd assumed that the contents of the safe deposit box—the papers presumably in the manila envelope that Karen had seen the secretive Giselle tuck into her bag outside the bank—had to do with Jane. That perhaps Giselle was changing her will or that she needed the documents for the trip to Montreal.

But perhaps Giselle had kept something in the safe deposit box in Portland that concerned Jacqui, something Jacqui was here to find, perhaps to do with her meeting with Nora in a short while.

There was yellow tape draped around the front of the cottage, but the lights were on inside. I didn't cross the crime-scene line to the front door, but retraced my steps from a few days ago around the back. The latch had been removed, but not replaced. Instead there was some tape across the sliding glass door, which someone had partially torn off, so that it dangled down. The door was open a crack. I knocked but there was no answer, so I slid the door open carefully and called a tentative, "Hello?"

A young woman was sitting on the sofa with a pile of papers on the coffee table in front of her, methodically flipping through them, pausing occasionally to read one or two at greater length. Rings were on every finger. After seeing photographs of her as a young child, I wasn't prepared for her rounded figure and full face. The only thing that was similar was the straight dark hair cut above her shoulders, and the bangs. But as she glanced up and stared at me on the threshold of the open door, I was struck by how she resembled the grainy picture of Alain LeMoyne with the slightly hooded eyes and large nose.

"Who are you and what do you want?" she asked. Her voice was higher than I'd expected, with a French-Canadian accent, a little unmodulated. But she didn't seem to be shocked to see me here, or particularly hostile. Perhaps because of that, I didn't offer the excuse I'd prepared, that I was a friend or neighbor just checking on the house when I saw the car outside.

"Cassandra Reilly," I introduced myself. "I knew Giselle Richard. I'm assuming she might have been your sister. I know Jane too. I'm a translator and they were publishing one of my authors. I had an appointment with Giselle here at the cottage the morning she was found. I'm afraid the police want me to stay in the area until the investigation is over." I paused. "That's why I was walking by. Just taking a walk."

Was she listening? She put the papers on the coffee table and stared at me.

"You said you're a translator? My mother was a translator. Did you know my mother? Do you want to come in and sit down?"

I came in, but continued standing. I contemplated saying I knew her mother. I felt unnerved by the steady stare, uncertain who I was dealing with. I began telling her about translating Luisa's book, perhaps with the notion of putting both of us at ease, but after a minute she interrupted me.

"My mother died here."

"Yes, I heard that."

"Giselle never told me the reason. I only found out later, like, four months later."

I tried not to show how taken aback I was. Four *months*?

"So, you didn't go to her funeral?" I said. I was thinking, Pauline wrote two suicide notes, one to Giselle and one to Nora. Wouldn't she have written to Jacqui?

"Giselle said she sent a message about the funeral, but it must have been addressed wrong, because I never got it. Sometimes I move and forget to let her know right away, she said that maybe was the reason." Jacqui brushed her dark hair from her eyes. I could see the photographs on the wall behind her: many of Pauline and Giselle, apart and together, but only the one of Jacqui with them, when she was a little girl. At that age she had looked more like her mother and sister, but her face now looked older than her years and vulnerable, with heavy lids and downturned mouth.

"Giselle was probably afraid of me coming to the service," Jacqui said. "Maybe that I would make a scene. I did make a lot of scenes once, when I was younger. I screamed and screamed as a baby, that's what they said."

I wondered if her air of detachment and flattened tone was the result of medication, prescribed or not. Whatever the cause, she did seem emotionally muted for someone who had been described to me as uncontrollable as a child and rebellious and angry as an adolescent.

"When was the last time you saw your sister then? In Montreal or Vancouver?"

"I hadn't seen her for a long time," she said, not quite answering. "Sometimes she sent me a check. When I asked. I moved around a lot. Into my boyfriend's place and then out again. And another boyfriend came along and we lived in a place together. I needed money for that and for other things. But she didn't always want to help me and him. She didn't like my boyfriends. She told me I should be learning to take care of myself. We had a fight, him and me. Now I don't have a boyfriend. Then, last September, she came to Montreal to see me after some meetings in New York. She was friendly. She said she wanted to help me. She said she wanted to see my artwork. I took her to a café where I was a dishwasher sometimes, some of my paintings were hanging on the walls. She said she liked them a lot. She asked me if I thought about studying art or taking college classes. If I might want to move out West to study. She helped me move here."

"You mean, west to British Columbia, to Vancouver?"

"No, to the Vancouver in Washington. There's a community college where I take classes in graphic art. I'm just taking one class now, I don't really like to do graphics that much though, I like painting my own stuff. Vancouver is right across the river from Portland. I moved there in October, Giselle found me an apartment. She bought me a used car."

I didn't know whether to be more surprised by the fact that Giselle seemed to have hidden Jacqui from Jane, continuing to pretend that her sister lived in Canada, or by the fact that no one I'd talked to in the course of this investigation seemed aware that Jacqui lived just across the Columbia River. Jane didn't seem to know, nor did Karen, nor did Nora. If they all thought Jacqui lived in Canada, why shouldn't I have assumed the same thing?

I'd seen the Washington state license plate on her car, but had assumed it was a rental she'd picked up in Portland at the airport. Two Vancouvers. That must have made it less likely that Giselle would slip up in referring to her sister. She could have kept Jacqui close enough to visit, but away from her life in Portland.

"Did you come here to talk to me about anything in particular?" Jacqui said in her high flat voice, and looking at me with unexpected sharpness. "Because I have to meet someone at five thirty."

"Oh, sorry," I said, falling back on one of my more recent fabrications, "Well, here's the thing: I've been asked to write an article about your mother and sister. As translators. Perhaps you could tell me something about them? The fact is, I only have a couple more days here before I go home. I live in London."

"London," she said, and for the first time I saw a glimmer of real interest. "I'd like to go to London someday."

"Maybe you will."

"My mother and Giselle always went places, flew around going places. But not me. I was only on an airplane for the first time in October. Giselle used to have a lot of money. But it's all gone now. She told me that she was running out. That she wouldn't be able to keep paying for my rent and classes next year unless I helped her. I had some money Mother left me in an account in Montreal for education and stuff like that. She said she was going to take the money out of that account and close it. Then we would both have some money, we could split it and she would manage my part for me. I said I just wanted the money, I didn't want her managing me anymore. She got mad. She yelled at me and said I had never been capable of managing anything, and I had been a burden ever since I was born."

"That's a very unkind thing to say ... When was this, that she told you this? Recently?"

But Jacqui didn't answer. She looked down at the papers on the coffee table. "It's not my fault," she muttered.

"What's not your fault, Jacqui?"

"The baby. I wanted to keep the baby. Mother wouldn't let me. It was my baby, and they took her. I've been looking for her ever since. I want to give the baby some money for her education. Giselle said she would help me. She knew something, where the baby went. The baby is in Montreal. I am going to back to Montreal to see her."

I thought it better not to point out that this baby must be at least fourteen or fifteen by now. I wondered how it had gone in the hospital after Jacqui had given birth. Perhaps they'd never even shown the baby to her. Perhaps the adoption had been arranged before the birth, and the child had gone immediately to the Martins.

Jacqui spoke calmly, but her hands twitched in her lap. "I'm not an idiot. I understand Mother was afraid to tell me about the adoption family because she thought I would try to find the baby, and I would scare everyone. I promised Giselle I wouldn't do that. I just wanted to know the baby was all right. But now I don't have to wait, I can see her."

I nodded, taking care to look sympathetic. I *felt* sympathetic actually, even though I also felt agitated. Had Giselle been trying to help her sister or just use her? I couldn't put all the pieces together. I kept thinking about Jane, how she had said she'd never met Jacqui before. Was that really likely? She *must* have known about Jacqui living across the river. Could I get the conversation around to Jane and their meeting on Thursday?

"Nobody cared about me," she said. "Mother hardly ever called me. I had to call her. After Mother died Giselle didn't call me even though she had my phone number. She never called me. I had to call her if I needed money, then she sent me a check. It was never enough."

"But you said she had tried to help you more recently," I said. "Brought you out to Vancouver, helped you enroll in community college, found you an apartment?" I didn't want to believe that Giselle had flown Jacqui all the way to the West Coast and then, after six or so months, told her she didn't have the funds to keep supporting her. Giselle as the grantor had the right to dissolve the trust and set up a different system to share the funds with Jacqui. It was possible that Jacqui was exaggerating Giselle's miserliness toward her, when in fact Giselle really *was* trying to make sure Jacqui would finish school and get a job and become more self-sustaining.

I continued, "Did Giselle ask you to come out here to the cottage this week to discuss her plan to close the account in Montreal? What did she say about your daughter and helping you find her? Did she say she had the family's name?" These were guesses, but if I expected Jacqui to react, I was disappointed.

"I even gave Giselle a painting," she said glumly. "It's hanging here on the wall." She pointed to a narrow wall leading to the bedroom downstairs, to a colorful canvas that showed a large cat with ruffled fur on a sofa. The cat was red and had fierce eyes.

"It's very striking," I said.

"I think in images," she said. "Not always words. Mother didn't even realize that for a long time. She was gone so much. She and Giselle were the smart ones, always talking in French and English, always reading, writing, translating. They thought I was stupid, they didn't understand that the words just didn't go in a straight line for me, they were all jumbled. It was Suzanne who taught me to read."

A shadow crossed her face.

"Tell me about Suzanne." I took off my jacket and put it over the back of a chair and sat down.

"My real father died, and Giselle's father didn't want me. Sometimes I thought maybe Mother wasn't my real mother either. That maybe Suzanne was. I felt safe when I was around her. I was happy at her house. Mother was so beautiful. But she didn't want me. She didn't really love me like her real child. At Suzanne's I was the only one for a while. Then she had two babies, and I felt like the older sister. It was nice at first."

"But something changed. When was that?"

"I don't remember some years very well. I had bad judgement." She spoke as if about someone else. "I made some bad friends. Took drugs and everything. I was mad with Suzanne. I didn't think she cared about me anymore. I left her house with some friends and we were just living on the street and everything, but then I got picked up by the police and they contacted Mother. I thought she was finally going to take care of me, now that I was having a baby. But she put me in a mental kind of home. I went to the hospital to give birth and came back to the mental place. I didn't know where the baby was. My baby was taken away. Mother only came to visit sometimes, then she moved to Portland. Giselle came once but she looked scared the whole time and never came again. She didn't live in Montreal. She lived in Boston. I didn't want to see either of them. I hated them. But just for a while. Then I tried to understand they were just doing their best. Mother said she loved me."

Jacqui fixed her eyes on the photograph of herself as a five-year-old with her mother and sister in Montreal. I could hardly blame her for feeling angry and bereft. She had missed out not only on her own childhood, but also on her baby's childhood.

"Mother tried to explain it to me, why she made her choice to put me in the mental place. And why my baby had to go to another family. She said there was more assistance available for me in Canada. She said she had to stay in Portland because of Grandfather. Then, after he died, she got cancer. She got it three times. The third time, she died. She died in this cottage, Giselle told me. At first she said Mother just died from cancer. But then Giselle said Mother suicided. Giselle said someone helped her, someone else." Jacqui's face suddenly twisted. "I miss my mother. Someone killed her, I think."

"Do you mean someone killed Giselle?" I asked carefully.

"Yes. Both." She said this with weird detachment. "I told the police. They don't know everything, you see."

I felt rattled now. There was a certain logic to Jacqui's mind, some pattern here, but I couldn't quite discern it. I wanted to go back to Jane for a moment.

"Did you tell Jane about your suspicions? When you met her a couple of days ago?"

"No. I wanted to see where Giselle lived and ask about the money in the bank, how to get it. She wanted to talk about Giselle's funeral service and my plans. She said she hadn't known until that morning that there was a bank account in Montreal. She said there was a lot she didn't know about Giselle. She wondered if I had talked to my sister before she died. I told her I was mad at Giselle because she was mean to me. I told her my sister didn't deserve a nice funeral. I couldn't afford that until I got my money. I asked her for a loan to help me out. She said she would try to figure something out and gave me forty dollars. I said Giselle used to give me a thousand but she said that was too much. I told her that Giselle was going to give me the information about the baby. She asked, *What baby?* So I told her what happened. She didn't know. She cried."

Jacqui said this with a vague sense of surprise. She was unlikely to know Jane's history. Or perhaps it was rare in her life that someone had cried to hear her story. It didn't seem as though Giselle had ever cared very much. How could she yell at Jacqui, and tell her she'd been a burden? Or maybe that was something Giselle was telling herself, to rationalize why she was planning to take some of the money that her mother had meant for Jacqui to keep her publishing company going and to expand it.

"Did you and Jane talk about anything else?"

"I asked her about the cottage," said Jacqui. "I wanted to know if this cottage is mine now." She paused and a look I couldn't decipher—was it anger or doubt?—appeared in her eyes. "Jane said she didn't know about that, it depended on the will, but she hadn't found the will yet. She said that Giselle had been working on the cottage to sell it. They needed to sell it because they had business debt. It sounded like she wanted the cottage for herself. But I could live here, couldn't I? I've never had a house. I don't know about business debt. Giselle knows about money, she used to help. Now I don't have anyone. Maybe Jane killed Giselle to get the cottage, I think that the police will find that out. You know, my mother died here," she repeated. "Someone killed her. Maybe Giselle, maybe someone else. I don't know."

I wondered how much of this Haakonssen had heard, and if he had discounted it as paranoid ramblings. Some of it sounded bizarre, but there might be a core of truth. Jane hadn't mentioned anything about expecting to keep the cottage for herself. She had been upset with Giselle for sure. But that didn't mean Jane had had anything to do with Giselle's death, did it?

"Why again do you think Jane wanted the cottage?"

"To sell to pay for the bills and things. Because Giselle used money from their business. She took their mixed money and sent it to the bank in Montreal." Jacqui kneaded her fingers stubbornly. "I can't give her *that* money, from the bank, it's for the baby when I find her. I'd rather give Jane the cottage."

"You don't have to give Jane anything," I said. "Anyway, until the will is found it's unclear who owns the cottage and everything. But you should still have the money in Montreal to live on. Your child is already taken care of. Of course you'll need some help to navigate all this."

She looked anxious and wistful for a moment, then almost indifferent. "I can't do stuff like that. Buy, sell, be smart with all the contracts and figures. It gives me a sick feeling in my stomach."

"You need a lawyer," I said. "Nora Longeran has a good one—a Mr. Tom Hoyt. He helped me get out of police custody a few days ago. You're having coffee soon with Nora, aren't you? She told me."

"You know Nora? She said she will talk to me about my mother. She was my mother's best friend, she says." Jacqui's dark eyes narrowed. "I don't know if I should trust her, if she will tell me anything. I remember she sent me all her books when I was growing up. But I couldn't read them until I got older. They were breathing underwater."

"I think Nora will help you, if she can."

Jacqui looked at the time on her phone. "I'd better go. Do you want to come with me? I can give you a ride."

"Nora mentioned I could join you. But if you don't mind, I'd love to go through Giselle's files a little bit. To learn more about her for my article."

I felt uneasy taking advantage of Jacqui, but I did want to look around the house and this was the only way I could think to manage it.

"Yes, you can stay for a little bit. I'll come back here later. I am looking for something. Papers and a special little key."

"The key to the safe deposit box?"

She nodded. "Giselle told me she had a safety deposit box, but the key was hidden. For a while. I know. I know where the key is now. I just have to go to the bank and ask for the box. There are papers about my baby. I asked Jane where the information is. Jane pretended she didn't know. Jane is not a nice person. She's a bad person. She was angry at Giselle. Jane is evil."

I wasn't sure why, maybe it was the use of the word *evil,* but I suddenly experienced a wave of distrust. Jane might, just might have pushed her lover over the bluff, but it would have been out of jealousy or despair that Giselle had rejected her. The Jane I'd talked with Thursday had been hurting with betrayal and grief. I could believe she'd cried when Jacqui told her about the baby who'd been adopted away. I couldn't believe she'd lie about the safe deposit box. Nor could I believe that Jane would go so far as to try to force Jacqui to give her this cottage. And maybe Jacqui's story about Giselle getting angry at her, saying she was a burden, was made up as well. Jacqui hadn't even answered my most basic question— When had she last talked with Giselle?

Because if it was here, on Monday, Haakonssen should know that if he didn't already.

So was I being played by Jacqui? Was this all a performance for my benefit? Or was there some truth to Jacqui's paranoia, and was it just the way she pronounced her words and her habit of repeating accusations that made them seem hardly credible? I owed her the benefit of the doubt, didn't I?

"Where would my sister hide a key, do you think?" she asked, getting up and making ready to leave. She looked over at the wall of photographs and my eyes followed hers to the one of Pauline with her two daughters.

She walked over to the sofa and lifted the frame off its hook. The cardboard backing was faded and buckled a little, and taped to it was a small brass key.

She peeled it off, put it in her pocket, and smiled, and in that smile, and in her eyes, was something unexpected: an unsettling, peculiar look of smugness.

The only way she could have gone right to that photograph was if someone had told her it was there. Or if she put it there herself.

26.

As soon as Jacqui left, I called the Newport police and asked to speak with Detective Haakonsen. They transferred me without my asking to Sergeant Jones.

"Good evening, Ms. Reilly," he said jovially. "We were wondering when we'd hear from you. Are you in Newport, by any chance? If so, we'd like to have you come by and answer a few more questions."

I suspected that Nora had told them that I was arriving today, and that this question was pure formality. "What questions?" I said.

"Oh, nothing serious," he said. "Just a couple of things we noticed in your statement. Once we clear those up, you can be on your way."

"To London?" I said hopefully.

"Well, not quite yet, but soon. Did you want to talk to Detective Haakonssen about anything in particular? Anything I can help you with?"

For some reason Pete Jones irritated me. Or maybe I was irritated by the fact that I'd been so taken in by his friendliness on my first visit to the police station. At any rate I didn't feel like chitchatting with him about being at the Richard cottage and having met Jacqui. He would surely advise me to get out of the house and not touch anything. Instead we agreed that I would come over at around six thirty.

That would give me a while to look around the cottage before I walked back to the hotel to get the car. To be honest, I wasn't sure why I had to solve this for the police. Except that my Wednesday flight was ever drawing closer, and Pete Jones seemed clueless that I might have a life to get on with.

Speaking of which, what was up with my editor? It seemed like weeks since I'd sent the first three chapters of *Baby's First Year* to Janneken, but it was actually just yesterday morning, Friday. I looked through my messages, and found one sent a few hours ago from London.

CR, Surprising turn of events. Angela's misfortune is your gain. You're set for Witteron, so get yourself back here on the double. PS Good job with the chapters, though I have some comments. Still think there's too much bloody whinging. JW

I wondered vaguely what had happened to Angela, but there was no time for that now. Jacqui had been flipping through a pile of papers when I came in and had left them on the table. They seemed to come from two file folders. I saw no signs in the folders of anything to do with an adoption, nor did I find any wills or a trust agreement. That didn't mean that they weren't in the cottage, but that they weren't among the papers here.

Correspondence with a publisher in Poland, sales reports, review clippings. I looked at the label on the empty folder on the table. The words TO DO reinforced my sense that Jacqui had picked up this folder randomly. There were other file folders on the table, including one with some recent acrimonious emails with Jane about financial matters, and another file with an itinerary of the Montreal trip and some correspondence with a bank manager about the trust account in the name of Richard confirming their appointment on the Friday just past. Frustratingly, there were no details of what they were going to discuss. But the itinerary checked out with what Karen had told me.

The last folder on the coffee table had held a few old letters from Nora to Pauline. They had been removed from their envelopes, smoothed out and arranged chronologically. The letters weren't complete, by any measure, considering how long the friends had known each other, so they must have been selected out for some reason. I skimmed them quickly, but all I could see was a line in a letter from Nora to Pauline sometime a few years before she died. Pauline must have been visiting Jacqui because Nora was writing consolingly but firmly, suggesting that Pauline keep her distance from Jacqui if she didn't want to be drawn into her craziness. That suggested Nora had known more than she let on, but it didn't seem suspicious.

The last item in the file had no envelope, but was a handwritten note on scrap paper, Pauline's draft copy perhaps, of the last letter she wrote to her friend Nora before she took her life. It was long only because many of the lines were crossed out and rewritten, and hard to read because the script was half illegible. Perhaps Pauline had already been drinking or had taken some of the pills when she wrote this draft. It was definitely a suicide note though. She said nothing about having discussed this plan with Nora in advance, but only talked about what the friendship had meant to her for almost sixty years. A few words were in French; they were words of love.

I supposed Giselle had seen this. If so, she would have realized that Nora had nothing to do with her mother's death. The question was, had Jacqui read the note? The scrap looked untouched at the bottom of the pile. Surely she would have been looking for information on the adoption or financial papers, not old letters between her mother and Nora.

I decided to look around a little more for whatever had been in the manila envelope that Giselle had removed from the safe deposit box. I was definitely going to be in trouble if Haakonssen found out I'd been in the cottage, so I'd better hurry. I kept thinking about the meaning of what Jacqui had said about Giselle being willing to help her find the child adopted by the Martins. Why would Giselle do that? She didn't need Jacqui's approval to dissolve the trust, but maybe she needed Jacqui's silence. Could this be the "bargaining chip" Giselle had mentioned to Karen in Portland? Information about the child in exchange for Jacqui keeping quiet about the trust?

Given a good lawyer, Jacqui could certainly contest Giselle stealing her inheritance. But I wondered if Giselle was less worried about legal action than worried about Jane or Karen finding out how dishonest she was. Jane especially would be disgusted to find out that Giselle planned to help herself to the money in the trust.

I pulled open the desk drawers and a few cupboards without finding anything interesting, then decided to quickly search the rest of the cottage. The kitchen looked like it had been already gone over; there was evidence of dusting for fingerprints around the sink, cupboards, and table. I went into the downstairs bath and saw that someone had stapled in a new sheet of heavy-duty gray plastic to replace the flapping plastic of last Tuesday morning, when I was here last. Did the police department have a carpenter on call?

The door to the downstairs bedroom was closed. When I walked in, I found the space dim and musty. Giselle probably slept upstairs, where she would have an expansive view. Had this been Pauline's room, then? On the first floor, with a bathroom next door? The bed had adjustable railings and a mechanism to raise and lower the head of the mattress. There were no pillows, nor bedclothes; it was starkly unmade. The closet had been mostly cleared out, except for a rain jacket and a pair of rubber boots, but there was cedar chest in the corner of the closet still. I opened it to find a few colorful turbans of the kind that Pauline was said to wear after her chemo treatment. Underneath the turban was an inexpensive wig, with artificial black hair, cut in the style that Giselle had favored. A short pageboy with heavy bangs down to the brows.

The wig surprised me, until I recalled the photo in the other room of Pauline with Nora and Giselle. Many women wore wigs after they lost their hair from chemo.

I took the wig over to a spotted oval mirror hanging on the wall and tugged it over my own whitening curls. My skin was too pale and freckled for solid black; I looked like Morticia in the Addams Family.

From the living room I heard my phone ringing in the pocket of the jacket I'd draped over a chair, and I rushed to answer it. I thought it might be Nora, telling me what she and Jacqui had talked about.

"Oh, there you are," Kim said. "Candace has been trying to Skype you all day. A neighbor called her around noon to say the blinds were still down."

"Oh," I said. "Yes, I suppose they are. I mean, I know they are. But that's intentional, because I probably won't be back to Portland until tomorrow sometime."

"You're not in Portland? You're supposed to be housesitting and you're not in Portland? Tell me there's not a woman involved."

"I'm obviously grateful to have had a place to stay in Portland," I answered with dignity, "But my real task here is not housesitting, but investigating what happened to Giselle Richard. I was called back to Newport this morning on urgent business. I watered the plants before I left," I lied.

"You need to let Candace know then," Kim said, only mildly mollified. "This reflects on *me*, Cassandra, if you're flaky. Are you sure you don't want me to fly up to Portland tonight? I'm willing."

"I know that and I appreciate it, but I think things are approaching resolution. One more day and I'll be back in Portland, and I'll figure things out from there. Sorry, Kim, I'm in the middle of something, bye."

I had been looking at the photograph of Pauline and her two daughters on the wall while talking to Kim, the one Jacqui had briefly removed, so she could peel off the little key. As I'd glimpsed earlier, the cardboard backing was slightly buckled.

I suddenly saw Giselle and Jacqui in the room Monday night. Giselle had been drinking before her meeting with Jacqui. They must have argued. Maybe Giselle had pointed to the photograph and said the adoption information was there, and Jacqui could have it if she didn't make a fuss about the money. That Giselle needed it. That Giselle would take care of her as she and her mother always had. But Jacqui had balked and maybe Jacqui had even followed Giselle outside and hit her on the head with a rock and pushed her over the side, or just pushed her.

I went over and lifted the photograph off the wall and pried open the backing just enough to see there were some sheets of paper behind the cardboard. I thought that maybe I shouldn't touch them, because it was evidence, but my curiosity was too strong.

Just then the Skype tones sounded. I saw the call was from Candace. I thought she was supposed to be hiking in Joshua Tree National Park? Without answering, I turned off my phone, put it in my jacket pocket, and tossed the jacket irritably on the sofa. But the interruption had made me come to my senses. I took the framed photograph over to the front door and leaned it against the wall. I'd quickly check around the second floor and then take the picture and whatever was behind it over to the police station. I'd just headed upstairs and was standing on the landing when I heard a step on the threshold of the still partially open sliding glass door and someone softly moving into the living room.

"Jacqui?" she said. "Are you here? I didn't see your car but I wanted to check. The door's open." The person stepped inside and paused. She must have heard me on the landing. "Jacqui, are you upstairs? I thought we could talk a little more. About—what we talked about in Portland?"

There was no hiding, and I descended the stairs.

Jane gasped. "What are you doing? Take that off!"

I removed the black wig and placed it gently on a table. "Sorry. I didn't mean to freak you out."

I was actually the one who was freaked out. I'd glimpsed something in Jane's expression that I hadn't seen at her house; not anger or grief, but fear. And fear could make people do things they'd regret.

I was sorry now I'd turned off my phone and thrown the jacket on the sofa.

"Where'd you get that? Why are you here? How did you get in? Where's Jacqui?"

She attempted to be stern, but her voice was shaking. Her long, white hair was bundled up under a large tweed cap with a brim, and she wore a hefty corduroy jacket, and sturdy hiking boots. Seen from the front she was Jane of course; but seen from the side or back, I wondered if she would be identifiable. She looked wetter than she should have if she'd only just gotten out of her car and walked to the sliding glass door. How long had she been out there?

In her hand was a briefcase. A briefcase?

I kept my voice calm. "The wig is Pauline's, I presume. I found it in her bedroom and tried it on for a lark to see what I looked like. I was here having a chat with Jacqui earlier, and she's gone off for a walk. She told me I could wait for her." I didn't want to bring Nora Longeran into this, or mention that Nora and Jacqui might be expecting me at the café. "Why are *you* here?"

"Jacqui was here? Where is she now?" Jane advanced into the room and looked around. She set the briefcase on the floor, took off the wet corduroy jacket, and seemed to brace herself, feet planted firmly, wide apart.

"Did Jacqui ask you to come?" I was playing for time, thinking about how to get past her to the front door. Were Jacqui and Jane in on something together? Was there any chance that Jane was freaking out because she was the one who bought the black wig and had put it on to walk down the beach after the murder?

"This is Giselle's cottage," she said, suddenly more aggressive, taking a deliberate stance with one leg forward. Did she have some kind of martial-arts training? "I can come here if I want. You're the one who has broken in. You're the one who doesn't belong here. What's your game, Cassandra? Why did you come back to Newport? Were you and Giselle having some kind of affair too? Did you leave something behind that would incriminate you?"

"Me?" I sputtered, in self-defense but growing panic. I didn't like the way that Jane was standing or the way she was glaring at me, not one bit. It made sense now. Jane was the killer. She'd had enough of Giselle's wandering eye, her affair with Karen, maybe affairs with others. Or maybe what had really set her off was learning about how Pauline and Giselle had treated Jacqui. Jane was an orphan, abandoned by her mother in a South Korean orphanage, adopted by strangers in another country. *Of course* the story of Jacqui's baby, adopted by strangers, would have affected her.

Maybe she hadn't just learned about Jacqui's baby and the adoption a couple of days ago, but had known for a while. Maybe she had found evidence of the trust account before Thursday morning. Maybe Jane had been planning to murder Giselle long before she came out here Monday evening.

Whether her reason was jealousy or anger about Jacqui, maybe Jane had turned up at the cottage, in the heavy fog. She'd brought a bottle of Scotch and encouraged Giselle to drink. When Giselle was woozy, Jane had persuaded her to go outside, and then Jane had thrown her over the guard rails and left her for dead. And then she'd returned to the cottage, removed the second glass, and staged the table with the bottle to look as if Giselle had been drinking alone.

After which she'd put on the black wig she'd brought with her and gone down to the beach and walked, so that someone like the beauty-salon owner would think it was Giselle.

Obviously it was Jane. Why hadn't I seen that?

In her present state of grimacing anger, with her arms raised in front of her chest, Jane looked very threatening indeed. This was not the time to confront her with her misdeeds. I needed to get away, fast.

She saw me looking toward the front door, and moved to block me. I changed direction and dashed into the bathroom, locked the door, and attempted to remove the heavy plastic around the window. I scrabbled with my fingernails, but they were too short. I'd need a knife. Maybe there were some scissors in the cabinet. I pulled open the drawers. Empty except for a dried up toothbrush.

I heard Jane give a last bang on the door, then retreat to the living room. What if she had the idea to go out to the front of the house with a kitchen knife and rip through the plastic from the outside?

I imagined her trying to drag me out through the window, or stabbing me, or shoving my head in the toilet bowl. It's not the kind of thing I'd ever imagined for my obituary in *The Guardian*, should I be fortunate enough to receive one.

I heard a phone ring. I thought it was mine, in the jacket on the sofa, and cursed my bad luck again for casually tossing it there. Then I realized it must be Jane's phone and she was talking to someone.

About me.

"Yes, she's, ah, hiding in the bathroom. Well, she *seemed* to be acting suspiciously. And then, I guess, we both panicked. Yes, I'll tell her you're expecting her at the station. We'll be here."

Her voice had been getting slightly louder as she carried on this conversation, until finally she came to the bathroom door.

"Cassandra, I'm sorry. I just panicked. I thought ... I'm really very sorry. That was Detective Haakonssen. He's waiting for you at the station. Can you come out?"

I was silent, weighing whether this might be a trick. I *had* heard the phone ring. But maybe it was still a trick.

"Look," she said, "I came to Newport to be re-interviewed and Detective Haakonssen asked me to bring the bank statements I told him about. I just came from the police station. He didn't say a lot but I was under the impression he suspected Jacqui, from the kinds of questions he asked. After I left the station I decided to come here and look for the key to the safe deposit box. I came to the door and heard something. I assumed Jacqui was here. Then I saw you on the stairs. In the wig. I sort of lost my head. I thought maybe he was all wrong. I thought maybe, it wasn't Jacqui. It was you. Won't you come out? I promise I won't hurt you."

Slowly, very slowly, I opened the bathroom door.

Jane stood there, looking contrite. But behind her loomed a male figure in the open sliding door, holding some sort of sinister tool.

"Hey," he said. "I'm the window guy. I'm here to fix the lock on the door and finish putting in the bathroom window. Sorry I couldn't get here sooner."

Jane and I both bolted for the front door. I grabbed the photograph on my way out.

27.

It wasn't until we were in Jane's car, pulling away from a white van with blue lettering (**THE WINDOW GUY: Serving Greater Newport Since 2006**), and speeding away down Coast Street, that we each took a breath and spoke.

"It probably wasn't him," I said.

"No, I realize that too."

"If you don't mind, I'd rather not go directly to the police station," I said. I told her briefly about my conversation with Jacqui. "When I arrived, she was leafing through some papers. She left me there to go have coffee with Nora. When I looked through the papers I saw some correspondence from Nora to Pauline, basically suggesting that Pauline keep her distance from Jacqui. And also a draft of Pauline's letter to Nora before she died. I'm not sure if Jacqui saw them, but they might have upset her. I'd like to just check and see if Nora's okay."

"I'll go with you. And if anything seems to be going wrong, I have the Newport police number right here."

When we pulled up in front of the café near the hotel, the sign on the door was turned to Closed. I was reminded of how the owner had rather pointedly been wiping counters down on Tuesday afternoon when Tom Hoyt and I were still there after five.

Had Jacqui and Nora gone elsewhere then? And if so, were they still together? I tried the phone number I had for Nora, but it went to voicemail.

"Would you mind dropping me at the Sylvia Beach?" I asked. "I can go inside and ask if they've seen them, or at least Nora. That would set my mind at rest. Then I can drive myself to the station afterwards."

"I'll go with you," she said, as she turned into the small lot across the street from the hotel. I hoped it wasn't because underneath Jane still harbored a small suspicion toward me, and thought I might do a runner. Or maybe because she'd promised Haakonssen on the phone that she'd deliver me and wanted to make sure she kept her word.

Yes, the receptionist had given Nora her key a while ago. Nora had a woman with her, dark hair. She hadn't seen them since.

She gave me my key. "And how are you enjoying Newport, Ms. Reilly?"

Jane and I were already at the bottom of the stairs. I was still holding the photograph. "Nice aquarium. And the Mark Twain room is ...?"

"Second floor."

Jane and I were both long-legged, but I got there first, spurred by anxiety. I knocked on the door and heard the sound of running water, a lot of water. This room had a clawfoot tub. Had Jacqui left already? Was Nora having a bath?

"Nora!" I whispered urgently, hitting the door with the flat of my hand. "It's Cassandra Reilly."

I thought I heard voices mixed in with the running water, a gurgled series of screeches. Two people or just one?

Jane looked at me and tried the doorknob. Creakily, it turned.

Jane and I pushed into the room together and headed to the bathroom past a magnificently mustached bronze bust of Mark Twain on the mantle.

"No, no, no," shouted someone above the noise of the tap. A terrible image from *The Sea-Breathers* flashed before me. Was Jacqui pushing Nora under the surface?

They were both wet, but to my relief, neither of them was actually *in* the clawfoot tub, which was only filled part-way. Jacqui sprawled on the bathroom floor, crying *No*, and writhing to get free under the weight of Nora, who, spry as she was, sat firmly on Jacqui's ample back, feet braced against the wall, with a determined look on her face.

"Thank God," she said. "I always thought I could depend on you, Cassandra."

Jane was already on the phone to Haakonssen.

It wasn't until later that evening, as Nora, Jane, and I sat around the brown-and-white Mark Twain room, with its unlit fireplace and a painting of Samuel Clemens lounging in his bed writing, that we could tell each other what we knew. Although Jacqui had at first been combative and screaming when Jane and I tried to pull her upright from the floor and put a towel around her, when she saw the uniformed police she'd crumpled into sobs.

"Didn't mean to hurt her," she cried inconsolably. "I want my mother. I want my mother."

We couldn't get any more out of her. Did she mean she hadn't meant to hurt Nora, or was she talking about her sister? Nora wasn't much help either, at first. Her spunkiness had perhaps saved her from drowning, but she seemed in shock and the sight of Jacqui crying on the bathroom floor made her cry as well.

After Jacqui was gone, Jane toweled off Nora's face and arms, and found her pale-green felted shawl with the sea creatures and wrapped it around her. I could see the tangle of octopus tentacles flowing over Nora's right shoulder.

I would have expected Jane to be in a right state as well, but she seemed more concerned about Nora than about herself. She asked the receptionist, who was hovering in alarm, if she could possibly bring us some hot tea.

Haakonssen stayed on for twenty minutes after Jacqui was led away, asking Nora with surprisingly gentleness what had happened.

"I hadn't met Jacqui before, so from the beginning it was upsetting in some way, maybe just that there was so little of Pauline in her." Nora's wrinkled face scrunched up around the eyes. "I couldn't help all the rush of feelings that came up for me, thinking about all Jacqui'd been through. Obviously she's not fully in her right mind but some things she said were clear enough. The café was closed but she started talking away, there on the sidewalk, about a lot of personal things: the baby, what Giselle had promised, and if her mother knew how Giselle was going to act she wouldn't have given Giselle everything."

Nora shivered under the shawl and the sea creatures shivered with her. "Well, this wouldn't do, all this ranting in public, so I said, let's go to my hotel room, it's just across the street. Obviously it never occurred to me that Jacqui presented any danger to me. Except emotionally. I was afraid, of course, what I might feel when we talked about Pauline, but I thought I owed it to Jacqui to tell her more about her mother and what I knew of how Pauline had made the choices she had."

Haakonssen nodded patiently. I was thinking, *Nora, didn't you realize you were taking a suspect up to your room?* But of course, I too had been alone with Jacqui just a short time ago, and hadn't feared for my life. I had felt sorry for her, and I supposed Nora had as well.

"I did tell her a few things, tried to be calm, said that Pauline had tried to take care of her as best she could. That she had her own parents to worry about, too. And she had to make a living. Some of this may have sunk in, most of it just seemed to go by her. Her face got redder, voice higher. She said she'd been reading a letter I wrote to her mother, saying it was good to separate from Jacqui and her craziness. She apparently found it today at the cottage, along with a draft of a suicide note. At first Jacqui thought it was the letter her mother had left for *her*, the letter she'd never gotten, then she realized it was for *me*. She felt upset about that and started accusing me of turning her mother against her. Then she started ranting about Giselle, and Giselle telling her this and that, and taking all her money, and now Jane wanted the cottage, and she would never give away the cottage, and everyone was lying to her and stealing from her and her mother wouldn't have let them if she had been here."

Nora grasped the two arms of the chair to steady herself. "The next thing I know she jumps up, and she's saying that she knows I killed her mother. That Giselle said I let her mother die."

Nora stopped, suddenly aware of what she'd said. As far as Haakonssen and the police knew, Nora had been completely ignorant of Pauline's intention to take an overdose.

Haakonssen nodded, prepared to overlook this. He said, "What happened then?"

Nora said, "Jacqui broke away and went into the bathroom. I heard the water running and after a couple of minutes, I realized it was the bathtub. I got up and knocked on the door, asked what she was doing. I still didn't feel in any danger, I thought only of her. When she didn't answer I opened the door. She was behind it and surprised me by grabbing me around the neck. She said something about the Sea-Breathers and now she'd see if I could really breathe in the sea, and started dragging me to the tub. She got my head underwater for a second. There wasn't that much water, but you don't need much to drown. For a minute I panicked, she was a lot heavier than me and stronger than I expected. But she slipped and fell backwards while we were struggling, and somehow or other I managed to sit on her. That's when Cassandra and Jane arrived. "

Nora was now shivering throughout her whole body, and Jane crouched and put an arm around her, murmuring, "It's okay, Nora. It's okay."

"We can hold Jacqui on assault charges," said Haakonssen, getting up and moving to the door. "But I think very soon we'll be booking her for the possible murder of her sister Giselle. We've been working on the evidence. And now we have the motivation."

"She needs a lawyer," said Nora. "I'll call Tom."

When I'd rushed into the Mark Twain room I'd tossed the framed photograph of Pauline and her daughters on a chair. Now I retrieved it and handed it over to Haakonssen. "The key to the safe deposit box was taped to the back," I said. "And there are papers under the backing."

By now, with all the rough handling, the cardboard was more than buckled, it was halfway off, but Haakonssen didn't accuse me of tampering. I added honestly, "I don't know what's there, but suppose it's the wills and trust agreement."

"We already found those legal documents," said Haakonssen, "when we did a more thorough search of the cottage yesterday. They were upstairs in a suitcase." He carefully removed some folded sheets of paper. "Adoption papers, it looks like." He straightened them out and a photograph fell out on the carpet.

It showed a young girl with a short dark haircut and confidant smile. "Pauline," breathed Nora.

"No," said Haakonssen, picking it up and reading the words on its other side. "Aimée Martin."

28.

After Haakonssen had gone, the three of us sat there for a minute without saying much, overseen by the bust of Mark Twain, with his overarching brows and thick moustache. Then came a knock at the door, and the receptionist brought some sandwiches from the kitchen and another pot of hot tea. I was the only one who seemed to have any appetite. Aside from an energy bar on the way to Newport, I had last eaten some twelve hours earlier, a fresh-egg omelet with Arlene Zink at her kitchen table.

But the arrival of the food shook us out of our stupor. Nora pulled a dry hoodie and jeans from her suitcase and went into the bathroom to change her clothes.

Jane said, "Haakonssen's a good detective. A good man. He gave me a talking-to last night on the phone." Somewhere in the rush to get out of the cottage or up the stairs of the hotel, she'd shed the tweed cap she'd been wearing. Her long white hair fell around strong cheekbones and jaw, softening their lines. "He thought I should have been forthright about my relationship with Giselle, right from the beginning. It would have saved him some time and energy, he said."

Jane crossed her arms to hold herself, rocking slightly, the way I remembered from her on the porch the other day.

"The first time he called me was Tuesday. He told me Giselle had fallen from the bluff, and asked me what our relationship was, since something in her wallet listed me as the person to call in an emergency. I was stunned, but my first impulse was to lie. To say we were business partners. Maybe it wasn't lying, exactly. We'd stopped being lovers around the time Karen came on the scene. But I've spent most of my life in the closet, and was never comfortable, even when I believed Giselle loved me, at being public about our relationship. So I lied, said we were in business together, that she used to live at my house temporarily, but had moved out. Even though her driver's license had my address in Portland as her residence. He asked why she was in Newport, and I told him she was living there full-time now, overseeing the remodel of her cottage. It didn't occur to me then that Giselle's death had been anything but an accident, especially when Haakonssen asked me if she was a drinker. I said yes, she drank. That wasn't completely true, it was only in the past few months it seemed like she was drinking more, not just wine, but Scotch. I thought it was from stress about finances. His asking that made me think that Giselle had been drunk and fallen somehow."

From the bathroom I heard Nora talking on the phone. If it had been me, I wouldn't have chosen to return to the spot where someone had recently tried to drown me, but Nora was obviously made of tougher stuff. She was probably calling Tom Hoyt.

Jane stroked one arm with the opposite hand. Again, that slight rocking, as if for comfort. "Haakonssen pushed me a little more, and— I'm ashamed to say this—I told him I thought Giselle and Karen, our publicist, might have been involved. I gave him her address. I'm very ashamed of that, that I tried to point them in the direction of Karen. Then Haakonssen said something about me coming to Newport to identify the body. I refused. I said she had a sister, Jaqueline Richard, though I'd never met her. I told Haakonssen she lived in Canada, that she had recently moved to Vancouver B.C. I went to Giselle's desk and found Jacqui's phone number and gave it to him. Even at the time I thought somewhere in the back of my brain that there was something wrong with the area code. I should have recognized it as Vancouver, Washington."

"So Haakonssen never actually thought that Jacqui lived in Canada?" I asked. "He must have called Jacqui in Vancouver and asked her to come to Newport to identify her sister?"

Jane's lips trembled. "Yes. It must have been so horrible for her. I mean, to have pushed her sister off the bluff, and then have to come back and identify her. How could she not have broken down right then?"

"Disassociated maybe?" I said. "Maybe only remembered parts of what happened? Enough to try to cover a few things up, to justify her actions, but not to completely understand what she did."

"So Jacqui was a suspect from the beginning," said Jane. "Yet they didn't charge her."

"If we were confused by her behavior, the police might have been as well," I said. "And there were other suspects: you, Karen, me, maybe Nora, maybe others. There were no eyewitnesses except that woman with the dog who thought she'd seen Giselle on the beach later, but it must have been Jacqui walking away from the cottage. Maybe she'd even gone down the bluff looking for her sister in the fog, didn't find her, and persuaded herself that Giselle was all right. No neighbors reported seeing Jacqui's car, so maybe she parked somewhere else. I can somehow imagine her getting in her car and driving back to Newport telling herself nothing had happened."

"Detective Haaksonssen called me Wednesday afternoon," said Jane. "A couple of hours after you'd been at the house, Cassandra. He asked me more about Jacqui, asked about Giselle's will or any other documents. That's what sent me to the bank files. He also asked me if Jacqui had contacted me yet about the funeral, and I told him we were having lunch the next day." Jane pushed her white hair from her tired face.

"You saw me after that lunch, Cassandra. It was hard, so hard when she told me about the baby. I really couldn't imagine Jacqui killing Giselle. I was more upset with Pauline and with Giselle than with Jacqui."

"Jacqui told me that you wanted her to give you the cottage," I said.

"No, I didn't say that. I tried to get out of her what she understood about the financial arrangements that her mother and then her sister had set up for her. I did suggest that I wouldn't be able to support her as they had done, that Giselle had left me with a lot of business debt. I said that if it did turn out she inherited the cottage, I would try to help her. I may have said something about her repaying the business for the cash Giselle had taken out to repair the windows and roof." Jane flushed with anger. "It was like she didn't hear me. Instead, she asked me for a thousand dollars. That was when she started talking about the baby that had been taken away. How could Pauline do that?"

Nora came out of the bathroom and heard the question. "I always thought I understood why Pauline did what she did. But now, when you see Jacqui, you can understand the long-term effects. Pauline was my dearest friend, but I'm grappling with her actions and, even more, Giselle's. I mean, Pauline felt guilty about placing the child with an adoptive family. But did Giselle ever feel guilt for anything?"

"Giselle could always rationalize her behavior," Jane said, and now there was no anger, only sadness. "Everything done for the press, for her mother's memory, was acceptable. She was so good at making people believe in her. And when they believed her she felt justified in trying to make what she wanted reality. That's probably why she believed it was fine to close the trust account and take most of the money for herself. She told herself it would be to keep publishing, the way Pauline would have wanted."

Tears gathered and fell from her eyes and Nora produced a round linen doily with cutwork in lieu of a handkerchief.

Nora said, "I imagine Giselle must have decided even as a young girl to always take her mother's side. We'll never know for sure what she was planning for Jacqui, but we do know it backfired. Jacqui probably didn't think about killing her sister. I imagine that Giselle might have been drinking and said some things that hurt her sister. Maybe they argued, and Giselle went outside and Jacqui followed her. I don't know if Jacqui herself even completely understands how it all happened."

I wasn't sure myself, but I remembered that smug look in Jacqui's eyes when she demonstrated that she knew where the key to the safe deposit box was. As if, for once, she'd outwitted her sister.

"I remember when I met Giselle," said Jane. "I went to a reading at Powell's. The author had written a book about dealing with the loss of a parent, and I thought there would be a large audience, but there were only about six of us, so it turned into more of a discussion group with the author. I sat next to Giselle. She was really torn up about Pauline's recent death, talked about it openly, how her mother was devastated to learn that the cancer had spread to her brain. She said her mother had talked about ending her life and Giselle had tried to talk her out of it. But Pauline had gone ahead anyway."

"She knew? She knew it was Pauline's choice?" said Nora. "Then why didn't she tell me that? Why did she distance herself from me? Act as if I had killed her mother?" Nora's voice thinned to a whisper and she had to sit down.

"I suspect Giselle couldn't believe that her mother would really commit suicide and leave her. She got it into her head that you'd talked her into it, even that you'd assisted her."

"But I *loved* her mother," Nora said. "I didn't want to lose her either."

"Giselle worked overtime to protect the memory of Pauline," said Jane, and sat up straighter, putting her arms at her sides. "She could have just forgiven her."

"What will you do now?" I asked, having walked Jane out to her car in the lot across the street from the Sylvia Beach. She had expected to drive back to Portland, but since it was after ten, Nora had insisted on booking her a room at the nearby Whaler's Inn.

It was no longer raining and the sky was full of stars and the smell of salt. The ocean roared distantly in the background.

She shook her head. "I don't know. My world doesn't feel the same." She looked up at the sky. ""I came to this country when I was only four, in the Sixties. From an orphanage outside of Seoul." She gave a half-smile. "At first I seemed to think the house in Portland was another kind of orphanage, it was so big. I kept looking for the other kids, my mom said—my new American mother, Judy. I was afraid to have a room by myself, and for a while I had to sleep in a large crib in their room. Eventually they got a small dog for me, and two cats, and a lot of stuffed animals, so my bedroom felt more populated. I don't remember all that, of course. Mom told me later." She stared out over the porch railing at the quiet street. "I don't have any real memories until kindergarten started. Then I remember two things. Some kids laughing and pointing at me, saying 'Chinkie,' and a girl in the class named Tammy, who stood up for me. She lived in the next block, and was my best friend all through school. For whatever reason, as soon as Tammy and I became friends, I never felt people messed with me at school. She brought out the best in people."

"Where's Tammy now?"

"Oh, she got married. She has two kids and a husband. They live outside Portland in Lake Oswego."

"Are you still in touch with her?"

"No. My choice. I was closeted for a long time. Eventually I dropped the lies about having a boyfriend or still thinking about marriage. My mother knew but we didn't talk about it. Mostly I just avoided people from my past. You don't like to see the look in their eye when they suddenly realize you're not like them."

"You need some friends," I said. "Not another lover, not yet. Just some friends."

"You'd be surprised how few lesbians I know," she said. "I wasn't part of any community, and then Giselle, well Giselle was funny that way. She was definitely gay and didn't hide it, but she didn't ever develop a strong lesbian identity. Like it was so normal you didn't need to make a big deal of it. But I noticed she sort of kept her distance from not just lesbians but, well, everyone. She was really outgoing, but it was as if she was content with acquaintances and didn't really need people. Like I do."

I remembered back to how alone Jane had looked, standing in the doorway of the house she'd come to as a four-year-old. I thought about the way she was bullied in kindergarten. I thought about Nicky and my other friends around the world, and about the attachment between Pauline and Nora that went back so far in time, from rivalry and envy to deep companionship and devotion, with love enough to see them through to the end.

"Why don't you call that old best friend of yours—Tammy?"

"I don't know. She probably wouldn't want to have anything to do with me." And Jane looked so stricken suddenly that my heart went out to her. I took her hand and pressed it.

"Don't wait. Find her. Call her. Tell her."

29.

The plane lifted off from San Francisco International Airport on time, Wednesday evening, into a sunset that threw glitter on the red arches of the Golden Gate Bridge and doused the choppy waters of the Bay with tangerine and rose.

It still felt like a surprise to be leaving.

Out the plane window I looked down on the surf crashing against the bare golden hills of the Marin headlands. We were flying north, toward Oregon, where I just came from this morning, in the direction of Michigan, where I'd grown up, where my mother and father were laid to rest, where one younger sister and a brother still lived. A state I never visited. But we wouldn't fly over Michigan. Instead it would be north to Edmonton, Hudson's Bay, Greenland, Iceland, and then south again, over the Hebrides and down to Heathrow and home.

Home, more or less, but more home than not. I had gotten an email from Nicky on Monday, in response to the stern message I'd sent Sunday, warning her about Russians buying up property in London.

Reilly, you of all people should understand a joke. I was having you on about the Russian making an offer. Just like you were taking the piss about not getting home right away because of a murder case in Oregon. You're not even in Oregon. And there's no need to panic, lassie. Now I'm back in London I see a few advantages for sticking it out here with the rest of you. For now anyway (let's keep the Scottish option open though, shall we, just in case we need to make a quick getaway?).

And as for Germany, well, I don't think I'd really noticed until I'd been there a week that no one understands a Glaswegian accent, much less a Glaswegian trying to speak some German. Was I going to be repeating every sentence I uttered day in, day out? Not bloody likely. At least in London people understand me when I'm speaking. You understand me anyway. And I would miss you too. A lot. See you Thursday morning. Love, N.

The plane was full, but I tuned out the noise of people settling, of flight attendants giving information as we started our climb. Good-bye again, America. *God mend thine every flaw.* As usual my trip left me feeling both as if I'd never left the States and as if I'd never been here before.

The plane was veering away from the Pacific, heading toward the interior, away from the coast. I'd remained at the Sylvia Beach through Monday morning, mainly because I was exhausted. After I returned to Portland, I had brunch with Candace, Jill, and Kim, who had taken a few days off work to retrieve Dora's Subaru.

It was a polite, somewhat awkward encounter at a nice café in their neighborhood. I'd brought Kim up to date on the investigation and Jacqui's arrest for her sister's murder. Jill seemed interested in knowing more, but Candace, I could tell, still held some ill will against me for not treating their home with the attentiveness it deserved.

While I ordered a liberal breakfast of buttermilk waffles with maple syrup and extra butter, a side of local thick-cut bacon, and cream and sugar for my coffee, everyone else asked for things like vegetarian eggs Benedict, toast with no butter, gluten-free pancakes, sides of fruit not hash browns, and decaf and water. There were jokes from Jill and Candace about paying the price for over-indulgence in Palm Springs, and shared stories of food allergies and trying to keep the weight off. Then the conversation turned to retirement.

Candace, the youngest at sixty, was fully retired, and she raved unashamedly about her freedom from the daily grind and her government pension—she had been a federal employee. Jill and Kim, several years her senior, were getting close to Medicare eligibility, but while Jill said something about wanting to continue on with her research as long as she could, Kim claimed she only planned to teach a couple more years. She wanted to travel, maybe buy a place in Mexico or Costa Rica, just lie in the sun and read. Dora loved this idea too, Kim said. The talk turned to IRAs and pensions, to real estate and the cost of living. It was harmless talk among friends. Probably Kim would go on teaching as long as possible, because she loved it. And she and Dora were unlikely to leave their community in Oakland.

"What about you, Cassandra?" said Kim finally, and to be contrary,

I said I was too broke to consider retiring and wouldn't enjoy having that much free time on my hands anyway. Leaving aside the fact that some good friends were in hospitals or graveyards, or slowed down by illness or disability, I insisted that I knew tons of older people who were still actively working. I bragged about an English friend who at seventy-seven was still a part-time editor at a publishing company, and another in Amsterdam who ran a large charity even though she was nearing eighty-five.

"But I'm sure you must have friends in England who are retired," Kim said. "What are they up to?"

I had to admit that I did know some people who were pensioners. If they lived in the countryside, they took long, bracing walks through muddy fields with their very muddy dogs, raised vegetables, busied themselves with trying to save the ancient hedgerows, or to decommission nuclear-power stations. If they lived in London they went to their Pilates classes, met in socialist study groups, and still turned up for worthwhile causes and demonstrations. In London or Brighton or the countryside they continued playing music, reading, knitting, gardening, tormenting the local councils, working with archivists on the history of the Women's Liberation organizations, and drinking whiskey and eating butter just as they always had. When I got off the tube at the Angel in Islington on Thursday morning and took the bus up to Nicky's, I would walk right back into that life. I'd get a few questions about my time on the West Coast, but no one except a few other expat friends would be much interested. Most considered the U.S. a crazed hotbed of right-wing religious nuts carrying guns. When they could be bothered, they reminded me that I wasn't really *very* American, that I wasn't like other Americans, that they never thought of me as one of *those* Americans.

I suspected the women at this table didn't really think of me as American either, not even Kim. And it was not just that I asked for a sticky cinnamon roll on top of my buttery, syrupy waffles. Or that I used words like *pensioner* and *local council*.

Too much time had passed. The decades when I could have lived somewhere in the States and built up the texture of a life were gone. My life as a part-time Londoner and full-time translator on the move had made me a different person from the young woman who first left Michigan for Madrid so long ago. By going east to Europe instead of west to California, I'd been changed. Probably irredeemably.

I wasn't a foreigner in the States and I was still an American citizen, for better or worse. But I couldn't go back in time and live the lives these women had lived. I thought of my freckled librarian and her urban chickens with a little regret. Arlene Zink had sent me an email while I was still in Newport, saying that she'd love to see me before I returned to London and asking me if I needed a ride to the airport.

I'd thanked her and said another friend had offered to give me a lift. That was Nora Longeran, with whom I stayed Monday and Tuesday nights in Portland.

Yes, right after I said good-bye to Kim with a big hug, and to Jill and Candace with friendly handshakes and yet another half-hearted apology about my incompetence as a housesitter—"But as you know, there *was* a murder investigation going on"—I headed up Thurston Street to Nora's, where I had already left my rolling suitcase and briefcase.

Here, in a second-floor guest room at the back of the large house, which looked out at the bright green leaves of a big maple, I finally had a little mental space to get to grips with *Baby's First Year*.

I'd been energized by an email from Janneken on Sunday with the news that on Friday Angela Cook had fallen down some stairs at the South Kensington tube station and had broken her leg. In three places. She was not, among other things, going to be able to participate in the panel with Claribel in Chipping Witteron.

Honestly, I felt bad for her.

But as Janneken said, in her no-nonsense way, "Well, at least *she's* out of the picture. Claribel says she will be pleased to have you translate the baby book. She knows you will do your best in English to capture its different levels of meaning."

Before my unexpected visit to Oregon and my involvement in the stories of women who did not bond with their babies or had to give up their babies, I might have scoffed at the notion that this novel had much depth. But gradually I'd begun to be affected by the narrator's very real depression and her painful inability to love the little being that came from her body with the tenderness that the baby deserved and needed.

I saw that in my own choice of words I could help the English reader to an understanding of the narrator's agonizing longing to love a child she also bitterly resented and blamed for her unhappiness. I could choose the right words and the right tone. For isn't it the task of the translator to help the author tell her story in new and nuanced language?

If Claribel wanted to call what I could do for her *capturing the levels of meaning*, that was fine.

I translated for several hours on Monday afternoon and much of Tuesday. In fact, I would have been happy just to stay a week or two longer in my new friend Nora's house, in this pale yellow room with its narrow bed, neat pine bookcases, easy chair and lamp, and desk facing the green window-wall of maple trees. I gravitate to houses like these, old-fashioned, cozy, un-remodeled, and to women like Nora whose lives are shaped by imagination. Everywhere in the house were books, photographs, posters, paintings, and gifts given by friends and family, some with a marine or maritime theme. A grandchild had painted starfish on the walls of one bathroom, and the shower curtain was printed with octopuses. Nora, still grappling with what had happened in Newport, still figuring out how she could support Jacqui through her arrest and trial, nevertheless found writing a solace and a necessity. After making coffee for us both and pointing me in the direction of the fridge and a frying pan, she disappeared into her room in the morning, only to come out for a walk later, and for a G & T promptly at 5:30 p.m. I gathered this was her usual schedule when she was working on a project.

"Retirement?" she said. "No time for that."

But of course I had to leave. The Witteron festival was this weekend, and I had a meeting scheduled with Janneken on Friday. We were to discuss *On Jupiter,* which Janneken was to publish, if the rights situation could be sorted out quickly with Jane and the Spanish publisher, early next year.

Luisa, grudging for form's sake ("I must consider my options, because Karen Morales—she is offering more money, you know."), was in reality over the moon about the prospect of a well-known British publisher taking her on. Make that a Galilean moon. I was back in her good graces, her darling, her *querida amiga,* her *cariña Cassandra.*

I had twisted Janneken's arm a little—well, a lot—by saying that if only I could find a publisher for *On Jupiter,* I would have the mental calm to proceed more rapidly on *Baby's First Year* and additionally would not ask for anything ever again.

"As long as I don't actually have to deal with Luisa," she finally said. "I do like the premise of the story. The remote mother, the daughters caught in her gravitational field. Lacan—a little old fashioned— but then there's the science-fiction angle. Do you think Luisa would be on board with promoting it that way?"

I thought of Señor Nic-Nac, and lied confidently. "Yes, I really think she's coming around to seeing herself as a foremother of Latin American science fiction. And she's using Asimov's stories about Lucky Starr as a postmodern jump-off point. Even quoting him directly," I added. "Which we'll acknowledge."

I gazed into the billowing clouds around us, blocking out the American landscape below, and opened my copy of *Baby's First Year* and my translation notebook, and I returned to the work I loved best, making words from other words, living in two languages, and somewhere in between.

ABOUT THE AUTHOR

Barbara Wilson is the author of seven previous mysteries, including *Gaudí Afternoon,* which introduced translator sleuth Cassandra Reilly and was made into a movie starring Judy Davis and Marcia Gay Hardin. She is a winner of two Lambda awards and the British Crime Writers' award for best thriller set in Europe. As Barbara Sjoholm, she is the author of fiction and narrative nonfiction, including *Incognito Street* and *The Pirate Queen.* Her translations from Norwegian and Danish have been awarded prizes and fellowships from the American-Scandinavian Foundation and the National Endowment for the Arts. She was also co-founder of Seal Press, a women's publishing company, and director of Women in Translation, a non-profit press specializing in translation. She lives in the Pacific Northwest.

Visit her online at barbarasjoholm.com and barbarawilsonmysteries.com.

CPSIA information can be obtained
at www.ICGtesting.com
Printed in the USA
LVHW112121291021
701929LV00011B/1337

9 780988 356764